Forbidde

MW01472452

Breaking Pack Rules: Book 1

Roxie Ray

Disclaimer

Contents

Chapter 1 - Marley 5
Chapter 2 - Cole 20
Chapter 3 - Marley 42
Chapter 4 - Cole 58
Chapter 5 - Marley 114
Chapter 6 - Cole 130
Chapter 7 - Marley 155
Chapter 8 - Cole 165
Chapter 9 - Marley 185
Chapter 10 - Cole 232
Chapter 11 - Marley 243
Chapter 12 - Cole 265
Chapter 13 - Marley 295
Chapter 14 - Cole 303
Chapter 15 - Marley 323
Chapter 16 - Cole 349
Chapter 17 - Marley 381
Chapter 18 - Cole 390
Chapter 19 - Marley 408
Chapter 20 - Cole 432
Chapter 21 - Marley 455
Chapter 22 - Cole 486
Chapter 23 - Marley 500
Chapter 24 - Cole 522
Chapter 25 - Marley 537

Chapter 26 - Cole 549
Chapter 27 - Marley 555
Chapter 28 - Cole 565
Chapter 29 - Marley 592
Chapter 30 - Cole 599
Chapter 31 - Marley 602
Chapter 32 - Cole....610
Chapter 33 – Marley 617

Chapter 1 - Marley

A year ago, if someone had told me I'd be working at a school filled with shifters, I would have said they were crazy.

Yet, here I was, sitting in a beachside bungalow *owned* by a shifter, wincing in the pre-dawn light over a seating chart for two dozen five-year-olds who were about to start their school career in Miss Cage's kindergarten class at the Polar Shift Academy.

That's me. I'm Miss Cage.

I didn't have anything against shifters. I wasn't prejudiced against the part of the community that could shift between a lupine form and a human one. In fact, I'd dated one of them for a while.

But that whole thing... it hadn't ended well. And it almost ruined my whole life.

I rubbed at the ache in my neck. I'd spent so much of the week sitting at the breakfast bar in the kitchen, hunched over student files, curriculum paperwork, and flashcards with each student's name on one side and whether they were shifters or not on the other side.

It was still surreal to be starting a job at a prestigious institution like Polar Shift. A school that fully integrated the lycan and human populations in a way that didn't alienate either population would have been absolutely unheard of in a place like Leighton Valley, Pennsylvania.

My upbringing in Leighton Valley had been pretty idyllic, but things took a dark twist when lycan folk came out of the "clawset" (I know—cute? Right?).

I'd always thought my hometown was pretty progressive. My neighbors were generally kind and generous, but they showed their true colors when lycans started revealing themselves.

Some of them were newcomers; some of them had lived among us for years. It made no difference to the people of Leighton Valley how new or old they were, though. Almost every single one of them was run straight out of town. It was an injustice that was easy to be complacent about when it wasn't staring you directly in the face, and for a long time, I didn't have to deal with the repercussions of the hatred toward them directly.

But all of that changed when I met Wyatt Pierce.

I was a few years out of high school, and Wyatt was older, charismatic, and charming. He was the first guy who'd ever really taken a true interest in me. Having such a powerful man, a powerful creature, desire me was almost like a drug.

The laws allowing shifters and humans to be together had just passed through the Supreme Court in DC, and sparks flew between us as we fell hard and fast into love with each other.

We kept the fact that he was a shifter a secret, which added to the allure of the relationship. Looking back, I think I was so used to being "Little Miss Perfect" that I wanted to live life a little more dangerously. I liked feeling like I was doing something my friends wouldn't approve of, and Wyatt encouraged that side of me.

But being a shifter made all the normal relationship stuff that much crazier—at least, that's what Wyatt always told me. Things were amazing for a few years—years I'd spent obsessed with him and wanting nothing but to marry him and pop out a litter of pups, start our family pack, and be the perfect stay-at-home mate.

I started to get hobbies and hang out with other people. I'd felt so comfortable and confident in my relationship with Wyatt, I never thought it would be a problem.

But I'd learned pretty quickly that Wyatt was jealous and possessive.

Pain skewered through my temple and settled behind my eyes.

I needed to stop thinking about this, or it would throw me. I couldn't put on a cheerful face to teach kids the alphabet and the seasons if I was sulking about my ex.

I checked my phone to see how long I had before I needed to get dressed and get on the road to POSHA—the Polar Shift Academy. It was only five-thirty, and with the academy's very progressive start time of nine in the morning, I'd have plenty of time to kill.

With so much pent-up, nervous energy in me, I decided to take a quick run through town. Running would help me get some of the nervous energy from starting my new job out of my system and would have the added benefit of loosening up all the tight muscles in my neck and shoulders before I had to spend the day running around and chasing children.

Sliding off the velvety seat cushion, I left my seating chart and files on the kitchen counter and walked back to my room to change.

It still threw me for a loop every time I walked into the bedroom of the quaint beach house. Looking out the huge windows and seeing the shoreline only a short walk away never got old, nor did falling asleep to the sound of the crashing waves each night and watching the sun peek up over the pinks and purples of the horizon.

I could never have afforded this by myself. It's not like kindergarten teachers make six-figure salaries (though I think we all should, thanks very much.) The only way I could live in such a perfect place was thanks to an unlikely run-in with a lycan who helped me get back on my feet when my life had all but fallen apart.

It was hard for me, after leaving an abusive relationship, to accept the act of kindness. Lana just *gave* me this place to live in as long as I paid the utilities and kept the place nice. She even gave me a small stipend when I first came out—called it *advanced house-sitting*.

For the first few months, I'd kept waiting for the other shoe to drop, kept waiting for Lana to snap and kick me out or get tired of how sad and broken I was after Wyatt.

But it never happened. Lana gave me the time I needed to heal both physically and mentally and even set me up with this brilliant job I was certain I was underqualified for.

That was Lana, though, I'd eventually learned. Aggressively, annoyingly, persistently generous—and if you ever dared say no to that kindness, she made sure to make you feel like an absolute villain within the space of a couple of hours.

Smiling at that, I shucked off my jeans and swapped them for a pair of stretchy jogging shorts. I abandoned my shirt in favor of a cropped tee and sports bra that wouldn't make me feel like I was going to melt in the sweltering heat of the South Carolina summer morning. I was careful not to look at the bite mark on my shoulder as I changed, not wanting to fall down another rabbit hole of self-pity and sadness.

I didn't like thinking about the days I'd spent healing from Wyatt's failed bite—an action that not only would have marked me as belonging to him forever but would have likely killed me if it had triggered a change into a lycan. I'd felt utterly alone in the hospital, the object of judgment and scorn of all the people I'd grown up with. I avoided thinking about it at all costs if I could help it.

Finally, I pulled my sandy hair into a high ponytail before grabbing my wireless earbuds and heading out the door.

My bedroom opened to a white-washed deck with stairs that led down to a driftwood pathway all the way to the shoreline. I slipped on my dew-dampened running shoes and tied them tightly, then headed down into the sandy pathway and onto the nearest sidewalk.

I waved at a few of my neighbors as they walked their dogs or sat on the benches that peppered the walkways, offering visitors a chance to sit and bask in the salty air or admire the sunrise. Each one knew me by my face, if not my name, and a couple wished me a good morning, which I was happy to return.

Once I was out of danger of being rude to anyone or accidentally missing a pleasant bit of chit-chat or a morning hello—Southern manners and all that—I put my earbuds in, set my jogging playlist to shuffle, and started running.

The playlist was full of high-tempo songs that made me feel like the hottest bitch around, which was an absolute necessity when you spent the morning getting sweaty in glorified pajamas.

Before long, I was on my usual trek through the little neighborhood parklet.

The parklet had a nice runner's path that weaved through a meticulously landscaped strip of land—probably the result of a city beautification project championed by the local housewives with too much time on their hands and not enough problems to keep them entertained. I was grateful it was so close to where I was living. I'd found comfort in a good run since freshman year in high school, and it was made all the better when you could see rabbits and gophers skittering through the tasteful vegetation. It made me feel like Snow White in running shoes.

As I ran deeper into the shaded parts of the path, however, I started to get a nagging feeling, a sort of tickle against the hairs on the back of my neck. I looked down at my arm and found it prickled with gooseflesh.

Slowing my pace a bit, I plucked one earbud out of my ear and looked behind me. When I did, I saw nothing but the stretches of the path I'd already traversed. Not a soul in sight—not even one of the rabbits.

I shook off the feeling. I was just being paranoid.

This sensation had happened a lot when I'd first come out to New Middle Bluff last year. I couldn't even count the number of times I'd begged Lana to come over and sniff around for Wyatt, like a kid asking their mommy to check their closet for monsters. Every single time, she always came up empty.

It was probably just the stress of starting at POSHA. At least that was what I told myself as I took a detour from my usual route through the neighborhood in favor of heading toward the city instead. There was no reason to stay in the relative quiet of my neighborhood when I could avail myself of the comfort of having a bunch of eyes on me in the city. It wasn't like someone would pull up on a busy street and shove me in a windowless van, right? Someone would probably stop them.

Hopefully.

I found it remarkable how quickly the suburbs gave way to the hustle and bustle of boulevards and business offices—how familiarity gave way to anonymity. I ran through the city, watching people from different walks of life going about their day: exhausted bartenders just finishing their night shift, yoga instructors perky with coffee and prescribed amphetamines heading into posh gyms, businessmen already rubbing their temples with the frustration du jour on the other end of their phones.

Having grown up in a small town like Leighton Valley, it never ceased to amaze me. Sometimes I came into town to people-watch on less busy days. Sometimes I wished I had an apartment in the city instead of on the beach—but only sometimes.

The only downside to running in the city was having to stop a lot more to wait for lights to change. Normally that was just par for the course when running in the city, but with each crosswalk and the thinning crowds of people as they went to work came a new wave of fresh paranoia that made me feel like I was going to jump out of my skin.

At each light, I looked around, trying to see if some creeper was ogling me from his car or if some old lady who had a problem with exposed midriffs was scowling at me. But, again, every time I looked, no one was paying me any mind.

I was nearing the end of my route, and the problem was worsening. I'd really wanted to avoid taking my emergency anxiety meds today, but it was becoming more and more apparent that if I wanted to function at all today, it would be a necessity.

I'd get to the Daily Grind, the local artisan coffee shop, go in for a chamomile tea to see if it would help ease my panic, then take the bus or a Lyft back home to avoid the anxiety of feeling like I was being followed all the way there.

It was a good plan, I decided as I checked over my shoulders for the hundredth time on this run that was supposed to make me feel better.

But I looked just a little too long—let my mind wander just a little too far—because out of nowhere, I jogged right into a brick wall. I bounced off it, the air knocked out of my lungs as I stumbled back. Before I could fall on my ass, a huge, firm hand caught my arm and steadied me.

I was still panting as my head spun. I tried to catch my bearings, looking for the evil wall that had dared get in my way as I was jogging. I realized, though, that I hadn't run into a wall.

I'd run into a man.

A huge, towering mountain of a man with perfect, slicked-back chocolatey brown hair. The meticulously groomed beard was the same shade as his hair but with a few amber hairs mixed among them. He was like the most beautiful lumberjack that ever lived, looking far too good in his tight black T-shirt.

Focus, Marley, focus!

He looked down at me with eyes the color of rich, dark-roasted coffee. His heavy brows knitted together as he examined me from head to toe.

"Whoa there, you okay? You hit me going about twenty miles an hour," he said.

I wobbled a bit, and he set down an empty coffee cup to use his other hand to steady me again.

"Easy, *easy,*" he said as he snapped his finger in front of my eyes. "You in there, Miss? Can you see how many fingers I'm holding up?"

He held up his thumb and first two fingers.

"Two fingers," I said.

His brow furrowed more, and I watched the corners of his mouth turn down in concern.

"O-one is a thumb," I stammered. "S-sorry, probably not the best time to joke about semantics."

His breath left him in a relieved gust before he let out a hearty laugh. "It's a good joke. I'm glad I don't have to call an ambulance for you. That would probably be the first time a paramedic had to deal with a head-on collision of two people."

It was then that I realized what I'd just done to the poor man.

"Oh! Oh my god! I just ran straight into you at full speed. Are you okay?"

Without thinking, I patted his torso, finding it wet and sticky. My hands slowed as I looked toward the coffee cup he'd just set down.

"Hey now, if you're going to try to get fresh with me, at least take me to dinner first," he said with a crooked grin.

I snapped my hand back as fast as if he'd burned me.

"First, I careen into you and ruin your morning coffee. Now I'm stealing your virtue," I croaked. "I'm so sorry. You must think I'm a complete idiot. Are you, though? All right, I mean? Did I burn you or anything? Crack a rib?"

He laughed, the sound warm and bright and tickling up my spine in a way that felt just right. "No, I think it'd take at least three of you to crack a rib. How about you, though? The light left your eyes there for a second. I was afraid you were going to faint."

I looked back over my shoulder like I had when I rammed into him at full speed. I couldn't tell if it was because of him or because whatever had followed me finally left me the hell alone, but the feeling that I was being watched or followed had vanished.

Note to self: to combat paranoia and anxiety, just find a hot guy and ruin his morning coffee.

I looked back up at him and nodded. "I'm fine. So sorry for ruining your morning."

"Believe me. This is the best morning I've had in a while," he said, lips curving into a smile. "This is my favorite coffee place. You should go in and get yourself a drink before you go running, just in case. You have a good day now."

"Wait, can I buy you another coffee?" I said.

"Another day, maybe, if we run into each other again—or if you run into me, I guess."

I gave a laugh that was just a little too eager. "Um, yeah. S-sounds good," I said awkwardly.

He picked up his near-empty cup and deposited it in a nearby trashcan. Giving another crooked smile, he turned and walked down the street.

I was left standing there, almost dumbfounded by what I'd just experienced.

Then I realized I didn't even get his name.

Chapter 2 - Cole

Well, this was the best day of my life.

It wasn't every morning that a beautiful woman ran into you like a speeding train, but I wasn't one to complain. At least not until I saw her blue eyes roll and flutter with the impact.

My coffee splattered all over my black T-shirt, seeping through to my skin. Lucky for morning-jog Barbie that my temperature tended to run a bit higher thanks to the lycan blood coursing through my veins. A toasty 104.9 was the standard temperature for a grown wolf, which made it harder for us to burn from warm liquids.

I'd be lying if I didn't say I was disappointed that the sexy little blonde didn't laugh at my joke straight away, but at the speed she was running, running into me probably felt a lot more like running into a solid oak tree rather than a person. When she wobbled a bit, I quickly grabbed her forearm to steady her.

What followed thereafter was an adorable litany of the small woman fretting over me. There was something strangely endearing about her fussing; her suggesting that someone so tiny could break a rib or even hurt me at all was an idea that brought no small amount of humor to the situation.

God, how long had it been since I flirted with someone? Ages, now that I thought about it. I'd sworn off women entirely while my son grew up. His mother had been a nightmare, but I knew it harmed him to grow up without a mother figure. However, everything about this woman gave me pause—the way she looked, the way she smelled... it all drew me in.

There was the pleasant musk of a woman who'd gone for a run. The sort of salty tang of her perspiration mixed with the lingering scents of laundry detergent, shower gel, and shampoo. But along with it, buried underneath all of that, was the acrid scent of fear. She'd been running from something, maybe from *someone*.

That immediately set me on edge. I looked behind her as I set down my empty coffee cup, putting my other hand on her shoulder, practically ready to move her behind me if this was a case of some creep having gotten too close with some knock-out drug before she managed to get away—her adrenaline helping her cling to her consciousness just long enough to get help.

She looked over her shoulder, back in the direction she had come from, and I smelled the faint twinge of her fear again. But the smell left as quickly as it came, whipped away in a breeze conjured by a passing car. When she looked up at me, her big doe eyes made me want to forget my stacked-up meetings and Noah's first day of school, throw her over my shoulder, and just spend the rest of the day showing her exactly how well my body could function even after our little fender bender.

I hadn't felt like that in years, and I had to remember feelings like that were dangerous. Feelings like that made me forget good sense. Feelings like that led to broken hearts.

"I'm fine, so sorry for ruining your morning," she said.

"Believe me, this is the best morning I've had in a while," I promised her with a smile, even as I realized I wouldn't be getting her number. Probably best not to even get her name. Now that she wasn't going to pass out in the street, she wouldn't have some creep coming after her. Best to cut this interaction short.

"This is my favorite coffee place. You should go in and get yourself a drink before you go running, just in case. You have a good day now." I finally said.

"W-wait, can I buy you another coffee?" she asked.

I almost wavered. Almost gave in.

But I didn't.

"Another day, maybe, if we run into each other again—or if you run into me, I guess."

"Um, yeah. S-sounds good," she said, and I tried not to read into what sounded almost like disappointment.

I turned from her and headed down the street to my car, then made my way home.

My home was my treasure. I'd built the entire thing from the foundation to the rooftop. Not single-handedly, of course. But I had drafted the plans, sourced the materials, hired the team to build it, and broke ground on the project when the time came.

I'd purchased the land back when I was still with Olivia, my son's biological mother—or egg donor, as I liked to call her. Back then, I was working as a foreman before I started up Fur Sure Solutions. Back then, I was so hopeful that I'd finally found *the one*. My mate for life. There was nothing sexier to me than Olivia, and the fact that she carried my son in her womb only made me more drawn to her—more reliant on her.

I'd had no idea just how fleeting her loyalty was. I'd been an idiot. But I knew better now.

My house wasn't all too far from the Daily Grind, perhaps a twenty or thirty-minute drive. I wasn't looking forward to Travis's inquiry about why I'd not come back with coffee—or why it was all over my shirt instead of in my hand. Hopefully, I'd find some way to dodge the question when I got home because Travis was never one to let the damned matter drop when it came to the subject of my love life.

Busybody human. I couldn't believe I'd let myself become best friends with him.

I pulled into my driveway, parking the Jeep next to my work truck. I hopped out of the car and made my way through the frosted-glass door in the carport, stepping into the comforting familiarity of my modern beach home. The first thing I saw was Travis sitting at my bar, holding a newspaper.

He was dressed in his customary black turtleneck and gray skinny jeans. Travis had worn pretty much the same thing since I met him in high school—back then, he sported band T-shirts, but the colors were always the same. He wore his blond hair in a tidy combover, a welcome change from his old grungy long hair from his teens and early twenties. Now, he really looked the part of my accountant and the vice president of my company.

He looked at me and arched a perfect blond brow. "Where is your coffee, bro?"

"DADDY! THINK FAST."

The second voice came from the stairs right next to the carport door. I looked up to see Noah, my son, standing about halfway up the stairs. His sneaker-clad feet were right at my eye level.

"Wait, Noah—"

Too late. He had already leaped into the air, flying down the stairs like a daredevil.

My arms shot up, almost with a mind of their own, it seemed and caught him mid-air, his laughter ringing through the air. His little dimples and the bounce of his shiny curls almost made me forget that we'd been working on getting him to stop jumping off the stairs. Almost.

"Noah, kiddo, what did we say about jumping down the stairs?"

"Daddy, I'm not gonna hurt myself," he said back to me. "I'm strong like you."

"Yes, you are, which means you can bust up my reclaimed wood floors, and then I would have a very expensive problem on my hands, wouldn't I?"

"But you have *lots* of money, Daddy," Noah said.

"He's not wrong," Travis said from his perch, turning the pages of his newspaper.

"Not helping, Trav. Wait, why is Noah dressed in jeans and a T-shirt?" I asked, looking back at him and hitching my son onto my hip. "I told you to get him dressed in his school clothes."

"Because, like *a certain someone*, he doesn't listen to anyone other than his favorite people."

"Ahh," I said, blowing a raspberry on my son's rounded cheek. "You weren't listening to Uncle Travis about what to wear, huh?"

Noah laughed and shook his head, but I could tell from the timid tilt of his head that he felt a little guilty at getting caught red-handed not listening to the grown-ups. I set him down on his light-up sneakers, then bent at the waist so I was eye-level with him.

"Go, get dressed in your special school clothes, okay? The ones I showed you."

Noah, as if needing to assert his authority as the resident kid one final time, shifted into his lupine form. I watched with amusement as he ambled along on his clumsy, large paws toward his room. I shook my head as I went to sit with Travis.

"So, boss, where's your coffee, hm?"

"Can't you take a hint and drop something for once?" I asked him. "You're as bad as Noah with all the questions and twice as bad at listening."

Travis laughed, folding his paper and setting it aside before leaning back on the granite surface. "Do you remember when Olivia kept trying to get her infant son to recite Shakespeare?"

I rolled my eyes and scoffed. "Yeah, I don't think she really ever understood children. She used to treat Noah like a chihuahua she could keep in her purse. God, remember that time she had a meltdown because Noah spit up on his onesie?"

"*It's Gucci, Coleson!!*" Travis imitated in a voice that was practically identical to the one she'd used back then. I laughed out loud, slapping Travis on the back. He coughed and sent me a withering look.

"We've been friends for fifteen years. When are you going to stop abusing my poor back?" he asked.

"As soon as you stop being funny," I promised with a grin. I looked toward Noah's room to make sure he didn't overhear. "I keep trying to wrap my head around it—Olivia and how she was as a mother. But I think she may have just not been built with the patience for children."

"Yeah, or a human soul," Travis said dryly. "Kids are perceptive, you know? They can tell when you don't want them around, when you're bothered, unhappy...I don't think it had anything to do with patience. I think it had to do with Olivia being a shittier person."

I nodded once and heaved a great sigh.

Even now, two years after Olivia split from our lives, it still hurt to think about it. I'd thought we were perfect for each other, that I'd finally found my life partner. Hell, I'd thought I was on my way to having a daughter before I learned she was carrying another man's baby.

"I wish I could just be done with that chapter of my life," I muttered under my breath. "That sham of a custody hearing ripped all the sutures open."

"I wish you'd get over it, too. The longer you're a workaholic, the longer I'll have to wait to get *my* dating life started," Travis said.

His tone was wry, but when I looked over at him, his mouth quirked in a way that told me he wasn't entirely joking. He was definitely joking about his dating life, but he wasn't being a jerk about me being hung up on the hurt Olivia had inflicted on me.

"You have to take the time," Travis finally said. "It's just one of those things you have to work through over time. It's like the flu. You gotta let it run its course."

I nodded. "Yeah, you're right."

Noah came out of his room a moment later, wearing his khakis, his slip-on navy shoes, and a matching navy polo with the POSHA emblem embroidered on a tiny pocket on the right side. I couldn't help the grin that spread on my face, and I held out my arms for him.

"C'mere, little wolf," I growled.

Noah smiled timidly before running over to me. I picked him up and plopped him down on my knee. I beamed at him, but he was tilting his head down, his mouth pursed in a familiar way, a way that only happened when he was worried about something.

"You nervous about today, bud?"

He shook his head, brown curls bouncing.

"Is it the clothes? Are you sad you can't wear your superhero sneakers?" I guessed again.

Again, he shook his head, not meeting my eyes.

I tucked my finger under his chin and made him look at me. When he did, his green eyes—his mother's eyes—met mine. They shone with tears. It broke my damn heart to see him so sad. I'd do anything to fix it.

"What if people at school ask me about my mom?" he asked.

The fact that my son even had to ask that question filled me with a sour tangle of anger and sadness. My throat ached, my stomach twisted, and I wanted to throw the nearest stone through my own glass window.

"You know, Noah," I said. "There are a lot of kids with only a dad or only a mom. Did you know that?"

Noah shook his head.

"Remember reading the Pinocchio picture book before bed?" I asked him.

He nodded.

"Remember how he only had his dad? Geppetto? And his best friend Jiminy?"

Another nod.

"Jiminy and Geppetto still loved Pinocchio just as much as any mother would, right? Geppetto got eaten whole by a *whale*. That's how much he loved his son. You remember?"

"Would you get eaten by a whale for me, Daddy?"

"You bet your little butt I would, kiddo," I said, nuzzling my nose against his. "I bet Travis would too."

"Hey, now, don't rope me into this!" Travis said.

"Well, I guess we'll have to figure out how to turn him into a cricket shifter, huh? So we can fit him in your shirt pocket," I said before pretending to stick something in his pocket. "Noah, if anyone asks about your mom, all you have to do is say that she's not with us anymore, okay? And if people keep asking, you're allowed to politely say that you don't want to talk about it."

"I can say that?"

"Yes, *politely,"* I said one more time to make sure it was fully emphasized. "Now, go and figure out what you want to have for breakfast while I tell Uncle Travis all the stuff we've got to do today."

"Kay!" Noah said, then scrambled off my knee and ran off.

"Walk with me. I need a new shirt," I told Tavis.

"I thought I smelled you *wearing* your coffee. Hit a bump going too fast in the Jeep?" he asked.

"Yep," I lied.

Having to explain the perfect girl I'd met in town was just not a conversation I wanted to have today.

***

About an hour later, Travis was fully briefed, my son was fed and snugly buckled into his car seat in the back of the Jeep, and we were on our way to Polar Shift Academy. Smiling, I watched Noah wiggling to The Beatles in the rearview mirror as I drove.

I couldn't believe how fast time had flown. It felt like only yesterday that I was cradling him, worried I'd break him because he was so fragile and tiny. Now he was starting his first day of kindergarten, learning to have his own interests and dreams.

He truly had become a little person before my eyes.

I fought back the lump in my throat as we made our way through town and pulled up to the state-of-the-art academy. The place was a source of pride for me, seeing as I'd had a hand in some of the plans and hiring to build such a progressive and advanced school.

My business, Fur Sure Solutions, specialized in shifter-friendly construction projects. We'd done everything from shifter parks and clubs to houses, apartment complexes, and Polar Shift Academy. I hoped that the school would be helpful in setting a precedent of fully integrated schools all across the country, but even five years after its conception, a lot of places were still fighting that idea tooth and nail—no pun intended.

It was rewarding to finally be in the position to place my son in school here, and I reflected on that as I helped get him out of his car seat.

I took his hand as we walked in the steel-and-glass front door. Parents were allowed to come in early on this particular day, what with a bunch of children starting school for the very first time. And besides wanting to give Noah a solid start to his first day, I had friends I wanted to see.

The foyer was one of the rooms I designed and sourced materials for. It was all stainless steel, reinforced glass, and warm wood with an open floor plan. A moving model of the solar system, nestled in a dome-shaped skylight, rotated slowly above our heads. I pointed it out to Noah.

"Kiddo, take a look at that. Do you know what that is?"

"The planets!" he said, delighted to know the answer to the question.

"That's right! Look at how the world is spinning around that big yellow one. That's the sun. Did you know it was that big?"

"Whoa!"

"I thought I heard a familiar pup," a friendly voice said behind us.

I turned to see Lana Gold, assistant vice principal of the school and a long-time friend since before we started the POSHA project together. I swore the woman didn't age—she still looked the same as when I met her years ago: cornsilk hair cut into a classy bob, pencil skirt, ironed blouse, and tasteful blazer.

"Hey, Lana," I said, pulling her into a one-armed hug. Noah glanced between us, face pulled into a frown.

"I haven't seen you since you were just about to turn three!" Lana said, backing from me to ruffle Noah's hair. "I bet you don't remember me, huh?"

Noah shook his head.

"Well, not to worry, we'll become good friends in no time," she promised. She looked at me. "Did you want to come and meet our new kindergarten teacher before you head out?"

"Yeah, that'd be great," I said, nodding toward the door that led out to the playground. "Lead the way."

Noah and I followed Lana out the side door. A young woman stood in the middle of a sea of five-year-olds who were all running, playing, and screaming. Her hair hung in loose curls to about the center of her back. She was dressed in a nice floral blouse and a pair of fitted black capris, her small feet contained in tasteful, practical flats.

Noah was practically vibrating at my side; I could tell he wanted to join the chaos. Indulging him, I released his hand to let him join in on the fun with the other kids.

Just as I was about to ask Lana about the new teacher, she got hailed on a walkie she had holstered to her hip.

"Copy, Miss Gold, do you copy?"

"I'm here," she said into the walkie. "What's up."

"We have a vomit situation in classroom ten. Can you come and help?"

Lana looked at me, pressing her lips together and sighing. "Duty calls," she said. "If I call you at the end of the day half-drunk, remind me that I love my job."

Laughing, I gave her another quick hug. "You got it," I promised. "Best of luck. I'll see you later if you're around when I come to get Noah."

"Yeah, see you later."

As Lana went back into the building, I stepped off to stand next to another parent. I stood next to the only other man there, a slight human fellow who looked up at me a little nervously. I gave him a closed-mouth smile, doing my best not to come off threatening. One thing I'd learned to do since lycans came out of the clawset was to be as unimposing as possible.

We all learned not to show our teeth, not to let our tempers get the best of us, and to be as close to human as we could manage. Even here at a progressive school, I needed to keep that in mind. It was one thing to see lycan pups play with human kids and support the unity in that idea—it was another thing entirely to stand next to a man who was genetically coded to be stronger, faster, and more ferocious.

Amused, I watched the poor new teacher checking her watch and trying to wrangle all the children together—class was set to start soon. I caught her scent on the wind. Human. She would definitely have her hands full at this school. There was something familiar about her scent, but I couldn't put a finger on it.

At least I couldn't until she turned to greet my son as he rammed head-first right into her legs.

My heart stuttered, and an animalistic hunger—fleeting but there—zipped through me from head to toe. It was the perfect girl from earlier that morning, the one who'd careened into me like a freight train and threw my whole morning for a loop.

She's my son's teacher?

Sometimes the world was just too damned small.

I watched as the poor girl looked around the rest of the playground, seeing her face fall as she realized most of the other teachers were getting their kids under control. A moment later, she put her thumb and finger in her mouth and whistled.

Every single shifter kid in a ten-foot radius whipped their head to look at her, but the human children kept doing whatever they were doing.

"Did you hear that?" I asked the father standing next to me.

"Hear what?" he said nervously, pushing up his glasses.

I shook my head in answer and crossed my arms over my chest.

Maybe she was a bit of a klutz, but she knew shifter kids, that was for sure. Something warmed in my chest at that.

Olivia could never quite keep up with Noah, even when he was a baby. I couldn't even count the number of times I had to take over caring for him because she had a meltdown. I could tell that the woman—Miss Cage, if I remembered the paperwork right—was overwhelmed but generally patient and understanding. It seemed like she just knew how to handle shifters, even though she wasn't one herself.

I decided to throw her a bit of a bone and stuck my fingers in my mouth the same way she had just a few moments ago, then gave a much louder whistle.

That one caught the attention of the human children and made the shifter kids wince and cover their ears. At the same time, Miss Cage's head whipped to look in my direction. Recognition bloomed on her face, and I was surprised at my satisfaction when I saw her face light up.

That look stoked a fire deep in my belly, a desire I hadn't felt in a long time.

She gathered all the children and talked to another adult—a brunette in a simple sundress of pale blue. The brunette nodded and started to lead the children toward the classroom. Many of the children looked somewhat confused but followed her anyway. The only exception was Noah, who suddenly seemed to realize that he would be separated from me and, in a panic, ran back to my side, hiding behind my leg.

Miss Cage looked at Noah and then at me.

I gave her an apologetic smile as I patted Noah's head.

"Go on, buddy. It's time for you to start your first day of school," I said, patting his back to encourage him toward her.

His fingers curled into my jeans, and he pressed his face into my leg.

"No more school. School's over," he said, his voice muffled against my jeans.

"Kiddo," I said, trying to kneel to his level.

He interpreted it as me trying to break away and upped his game. He wrapped his arms and legs around me. I tried to pry him off, tried to move, but somehow, I'd been rendered entirely immobile by a five-year-old.

"Buddy. Noah. Come on."

His teacher hesitated for a moment, then looked over her shoulder to watch the assistant taking the children inside. Once satisfied that it was going well, she walked toward me.

I couldn't decide if I was grateful or embarrassed.

Chapter 3 - Marley

I couldn't believe it.

The hot lumberjack I'd plowed into earlier that morning was standing right there.

And he'd just whistled loud enough to bring a speeding freeway to a screeching stop.

Rounding up the kids, I made my way over to Paulette and discreetly asked if she could take them inside. I wanted to say hello to the handsome stranger and at least get a name.

All throughout the morning, I'd struggled to get that crooked smile and the smell of him off my mind. I'd done just about a million other things that morning to get ready for my first day. I got that chamomile tea and took a Lyft home, where I took a scalding shower, got dressed, and prepared goodie bags for the kids before finally hopping in my car to drive to work.

All that time, I couldn't stop thinking about him. I regretted not getting a name or at least buying him another coffee to make up for the one I ruined.

If he was here, that meant he was a parent. That was confirmed when one of the kids broke off from the group and ran toward the man. It was the perfect opportunity to finally get his name and stop obsessing over the chance meeting.

I approached him just as the boy clung to his father's leg like a baby monkey. I couldn't help but giggle as I walked up to them.

"I, uh, think you've got a little something on your leg there," I teased.

"What, this old thing?" He lifted his leg and wiggled it a little, eliciting a squeal of laughter from the boy. "It's all the rage in Paris these days."

I laughed and shook my head. "Got an eye for fashion, huh?"

"Oh, I definitely have an eye for when something looks good," he said.

I bit down on my lower lip, perhaps a little too hard, feeling my face and ears flush.

Focus, Marley. Focus.

I knew I couldn't entertain the flirtation, so I cleared my throat and ran a hand through my hair. The other parents were trickling out of the school after seeing their children safely transported into their classroom.

"Can I help?" I asked.

"Please," he begged. "I think he thought school was a trip to the playground and then a drive back home."

I laughed. "Yeah, happens every year with the kindergarteners. I don't think it matters if you're a shifter or a human. The first day of school is scary for everyone."

I knelt on one knee and pressed a gentle hand to the boy's back, patting it slightly. "Hey there, kiddo. What's your name?"

He only peeked at me from where he clung to his father's leg.

"My name is Miss Cage. I'm really excited to meet you and be your friend," I said. "But it will be a lot easier for us to play together if you tell me your name."

It was a few seconds before he answered, but he finally said a skeptical, "Noah."

"Nice to meet you, Noah," I said with the biggest, most encouraging smile I could muster. "Now, Miss Paulette is inside with all of the new friends you were playing with, and she's giving everyone goodie bags for when we sit down for circle time. Do you like goodie bags?"

He took his face fully away from his father's leg now, eyes wide and interested. "Goodie bags?"

His father brushed his hand through his thick curls. "Remember when you went to Cousin Riley's birthday party, and you got that bag with the toys and candy in it?" he asked. "Sounds like your pretty teacher made special goodie bags for everyone in your class."

"That's right," I said brightly. "Because school is just like a birthday party! We get to play with friends, make art, and learn new and fun stories. And we get to eat tasty snacks."

Noah looked up at his father.

"Daddy, can I go to the school party with Miss Cage?"

I smiled and looked up at his dad. He looked almost incredulous as he looked down at his son.

"Yeah, buddy. Go get 'em and have a great day. I'll be back to get you before you even realize the day has passed, all right?"

Noah nodded and finally relinquished his father's leg. I pointed to the classroom door that I'd decorated in moons and stars, each of them with the name of one of my students.

"See that door over there with the moons and stars?"

Noah gave a timid nod.

"That's where we're going. You run ahead, and I'll be there right behind you, okay?"

"Okay!"

The boy took off, dark curls bouncing as he ran. He stopped in the middle of the playground and turned around, looking at his dad.

"I LOVE YOU, DADDY!" he screamed as if trying to be heard across a valley. Then, he abruptly turned again and ran the rest of the way to the classroom.

It shocked me so much that laughter bubbled up from my throat, unbidden and a little too much.

"Love you too, kiddo!" his father called back through a laugh of his own.

I stood up and smiled at Noah's father as I offered my hand.

"I'm Marley... uh, Miss Cage, I guess," I said a little awkwardly. "I guess we ran into each other again, so I really do owe you a coffee."

His hand dwarfed mine as he gave it a good, firm shake.

"Cole Lucas," he said with that crooked smile. "Seriously, though, don't worry about the coffee. It's bad for my blood pressure anyway."

I scanned his body, every inch muscular and toned.

"You don't look like you have to worry that much about your blood pressure, Mr. Lucas."

He laughed warmly, the sound of it almost musical. That husky laughter tickled the hairs on the back of my neck, just like it had this morning. "No, I don't need to worry about my blood pressure," he said. "And you can just call me Cole. Never liked being called mister anything."

"Then I insist you call me Marley," I said.

His gaze slid down my body, and not in the same way it had when he'd looked me over that morning. I guess it was only fair for him to ogle me after I'd just so blatantly ogled him. My thighs squeezed together involuntarily, and I found myself hoping he wasn't a shifter, even if his son was.

Then I found myself remembering that whether or not he was a shifter, he was still a parent of one of my students. My employee handbook emphasized multiple times in bold and italics that parents of students were strictly off limits for any kind of romantic involvement.

With all the stories in the news of shifter and human romances going awry, POSHA was extremely careful about inviting that PR nightmare upon themselves, especially during a year when their accreditation was on the line. The pressure was on *everyone,* from lunch ladies to principals, to play by the rules. If I fell to temptation it wouldn't only be my reputation on the line, but Lana's as well.

"Marley, then," Cole said, his gaze sweeping over me again. "Well, listen. Noah had a bit of a crisis this morning about his mother. Could you keep an eye on him today and make sure none of the kids ask him any funny questions about his parents?"

"Oh, is his mom okay?" I asked, heart sinking a bit at the fact that I'd just thirsted over a man who was apparently spoken for.

"Hell, if I know, but she's out of the picture. Noah and I talked about Pinocchio this morning—"

"Oh, yeah. That's a great way to think about it. Pinocchio only has his dad, too."

He looked at me a bit strangely, and I immediately felt embarrassed.

"Wait, was that not what you were getting at when you talked about it?" I asked, my face heating.

"No, no. Sorry, that's exactly what I said to him...I was just surprised, I mean..." he trailed off, then continued. "You really understand kids, don't you? I mean, I guess you'd have to in this job, but... you really have a knack for it."

Pride stirred in me at the compliment, and I had to look away, suddenly bashful. "I've always loved kids. The way they see the world is just so pure and full of love. It's a nice break from all the hatred and distrust in the world, you know?"

"Yeah," Cole said, looking toward my classroom.

I followed his gaze before looking up at him again.

When I was with Wyatt, he always called himself an *alpha*. I doubted he understood what that word meant. The way he'd spun the idea was like he was going to be the boss of the household, and I would be his humble servant—spitting out babies, cooking for him, and rubbing his feet.

But seeing how much love and concern Cole had for Noah made me see a new side of that idea. An alpha wasn't someone who sat on his ass and got his way—it was a father who set aside everything, even his own comfort, to provide for the people most dear to him. I didn't know if Cole was a shifter, but he had big alpha energy, nonetheless.

I leaned forward a bit and smiled up at Cole.

"So," I said somewhat teasingly. "Now is the part where the parents go back home or go to work...or maybe get a replacement for the coffee someone ruined for them earlier this morning."

Cole jerked as if remembering himself.

"Right. Jeez, I'm no better than my son, am I?" he asked with a startled laugh.

"I guess you guys are just made for each other," I joked. "Class will be done at two. You can come and wait for him here if you want."

"Yeah, that sounds good. Thank you again, Miss Ca—Marley. I'll see you both at two. Just let me know if you need anything. If he gets upset or needs something—"

"Everything will be *fine*," I promised him with a reassuring smile. "Have a nice day."

Cole looked toward the classroom one last time before he nodded, pressing his lips together and stiffly turning to leave.

I'd be lying if I said I didn't watch him go.

Thank God for well-fitted jeans.

***

The morning went smoothly enough.

Paulette handed out the goodie bags that were filled with some healthy, allergy-friendly snacks along with some toys that would help us with one of our first lessons: colors.

I'd had the idea to pick up a bunch of small squishy toys, each of them in a color of the rainbow. The nice thing about squishy toys was that they were popular among the kids, couldn't hurt anyone if they got thrown, and had the added benefit of being a great source of sensory input when kids got antsy or upset.

We taught them a fun song about the colors in the rainbow, and I had the children lift the right colored toy as we sang through the colors. Then, we moved on to secondary colors by having the kids mix different colors together with wads of play dough.

Finally, we started learning the alphabet, the foundation for learning basic sentence structure, nouns, prepositions, basic capitalization, and punctuation.

The day already felt incredibly full by the time the bell rang for recess. I was happy to have a little bit of unstructured time myself, so I could only imagine how the children felt. Paulette and I led them back out to the playground in a line, emphasizing the importance of listening to directions, then we let the adorable little monsters loose.

Picking a spot on the playground where I would have ample view of all the kids, I sighed and rolled back my shoulders. Paulette came to join me, and we watched the kids in silence as we both came down from the busy morning.

Paulette was a shifter. Specifically, she was the shifter assigned to me just in case any of the kiddos got out of hand or shifted and started causing problems for the rest of the children. As an adult shifter, she could make up for some of the authority I lacked as a human.

It wasn't necessarily that shifter children were barbaric or even wildcards. Some of these things were just biological. There had been studies in the past few years that showed when shifters were too far gone in their animal side, they could no longer understand human speech or even social cues. Studies also showed that lycans had to be pushed past their limit pretty far to get to that point, but with children at this age, every emotion was so large that it was important to have a shifter on hand who could calm them down when I couldn't.

We stepped in every now and then when kids fought over whose turn it was to use the swings or to stop kids from wrestling in their lycan forms on the blacktop. When the playground had become less chaotic, Paulette turned to me.

"Okay, I've stayed quiet about it as long as I possibly can. I saw you talking to Cole Lucas this morning—like really, really talking to him," she gushed. "Are you guys good friends or something?"

"What?" I blurted, surprised by the sudden question. "No, not at all. I only met him today. I kind of careened into him on my run this morning and destroyed his coffee."

Paulette brought her hand up to her mouth in surprise, leaning in like a gossip. "You *didn't*," she said conspiratorially. "What did he do? Was he mad?"

"As far as I can tell, no." I shrugged. "I tried to buy him a new one to apologize for the mistake, but before I knew it, he was on his way. I didn't even get his name until earlier when he dropped Noah off."

"No way. Girl, you are so lucky. It's like some cheesy romance meet-cute."

"Meet-what?" I asked.

"You know, a meet-cute, like when the two love interests meet for the first time because their dog's leashes get tangled, or they reach for the same book in the library—"

"I'd hardly call splashing an unsuspecting man with scalding coffee while I'm drenched in sweat a - *meet-cute*, Paulette. Besides, you know we're not allowed to have relationships with any of the parents."

"But the chemistry," she squealed. "I could see it on his face! He was *into* you."

I snorted, smiling at my assistant and friend. "Paulette, he was just a concerned father making sure his son was set up for success on his first day of school in his life, okay?" I said. "He's not flirting with me. We didn't have a meet-cute. I just rammed into him and embarrassed the heck out of myself."

Paulette pouted. "You didn't even let me list his qualifications."

"Qualifications for what?"

"For hooking up with you, obviously!"

I looked quickly around us to make sure there were no children in earshot—then I realized that half of the kids on the playground had supersonic hearing. My face warmed as I elbowed Paulette in the ribs.

"Watch what you say around the kids. I don't want anyone going home and asking their parents what 'hooking up' means."

"I'm just saying that just because you can't uh... Hmm... *Buy a coffee machine* doesn't mean you can't *get a nice latte* once in a while."

The euphemism flustered me more than I liked to admit. I shook my head and looked out at the kids on the playground, trying to find something to do that would get me off the hook from this conversation—no pun intended.

When I did, however, my eyes didn't land on any of the children on the swings or the jungle gym. Instead, my gaze stopped on a shadowy figure loitering near the farthest corner of the brick and stainless steel gate around the property.

He was far enough away that I couldn't really make out his features, aside from the fact that he was rail thin and seemed kind of young, like he was a first-year college student or something. His long, dark coat made him stand out like a sore thumb against the vibrant colors of the children and their school uniforms. Even from that distance, though, I had the sense that he was staring directly at me.

In fact, it was eerily similar to what I'd felt that morning—a set of heavy eyes boring into me from somewhere I couldn't see.

"Who is that guy?" Paulette asked. "Isn't it a little weird for him to be hanging around a school like that?"

And then, as if cued by Paulette's question, the shadowy figure turned and strode away, not sparing us or anyone else a glance. His pace was casual, unhurried, and almost made me feel like I was being paranoid...almost.

I'd learned from my relationship with Wyatt that paranoia was often justified. I'd gaslit myself for so long, even after leaving Pennsylvania. This time, I wasn't letting it go.

"I'll talk to Lana after school and see if there have been any reports of creeps in the area and make sure she knows someone was lurking near the playground," I said. "He seems gone for now, but let's make sure the kids are staying away from the gates."

Paulette's brow bunched as she watched the man vanish down the street. She nodded once. "Yeah, let's start herding them closer to the classroom. You never know what kind of psychos are out here these days."

I nodded but found myself unable to move as Paulette started to corral the children toward our classroom door, enticing them with the promise of playing with glittery slime for the rest of recess.

I wasn't sure what was going on.

But I knew something was wrong.

Chapter 4 - Cole

It was strange to walk up the stairs and into the office without Noah clinging to me like a little koala bear.

Sylvia, my administrative assistant, was at her desk and gave me a knowing look when she saw me.

"How's our boy doing?" she asked.

"There was a moment where he latched onto my leg—first-day nerves and all that. His teacher is really great with him, though. Got him to go in willingly. No tears at all."

"I'm glad Noah's doing well, Cole, but I was asking about *you*."

I blinked, momentarily confused, then laughed. I sat on the edge of her desk, bending one knee. "Is it that obvious?"

"I've known you since before Noah was born, so I do like to think I have an eye for your moods." Sylvia's eyes crinkled. "Plus, I've raised a litter of my own. I remember the first day of school very well."

I nodded and exhaled heavily. “I feel like I’m missing a limb. It’s taking just about everything in me not to turn around and take him out of school.”

“You’ll get used to it in no time, especially when the art projects start rolling in. All the macaroni necklaces and portraits. You’ll love it too much to give it up. You’ll also get used to having some grown-up time all to yourself surprisingly fast,” she said with a laugh. “By the time summer rolls around, you’ll be begging me for help again like when you were a brand-new father.”

“Have I thanked you for that lately, by the way?”

“Every chance you get, sweetheart,” Sylvia said with a roll of her eyes. “But don’t worry about it. It’s been a pleasure to help you learn how to be a father and watch Noah grow up. I’m so proud of you both.”

In some ways, Sylvia was like a second mother to me. She’d been in her late forties back when I hired her as a secretary, and as I grew up and became a father, she came to fill the role of both employee and mentor. I’d tried multiple times to give her a promotion to chief operations officer, but every time I’d offered it to her, she politely declined. She said a role as COO would be like marrying her job, and she had no interest in being married to her job.

Regardless, she still did much of the work a COO would do, but she liked not being obligated to do it.

I was happy to pay her an executive's salary regardless of what we called her. Sylvia was an invaluable part of my team, and many of the efficiencies my company could tout came directly from her. She was a genius when it came to logistics.

Speaking of logistics...

"How are preparations going for the meeting with Lennon Brooks this week? Are we still on to talk about purchasing the plot of land in town?"

"Travis didn't tell you?" she asked. "The meeting got canceled in a...fairly dramatic way."

"Uh, no. Travis didn't tell me."

"Because I was waiting for him to be less stressed. But thanks for that, Syl," Travis said from behind me. "You're already on edge. I didn't want to make it any worse."

"What's going on?" I asked, my inner wolf rankling.

Travis approached the desk. He crossed his arms and shifted his weight to one foot.

"Brooks let slip that we're a wolf-owned business," Travis said. "Apparently, the property owners aren't interested in doing business with 'filthy mongrels.'"

I inhaled deeply, flexing my hands to rid myself of some of the tension building in my body. I rolled my shoulders and neck as a flare of fury ripped through me, and I exhaled nice and slow. When I was a kid, I'd struggled to keep my temper in check, but when I became a man and a father, I'd worked a lot harder to regulate myself.

I wanted to scream at Travis, but Travis wasn't the bigoted prick. I wanted to tear into the jerk who turned us down, but that would only prove him right in refusing to deal with lycans.

"Does the owner of the property realize the Supreme Court made it illegal to refuse the sale of property to lycans?" I asked, my words clipped and snappy.

"I'm sure he does," Sylvia said. "Because when I called him to discuss it with him, he told me we could take him to court if we had a problem with it."

"Fantastic, that's something we absolutely have the money to do," I seethed. "When is this shit going to stop being a problem for us?"

"Well...probably a lot longer than the month or so we have to locate a place to build. And we really don't have the money to take a real-estate mogul to court. They will absolutely out-lawyer us," Travis said.

He was right, of course. "It's just the principle of it," I griped.

"We will be reporting it to the proper bureaucratic channels, but you know how long it takes for those things to go through." Sylvia handed me a folder with our logo embossed on the outside. "I've already put together a list of alternate locations—all vetted to make sure they aren't owned by other lycanphobic asshats. Go with Travis to tour them. You always feel better when you take an active role in solving a problem."

I took the folder and opened it, finding a dossier of about a half-dozen locations in far less-centralized areas. Each address was paired with a list of pros and cons, the asking price, as well as a summary of the environmental reports—primarily the information that would impact our ability to build an office that represented us as a company.

"I adore you, Syl. Unbelievable work, as always," I said.

"And, as per usual, I prefer the single life," she responded. It was a running joke after the many times I'd jokingly threatened to marry her sheerly for how helpful she was to me and Noah.

I was still pissed, but I did manage to quirk a small smile. She was right. I'd be better suited to getting to work on finding another place, even if I shouldn't have to.

"Trav, let's hit the road, yeah?" I said.

"You got it, chief," Travis said, picking up the keys for the work truck out of the bowl we use as a catch-all for office resources: car keys, business cards, things like that.

We descended the stairs together and got into the work truck, a large, charcoal four-seater beast of a truck with four-wheel drive. Travis got into the driver's seat, and I settled in the passenger seat. When he first started driving the work truck, Travis was a nervous wreck about it. He'd been a long-time lover of sporty coupes and was convinced he'd kill someone with the truck. It took me forcing him to drive the truck whenever we had to go somewhere together for him to get used to it. Now, it was habit to have him drive any time we went somewhere together, truck or not.

There was a bit of an awkward silence as we drove, and I was pretty sure I knew why. Travis sometimes got a little nervous when I was on edge. He'd witnessed some pretty ugly moments in our teens. Times I really flew off the handle. Never directed at him, of course, but a wolf in a fit of rage wasn't easy to handle, even as a friend or bystander.

Travis learned pretty early on that the best option was to just let me stew, that trying to rationalize with me or calm me down only made things harder for me because I felt like I had to defend my feelings.

All the same, it always made me feel a bit guilty when Travis clammed up. I'd come a long way since my tumultuous youth, but I knew his behavior was a holdover from times I'd either frightened him or placed a burden on him he didn't deserve.

"Hey," I said.

"Yeah?"

"I'm fine, Trav. I mean, all things considered. I'm pissed off, sure. But I'm not about to go all aggro, okay?"

Travis nodded and exhaled. "Yeah, I'm sorry. I clammed up again, huh?"

"A bit," I said. "But I was also telegraphing a lot of anger back at the office."

"For good reason," Travis said. "I don't want you to feel like you can't be real with me, Cole. It's just...I mean, you haven't had a good run in a while, right? Things have been so busy with work, looking for a place to build the new office, and getting Noah ready to start school. I'm just worried that you're getting a little...pent-up."

I rubbed my jaw. I really hadn't shifted in a long time, and Travis's concern was fair. It wasn't always good for shifters to stay in one form for too long. Lycans who stayed in their lupine forms for too long often found themselves having a hard time socializing normally in society, and those of us who forgot to give in to those wilder instincts sometimes experienced problems with rage and cruelty in our dealings with other people.

"I think it's been...a few months, maybe? You're probably right. I'm due for a shift," I said.

"A shift and a stiff drink, I think," Travis said. "So, after we look at these places, why don't I drop you off at the shifter reserve, and then we'll go out for drinks tonight."

"Tonight? It's a Wednesday, Trav," I said.

"And your parents have been begging to see Noah, and you are the boss, so you can sleep in if you want."

"But *you* can't," I pointed out. "You're not the boss, so what will you do tomorrow?"

"Obviously, I'll call out sick. My boss is a fucking idiot. He won't care," Travis said with his perfect deadpan delivery.

I shook my head. "You're a ridiculous clown."

"And you're a tightwad in need of a break. You're lucky you have me."

"Ah, yes. My humble, kind friend," I joked.

Travis grinned as he stared at the road ahead. "Humility is for chumps."

"Right."

Touring the other options Sylvia had prepared for us was much less painful than I'd thought it would be. None of the options were as perfect a choice as the one we'd already placed an offer on, but all were workable.

My favorite of the options was only a five-minute drive from POSHA, which would be great when Noah got old enough to walk to and from school. The old dental office had been vacant for some time, complete with outdated green vinyl flooring, X-ray lights embedded in the walls, and the perpetual smell of amalgam filling material and hospital-grade disinfectants.

The demo would be pretty substantial, and with how old the building was, we'd have to hire people to deal with old wiring and plumbing issues.

All told, we'd have to recalculate the budget for the project, which was unfortunate and likely meant I wouldn't be getting a Christmas bonus this year. That's how it went, though. When you owned your own business, it was always an experiment in Murphy's Law—anything that could go wrong, would go wrong.

We called our realtor and told him to put in an offer for the place, and with Travis's blessing, we came in at a little over asking price—luckily, we had liquid cash to spare.

When all was said and done, it was nearly one in the afternoon, which left me about an hour and a half before I needed to pick Noah up.

"Do you think it's enough time?" Travis asked me when he checked the clock on the dash. "I was hoping you'd have a little longer to go beast mode, but these things always take more time than I want."

"I'll be fine. Why don't you just drop me off and grab some lunch? Pick me up when you're done, then we'll go get Noah and take him to my folks' place."

"Yeah, that sounds good," he said.

He dropped me off at the reserve and drove away, promising to grab some lunch for me. As the truck headed down the street, I turned to enter, as I rolled my shoulders.

Shifter reserves were a relatively new concept and only found in progressive, shifter-friendly areas of the country. Ours in New Middle Bluff was especially nice and a project championed by a coalition of local shifters. The New Middle Bluff Shifter Reserve was sort of narrow, but it had a large radius of about four square miles. If I were to compare it to something, it was similar to a giant running track, only with tall grass, trees, and patches of sand instead of latex or polyurethane paving.

It wasn't very busy in the middle of a typical workday. There were perhaps only about six wolves I could hear nearby. Most of them were running—there wasn't much else to do in a reserve so close to a city. In some more remote places, shifters often would gather for hunting retreats where they gave in to their wilder side by taking down massive elks in traveling packs.

I didn't really need to do that to take the edge off, though. I could find a lot of peace in feeling the mossy earth beneath my paws and the wind through my coat.

It was always a little tricky to shift when it had been a while since the last shift, kind of like going from being sedentary to suddenly starting up your old routine of going for a jog every day or doing yoga each morning. It was much easier for my son to shift in and out because he had a much smaller body, but as you aged, it required more of your metabolism to shift.

I took off my shoes—not that I had to, considering my clothes would just go wherever my human form went when I shifted, but I wanted to feel the grass beneath my feet. Grounding myself always helped to bring me closer to my wilder side.

The word *shift* was a bit of a misnomer when it came to what we did. Shifting made it sound like our body cracked and changed into a different one, but it wasn't like that.

When we shifted, it was more like one form replaced the other rather than our bodies changing form. That's why we could do it so quickly. It happened in the blink of an eye because that was all that was needed to call upon that part of ourselves.

Scientists had been trying to explain it for years; some astrophysicists even speculated that it caused a bend in reality or called an alternate form from a parallel universe. Some of them said that when we took our lupine forms here, they took their human forms there and vice versa.

But I was just a contractor. All of that went straight over my head. I just called it magic because that's pretty much what it was until some egghead in a lab decided otherwise.

I drew in a deep breath as I closed my eyes, focusing on the sensations around me: the breeze rustling through the trees, the distant honk of a car horn probably a mile away, the rhythmic panting of another wolf somewhere farther in the reserve as they sprinted through the tall grass.

I dug my toes into the damp dirt under the cushion of the grass, smelled the loamy quality of it, and scented the dew still collected on the leaves in the shade of the tree canopies.

The beast inside me reached out, and I welcomed it, letting that wild, instinctual quality race through my veins.

When I opened my eyes again, I was a wolf.

I tore off into the greenery, shoes forgotten behind me. The concerns of my human life were no longer. There was no lycanphobic asshole making my life hard, no irritating, expensive demo, and no worry over my son growing up too fast.

Okay, perhaps there was some of that last one. Because as I ran, I caught Noah's scent and found myself gravitating toward his school.

The reserve bordered the school, and as I raced over grassy bridges that sloped over cars driving on the streets below them, Noah's scent became stronger and stronger. Finally, after a spirited twenty-minute run, I found myself at the academy.

It was almost fifty yards away, but my keen eyes allowed me to clearly see Noah through his classroom window. He sat with the other children at a round table, smiling and laughing as he smushed balls of play dough together. Near the front of the class, I could see the beautiful Miss Cage. She held up big circles of colorful paper. They were learning to mix colors. I glanced over at Noah. Based on the gleeful expression on his face, Noah was loving it.

Despite the fact that I'd come all this way to check on my son and despite the fact that I'd been worried about him since dropping him off, I found myself staring, not at him, but at his teacher.

My sense of smell was always strong, even in my human form, but as a wolf, it was tenfold. Her scent drifted through the open windows. The sweetness of honey and soft pink roses carried on the air like flower petals in the spring.

Her smile was so radiant, and her hair burnished like some fine Greek statue devoted to a goddess. I wanted to smooth my hands over that warm, tanned skin—wanted to feel the downy lightness of her in my arms. I wanted to—

Over the din of my desire, I heard the distant call of my name. No, not my name.

"Daddy, Daddy, Daddy!"

Shit. Fuck.

I looked back to see my son get up from his chair and run over to the window I was staring through like a peeping tom. Marley looked out the window in surprise—the class thoroughly disrupted, thanks to me and my silly, wonderful son.

As she came to the window, Noah pressed his hands and nose to the glass, scanning the reserve for me after he'd no doubt caught a whiff of my scent. Even from this distance, I could tell Marley had seen me.

I was ashamed to admit it, but I tucked tail and ran away like a coward.

I couldn't describe why, but it felt like I'd been caught doing something bad. Well, maybe I had been—I didn't see any other parents sneaking around to check in on their kids like some weirdo. Embarrassment blazed through me as I sprinted through the reserve. I suddenly dreaded seeing Marley when I went to pick up my son.

Maybe I could just send Travis in to get him?

No, that was even more cowardly.

I groaned internally and forced my legs to go faster and faster as if I could outrun my own humiliation. Why did I even care what a kindergarten teacher thought of me?

Because it wasn't just any kindergarten teacher, was it?

There had been another teacher looking out the window, too, I realized. The shifter teacher. But my embarrassment didn't extend to her. No, just to the perfect sandy blonde who smelled like honey and roses.

Fuck.

I didn't have time for this, and the last thing I needed to do was complicate Noah's school experience by becoming interested in his teacher. Yet, more and more, I found that my interest in Marley was more than just cursory. It was hardwired into me biologically. Something about her just turned my wolf into a puppy who wanted nothing more than belly rubs and ear scratches.

By the time I'd circled the reserve, I was panting, my tongue lolling out of the side of my mouth. I sniffed around until I found my shoes, then plopped down into the grass with a deep sigh.

After I'd caught my breath, I shifted back to my human form and checked the watch on my wrist. Just as I registered the time, a face came into view, hovering over me.

"Did you overdo it, old man?" Travis asked.

"Don't call me an old man, jackass. We're the same age."

"I don't have to lay on the ground after going for a jog, old man."

"This old man is about to get up and kick your ass," I grumbled as I propped myself up on my elbows. "How was lunch?"

"Middling," he replied, then thrust a plastic bag at me. "We really need to find some new places to eat. All of the old haunts are getting boring... or complacent."

I sat up and took the bag, setting it aside to put on my shoes. "You just have a strange relationship with food. I've never met someone so opinionated about salad dressing before."

"Would you let that go? That poor locally grown romaine was swimming in Caesar dressing. *Swimming!* It's a salad, not a dressing soup with a bit of lettuce thrown in as a treat."

I leveled him with a look.

"I did it again, didn't I?"

"What? Prove me right?"

"Yes, I hate when I do that." He offered me his hand. "Come on. We have a few more errands to run before we go and get Noah."

I chuckled as I took his hand and let him help me to my feet.

I ate the burger and fries Travis had picked up for me as we finished the mundane errands—picking up some new checkbooks and Sylvia's preferred brand of coffee for the office, snacks to have on hand for clients, and those little sticky notes that looked like tiny arrows to help people find where to sign the contracts.

Then, it was time to get Noah.

That dreaded, awful time.

"What's got you so keyed up? I can feel the tension rolling off you, man," Travis asked when he turned onto the street to the academy.

"Is it that obvious?" I asked, straightening and trying to look as casual as possible.

"Yeah, and don't do that. It makes you look worse," he said.

"Fuck me." I groaned. "When I went on my run, I caught Noah's scent and came to check on him. When I did, he scented me and ran straight to the window. I think his teacher saw me peeping."

"So, someone who's never seen your lupine form before saw you through a window? I mean, I think you have a decent amount of deniability there."

"Sure, if Noah hadn't been screaming 'Daddy, Daddy, Daddy!'"

Travis winced.

"Yeah, so I'm a weird, creepy man—"

"Weird, creepy, *old* man—"

"You really want me to kick your ass today, don't you?"

Travis laughed and shook his head.

"Cole. You need to relax. You are not the first parent to peek through the windows on the first day of kindergarten, and I'm positive you will not be the last Noah's teacher ever encounters. Since when do you even care what someone thinks about you? That's not like you," he said.

I shifted uncomfortably in my seat. This was the second time today I was trying to avoid talking about Marley—only this time, I wouldn't be able to escape it with a well-timed lie.

"Oh, *I see,"* Travis said. "You're freaking out because you're into her."

"I am not *into her*. She is my son's teacher," I said.

"Cole, you don't get nervous around women. You make them nervous. You're into her."

"Okay, she's fucking pretty, and she smells good. What do you want from me?" I asked. "Do you know how confusing it would be for Noah if I started dating his teacher? He'll start every school year thinking all his teachers are surrogate mothers or tell them to kiss me or something."

Travis pulled into a parking spot and waggled his eyebrows at me. I resisted the urge to punch him in the face.

"I could think of worse things for those teachers. So, what is it about her, Cole? You into the denim skirt and athletic sneaker look these days? The smell of baby wipes and dry-erase markers really doing it for you?"

"Oh, fuck you. She doesn't look like that, asshole."

Travis devolved into a fit of laughter. Anger roiled in me, hot and bitter, along with a misplaced sense of protective brutality.

"You know what, asshat? Come on. You're coming with me."

His laughter died abruptly. "Oh no. I don't do kids. This is a Noah-Only zone. That's the agreement we've always had."

"Well, the agreement is null and void when you imply I'm trying to fool around with a Sunday school teacher."

"So, you *do* want to fool around with your son's teacher?"

"Don't change the subject. Out of the car. Now."

Travis huffed, the mirth leaving his expression as quickly as it came. I got out of the car, and he followed after me sullenly.

Kindergarten got out before the rest of the school, which was pretty par for the course, as far as I was aware. The school was still mostly quiet as we entered through the foyer with the model of the solar system and through the side door that led to the playground.

"Nice digs," Travis said. "I haven't seen this place since we'd just gotten the bones of the thing up."

"It's a great school," I said in agreement.

"With hot teachers, apparently."

"Would you quiet the hell down? Half the students and faculty are shifters," I hissed.

"I could just go back to the car if I'm embarrassing you?"

I gave him a withering glare.

"Is that a no, then?" he asked.

"It's a no."

We joined the other parents just as the bell signaling the end of the school day for the little ones tolled. I heard Marley's voice straining through the open door as she tried to herd the kids and make them listen to her.

"The bell doesn't dismiss—hey! Hey! Hold on. Single file li—*urgh*."

Despite the shifter kids' keen sense of hearing, all the children, including mine, seemed to deafen to

Marley's instructions. They ran out of the classroom, each child scanning the crowd before hurrying to their parents.

Noah ran at me, and I laughed, scooping him up into my arms.

"Hey, kiddo, how was your first day of school?" I asked.

"We learned colors! And sang ABCs. And Miss Cage said I'm really good at my alphabet."

"That's 'cause we practice all the time. We learned over the summer, remember?"

"Yeah!" he said. "Daddy, I made you a wolf out of play dough, but Miss Cage says we can't take it home until tomorrow 'cause it has to dry."

"That's amazing, kiddo. I can't wait to see it."

"How come Uncle Travis is here?"

"I asked him the same thing, my du—holy shit," Travis blurted.

I glanced at Travis, then followed his gaze to the classroom door where Marley was coming out of the classroom. There she was in her tight capris and flowery blouse. She was resplendent, and even though she seemed a little tired and frazzled from the day, she was still a ten. Maybe even an eleven.

"I told you," I muttered.

"Daddy, Uncle Travis said a bad word."

"Noah, you are entirely right. He did."

"Yeah, loud enough for all the shifter children to hear it too. Real nice," said another parent—a short woman with a cropped haircut.

"My bad," Travis said in a voice that sounded in no way sorry or remorseful.

The woman scoffed and picked up her child before hurrying out of the playground.

Travis rolled his eyes. "What a bitch," he said with a shit-eating grin.

"You're such a jerk," I said through an incredulous laugh.

No one else seemed to mind the momentary lapse into profanity, for which I was grateful. Well, no one else, aside from Noah, anyway, who told Travis that he would have to wash his mouth out with soap. Perplexed, I asked him where he got that idea because I certainly had never done something like that. Cartoons, apparently, was the answer.

Once Noah had finished scolding Travis, he insisted on showing me his school. I explained that I'd just seen it with him that morning—even explained that I'd helped build it—but Noah wasn't taking no for an answer.

I let him take my hand and lead me around the playground. He was intent on walking himself rather than having me carry him, so I had to bend slightly at the waist to accommodate my son's length.

I did my due diligence of reacting strongly enough to look sufficiently impressed. I nodded eagerly and extended as many vowels as I could. When Noah was satisfied with a job well done on his tour, he took to playing on the jungle gym. Most of the children and parents had already taken their leave, and Travis was talking to Marley and the shifter teacher.

I'd been so distracted that I hadn't heard what they were talking about for the last ten or fifteen minutes, and just as I started to head over to them, Marley suddenly sputtered a laugh.

She bent over, holding her sides as her laughter rand through the air. Travis smiled awkwardly as he rubbed his nape, and the other teacher looked over at me and quickly jostled Marley's shoulder.

I smiled as I approached. "What's so funny?"

"N-nothing," the other shifter said.

Marley put a hand on her friend's shoulder as she tried to straighten again.

"F-Fur Sure Solutions?" she sputtered. "Oh my god, it's like a bad dad joke."

"*Marley*," the shifter hissed, eyeballing me like she was worried about offending me.

I wasn't, though. If anything, I was happy to see Marley laughing so hard at something so small. Olivia never laughed—not at dad jokes, not at comedies. She'd always just roll her eyes and call everything stupid. When I named my company, she called that stupid too.

"That funny, huh?" I asked, cracking a smile of my own.

"Sorry. I'm so sorry," she gasped through her laughter. "It's just so...dorky. You look like a cross between a lumberjack and a menacing member of a motorcycle gang and... Fur Sure? I just—"

Travis met my eyes, and I gave a good-humored shake of my head.

"If you think that one's funny, you're going to love my other dad jokes," I said with a quirk of my eyebrow.

"Please, no. I need to recover from this one first." She wiped at the corner of her eye. "I'm so sorry. I'm not being professional at all right now."

"Hey, school day's over. You can let your hair down. Won't bother me a bit," I said.

Noah suddenly called from behind me from his perch on the jungle gym. "Daddy, I have to pee!"

I blew out a breath and turned to look at him while Marley stifled another fit of laughter. "Good to know, champ! Come down the slide, and we'll find the bathroom, buddy."

Travis scoffed as Noah ran toward us. "I'll take him and get him buckled in the car," he said. He looked pointedly at Marley and then back at me, raising his eyebrows in silent communication.

Travis and his damned, relentless wing-manning.

"Thanks," I said with a nod. "Be right out."

Travis ruffled Noah's hair. "Come on, kid. You wanna go see your grandparents?"

"Nanny and Gramps? Yeah!" Noah shouted, leaping lightly into the air as he and Travis went to seek out a bathroom.

Once Noah was sufficiently out of earshot for his wolf ears, Marley turned to me with a kind smile. "So, I just wanted to let you know that if you are curious about what we do in class during the day, you can absolutely drop in once in a while. You can either volunteer or bring by lunch or come in as a parent aid."

First, I cringed internally, and then I cringed externally.

"I was really hoping you hadn't seen me," I said, rubbing my hand over my chin. "You probably think I'm an idiot. Or a creep."

She shook her head, her kind smile widening to reveal a row of perfect white teeth. "No, it's sweet. A lot of dads feel awkward about showing their hand when it comes to how much they love their children, so it's nice that you came and checked on him."

And then, like a teenage boy, all my blood rushed to my face.

"Well, ah, aside from his father disrupting the entire class during your lesson on colors, how did he do today? Any problems?"

Marley shook her head. "Noah is a very bright boy. He's super friendly and imaginative. We're going to work on talking over others—learning to take turns—but that's a pretty standard developmental concern that we address in kindergarten. Noah isn't the only one who will need to learn that," Marley said. "Don't worry too much. He'll do great this year.

"That's good. I'm glad he's being nice to the other kids," I said, sighing with relief. "It's been a long day. Noah is my only son. It's difficult to accept that he's growing up, you know? It feels like only yesterday I was teaching him how to walk."

Marley nodded. "I've been working as a teacher for a long time, so I know exactly what you mean. I hope you can at least take heart in knowing that you're handling the transition pretty well, all things considered."

"I don't really feel like I am."

"Well, I've seen everything from parents peeking in the windows to parents crying at drop-off. I'd say you're handling it well."

"Maybe." I tilted my head. "Maybe I'll believe you if you tell me your worst parent story."

Marley gave me a cute little conspiratorial smile.

"Mr. Lucas, are you a gossip?"

"I've been known to enjoy a bit of a story. Although, I'd completely understand if you didn't feel up to indulging my morbid curiosity."

"Ah, well, this story happened out in Pennsylvania," she said. "So, I guess it wouldn't be such a scandal to share it. It's not like you're going to tattle on me." She paused, her eyes narrowing theatrically. "Are you?"

I crossed my fingers over my heart, then lifted the same hand in a sort of scout-like pledge. "I solemnly swear to take this to the grave."

That oath seemed to satisfy her because she nodded sagely and leaned toward me.

"The wildest experience I ever had with a helicopter parent was the stay-at-home mother who insisted on coming to each and every class with her son. She did that for close to two weeks, sometimes interrupting my lessons to correct me. I finally got the principal to step in during the third week."

I chuckled in disbelief. "I can't believe it took them that long to do it. Why did you put up with it?"

"It was my first year teaching. I didn't want to get in trouble by having a parent complain about me so early on. But when it started affecting the other children's learning experience, it became about more than just me, you know?" she said. "I've always been better at standing up for other people than standing up for myself."

I didn't know Marley very well. I'd only run into her for the first time that morning. Yet, I entirely believed that a woman with such a sweet disposition would absolutely take a bullet for someone before she'd ask a waiter to fix her meal. She just had that way about her.

"Well, listen, I won't keep you any longer. I'm sure you have plenty to do and want to get home after handling a gaggle of kids all day. Thanks for not making me feel like a creep. I'm glad I'm not the worst parent you've had to contend with."

"I don't think you can look the way you look and be considered a creep. Not that you have to look bad to be a creep... just that you definitely don't look like—"

I watched Marley's expression change from kind, to aghast, to mortified, and finally settling on a mixture of embarrassment and struggle.

"I think I'll stop talking before my foot makes it from my mouth all the way down to my stomach."

The silly look on her face and her endearing nature when she was trying, and failing, at being coy had me laughing before I could stop myself. Truthfully, watching her fumble like that made me want to take a bite out of her. I composed myself, though, not wanting her to think I was having a laugh at her expense.

"I guess I'll see you tomorrow," I said, letting us both off the hook.

"See you tomorrow, Mr. Lucas."

"Just Cole," I said. "Remember, I don't like being 'mister' anything."

"Right. Cole."

"Atta girl, Marley," I said, winking at her.

Before I could get myself into any more trouble, I went to join Travis and my son at the car.

***

Taking Noah to my folks' place was always a treat for everyone involved. I usually got to eat an amazing homecooked meal with my parents, Noah got to be spoiled by his grandparents, and Mom and Dad got a chance to spend time with their only grandson.

My mother, while identifying primarily as a shifter, had a lot of Italian heritage in her bloodline. In fact, she was the first generation born in the States to my late grandparents after they immigrated. Because of that, food had always been equated with love in my household, and we ate a lot of amazing food.

Now that my parents were retired, my mother spent most of her time improving old recipes. Buying her a pasta press for Christmas a couple of years prior was the best and worst decision I ever made.

When we pulled up outside of the house, even Travis could smell the fresh garlic and butter from outside their beachfront bungalow.

"Holy shit," he said as we climbed out of the car.

"Uncle Travis! Bad word!"

"I know, I know, but I had to, kiddo. If that food smells good to me, it must be otherworldly for you and your dad, right?"

"I want dino nuggets," Noah said as Travis helped him out of his car seat.

"How about something kind of like dino nuggets, but with pasta and not shaped like a dinosaur?" I asked him.

"No! Dino nuggets!"

I stifled a groan as Travis set Noah on his feet. I ruffled his hair before squatting next to him to meet his eyes. "You know Grandma gets really sad when you don't eat like a big boy, so if you eat like a big boy tonight, I promise we'll do dino nuggets *and* potato smileys tomorrow."

"Both?" Noah exclaimed. "Yeah!"

He took off running up the stairs to the front door of my parents' house, fully bribed into behaving. I stood to my full height again and huffed, looking at Travis.

"Want to stay for some dinner before we go out drinking?" I asked.

"Why would you even insult me by asking that? As if your mother doesn't already love me more than she loves you. As if I would ever turn down your mother's cooking in this, the year of our Lord—"

"All right, all right," I interrupted. "I don't need the monologue. Come on."

My parents' place wasn't too far from my own, in the same neighborhood, in fact. I bought the small plot of land and built them a house as an anniversary gift when my business had turned a decent profit.

They had been living in a mobile home for a while at that point, having downsized after my sister and I left them with an empty nest. But the rent for the plot had been getting out of hand, and while they never told me directly, I knew they'd been struggling to make ends meet. It had become especially clear when I visited, and Mom didn't offer to make me a meal.

The way I'd seen it was that they'd given everything to give me and my sister a great start in life. It was now my job to help take care of them in their retirement and as they aged.

When Travis and I stepped inside, our senses were assaulted by even more mouthwatering scents of tomato, capers, milk, cheese, and prosciutto. A happy warmth filled me as my mother called from the large kitchen.

"Is that my favorite son?" she called.

"You bet it is, Mrs. Lucas!" Travis responded without a beat.

I punched his arm lightly as my mother poked her head out above the breakfast bar. She grinned at us.

"Come on in. I made chicken parmesan!"

We migrated toward the kitchen where my mother stood cooking. My father sat a few feet away at the breakfast table, sipping on a bottle of beer. My mom leaned down, opening her arms up to Noah for a hug. Obliging her, her ran to her. She peppered kisses all over his face and the top of his head.

"You get bigger every time I see you, you little monster," she said, tickling him. "Do me a favor and stop growing up, would you? It makes me feel old!"

"But, Nanny, you *are* old!"

"Noah!" I chastised. His mouth pulled down, and he shrunk into himself as he looked at me.

"Out of the mouths of babes." Dad chuckled.

"Oh, don't encourage him, you," my mother said. "You're older than I am, after all."

"No one needs to tell him that," he retorted.

"Gramps is old! Gramps is old!"

"Not so pleasant when it's you, is it?" Mom asked with a satisfied smirk. "Anyway, Noah, I made special chicken parmesan for you. Want to see it?"

"Okay!"

My mother grunted as she picked Noah up and carried him over to the island counter, where a small collection of chicken cutlets was already cooling on a plate. Noah cried out with delight.

"Nanny made dino nuggets!" he squealed.

And sure enough, she had. On the plate were the most gourmet-looking dinosaur-shaped chicken nuggets I had ever seen.

"Mom, you didn't have to go through all the trouble," I said.

"It wasn't any trouble," she said with a dismissive wave of her hand. "I needed a new challenge. It's good for me, keeps the ol' brain chugging along."

"What do you say, Noah?" I prompted my son. Manners were a newer lesson for him now that he was coming into his boyhood. But I'd be damned if my kid was going to be a rude little shit.

"Thank you, Nanny," he said, wrapping his arms around her neck.

She smiled and squeezed him tight. "Anything for my sweet little pup. Now, go sit with Gramps. Dinner will be ready soon." She let him scramble down her body, and he hurried off to give my dad a hug. Then she looked at me and Travis.

"You two going to stay for dinner, or are you heading right out?"

"I thought we could stay if you have enough," I said.

"It's like my own son doesn't know me at all. You both go take a seat. Help yourself to a drink from the fridge if you like."

"Thanks, Mom." I grabbed a beer for myself and Travis from the stainless-steel refrigerator and chocolate milk for Noah. It was always a toss-up on whether Noah would actually eat what was served to him, and even if he was excited about my mother's homemade chicken nuggets, it was best to make sure he got some protein from a glass of chocolate milk.

I sat down, rubbing the back of my neck as I took a sip of my cold beer. I was in a decent mood, but I was still wearing a lot of the stress of the day in my shoulders. If a night of drinking didn't fix this, then a massage would be needed in short order.

"What's wrong?" my mother asked.

"Wrong? Who said anything was wrong?" I looked over to where she stood, stirring a pot of sauce on the stove.

"I'm your mother, Cole. I know when something is bothering you," she said, pointing her stained wooden spoon at me.

"Long day. Noah's first day of school and some...stupid work stuff," I said.

"Stupid work stuff? Something wrong?"

"Just some jackass refusing to sell to us because of—" I cut myself off, looking at Noah, who was playing with some dinosaur toys that my parents kept for him. I didn't want to talk about the elephant in the room with Noah in the vicinity. After all, by the time he was old enough to understand prejudice, there was a chance there would be less of it toward our kind. "Well, you know," I said vaguely.

"Ah...I thought that was illegal these days."

"It is," Travis said. "We told him as much, and he told us to take him to court."

"Well, he sounds delightful. Seems like you dodged a bullet then."

"Yeah, I guess. It just puts us in a tough spot for the new office," I said. "How's Ginge doing?"

"Your sister's fine—busy as ever in the shifter division. I've only really talked to her on the phone. Between the department and heading to the state capital to lobby for better working conditions and a restructuring of the police force to account for shifters, she's barely had any time for herself or for anyone else."

"Really? She's getting into politics?" I asked.

"You know how stubborn your sister is—if something is broken, she wants to fix it." Mom tasted the sauce, mouth working for a moment. Then she grabbed a fresh sprig of oregano from her herb planters on the windowsill and crushed it into the mixture. "I guess you're both that way. Your sister fixes society, and you fix homes and businesses to be more accommodating to us shifters. You must have gotten it from your father."

Dad snorted and shook his head, quiet as ever. "I don't know about that."

My father was an analytical, thoughtful guy. When he and my mom were young wolves, after they mated and started facing the world together, people didn't really know about shifters. We hadn't come out of the clawset yet. If things were hard now, they were even harder then.

Shifting had been so perilous that many packs were forced to live on the outskirts of society. Abuse and assault ran rampant for decades because a woman coming forward about her abuse ostensibly meant selling out the existence of shifters as a whole. There were still women my mother had known growing up who were missing, likely dead, but we couldn't be sure.

Dad wasn't a particularly strong male—some would call him a beta. Just a quiet guy with a penchant for chess who ran a specialty watch-and-clock repair shop for most of his life.

Still, Dad was one of the good ones, according to my mother, and managed to somehow get them situated in a cushy city life even though it had been risky. They both stayed as far away from pack politics as they could, which had been a big deal in the beginning. My grandfather, Victor, was actually the alpha of a pack in Georgia, and it was sort of the logical next step for my dad to take over that position. But instead, he left the pack to be with my mom and make his own way. For a good portion of my childhood, whenever I asked about my grandparents, things always got really tense.

I didn't meet my grandfather until I was in my freshman year of high school, but I think we were all better off for it, especially when I overheard how the pack elders talked about my sister when she was barely starting puberty—like she was breeding stock for a prized horse. Sometimes, back when we were teenagers, my sister and I resented our parents for not keeping us closer to pack culture, but the more I saw of all that garbage, the less I liked it.

As it was, more and more people were moving away from that these days.

"You know, Cole, you'll probably fare better in a different location anyway," my dad said. "After all, people like him? If they're ignorant about one thing, they're usually ignorant about a lot more."

"Yeah." I took another swig of my beer. "It just rubs me the wrong way. It's the principle of it, you know?"

He nodded in understanding but also knew that there was nothing to be done about it.

The skin under my collar was just starting to prickle with irritation when my mother approached the table with an armful of expertly balanced plates of chicken parmesan. She'd been a waitress for most of her life until Dad was able to keep us afloat on his own. Then she became a stay-at-home mom.

"Cole, I'm marrying your mom," Travis said as he picked up his fork.

"I'm taken, kiddo," Mom said, the nickname a holdover from our time in high school together.

Travis pointed a fork at my father. "If you ever mess this whole thing up, just remember that I'm waiting in the wings."

"You know, between Cole joking about marrying Sylvia and you always vowing to marry my wife, I sometimes worry about you boys. Aren't there any women your own age who are interested in you?" Dad said.

I snorted a laugh as I tucked into my food, shaking my head.

"No, Pops. But now that you mention it, Cole has his eye on a certain someone."

I dropped my hand, fork clattering forcefully on the plate. "Don't," I threatened.

"Too late, I already heard it," my mother said as she sat with us. She tucked a napkin into the neckline of Noah's shirt, who seemed blissfully unaware as he dunked dino-shaped chicken into red sauce and munched on buttered noodles. "Spill," she commanded.

I shot Travis a withering look before gesturing for him to continue. Now that my mother was on the subject, she wouldn't drop it. She'd been pushing me to start dating ever since Olivia and I split.

"Well, her name is Marley, and she is a certain someone's T-E-A-C-H-E-R," Travis said. "She's very cute and laughs at your son's stupid jokes."

"Oh, really? That would be convenient, wouldn't it? You could see her almost every day."

"Or really inconvenient if it goes poorly. Besides, I'm pretty sure Lana said there's a no-dating policy for the tea—" I looked down at Noah, who was now making two dino nuggets fight in a fierce battle of violence and domination. "The point is moot, basically. She's very pretty, but it would never work."

"Well, that's convenient too—only in a way I don't like." My mother frowned. "Honey, you shouldn't be complacent about dating. Believe me, it's only going to get harder as Noah gets older. And you deserve to be happy. Not everyone is going to turn out like…like you-know-who.”

I pressed my lips into a tight line—even now, thinking of Olivia just pissed me off. I would never understand her and the people who were like her.

“I don’t know, Mom. I’ll think about it. Let’s just drop it for now. I don’t want things to get…” I looked at Noah again, still blissfully unaware for now. “I just don’t want to talk about confusing stuff.”

“Fine,” she said, lifting her brows in concern. “We’ll drop it for now.”

The rest of dinner went easily enough, and by the time Noah’s food was almost finished, he was already starting to get a little drowsy. Since it was still early for him to be going to bed, my dad took him to play with knick-knacks in his workroom.

The sun was beginning to set when Travis and I hugged and kissed my mother goodbye.

“You guys have fun tonight and drive safely. If you need to run home, just do that.”

“Mom, I’m a grown man. You don’t have to remind me not to drink and drive,” I teased.

“I don’t have to, that’s true, but I will anyway,” she said with a wink. “Don’t worry about Noah. We’ll take him to school in the morning. We want to see the place anyway. We haven't seen it since the ribbon-cutting ceremony."

"A lot has changed since then, too. Make sure you go in and check out the model of the solar system in the lobby. It's amazing."

"Your dad will love that," she said. "Love you."

"Love you too," I said as I trotted down the front steps and got into the car.

"So, back home to freshen up for the ladies? Or straight there?" Travis asked me.

I snorted. "Ladies? Dude, we're just going to get a couple of beers, maybe one or two shots. Unless you're trying to tell me I smell bad?"

"You know you don't smell bad. I know you know that because your nose is a thousand times stronger than mine, which leads me to believe you are fishing for a compliment. And I am not taking the bait. If you're set on a sausage party, then you won't hear any bitching from me. We can rough it."

"Travis, you are an enigma, truly. How is it that one man who does nothing but think about women remains so single?"

Travis tossed his head back as if flipping non-existent hair out of his face. "None of these people deserve me."

I choked back a laugh and shook my head. "All right, Grace Kelly, let's get a move on, yeah?"

"You got it, Mr. Daisy."

Our usual haunt was a brewery in town owned by a local and a long-time friend of Travis. It had all the standard trappings you'd expect at a brewery. Atmospheric orangey lighting, rustic wooden interior and fixtures, comfortable booths in tasteful black vinyl and—

"Travis, you missed the turn," I said as we sped past the street that would take us to the brewery.

"We aren't going to Beards and Brews today."

"Well then, where the hell are we going?"

"The Night Shift," he said.

I balked. "The Night Shift? As in the shifters' bar and dance club?"

"That would be the one," he said casually.

"But you *hate* shifter clubs," I said. "The last time we went to one, you almost got your throat ripped out for dancing with someone's mate."

"Listen, Cole. I am nothing if not a stubborn idiot. Maybe this one is different. That last shifter club we went to was more like a biker bar, anyway. Didn't you say the biker packs are kind of old school and weird?"

"How is this one any different?"

"Uh, it's in New Middle Bluff, and it is *chic*. Fuckin' light shows and shit," he said.

"But—"

"Bro, would you please, for the love of all that is good in this world, just shut your trap and try to have a good night? We're going somewhere that will allow you to be yourself after a day where you had doors slammed in your face for being what you are, okay? I am your best friend. Let me be self-sacrificing once in a while, you ass."

I inhaled to speak again and promptly let the words vanish, my breath leaving me in a huff.

"Fine. But you better not try and get me to dance with anyone. I see what you and Mom are up to."

"Scout's honor, I will not make you use your two gigantic left feet on this night." He held his hand up in a pledge the same way I had with Marley earlier that day.

After about twenty minutes, we arrived at the club. Travis was right; the place was trendy. The signage was made of silvery neon lights depicting a huge, full moon and the name of the club written in cursive. There were no real windows, but as I looked past the bouncer at the door, I could see stainless steel, dancing poles, and violet and pink lighting the dim interior.

"It looks...kind of girly," I said.

"Oh, so clubs are gendered now? Stop being a pig and get out of the car," he said.

Rolling my eyes, I slid out of my seat and reluctantly walked toward the entrance. Travis, hilariously, was carded at the door. I teased him for a good ten minutes about looking like a teenager, but only because I was so uncomfortable. The place was nice enough, just not really my vibe. At least they had some good pale ales on tap, so I ordered a round of those as we got settled in.

What bug had gotten up Travis's ass? Why was he suddenly trying to get me into shifter spaces? Or at least, shifter spaces like this—trendy and obnoxiously dark, with overpriced cocktails served with clouds of cotton candy around the glasses. This wasn't our vibe, shifter club or not.

We sat and shot the shit for a while, talking about work and brainstorming a nice gift for Sylvia's upcoming fifty-fifth birthday.

Then it happened.

I caught the scent of roses and honey on the breeze coming through the door.

I whipped my head around, looking for the owner of that familiar yet entirely unique scent. The place had gotten a lot more crowded, but my eyes quickly found her.

Marley Cage stood just a few steps from the entrance, looking around the place with Lana and Noah's other teacher. Marley had changed out of the capris and flowery blouse into something more feminine. Tighter. She tugged awkwardly at the hem of her skirt like it wasn't hers, and she didn't exactly know how to wear it. Still, she looked delicious in it.

The shirt was lace, showing off a lacy bralette that cradled her perfect breasts with care. Long sleeves connected to a pair of silver rings, one on each middle finger. A pencil skirt hugged her ample hips and thighs, the skirt's slip just barely allowing her thigh to escape when she shifted her weight to one hip. She'd put on some flashier makeup, too—glitter and gloss—and even curled her hair a bit more.

She was perfect.

And I was annoyed.

I looked over to Travis, who was studying the ceiling tile a little too intently.

"A place to be myself, huh?" I griped.

He looked over his shoulder and made a horrible show of looking surprised. "Oh, my goodness! What a coincidence. Small world, huh?"

"You did this on purpose, asshat."

"I may or may not have heard from her that she was coming here with her friends to celebrate the first day of school while Noah was giving you the grand tour of the playground," he said. "And I may or may not have decided that it would be good for the two of you to talk when you were both a few drinks in."

"Can you do me a favor and...stop doing me fucking favors?"

He leveled me with a deadpan stare. "That is a paradox, Cole. Are you trying to make me explode?"

"Are you implying that you're secretly a robot?"

"I mean, have you ever seen me and a robot together in the same room? I could be."

Despite my frustration, I looked over to Marley again. I watched as Lana directed her to a nearby booth, then I watched as every other unpaired male in the room watched her and her friends walk over to it.

I felt Travis's eyes on me.

"What?" I said a bit too sharply.

"You want to go talk to her, don't you?"

"I want to do way more than talk, and you know it. You *also* know I'm trying pretty hard not to confuse my son, and I don't know why you are actively sabotaging me in that."

"Because this is the first girl you've given more than a passing glance in five years? Because you both have really great chemistry? Because she's got the face of an angel and a body made for sin?"

"You need to lay off the romance novels, Trav."

"Excuse me. They are the way to a woman's...uh...heart. And a few other places. But enough about me," he said as he gave my arm a push. "Go and say hi. Go and charm her. It's not a damned marriage proposal. It's just a nice, fun night. Fuck the consequences."

I looked back at Marley, laughing and talking with the other women. "You are a terrible influence. You know that?"

"It's why you love me." He raised his beer. "Go get 'em, tiger."

I rolled my eyes and stood up. After a second's hesitation, I walked over to their table, trying not to feel like the world's biggest creep. I ran through a couple of potential greetings in my head before settling on one.

Marley was sitting between her friends. She looked up at me as I approached, her head dipping down just ever so slightly so that she looked at me through her long lashes.

I gave her my most charming smile.

"We have to stop running into each other like this," I said.

"I'd ask if you were following me, but I technically ran into you first," she said with a cute, restrained smile.

"Are you flirting with my teacher, Mr. Lucas?" Lana asked coyly.

"I'm flirting with Marley, Lana. Unless I'm supposed to call you Miss Gold?"

"Ew, no," Lana said, drawing a laugh from the other woman.

As I stood there, a waiter approached, delivering some of those ridiculous cocktails haloed with sprinkled donuts and cotton candy. He put one drink each in front of each of them. "From the blond gentleman at the bar."

I glanced over my shoulder to see Travis raising his glass to us.

"Wow, these drinks are, uh..." Lana said, her nose wrinkled slightly in disgust.

"They're on us," I said. "If you hate those, just order other ones." I turned to the waiter. "Sir, can you put whatever they order on our tab, please?"

"Under Lucas, right? You got it."

The girls all looked at each other, seeming like they wanted to gush and gab.

"I don't want to intrude on ladies' night, so if you need me, you know where to find me," I said. "I just wanted to come and say hi. Seemed rude not to."

"Well... thank you. You're being very generous," Marley said. "You don't have to buy our drinks—"

"Girl, speak for yourself!" the third woman said. "Drinks are expensive here. And this one tastes like a rainbow." She sipped her cocktail with flashing ice cubes, making it light up like the dance floor.

I chuckled, my eyes meeting Marley's. For a moment, the club faded around me. I wasn't sure if it was the magic of the darker hour or the few beers I already had in my system, but I just...wanted her.

In fact, it felt like I needed her.

Maybe I should have just said damn the consequences—maybe I ought to have asked her out on a proper date. Well, maybe when her boss wasn't there to see it. But Travis was right—I hadn't felt a connection like this to anyone in years. I knew it was senseless. I knew it was entirely physical. I knew I was thinking with my dick more than anything else. But couldn't something great start that way?

I let my gaze linger on her just a little while longer before I headed back to my seat at the bar.

No matter what happened the rest of the night, I knew one thing for sure.

For tonight, Marley was mine.

If anyone else tried to encroach on that, I would be sure to correct it immediately.

Chapter 5 - Marley

We really had to stop bumping into each other.

Every single time I ran into Cole Lucas, it got harder and harder to say no to him—to myself. I wondered if he was aware of the way the world around me had gone quiet when I saw him looking at me from the bar. I wondered if he could hear the way my heart had pounded against my sternum when he slid off of his barstool and walked over to our table.

“We have to stop running into each other like this,” he said, looking right.

My heart throttled as alarm bells went off in my mind. This man was a shifter, the very thing I’d sworn myself off of after Wyatt. More than that, he was the father of one of my students. I’d only just got my life back. I couldn’t risk losing it again.

But the power and confidence about him... The perfect body and flawlessly groomed facial hair... The smell of him. It felt as if I was wandering through a desert, starving and parched, and he was a spread of the most decadent foods and the promise of a cold drink of water.

"I'd ask if you were following me, but I technically ran into you first," I said, nibbling on the inside of my lip.

I could feel Paulette and Lana looking at me, and my fingers tightened into the fabric of the skirt I'd borrowed from Lana. She'd encouraged me to come to the club looking cute tonight, but now I couldn't decide if I regretted it or not with how Cole's eyes were glued to me.

"Are you flirting with my teacher, Mr. Lucas?" Lana asked.

Cole looked at her and gave me momentary respite from the weight of his gaze.

"I'm flirting with Marley, Lana. Unless I'm supposed to call you Miss Gold?"

"Ew, no," Lana said. Paulette giggled from beside me. I didn't know if she was intentionally leaning toward Cole, but a brief, irrational pang of jealousy skewered through me as she ogled him.

I was thankful when the waiter came and delivered our drinks. If nothing else, it gave me a moment to catch myself being an idiot. What was I even feeling possessive about? Cole wasn't mine. I couldn't even call him a friend. I'd only met him today. If Paulette wanted to pursue him and risk her job, it was no one's business but her own.

So why did the mere idea of that make my stomach churn?

Lana's apparent disgust at the girly drinks brought to us shook me out of my reverie. I looked at her as she took the straw and poked at the cocktail like it was going to sprout wings and attack her.

"Wow, these drinks are uh..."

I looked at my own drink now, pink with edible glitter floating inside and a pink-sprinkles donut resting on top like a garish sugared rim.

"They're on us," Cole said. "And if you hate those, just order other ones. Sir, can you put whatever they order on our tab, please?"

The man was insane! The drinks here were almost twenty bucks a pop.

"Under Lucas, right? You got it," the waiter said.

I looked at Lana, who was looking at Paulette like they were about to go on a mad shopping spree, one that would end with three hungover educators on the second day of the school year.

"I don't want to intrude on ladies' night, so if you need me, you know where to find me," Cole said as he peered briefly at a handsome blond man sitting at the bar. "I just wanted to come and say hi. Seemed rude not to."

"Well… thank you. You're being very generous," I said. "You don't have to buy our drinks—"

"Girl, speak for yourself!" Paulette retorted. "Drinks are expensive here. And this one tastes like a rainbow."

I forced a laugh and watched as Cole walked away. Once again, I marveled at the way his jeans hugged his ass in all the right places. I bit my lower lip in lieu of what I actually wanted to bite.

"You hate to see him go," Lana said quietly.

"But you love to watch him leave, God *damn*," Paulette finished.

"You guys are awful. Lana, you're even worse! You know we can't date parents," I hissed.

"Uh, first of all… For a man that looks like that, I would risk it for the biscuit, thank you very much," Lana said. "Secondly, hooking up isn't dating."

"I love the way you think," Paulette said.

"Also, Marley, when were you going to tell me that the most eligible bachelor in New Middle Bluff was giving you *that* look?" Lana pressed.

"You should have seen them this morning. Sparks were flying. I thought he'd try to claim her right there on the blacktop."

The conversation had officially veered into a territory that made me uncomfortable. I had been with a man who loved nothing more than claiming me, marking me. Sometimes he did it in ways that weren't particularly kind—scratches, bruises, cigarette burns. Some of those scars were more psychological than anything else and left me with a general feeling that I would never be able to function without him.

I almost lost myself in a spiral of flashbacks when I felt Lana jostle my shoulder gently.

"...ey—Hey, Marley? You okay?"

I looked at her, blinking those ugly visions of the past out of my eyes. "Oh, sorry," I said.

"No, it's okay. I was stupid to say something like that, especially with what I know about you. Do you want to go home? Need some air?"

I shook my head. There was a time, when I first got into town, that I would have spiraled right into a panic attack after a flashback. But that was almost a year ago now, and I was doing much better.

"No, I'm fine. Thank you, Lana." I gave her an encouraging smile. "I just...don't want to put myself in that position again."

"I'm not saying this to pressure you," Lana said, "but I can promise you that Cole is good people. I've known him for a long time, and he would never even so much as touch you without asking first. He's one of the good ones."

Paulette sighed longingly as she looked across the room at Cole.

"Marley, you're *so* lucky." She pouted. "There are so many shitty alpha-bros in the shifter dating scene. I would die if Cole were into me. I'd give up my job in a heartbeat if the shoe were on the other foot."

I tried not to feel irritated at Paulette's casual admission. She wasn't privy to everything I'd shared with Lana about me and Wyatt and how traumatic all of that had been for me. I didn't like hanging my dirty laundry out for everyone to see if I could help it. Besides, being a homemaker was an entirely valid thing if you loved someone who respected you. But I'd fought so hard to salvage the scraps of my old life, and I was not going to risk it all on another shifter.

It was one thing to stay at home with the pups if you wanted that for yourself.

It was another thing entirely to have that decision forced down your throat.

Before I could sink back into the panic and distress at the old memories of Wyatt, the waiter made another appearance. This time, he came with a tray laden with food. He set down a charcuterie board with a gorgeous spread of cured meats, soft cheeses, and fruit preserves. Following that, a bowl of spinach and artichoke dip and a plate of fresh oysters served on half-shells with lemon.

I looked up to see Cole smiling at me.

I smiled back, lifting my glass to him before taking a sip of the too-sweet drink.

"God, a man who sends food absolutely trumps a man who sends drinks. I'm in heaven," Paulette said as she reached for a slice of prosciutto and an artisan cracker.

"I feel bad that he's spending so much on us," I said quietly.

"Don't feel bad," Lana said, scooping a chip into the artichoke dip. "He has the money, girl."

When I looked back over at Cole, he wasn't looking at us. Apparently, this kind of spending really was a drop in the bucket for him. I decided it was too much work to worry about something like drinks and apps at a bar on a Wednesday night. Worst-case scenario, I'd have some answering to do later with some higher-up at the school, or maybe Cole feeling led on or something.

But tonight? Tonight, I could just have fun. I could enjoy a fancy cheese platter and fruity drinks and a handsome shifter watching me from the bar.

It had been a long time since I'd allowed myself to feel cute, much less desirable. Engaging in that part of myself had led to so much danger and hurt that I'd corralled it into a tiny corner of my brain.

But, hell, I was twenty-eight years old. And I was cute. And smart. Sometimes funny, though rarely ever intentionally. And if a hot shifter dad wanted to spoil me with drinks and appetizers, I was going to fucking enjoy it.

At least, that was what I told myself as the alcohol-fueled bravado began to kick in.

Unfortunately for me, however, before it could fully kick in, we became the subject of unwanted attention.

As we talked about everything and nothing, a man approached the table. I wasn't sure if he was just bad at reading the room or if he'd taken our general good moods as an invitation to butt into our conversation. Either way, our conversation came to a screeching halt as he put his hands on the table and leaned so close toward Lana that even *I* could smell the sharp scent of cheap cologne and whiskey wafting off him.

His black hair was an oil slick, combed straight back with way too much pomade. He wore a leather jacket, distressed gray jeans, and heavy lace-up boots. An arrogant expression completed the look. Where Cole radiated power and dominance, this guy felt like a caricature of machismo. It was almost embarrassing.

"Can I help you?" Lana said, leaning away and contorting her face in displeasure.

"Maybe," he said.

Like some kind of mongrel, he reached over and helped himself to one of our fresh oysters, slurping it down and chewing slowly as he made awkward eye contact with Lana. I caught Paulette's gaze as he did and could immediately tell that the man was dead to her as of that moment.

"What you got going on tonight, love? Looking for a little fun?"

He had an accent—British of some sort, but not a Londoner. He didn't sound posh, more like a bumpkin.

"I'm not your love, and as you can see, it's fucking girls' night. Now that you've contaminated our food, why don't you crawl back to the hole you came from and leave us the hell alone?" Lana said.

"Aw, you're cute, but you've clearly got something shoved so far up your own ass that you wouldn't have room in there for me anyway."

Paulette clicked her tongue in disgust, which only made him focus on her.

"And what about you?" he asked, extending a finger to reach for her face.

She recoiled before he could make contact and smiled condescendingly. "I have a mate," she lied.

Black eyes slid to me, and I had to fight the urge to slide down in my seat. I wasn't a shifter. I didn't exude the same primal confidence and capability that Lana or Paulette did. If this guy set his sights on me and didn't want to let it go, it would be over for me. It wasn't unheard of for female shifters to change and fight off creepy guys, but what the hell could I do? I didn't have the ability to shift. I was shit out of luck.

"And what about you, sweet thing?" he asked me. "Pretty human girl like you hanging out in a shifter club? Fancy a little trip to the loo with me? I know you human girls like it rough. That's why you come here, right? To get fucked quick and dirty while someone pulls your hair?"

Lana and Paulette both growled, but his eyes remained fixed on me. Just before my friends could bolt up from their seats, a hand fell onto the stranger's shoulder.

He stiffened before turning to look at who had grabbed him, finding the blond man who had been sitting at the bar with Cole.

"Hey, mate," Travis said.

Before the pig of a shifter could get a word in, though, Cole's friend's fist connected with the shifter's jaw. There was an audible crunch. To probably everyone's surprise, the shifter crumpled into a heap on the ground, unconscious.

Travis shook his hand, and I realized at precisely the same time that Lana and Paulette did that the sickening crunch we heard wasn't the shifter's jaw. It was Travis's hand.

"Holy shit, are you all right?" Lana said, standing up to take his hand in hers.

"Yeah, I'm fine."

"Your heart is racing. Are you going to have a heart attack?" she said.

"Nah, beautiful women and sucker-punching strangers just have that effect on me," he said through gritted teeth. Lana pressed on his hand, and he winced, the muscles in his jaw clenching.

"Why would you even do that? Are you out of your mind? The guy could have eaten you. Literally," Lana said. I was surprised at the genuine concern in her tone, in the curve of her brow.

"Listen, it was either I come to punch his lights out, or Cole would have done it. The guy was being a fucking creep," Travis said. "Anyway, what's the prognosis, Doc?"

"I don't think it's broken, but you busted your knuckle pretty bad," she said. "Come with me to the bathroom, so I can get you cleaned up."

Paulette grimaced at the unconscious wolf on the ground. "I'm going to grab the bouncer to take out the trash. Will you be okay by yourself for a few minutes?"

"Uhm, yeah. But won't they call the cops or something? Travis just knocked a man out cold."

"Nah," Paulette said. "This is one of those things that just got settled like one of those old-school duels. Honestly, even if this douchebag *did* call the cops, he'd be laughed out of every shifter circle from here to Boston. Imagine calling the cops to fight your battles against a *human*. This is a humiliation he'll be happy to bury, trust me."

I nodded.

Paulette scooted out of the seat and hurried to the door to fetch one of the bouncers, leaving me alone at the booth with a man crumpled in a heap a few feet away. I shifted uncomfortably before lifting my gaze to look at the bar where Travis and Cole had been sitting.

Cole's eyes met mine, and my gaze instinctually dropped to his hands. He kept opening and closing them. After flexing his hands a few more times, flexing his hands a few more times, he stood and came over to me.

For a moment, I was worried he was coming over to exact more violence, but he didn't even spare the creep a glance. He only offered his hand to me.

"Come on. Let's get you away from this sack of shit."

Though his voice was calm, there was an edge to it—a sort of barely restrained fury.

I stared at him, almost frozen to the spot. I wasn't exactly sure why at first, and then as if my mouth was advocating on behalf of my brain, I blurted, "You're angry."

He dropped his hand. "I am. He disrespected you and treated you like a toy instead of the lovely young woman that you are. That shit doesn't sit well with me."

"But you don't even know me," I said. "For all you know, I could be exactly that kind of girl."

"Is that so?" he asked. "I suppose you could be, but I've met my fair share of the type, and I usually don't hear their heart thundering or smell their fear when they're approached like that."

I dropped my gaze to the charcuterie board at the empty spot on the ice where the oyster the stranger took once sat. Cole fell silent, allowing me to process, I think. But even I didn't know what I was getting at with my little accusation. Maybe I was just fearful of another shifter taking ownership of me all over again. Maybe I was worried this would blow up in my face.

Maybe I was just afraid to catch feelings for anyone, shifter or human. Cole had been the first man in almost a year for whom I felt even a passing attraction, and every time we talked, the pull toward him felt harder to resist. For Christ's sake, I'd only met him *today*.

When I finally looked up at him, he was watching me. There was no expectant stare on his face, no hint of irritation or impatience. The fact was that Cole wasn't the run-of-the-mill alpha-bro like the guy snoring at his feet or like Wyatt. He was different in a way I couldn't tell just by looking at him.

There was only one way to learn what kind of man Cole was, and that was to get to know him.

It wasn't a commitment. It wasn't a relationship. Or even friends with benefits. It was just a simple dose of curiosity, and a little curiosity never hurt anyone. Right?

"So, Cole," I finally said after the silence had stretched for too long. "Do you like to dance?"

Chapter 6 - Cole

God, to be a fly on the wall of Marley's mind. I didn't know how long I stood there, watching her wheels turn, but it was long enough to sus out that she had an aversion to shifters.

I knew better than to think it was prejudice or even a phobia. I'd seen lycanphobic people around shifter children. Those assholes always seemed uncomfortable and awkward around them. I'd noticed it when Noah was around. Men and women gave him wary looks like he was a rabid animal about to lash out. Marley wasn't like that. I recognized something in Marley. Someone wounded.

It pained me to think of what could have happened in the past to make her that way. I wanted to heal those old wounds, heal them in myself.

But for now, Marley wanted to dance, and I could do that.

I offered her my hand and a smile, and she took both. Our fingers twined together as I pulled her past the dining area to the dance floor. The music was loud and had a bass line so deep we could feel it in our chests.

As we reached the floor, Marley took the lead and pulled me all the way into the center of the chaos. Everything was a mashup of smells and sensations. The two shots I'd downed to try and get myself in check so I didn't rip that shifter's throat out started to really hit right as Marley stopped and turned toward me.

She put my hand on her waist, and God, she felt like absolute heaven in my hands. So small and perfect, I wanted nothing more than to lift her into my arms and bury my nose in her beautiful sandy hair, taste her sun-kissed skin, and hear the delicate noises of bliss I could coax from her if given the chance. This woman was beautiful, and tonight she was mine, and I wouldn't let anyone or anything get in the way of that.

If she'd been willing at that moment, I probably would have marked her—bitten her to seal our mating bond. The draw I felt to her was downright biological, from the moment she careened into me on the street to this very moment right now. I wanted her—no, needed her—to need me.

Some distant, more logical part of my mind reminded me how dangerous that could be. How lost I could get to my wolf and how sick it could make her. Luckily, I wasn't drunk enough to do something that stupid. Marking a girl you'd just met was just about as wise as running off to Las Vegas to one of those twenty-four-hour chapels. It just wasn't a sensible thing to do.

Still, as Marley pressed her perfect body against mine, I had to resist the urge to devour her. Her breasts were warm against my chest, and my hands felt perfectly suited for her ample ass. I would do anything to wrap her curvy thighs around my head and give her the ride of her life.

The pleasant musk of her own arousal coming off her told me she felt the same. I could hear it in the cloying soft breaths she exhaled as I ground my hips against her.

I lowered my mouth to her ear and whispered, "Do you like torturing the men who find you irresistible?"

She whimpered, her head lolling to the side.

I caught it, cupping her face and bending my neck to breathe in that intoxicating scent of honey and roses. Fuck, I wanted her so badly. I was ready to haul her over my shoulder and take her home if she would let me. I would show her just how a powerful shifter could worship every inch of her perfect body.

But then, over the thrum of the music, I heard a voice that brought me hurtling back to reality—back to the realization that neither of us had arrived here on our own. It was Lana and Travis, and they were calling our names.

Marley's head was still cradled in my hand, and she looked blissed out beyond belief. With her human ears, she couldn't hear Travis and Lana calling us. My lips flattened into a thin line as I ground my teeth.

"Fuck," I hissed.

The sudden expletive shook Marley out of her trance immediately. "What... What is it?"

"Travis and Lana are looking for us," I said.

"Oh! We totally left them hanging after Lana went off to help Travis," she said, straightening to look past me to see if she could catch a glimpse of them. "Maybe we ought to go back and hang out with them?"

There was a momentary hesitation as she suggested going back to the group—a clear expression of her nerves at ending our clandestine escape. I watched as her eyes danced, looking at my face and then my body as if checking for some kind of sign that I was going to blow up at her.

I wanted to ask her what the look was about, but I held off. Instead, I tried my best to look encouraging without being piteous. "Yeah, better not to give anyone a reason to gossip."

I offered her my hand again, and she quirked an adorably crooked smile before taking it and letting me lead her away from the dance floor.

Being slightly more imposing in size than Marley, it was easier for me to navigate us out of the chaos. People tended to move out of your way when you stood at six-foot-something. I moved her through the parting crowd and almost immediately caught sight of Lana and Travis, raising a hand to indicate where we were in addition to letting them know all was well.

Lana raised an eyebrow at our joined hands, but I didn't relinquish my grip on Marley's hand. It was my only consolation after having my dance cut short.

"How's the hand?" I asked Travis.

"Entirely fine, thanks to Nurse Lana," he said.

Lana rolled her eyes. "Don't call me that," she said, though she didn't sound particularly offended or bothered by it. "We were thinking about getting out of here before creepy guy comes to. You guys want to come with us?"

"Where are you thinking of going?" Marley asked.

"Another shifter bar. Closer to downtown, trendier," Lana answered.

Trendier? Holy hell, I didn't think I'd be able to keep up. Since becoming a dad, I felt more and more disconnected from the youths of today.

"To be honest, I think I had enough excitement for the entire year already," Marley said.

I could have kissed her on the mouth.

Lana's lips pursed in a very dramatic pout. "But Mar, you drove. If you go home, we all have to go home."

"Cole and I have enough room in the truck," Travis offered.

"I hate to be the bearer of bad news, but I don't think I'm game for an even trendier place than this," I said. "I do have to attempt to function tomorrow."

"Bro! Come on, we came out for a nice time. It's been what, an hour?" Travis argued.

"Yes, and in that hour, we have already knocked a man out and gotten three rounds of drinks in. I am an old man."

"You're thirty," Travis rebutted.

"Okay, you clearly want to stay out. Just keep the truck and drive the girls around. I can shift and run back home. Go have fun with Lana and her friend."

"Paulette," Marley assisted.

"Yeah, Paulette. Go have fun with them, drink all the Jager bombs your irritable bowels can handle, and I'll make sure Syl's favorite Broadway musicals are blasting from the company speakers when you arrive tomorrow," I joked.

Marley made a sound of something between a snort and a laugh. I slid her a conspiratorial look before winking.

"You know what? I think I will take the truck and sub those Jager bombs out for sake bombs. Challenge accepted." Travis did have the courtesy to give me a slightly concerned look, though. "Are you sure you don't mind getting yourself home? It's a bit of a trek to get back to the shore."

"The shore?" Marley asked. "I live out that way. I can just give you a ride if you like."

I bit back the urge to say something suggestive, opting to smile at Marley instead. "I'd really appreciate that if you're sure you don't mind. Whereabouts do you live?"

"She's in my bungalow on the beach," Lana said.

I was familiar with Lana's beach house, having done some work on the kitchen.

"Oh, that's perfect. I'll just come with you to the house and shift there to run to my place," I said.

"If you're sure," Marley said. "I don't mind taking you all the way home."

"It's fine. Honestly, I could use the run. Especially after I embarrassed myself earlier during my reserve visit," I said.

Marley smiled and nodded.

"Well, fine," Lana said, still pouting. "I wanted to see you let loose a little bit more tonight, Mar... but I will let you escape tonight if for no other reason than because you at least tried to have a good time before Creeper McFuckFace ruined it."

Marley laughed and pulled a shoulder up in a shrug. "Maybe next time. We'll go on a weekend so I don't have to try herding a bunch of shifter children with a hangover when I go to work the next day, hm?"

"A very valid point," I said. "After all, one of those shifter children is my son."

"Your son is a little angel from what I hear," Lana said, looking pointedly at Marley.

I glanced at Marley just in time to catch her flushing and averting her eyes.

"Well, you guys go on ahead. We won't keep you. I'll settle the tab with Marley on the way out. You kids go have fun."

Travis rolled his eyes and placed a hand on the small of Lana's back as they made the walk to the exit. "I don't know about you, but I feel like it should be illegal for someone who is the same age as you to say, 'You kids go have fun.'"

"It is giving weird old-man energy," Lana said as she turned to give me an amused look. "Marley, be good! Don't pass up on anything I would do—especially if it's *steamy*."

I chuckled. Marley's face had taken on a shade of crimson so bright I could even see it in the dim lighting of the club.

"She's...drunk," Marley said. "So, I guess...uh, give everything she says very little thought."

"I will make every effort not to think about doing something *steamy* with you," I said, imitating Lana's tone. "Come on, let's go settle the tab."

I placed my hand between her shoulders to lead her toward the same passage Lana and Travis had just vanished through.

The Night Shift had become much more crowded since we first arrived, so it took considerable effort to actually make it to the bar. When we finally did, it took us nearly another fifteen minutes to actually settle the tab and get my card back from the bartender. The club had officially become slammed, busier than any other place I'd seen.

At last, we made it outside to the cool night air. It was a relief to be away from the overstimulating sounds and smells. I dragged in a deep breath of the clean, crisp breeze.

"It's overwhelming for me to be in a club like that," Marley said. "I can't imagine what it must be like for you."

"You kinda get used to things like that," I said. "Still, it's nice to get outside and get a break from it when you can. Nothing like a coastal breeze, especially at night."

Marley nodded, bouncing a bit on her heels. "Uhm, my car is this way. It's pretty small, sorry. I don't usually drive lumberjacks around, so I got a compact."

I laughed warmly. "So that's all I am to you, huh? A lumberjack?"

"I guess you would be more of a timber wolf?" she said, tapping her chin with the tip of her finger.

"And you say *I* tell bad dad jokes?" I asked incredulously. "That one blows Fur Sure Solutions right out of the water."

Marley giggled. "What? I thought it was clever."

"The joke, much like you, was very clever," I said indulgently. "But it was also very bad."

"I think I'll take that."

Now that we were getting some distance from the club and from our friends, Marley seemed to be lightening up a bit. It excited me to see a different side of her—I was curious about exploring each facet of who Marley was as a person. I'd already seen her in a professional capacity, seen her out of her element, seen her frazzled and frightened, and now I was seeing her at ease.

At least, I hoped she was at ease.

She was right about her car. The practical little hatchback was slate gray and *tiny*. The rear window had a sticker with the Polar Shift logo on it as well as some remnants of old stickers she hadn't bothered to scrape off properly. In a moment of reflexive caretaking, I almost offered to get it off with the proper car-detailing tools and products but thought better of it. It probably would have been weird to offer to do something like that.

She unlocked the car, and I slid into the passenger seat, my knees bumping against the dashboard.

"Sorry!" she said frantically.

"No worries," I said. "Do you mind if I adjust it?"

"No, of course not. Make yourself at home."

I adjusted the seat, scooting it all the way back. The struggles of having long legs.

Marley started the car as I buckled my seatbelt, and we were on our way.

Her car's radio connected to her phone and started playing some loud, party-girl music. She winced and scrambled to turn it down as we came up on a red light just outside of the parking lot for The Night Shift.

"Sorry," she said, changing the song. "That's Paulette's music. She said we had to get in the partying spirit."

"Paulette and Travis sound a lot alike," I said. "I guess we have our token human and shifter friends, huh?"

Marley laughed, shaking her head slightly. "Paulette is a lot of fun. One of those girls who just loves everything to be fun and exciting. Is Travis that way?"

I shrugged. "He tries to get me out of my shell a lot. For better or worse."

Marley nodded. "Yeah, Lana and Paulette *both* do that. They have since I moved here. To be honest, this is the first time I've gone out in years. I think that's why I ran out of steam so quickly—I forgot what it's like."

"I haven't been out to a place like that in a long time, either. Not since before Noah was born," I said. "Not entirely sure I prefer it. I'm happier at a little brewery or a wine cellar."

"Or just really, *really* good food," Marley said.

"You know what? Yeah. Really good food trumps all the alcohol in the world."

"Nothing good has ever happened because of alcohol. But there are lots of great things that have happened over meals," Marley agreed.

"Our founding fathers made decisions over dinners," I said, "Consolidating debt, picking out the location of the capital."

"Stone soup—I use that one to teach the kids the importance of sharing."

"That's adorable," I said, unable to stop my grin. "The last supper?"

"Oof, maybe not that one," she said with a wince.

"Actually, yeah, you're right."

A comfortable silence fell between us, and I concentrated on the music. I've always felt that you could learn a lot about a person by the kind of music they listen to. Travis was always a sort of pop-punk-emo listener. In fact, when I'd first met him, he had the full emo aesthetic, except with blonde hair because his parents wouldn't let him dye it black.

Marley's music suited her gentle nature. Lots of quiet plucking of single acoustic guitars, breathy vocals, and slow tempos. The music seemed to wander and flourish between jazzy instrumentals, atmospheric low-fidelity tracks, and folk musicians of various kinds. It was the kind of music you might listen to after a long, noisy, chaotic day—which I imagined Marley experienced a lot since she taught young children.

"This is nice," I said.

"What is? The drive or the music?"

"Both, but mostly the music."

"I love this band," she said. "The Winterests. Have you listened to them before?"

I shook my head. "No, but I think I might start to," I said. "The lead singer has a really distinctive voice."

"He's amazing live if you love witty banter," she said. "Ugh, I miss live music. I haven't been to a concert in forever."

"We ought to go see one together. I've been due for some live music for a while," I said.

She hesitated, her legs shifting a little before she tugged at the hem of her skirt.

I kept my voice casual when I spoke. "We don't have to go together. It was just a suggestion. I'm not trying to be pushy."

"I didn't think you were trying to be pushy," she said. "You've been nothing but polite to me during all of the—what—four interactions we had today?"

I nodded, waiting for the caveat I knew was in coming.

"But..."

There we go.

"I mean, I don't know if they talk about this with the parents, but teachers aren't really supposed to date the parents of students. Especially across species lines—"

"Especially?" I asked.

"I... Listen, I'm not lycanphobic. I promise—"

"I know you aren't," I said gently. "I just wonder why *especially*."

"If something bad were to happen—any kind of PR disaster—it could be the end of POSHA. And with the school paving the way and setting all the precedents for integrated schools, it could set the entire effort being made back for years, you know?"

I nodded. She turned down the street that would take us out of the city and toward the beachside suburb.

"I don't think I could live with myself if I single-handedly set back the progression of shifter rights," she said, a keening warble in her voice.

I smiled, even though I was being rejected. She was just so sweet... too sweet. Which, of course, only made me want her more.

"I know there's a rule against dating, but are there rules against being friends?" I asked.

I studied her profile as she kept her eyes pointedly ahead, her mouth working for a moment as the cogs of her mind churned.

"No, there's no rule against us being friends," she finally said.

I nodded. "And two friends can go see a Winterests concert together, right?"

She exhaled, long and low, as she came up to a stop sign. When she came to a full stop, she looked over at me.

"You only want to be friends?"

"*Only?* That's a strange word to use."

"I just mean...that. Is that really all you want?"

It wasn't all I wanted, and I was certain she knew that. Marley was a smart woman. There was no need to spell it out for her. I didn't need to insult her or myself that way.

"What matters is what *you* want, Marley," I said.

Her throat bobbed as she swallowed. She continued looking at me as we idled at the stop sign, much longer than necessary.

"I think I want more than I should," she said finally. "Did...did Lana tell you anything about me? About my history?"

I gave a slight shake of my head. "No, that's not Lana's way. She would never divulge private information about someone without their permission. She's a loyal friend."

Marley nodded, then took her foot off the brake and started navigating toward Lana's bungalow. I had the feeling she was driving again just to avoid looking at me as she talked.

"My ex is a shifter," she finally said. "I dated him for close to five years, and it...it just ended really badly."

I let that sink in, silence swirling around us until I spoke. "So, you don't want to be involved with another shifter."

It wasn't a question, more of a clarifying statement.

"I don't want to be involved with *anyone*," she said without missing a beat. "I'm still trying to figure out who I even am anymore. And it's not that you're not a gorgeous, desirable man. I'd have to be an idiot not to see the appeal, but... I just—"

She let out a frustrated sigh, and I chuckled.

"I get it, Marley," I said. "I truly do. My ex—Noah's mother—did a number on me. I don't blame you in the slightest. And again, I am not exactly looking for anything either."

"But?" she prompted.

"*But,*" I said, taking the bait. "I would also be an idiot if I didn't think you looked good enough to eat."

Her throat bobbed again, and her face reddened.

"We can't. We shouldn't even be entertaining this. You're one of my student's fathers."

"I am—until next summer—and then I'll just be Cole."

She bit her lower lip, and I had to stop myself from doing the same—from leaning over the center console and taking her face in my hands, claiming her with all the fervor and want that a wolf would claim its meal.

A low growl came from my throat as I forced myself to look away.

We said nothing until we pulled into her driveway, the only sound in the car the calm, textured voice of the lead singer of the Winterests.

She put the car in park.

She took the key out of the ignition.

She let out a long, heavy breath.

Then, just when I was about to excuse myself and leave the car, just when I was getting ready to shift into my wolf form and run away with my tail tucked between my legs, Marley reached over and curled her perfect fingers into the fabric of my shirt, tugging me wordlessly toward her.

I didn't wait for her to change her mind. Heart racing, I obliged her, leaning over to meet her.

Our mouths clashed in a clumsy and messy kiss, the seal imperfect and needy. My lips tried desperately to latch onto hers, only to miss a step in the choreography. I growled, not even parting from her to reach down between us to unfasten her seatbelt.

I parted just long enough to draw the strip of woven nylon away from her. Then I grabbed her, one hand on her perfect thigh, the other on the lovely dip of her waist, and pulled her over into the passenger seat.

A small sound escaped her throat as I roughly positioned her on me, pulling her knees apart and placing them on either side of my lap so she straddled me. I moaned at the soft curves of her pressing against my thighs, my cock.

"You're fucking perfect," I moaned.

"*Shut up,*" she commanded, then our mouths met again.

This time, the seal was perfect. Lips and tongues mingled in perfect rhythm. She scooped her hand into the hair at the back of my head, rounded nails raking pleasantly across my scalp at the same moment that she seized my lower lip between her teeth.

I shifted my hips, my cock straining against my jeans. She ground her hips down on me in a moment of blissful torture.

Digging my fingers into the soft skin of her thighs, I pressed my forehead to hers.

"I need to fuck you, so decide if you want to ride my cock here in this car or if you want me to take care of you in your bed like a good boy," I growled.

She panted against my mouth before undoing my seatbelt and opening the car door.

I didn't dare let her climb off me. I quickly finagled myself out of the seatbelt and pulled her tight against me, my hands cupping the generous curves of her ass as I hefted her out of the vehicle with ease. I kicked the car door shut, and Marley lowered her mouth to claim the sensitive skin of my neck as I carried her across the driftwood walkway toward the front door.

Marley kissed my neck with a new intensity, the faint pressure from before ramping up with dizzying force.

"Now, now," I grunted. "Not hard enough to mark, you little minx."

She stopped nibbling me and huffed against my damp skin.

"I'm sorry. It's just been forever," she whispered.

"Believe me," I said as I neared the door. "I get it more than you know."

I adjusted her slightly so I could hold her against me with one arm. With my free hand, I guided her chin up. Her eyes were gorgeous and dreamy as she looked at me, cupping my face with her small hand.

"Are you sure this is okay?" she asked.

"That's my line," I joked. "I was just about to ask you if you were sure you wanted to do this."

"I'm sure I want to do this," she said. "I'm just not sure if I'm going to regret it tomorrow."

"Because you're not sure about me?"

“Oh, no. I was sure of you the moment I rammed into you like a bulldozer.”

I laughed as I leaned in to kiss her neck. She let out short breaths that punctuated her continuing thoughts. “I just mean…” she said as I pinned her against the wall. “What if this blows up in my face?”

“It won’t,” I said as I pressed a kiss against the point where her neck met her jaw. “I’m clear on what you don’t want, and I’m about to learn very intimately what you do want.”

She let out an airy laugh. “Take me to the door. There’s a code.”

“Thank God for technology,” I growled into her ear as I picked her up and pushed her against the door.

Instead of being met by the solid force of a locked door, however, we almost tumbled to the floor. I had to take a few clumsy steps as we pushed right through the doorway. My stomach flipped as Marley yelped, but I managed to catch our balance before we went hurdling to the ground.

“Easy, easy,” I said. “I got you.”

“I locked all the doors when I left,” she said.

She stiffened in my arms as her head started whipping around.

"Can you get a light? I can hardly see."

I didn't have to get a light. I could smell who had been here easily enough. It was unmistakable in the throes of my desire for Marley—in my possessive and protective instincts over her.

It was the smell of another wolf. A male, to be precise.

Fuck.

"Marley," I said, willing my voice to stay calm. "I'm going to walk you back to your car. When you get there, I want you to lock the doors and call the police. Ask for Ginger Lucas."

Her fingers curled into my shirt. I could hear her heart kicking up at a fearful tempo and smell the anxiety and stress coming off her.

"Why?" she asked, but the tone of her voice told me she already knew the answer.

"Because a shifter has broken into your place."

Chapter 7 - Marley

I was so freaked out that I couldn't even follow Cole's instructions properly. Truth be told, I couldn't even remember getting in the car with how quickly I descended into a complete and utter panic.

Someone—a shifter—had come into my house. It must have been Wyatt, but I couldn't be sure. Even if Cole described every nuance of the scent he'd caught, there was no way that I could have confirmed whether it was Wyatt.

My mind raced as the past year of careful repression surged through me. I realized I had only been barely holding it together. This whole time I'd been waiting for the other shoe to drop, and here it finally was. Somehow, Wyatt had tailed me all the way to New Middle Bluff, and now he would ruin my life here too.

I ran through a million scenarios in my head. I would probably have to leave the state and start anew in some other city, and I probably wouldn't get as lucky this time. There was no way I'd find someone like Lana who would drop everything and put me up in a place, give me a job, and introduce me to people in town.

I was fucked. I was so fucked.

I pinched the bridge of my nose as a sharp pain pierced the backs of my eyes. I winced and shuddered out a shaky breath. Just then, I felt a heavy, familiar comfort settle on my shoulders. I opened my eyes and found Cole kneeling before the ottoman I was sitting on, my favorite blanket wrapped around my shoulders. He tugged the blanket tight around me as he looked up at me.

"Hey," he said, his voice quiet and unobstructive. "No sign of him on this blanket, so he didn't touch everything, all right? The police are looking around now, seeing if they can track him or not, but it seems like he might have jumped into the ocean after he left."

"What's that mean?" I asked.

"If he hopped into the water, we'll lose his scent, even if it was just to get on a jet ski to make a getaway," he said.

I nodded, not really sure what else to say. Behind Cole, a woman who looked the spitting image of him in a female body hovered patiently. I lifted my gaze to look back at her, and Cole looked that way, also.

"Marley, this is my kid sister, Ginger," he said.

"Kid sister? Really?" she asked dryly.

"My *very professional* sister just wants to ask you a few things," he said pointedly. "Are you up for that?"

"Do I have a choice?" I asked.

Ginger's brow tensed, and she tilted her head. "You always have a choice, Miss Cage."

I chewed on the inside of my cheek, realizing how pitiful I must have just sounded. Regardless, I nodded, and Ginger came to stand next to Cole, who kept a supportive hand on my knee. Notebook in hand, Ginger eyeballed him. It seemed like she was trying to sus out who we were to each other. Good luck with that, I thought. I didn't even know.

I appreciated Cole's steady presence. For once, I didn't feel entirely alone in a crisis. It was a complete departure from my experience after fighting Wyatt off when he'd tried to claim me. Not even my parents wanted anything to do with me.

Still, even though Ginger was a shifter and Cole's sister, I could sense the same indifference from her as I'd experienced with the police back in Leighton Valley. Maybe it was just part of the job—maybe she had seen so much that someone breaking and entering into a human woman's home didn't faze her. Still, she could have at least tried to appear concerned.

"How long have you occupied this residence, Miss Cage?" she asked.

"A little over a year," I said.

"And you don't own the property?"

"No," I said. "It belongs to my friend Lana Gold."

Ginger nodded and took notes in her notebook. "Have you noticed any strangers lurking around lately? Anyone who seems to be following you? Anyone you've noticed in more than one place you've been to?"

I shook my head. "No, but I have been feeling like someone has been watching me or following me lately. And there was someone who seemed to be watching me at the school today."

"Do you have a physical description of the person? Where do you work?"

"I work at Polar Shift Academy. It was our first day of school today. I saw the person at recess, so I didn't get a good look at them."

"So, it could have been a parent?"

I stiffened and bit on the inside of my lip. "It could have been, but I don't think it was."

"But we can't rule it out," she insisted. "We can't rule out that it was just a parent checking on their child?"

"Ginge," Cole said, a hint of warning in his tone.

"Detective Lucas," she corrected. "And regardless of whether you like this girl, I have to do my job the way I do it for everyone else. If we see hoof prints, we need to start with horses, not zebras."

"Occam's razor," I said flatly before giving a humorless laugh. "The cops in Leighton Valley said the same thing after—"

I shook my head.

"Never mind. You're right. We can't rule out that it was a parent checking, but I didn't see the person at this morning's drop-off, and I made a point to introduce myself to as many parents as I could."

Detective Lucas nodded and jotted something down in her notebook. “Can you come with me and take a look around? Let me know if you see anything missing or out of place, and take a look at a couple of other things?”

I nodded. “Sure.”

I stood and hugged the blanket closer to me, using it as a shield as we started to walk through.

It looked like the intruder had fussed with the security lighting because the sensors were no longer tripping them in the front or the back. Whoever had come in had left most of my stuff untouched except for little things: a tilted picture frame, a perfume bottle out of its usual place, and my toothbrush on the counter instead of in the holder.

All they had to go off was a scent, an open door, and a sabotaged lighting system, it seemed, at least, until we went into the kitchen.

A simple handwritten note had been pinned to my fridge with one of my alphabet magnets—the ‘M’ magnet, specifically. The words on the note chilled me to the bone.

Go home, Marley. Where you belong.

The cops took the note as evidence, but when all was said and done, they didn't seem particularly encouraged about the investigation.

"We'll do what we can, Miss Cage. But the fact remains that all we have on the perpetrator is a scent, a note, and a door that may or may not have been locked. The most we can likely charge this person with is trespassing," Detective Lucas said.

"But they broke into my residence."

"They didn't steal anything. We can't even confirm that they touched anything. Even the note was written on stationery you don't possess. I'm sorry, Miss Cage, but this is all we can do until there's another incident."

My throat tightened, my lungs constricting. "So, you're telling me I have to let them break in again? What if I'm here? How am I supposed to protect myself from a shifter?"

Ginger sighed as her officers exited the house. "I'm sorry, Miss Cage. I wish you luck and safety. Maybe invest in a proper security system and some cameras for some peace of mind."

Tears burned my eyes as I shook my head. "That's it? I just have to try to sleep here tonight, even though a strange man I don't even know has come into my home?"

"Your decisions on that matter are your own, Miss Cage. I'm sorry I can't be of more help—"

"You can spend the night at my place, Marley," Cole said. "Noah's with my parents tonight, and I have a couple of guest rooms you can choose from. My house has a complete security system. I'll make sure no one bothers you tonight, okay?"

"Cole," Ginger said sharply, but she shrank back a little when I cut my gaze to her. "I mean, didn't you say you just met this woman today? It's one thing to hook up with a girl you just met, but inviting her to your home?"

As much as I was irritated with Detective Lucas and embarrassed that she was calling me out for making out with her brother, she had a point. I couldn't just crash at a student's home, no matter the circumstances.

"It's okay, Cole. I can just stay with Lana or Paulette."

He shook his head. "This is a male wolf, Marley. If he decides to tail you or attack, Lana or Paulette will still have a hard time fighting him off. I don't want to put any other women at risk tonight if we can help it," he said. "If you're not comfortable with staying in my home, at least let me take you to a hotel and get a room next to you."

God, what a nightmare. A hotel would be so expensive.

But I couldn't deny the logic in what he was saying. I wouldn't be able to live with myself if something happened to Paulette or Lana because of me. Still though, when we'd arrived here, we were about to…we almost slept together. I'd almost put everything on the line for a moment of lust. What would happen once we were alone again? What if I really couldn't help myself? And what if Wyatt really was watching me? I didn't want Cole to get hurt, either.

Regardless, I couldn't stay here. I couldn't afford a hotel, and I wouldn't make Cole go through all that trouble for me.

Finally, I relented.

"Okay," I said. "Thank you, Cole. I can't believe how kind and generous you're being. I really don't deserve it."

"You do," he said without any hesitation. "Please don't worry about it. Just let me help you through this rough night. We'll figure out the next steps tomorrow, okay? For now, let's just get you a hot shower and a warm bed."

I pressed my lips tight together to keep them from quivering. Nodding, I said, "I'll just grab a few things, and then we can go if that's all right with you?"

He flashed an encouraging smile. "Yeah, take as long as you need."

It was only a short while later, when I climbed in my car, this time on the passenger side—I was too shaky to drive—that I realized I was going to sleep at the house of a man I'd only met that morning.

Chapter 8 - Cole

I was relieved Marley had agreed to spend the night at my house. If she'd refused, I would have just patrolled her house—or wherever she'd intended to stay—all night. I could protect her better at my place, and I would feel like a creepy stalker prowling around outside her home. And since Noah was at my parents' house until morning, there wouldn't be any awkward questions about why his teacher was sleeping over.

Marley's brightness had left her when I'd told her about the intruder. All the color had drained from her face, and fear shone from her exhausted eyes. Just how badly had her ex treated her for her to be so terrified that he might have followed her to New Middle Bluff?

Then again, I could only speculate as to how complicated my feelings would be if Olivia broke into my house and made herself comfortable. How unnerving it would be if she pointedly avoided doing anything that could get her in any real legal trouble. It was absolutely ludicrous that Marley's stalker could get off with nothing but a misdemeanor just because he didn't steal or break anything.

What about her sense of security? Or feeling at peace in her own home?

As I drove Marley's car to my house, I let out a heavy breath to dispel the rage coiled around my every nerve. I flexed my hands and rolled my neck from side to side to loosen my bunched-up muscles.

"Are you angry at me?" Marley asked.

Her voice sounded so small, so fragile. It broke my damn heart.

"No, Marley. I'm not angry or annoyed or anything else like that," I promised. "More just irate with my sister. I'd hoped she would take care of you, but she kind of let me down in that regard."

"I'm used to that kind of thing."

"You shouldn't be used to something like that, Marley," I said softly. "No one should be."

"I guess it depends on where you are in the world. It was even worse back in Leighton Valley," she said.

I pulled into the driveway that led to my office entrance. "Is that where you're from?"

"Yep. And when the shit hit the fan there, they basically said the same thing. Actually, it was worse. They told me it was my fault."

She wasn't looking at me, but I could see her profile. Her lower lip quivered, and a single tear tracked its way down her cheek. She quickly wiped it away with the blanket that was still wrapped around her shoulders, but it was no use because two more took its place.

"Was this regarding your ex?" I asked as I put the car in park and took the keys out of the ignition.

Her nod was barely perceptible.

"Do you want to talk about it?" I asked, hoping my tone was soft enough so as not to pressure her.

A shake of her head. I leaned forward and brushed a kiss over her temple. She didn't shy away from me, which I was glad for, but it didn't seem to help much either.

I pressed my head against hers.

"Marley, no matter what happens, I will always believe you. No matter what anyone says about your past, no matter what happened. I believe you."

A sob burst from her mouth as she buried her face in the blanket. I wrapped an arm around her and rubbed her shoulder.

We stayed like that for a while, Marley crying and me just holding a quiet vigil for her. I wondered if she'd ever allowed herself to have a good, cathartic cry. I didn't press her for information or give her empty platitudes just to make her feel better. It seemed like she needed someone to hold her while she fell apart without risking losing herself completely.

I don't know how long we sat there, but her crying eventually slowed to little hiccups and sniffles.

"Do you want to go inside?" I asked her after she had quieted.

She nodded.

"Let me take your bag." I leaned back and held out a hand. She relinquished the handle of a colorful duffle bag in oranges and yellows that seemed to just scream *Marley*. I got out of the car and swung the bag over my shoulder, then stepped around the car to open the passenger door. Marley hesitantly climbed out as I nodded toward my house.

"I run my business from home, so we have an alarm system, cameras on every door, and both biometric and traditional locks," I said. "The only people who can get in are my trusted employees, me, and my family."

Again, she just nodded and didn't say a word, but I didn't miss the way her shoulders sagged with quiet relief.

I ushered her ahead of me, entering my house through the same door I had earlier that morning when Noah flew down the stairs toward me. It felt strange to bring a woman in here after the space had been dedicated to my family and business for so long.

As soon as we entered, the lights turned on automatically, transitioning from darkness to a warm evening glow. I placed her bag and keys on my breakfast bar.

She sniffled. "Nice place."

"Thanks," I said, smiling softly. "How about I set you up in my *very* luxurious shower and make you a cup of chamomile tea so you can relax?"

"Sh-shower by myself, right?" she asked.

I nodded. "I know things between us got hot and heavy back at your place, but believe me, I don't take advantage of women when they're as distressed as you are. Seduction is the last thing I'm thinking about. I just want you to feel comfortable and, hopefully, get some sleep. It was a crazy day."

A breath stuttered out of her. "I'm sorry that I keep acting like you're going to be a creep. I just—"

I put up my hand to stop her. "You don't have to apologize. I completely understand. Come on, let me show you the bathroom."

We walked down the hallway, past Noah's room, past the room she'd likely sleep in, all the way to the end of the hall into my bedroom. When I'd built the house, I'd wanted an especially large master bedroom. I wasn't sure why, but I figured my younger self had seen it as a sign of status when really it was just more space to keep clean.

I didn't regret any part of my decision to put together a luxurious bathroom, though. The sandy tile floors were heated and on a timer, so when I woke in the morning, I wouldn't have to brave the dreaded cold tile against my bare feet. Stained concrete fixtures were an unconventional but stylish touch. I'd had his-and-hers sinks put in because I'd originally designed the place when I was still with Olivia, but it was still a nice feature when Noah wanted to pretend to shave.

The pièce de résistance, though? The *shower*.

One of the common ailments many shifters had to deal with was muscle soreness, not just from shifting but also because we had so much more going on internally than the average human. A nice, hot shower helped with the aches and pains of my everyday life.

The shower was a large square, about five feet by five feet. It had a huge showerhead in the ceiling that had four settings—mist, rain, curtain, and waterfall. Two smaller showerheads embedded in the walls added more overall coverage to the body, and a movable showerhead sat in a holster on the wall, which only turned on if it was grabbed.

The bathroom had a tub as well, big enough to fit my leggy frame and a partner, but it rarely got any use.

“Do you prefer a shower or a bath?” I asked Marley.

She was openly gawking, and I’d be lying if I said it didn’t make me a little proud.

“You like it?” I asked.

“It’s like a spa. All it’s missing is a mud bath,” she said.

Shrugging, I said, "I like having a nice shower."

"No kidding." She gaped at me. I was relieved to see some of the color returning to her face.

"Bubble bath?" I offered, circling back to the original question.

"Tempting," she admitted. "But it's getting late, and I still want to make it into work tomorrow. I think a shower would be just fine."

I nodded, walking over to the wall where the external controls for the shower were installed. I showed her how to use them and indulged in her controlled giddiness. This wasn't saving her life or even making her day, but I hoped it was at least cheering her up after a horrible night.

"When you're done, come back out to the kitchen. I'll have some tea ready for you and a fire going in the living room so you can wind down before bed."

"You really don't have to do all of this. Just hosting me is more than enough," Marley said.

"I know I don't have to do it," I said. "But I like taking care of people. It's just how I am. So don't worry, I'm enjoying this in a weird way—even if the circumstances are kinda shitty."

I walked over to a hidden cupboard in the bathroom and pulled out two fluffy towels, as well as some shampoo and body wash I kept stocked for Ginger and Sylvia—not that either of them took many showers at my place, but with an infant running around and the shoreline just a few feet away, it was best to be prepared. I also took out a toothbrush still in its packaging just in case she forgot to pack hers.

"Uh, it's a kids' one from Noah's last dentist visit, so it's a little small," I said.

"I totally forgot to grab mine or any of my shower stuff, so it's perfect. Thank you," she said.

"No problem, just let me know if you need anything."

She nodded and sighed in what I thought was relief. "All right. I'll, uh...see you in a few?"

"See you in a few," I confirmed before leaving her to her own devices.

I went back to the kitchen, where I set up two coffee mugs with chamomile-lavender teabags and filled my electric kettle with water, but waited on starting it until I heard the shower turn off. She'd probably need just as much time after getting out of the shower to get dried off and dressed as it took to boil the water for the tea.

In the meantime, I lit the fire in my fireplace and turned on some relaxing music similar in vein to what Marley had been playing in her car.

Marley spent almost half an hour in the shower. I didn't blame her; she must have felt like she had that strange wolf's scent all over her and was trying to wash the feeling of the violation off her skin. I could only imagine what it must have been like for her to discover her home had been broken into after everything she'd been through.

I didn't know every detail about what happened between her and her ex, but I knew enough about how some shifters could be to know it must have been really bad if she had to leave town to get away from it. I'd heard some real horror stories on the news. Women being imprisoned and bitten against their will, women dying because their abusive boyfriends tried to force them through the change into a shifter.

The thought that something like that might have been done to someone as sweet and gentle as Marley cracked something deep inside of me—something I'd not felt in a long, long time. It had been building up since we talked on the playground, and it was becoming something I couldn't ignore.

Becoming. That was the keyword. It wasn't all the way there yet. I could keep those feelings buried if needed.

I poked at the wood as it started to crackle, the pleasant birch scent filling the room and making it feel more like a cold winter night rather than an evening in early fall. It made me feel comfortable and cozy, and I hoped it would do the same for Marley.

I set up some plush blankets on the couch for her to snuggle up in. My sister once told me that, after experiencing shock or trauma, a lot of people often felt cold once the adrenaline was out of their system and the threat was gone. Sometimes their body temperature would even drop as all their resources were diverted to the vital organs of the body, thus leaving the extremities to the cold.

I hoped the tea, the blankets, and the fire would help her feel safe.

After getting all that done, I heard the water cut off in the bathroom, so I flicked on the electric kettle. By the time she was walking down the hallway in her pajamas, the tea was already steeping.

Marley in pajamas was nothing short of adorable.

Olivia always wore silky negligees and lacy little things to bed. They were nice, don't get me wrong. A beautiful body in lingerie is always a great thing, but sometimes the extra effort it took to get her to dress down was a pain. She simply couldn't have a lazy sweats day.

Marley, though? Marley came out of the bathroom in a matching set of flannel pajamas, pink and covered with pencils, pens, rulers, and cats with glasses. I had to suppress the urge to chuckle; it was just too cute to handle.

"It smells amazing in here," she said with a sigh. "It's so cozy."

I smiled. "You want some milk in your tea?"

"I've, uh, never had it in tea. Is it good?"

"Absolutely. Go sit, and I'll bring it over to you."

She padded over to the sofa and bundled herself up in the blankets and pillow I'd set up for her comfort. It gave me the same joy I imagined a cat had when it curled up on a comfy pillow.

I fixed her tea and brought it over before sitting on the opposite side of the couch. I wanted to give her space and get some much-needed rest of my own after the day's events.

I sipped my tea, enjoying the warmth and aromas. Marley and I watched the fire, and a natural silence settled over us as we basked in its comfort.

"Do you think I should move?" Marley suddenly asked.

I looked over at her, surprised by the sudden question after we had been completely quiet for about twenty minutes.

"You're asking me?" I said.

I wanted to slap myself. It was the first thing that popped into my mind, and in my sobering, exhausted trance, I'd just let it fall right out of my mouth.

She looked down at her teacup, her finger sliding along the ceramic as she hedged a little bit.

"I guess it's kind of dumb to be asking you. I just... I know Lana and Paulette will say I shouldn't, but I'm worried it's my ex. I'm worried he's going to try to ruin my life."

"So, you're asking if I think you should leave town?" I clarified.

She didn't look at me, just gave a sharp nod.

I mulled it over, taking a sip of my tea to give me enough time to formulate what I thought.

"Well," I said. "For starters, I don't think we know for sure that whoever broke in was your ex. We know it was another male shifter, but it could have been coincidental. Of course, the note makes that unlikely, but it's possible it wasn't him. I mean, you were with him for a while, right? Would you recognize his handwriting?"

"It's been a while since I've looked at it," she said. "But yeah, I guess it was kind of messy compared to my ex's handwriting."

I rubbed my hand over my jaw as I considered. "But—just for this hypothetical—let's just say it is the worst-case scenario, and it *is* your ex pestering you," I said. "I think if you ditched town now, you would be on the run for the rest of your life.

"I know he spooked you out of your hometown, and I know the people in your hometown weren't very kind or tolerant people. But you've built a decent life for yourself here in New Middle Bluff. And if this asshole is anything like the other bullshit alpha-bros I've met, you going on the lam will only embolden him. He'll think he's got you."

"What if he does have me?" Marley asked. "What if he's right? What if there's nothing I can do but what he wants?"

"I think you have enough shifters in your corner for that thought not to even cross your mind," I said. "I think you're too smart and too sweet to let this dickhead ruin your life for you."

"What if...what if he's the violent type?" Marley said so quietly that I was certain I wouldn't have been able to hear her without my keener senses.

The question twisted in my gut and made the hair on the back of my neck stand on end. If anyone tried to hurt her—if anyone so much as laid a finger on a single hair on Marley's perfect little head—I would gut them. I would tear their throat out and relish every minute of it. I would—

Easy, Cole. Easy.

"If he is the violent type, then you can at least count on Lana and me to watch your six," I said. "And we can at least prepare you for the worst-case scenario if neither of us is around. We'll set up a panic button system and get you some bear spray. Hell, I'll reinforce your door with steel myself."

She didn't seem convinced, still staring down into her tea, all bundled up like a sad little burrito.

"Marley, there's no need to figure this out tonight," I said. "Tonight, just focus on recovering from the shock of having your home violated. Focus on getting sleep so the kids don't run you completely ragged tomorrow. But just remember that you're not alone in this, all right? You have people in your life who care about you. Don't isolate yourself from them."

I was careful not to presume to include myself in that group, even if I counted myself among them.

Marley chewed on her thumbnail as she gave another slight nod.

I drained the last of my tea before stretching my arms over my head. "I'm going to try and get some shut-eye. Help yourself to any room you like. You can even sleep out here if you'd like," I said. "My room is just down the hall if you need me."

Finally, she looked at me and rewarded me with the slightest curve of a smile.

"Thank you again for everything, Cole. I really appreciate you."

"Any time, sweetheart," I said without thinking.

I chastised myself internally with every step I took toward my bedroom, even forgetting to put my empty mug in the sink.

A few hours later, I was still tossing and turning. I'd heard Marley get up and go to bed in the guest room right next to mine. I'd heard her slide under the covers and, presumably, go to sleep.

I'd gotten up to bank the fire, fairly sure that Marley didn't know how to do it, and grabbed a snack, thinking it was hunger that was keeping me from falling asleep.

But that had been an hour and a half ago, and sleep had yet to take me.

I just couldn't get my mind to shut up and leave me alone. My mind wavered between the irresistible urge to carry Marley to my bed and kiss her fear away and the terrible sensation that I was dangling off a cliff with greasy fingers. I'd only met Marley that day, and I was already hooked on her. The idea of her heading home or heading into work by herself made my skin crawl.

I had no right to be so worried about her. I had no right to even care. She'd made it quite clear that she had plenty of trauma in her past thanks to her ex, and I didn't want her to have to face that every time she kissed me.

Then there was the other elephant in the room. I couldn't pursue her—not only because she was my son's teacher and it would put her job at risk—but because doing so would force Noah and me to open our hearts to that disappointment. I couldn't do that to Noah again, couldn't leave him more and more confused.

I needed to be careful. I needed to be wise. I couldn't just worry about my own life, and it wasn't just my heart I had to protect. And what did I even know about Marley, really? That she was good with kids? That she was nice? It wasn't as if she was going to act cold-hearted right off the bat.

She could be as manipulative as Olivia. This could all be for show—an enticing honey pot that would spoil as soon as things settled around us.

I needed to keep my wits about me. I needed to stay alert and guarded. I needed to—

There was a knock at my door.

Anyone else would have easily mistaken it for the usual ambient sounds within a house at nighttime, but I knew the sound of a knuckle against my door.

I threw back the covers and grabbed a T-shirt from a folded stack in my drawer, and pulled it on. I was still tugging the hem of my shirt down when I opened the door.

As expected, Marley stood there. Her hair was braided now, but the braids were disheveled as if she'd been rolling around in bed this entire time. Her back was to me like she had started to walk back to the guest room before I opened the door.

"D-did I wake you?" she asked, fidgeting with her fingers.

I shook my head. "No."

"Have I been keeping you up with my restlessness?"

"No," I said again.

She looked at me for a long time, then back to the guest room like a little kid. When she met my eyes again, hers were rimmed with tears.

"I'm so sorry, but I can't sleep," she said. "Every time I close my eyes, I see my ex. The few times I've dozed off, I'm plagued with nightmares that he's breaking into your house and—"

Before she could finish her sentence, I offered her my hand.

She stopped short, sniffling and quickly wiping the wetness away from her face.

"Just to sleep, though," she said.

"Just to sleep," I promised. "Can't have our nation's future being taught a sleepy teacher, right?"

A wet laugh escaped her as she took my hand.

"Thank you," she said as she stepped over the threshold of my bedroom.

I tucked my many anxieties and fears deeper into my heart as I closed my door behind her.

Chapter 9 - Marley

What on earth was I thinking? What was I, a seven-year-old, knocking on Cole's door because I was having nightmares? God, I was ridiculous.

But he didn't even bat an eye. He didn't even make me talk my foot into my stomach, just held out his strong hand and let me into his room.

Now I was in his bed.

His huge, insanely comfortable bed.

Holy crap, was this what it was like to sleep on a cloud? I'd never been on such a comfortable bed before in my life. I lay down and immediately felt cradled by the soft memory foam and pillowy cushioning beneath me.

"You a back sleeper? Side sleeper?" Cole asked.

"Side. Is that okay?"

He huffed a laugh and shook his head. "Marley, you know that not every question posed to you is done so to evaluate you, right?" he asked before handing me a pillow. "I just wanted to make sure your pillow was supportive enough."

"Oh, thank you," I said, accepting the pillow and placing it under my head.

He took the other pillow and chucked it off the side of the bed.

"Wait," I said.

He looked over at me, a single brow raised. "Are you one of those monsters that sleeps with eighteen pillows?"

"I... only *two*," I said. "I just like to have one to cuddle, that's all."

He looked at the pillow once more before he slid his gaze to me again, and this time his expression was different. It had a sort of smug, teasing quality to it. "I like to think that I can cuddle better than an inanimate object."

My face heated, and I pulled my collar up to my mouth in an attempt to hide my blush.

"Unless cuddling counts as more than sleeping, that is," he said.

"I have been known to enjoy cuddling once in a while," I said, my voice muffled against my shirt.

He grinned and patted the bed next to him. I turned onto my side and scooched back. Cole met me halfway, coming up close behind me and wrapping an arm around my waist. He bent his legs and rested them against the backs of mine. His warm breath rushed down the back of my neck. I shivered at the sensation.

"Cold?" he asked, pulling the blankets up and tucking them around me.

"Maybe a little," I mumbled noncommittally.

"I'm glad you knocked," he said quietly.

"Oh?"

I felt him nod and heard him yawn as he pulled me tighter against him. I could feel every line and plane of his body against my backside, and the warmth of him was a welcoming comfort. His arms around me were strong bands of muscle, yet his embrace was gentle.

"I don't think I would have been able to sleep if I was left to toss and turn in my bed all night," he said, his voice becoming gravelly with sleep.

"Because you were worried about someone breaking in for me?" I asked.

"No, no, no," he said. "Because I just would have been wanting to touch you so bad." He nuzzled into the back of my hair, inhaling deeply. "Because you smell so good. Because you're so beautiful."

I giggled breathlessly, my heart fluttering at the sweet words.

"Are you sleepy now?" I asked.

"So. Fucking. Sleepy."

"Then go to sleep," I said, smoothing my hand down his arm.

He nuzzled the back of my head again and let out a long and slow exhale. His limbs became comfortably heavy around me, almost like a weighted blanket. I felt the steady beat of his heart against my back, a faint rhythmic thumping through the thin fabric of his shirt.

As I lay there with him, I felt slightly unnerved. Like I was waiting for something to happen—some conversation to blow up or get out of hand. Wait for him to snap and call me names or start demanding things from me. I'd only just met him—it was easy to pretend to be reasonable and normal from the start, I supposed. But even when I'd first met Wyatt, I never felt as relaxed as I did with Cole.

With Cole, everything just felt so *easy*.

I was certain that if I'd ever run into Wyatt while he was holding a latte, he would have never let me live it down. He would have screamed at me for hours, then held it against me in every argument for the rest of my life. I'd sworn myself off dating shifters because of how aggressive and bullheaded he could be.

But now, with Cole's arms around me, his slow, steady breaths stirring my hair, and the gentle undulations of his chest rising and falling, I wondered if it wasn't shifters I ought to be avoiding. Maybe I'd just met the worst of not only shifters but of men in general.

My relationship with Wyatt had existed inside a vacuum. I could never get outside input because we had to keep so much of our relationship a secret. By the time the truth came out, I was already in so deep and so defensive of him against my parents and my friends that I had no room to even ask for help. Each time I reached out to ask about a situation, the conversation always turned to the fact that Wyatt was a shifter, so what else could I expect?

But Wyatt wasn't just a shifter. He was also an abuser.

It was the first time I really let myself accept that.

He wasn't a good person; I knew that much. I knew he was a jerk and that he was sexist and cruel. But I had always just thought that I had turned him into that—that I'd somehow ruined the relationship to the point of Wyatt having to be that way toward me. At least, that's how he'd made me feel.

Cole wasn't like that. Cole wasn't sour that our heated moment had been ruined. Cole wasn't bothered about letting me stay here tonight. Cole didn't press me about my past or push me to talk about anything that made me upset. He wanted to meet me where I was, and I couldn't say the same thing for Wyatt.

With Wyatt, it had always been like I was there for his pleasure and comfort. It felt like he relished making my life chaotic.

With Cole, even the difficult things felt easier. He made the massive overwhelm of the night feel digestible. His calm suggestions of tea, a nice shower, the warm fire, and the calm music all gave me the space to process the trauma of the night and parse my thoughts. Now, his calm breathing was like a metronome, lulling me to sleep.

My eyelids grew heavy, and I turned to face him. He opened his arms, and my legs tangled with his. He gathered me close, still sleeping from what I could tell, and I wrapped my arm around him, finally letting sleep claim me.

I woke the next morning to the smell of fresh coffee and melting butter. My eyes fluttered open, and for a moment, I didn't remember how I'd gotten into a huge, comfy bed. Then the previous night came rushing back in vivid detail. Fresh anxiety coursed through my veins, a sort of feeling of displacement in not being safe in my own home.

But as I forced myself to slow my breathing and close my eyes, as I remembered the gentle care Cole had provided, I was able to calm myself.

I rolled out of bed and padded out of the room, hearing the low sound of Cole humming along to some soft music. When I came into the open-concept living room, I saw him at the stove in the kitchen, flipping a pancake.

As soon as my foot hit the tile, Cole glanced over his shoulder, his face breaking into a smile.

"Good morning, beautiful," Cole said. "Hungry?"

I reached up to take out the elastics at the ends of my braids and started undoing them, working my fingers through my hair. "I'm usually not that hungry in the morning, but it smells really good."

"Mama Lucas's secret recipe pancakes," he said, pointing to a huge stack resting on a plate.

"Oh my god, are you feeding an army?" I asked on a laugh.

"When you're a shifter with a shifter son, you're always feeding an army. I freeze these bad boys and pop them in the toaster oven for an easy, five-year-old-friendly breakfast when the time requires," he said.

I leaned against the counter. "So, what's the secret?"

"Well, if I told you, it wouldn't be a secret, would it?" He winked. "I'm afraid that's privileged information."

"I see, you could tell me, but you'd have to kill me," I teased.

"Kill you or marry you," he said off-handedly.

We both stiffened at the same time.

"Because, you know, it's a family secret. It's a joke," he said.

I lifted a hand, dismissing his worry.

"Don't worry about it," I said. "It was cute."

"So, my parents are taking Noah to school today," he said, changing the subject. "I noticed you didn't grab any school things when we left your place. Do you want me to come with you so you can grab your work things?"

"My lessons are already set up in the classroom," I said. "I just need to salvage my bedhead and get dressed. Slap on a little makeup, and I'm good to go."

"Your bedhead is adorable," he said.

"My bedhead is unprofessional," I countered.

"Your clients are five-year-olds. How picky can they be?"

"My real *clients,"* I said, teasing his choice of words. "Are the parents. And parents usually like to think that their kids' teacher is at least a little put-together and not living in their car. Also, what do you mean? Five-year-olds are *notoriously* picky."

"Those parents sound boring, and also, touché," he said.

"It's hard to imagine a parent more entertaining than you," I said without missing a beat.

He rewarded me for that comment with a perfect smile and another wink that threatened to make my knees weak. "That's right, and don't you forget it. Now, go and take a seat and let me serve you some breakfast. I've been told it's the most important meal of the day."

"I think the most important meal is dessert," I said.

"Now, that is something I can get behind," he said.

I hoisted myself up on a bar stool and grabbed the carafe of coffee on the counter, pouring some into a mug that was set out on the countertop and tossing in a splash of milk. I looked around for a bowl of sugar, and before I could ask, Cole brought over a small dish filled with various kinds of sugars and artificial sweeteners, along with a plate of glorious-looking pancakes, complete with a whipped cream smiley face and a sprinkle of powdered sugar.

"Oh my god, adorable," I said.

"You better eat it before his face melts. Not a pretty sight, trust me," he said.

I took a couple of packets of raw sugar and dumped the contents in my coffee as Cole set down some cutlery next to my plate. I stirred my coffee with my fork before cutting through a wedge of the pancakes and taking a bite.

"Mmm," I moaned.

They were perfectly fluffy, delicately sweet, with a slightly crispy edge.

"How do you do that? How do you get them nice and crispy around the edges?"

"Butter," he said. "The low smoke point helps the sugars caramelize. Some people don't like it, but I prefer it that way."

"I love it," I said, shoveling another bite into my mouth. I didn't realize how hungry I actually was until the food started hitting my stomach.

Wyatt had always made derogatory jabs when I ate too fast or too much. Little Piggy was a favorite of his. But Cole didn't seem to mind as I chowed down. He only leaned against the kitchen island and sipped from a travel mug. When I was nearly done, he gave me a sidelong glance.

"You still hungry? Want some more?"

"No, thank you, though," I said. "If I eat too heavy of a breakfast, I'll feel like a zombie rolling into work."

He set down his coffee and crossed his muscular arms over his torso. He was wearing a long sleeve sweater today rolled up to his elbows and some dark gray jeans. He looked way too good.

"I want to talk to you about the security situation at your place. I thought I could take some initiative today and start installing some cameras, and a few more locks, get my buddy from the security company to come out and take a look."

"I...don't think I can afford all of that," I said. "Not only that, it's not technically my place, it's Lana's, so I kind of have to talk to her."

He nodded and rubbed his hand over his chin. "Why don't you talk to her today and let me know? Don't worry about the cost. I have a lot of the stuff sitting around on hand, and my buddy owes me a favor that I can cash in. Consider it on me."

I shifted a little in my seat. "Cole, you keep offering to do way too much. I really have no way to pay you back for any of it or even any way to make it up to you," I said. "You seem like you're a kind and generous person by nature, but I don't want you to wind up feeling like I'm taking advantage of you."

"I can assure you I don't feel that way. You haven't asked me for anything—I offered. It would be stupid of me to offer you something as a favor and then expect you to repay it down the line."

Would it be stupid? Wyatt used to do that all the time. Any kind act or gift he gave me would have to be paid for at one point or another. Whether that was with my obedience, my money, or anything else was always a mystery until he brought the act of kindness up.

"If...if you're really sure," I said. "I just don't want it to impact our friendship or my rapport with you or your son."

He held up his hand in a scout's honor pose. "I promise you. I will not come skulking around like the shifter mafia looking for favors to be repaid," he said with a wry smile. "I told you, Marley. I just like taking care of people."

I smiled and brought my mug of coffee closer to me, relishing its warmth on my hands. "Well then. I'll talk to Lana when I get to school today and keep you updated."

"Sounds good," he said. "Travis and my secretary should be showing up any moment now to start work. Do you need anything before they undoubtedly start pulling me in a hundred different directions?"

"Wait, they're coming here? To your house?" I asked panic coiling in my gut. I wasn't even wearing a bra. I hadn't even brushed my hair or teeth. What would they think of me looking like this?"

"Oh, no, not like *here*, here. I'm sorry I didn't mention it sooner. I run my business out of the top floor of my home. There's a separate entrance for my clients and everything. No one will be seeing you in your very adorable pajamas, I promise. That is a unique joy for my eyes only."

Heat rose to my face as I looked down at my pajamas.

God, what had I even been *thinking* bringing these pajamas? I hadn't even registered what I grabbed when I packed the night before.

"Th-these are my...pajama-day pajamas," I said sheepishly. "I got them for spirit week at school."

"You don't have to explain. Like I said, they're adorable. And I like that I'm the only one getting to see you in them—at least until pajama day rolls around," he said.

My stomach did somersaults as his eyes roved over me, hunger flashing in his eyes. I saw a flash of his tongue as he wet his lips before he said, "Anyway... do you?" he said, reminding me of the original question. "Need anything, that is."

I ran a hand through my tangled hair, feeling like a hideous goblin in my bedhead and PJs. "No, thank you. I'm just going to get ready for work and head on in. If you leave the dishes, I'll take care of them before I head out."

He shook his head. "Nah, don't worry about it. I'll see you at school this afternoon, and we can make a plan based on whatever Lana tells you, all right?"

"Yeah, that's fine," I said.

There was an awkward moment, a sort of hovering we both seemed to do. It felt so much like a parting between a boyfriend and girlfriend or a husband and wife. Like there was some missing phrase hanging in the air between us or the urge to give each other a quick, goodbye kiss on the cheek. But of course, that was madness—we'd only just met, for God's sake.

“Well, uh… h-have a good day at work, I guess,” I said.

He cleared his throat and nodded. “Yeah. Yes. You too. I’ll be right upstairs if you need something, or you can just text me—wait, do you even have my number?”

I shook my head, gesturing over to my phone on the counter. I’d plugged it in the night before when the battery had run low.

He grabbed the phone and handed it to me. I unlocked it and opened up a new contact for him to fill out, which he did quickly before handing it back to me.

“There we go. Perfect,” I said.

“I texted myself, so I have your number. I hope that’s okay?” he said.

“Yeah, of course, it is,” I said.

He patted the counter twice. “All right, bye for real this time.”

I huffed a smile and nodded. “Bye for real.”

He patted his counter again, adorably awkward for once instead of seeming perpetually self-assured. Then he turned and went up the stairs out of my line of sight, the sound of some unseen door following a few moments later.

My breath rushed out of me once I was alone—not exactly in relief but in some sort of deflation. Cole made me feel…a lot. Too much to actually describe succinctly in a single sentence. I wasn't sure if it was a good or a bad thing. Maybe it was neither. Maybe both. I wondered if I could trust him or if he was like Wyatt.

Wyatt had love-bombed me in the beginning. He'd taken me on thoughtful dates, made grand gestures, bought me gifts, and showered me with praise. But that treatment vanished pretty quickly. After about a year, I'd spent every moment trying to get back to that version of him to no avail.

According to Lana, the reason I couldn't get old Wyatt back was because old Wyatt never existed. But what if the Cole I was experiencing wasn't the real Cole either? How could I trust him, really? Just because Lana said I could?

It wasn't like Lana knew how Cole was in a relationship.

I got up, and even though he said not to worry about it, I cleaned the breakfast dishes. It was only a small gesture, but at least I could be sure that in the tally of things he was doing for me, he couldn't include cleaning up after me.

It was just enough effort to make me feel a little less anxious about Cole's kindness biting me in the ass later.

After that, I did what I could to get ready for the day. I dressed in the clothes I'd brought—a tea-length sundress in pale yellow with a white Peter Pan collar and pearly buttons. I paired it with some white flats and put my hair up in a loose approximation of a French twist so I didn't have to worry about the wild bedhead I was sporting. When I was sure I was put together enough, I tossed my overnight bag into the trunk of my car.

I had some time before I had to head to the school, but I was starting to feel restless about taking too much of Cole's hospitality, so I left early, dialing Lana with my car's Bluetooth.

"Hello, this is your hot shifter-sex hotline. How can I assist?"

I rolled my eyes in exasperation. "Lana, nothing happened."

"Are you kidding me? I was really hoping I would have to transfer Noah out of your class today," she griped. "Girl, Cole was all over you last night. Why wouldn't you hit that?"

"Because of what you just said! I don't want to lose any of my students because of a hookup, Lana. Come on, you know me better than that."

Lana grumbled. "Well, if you didn't call to kiss and tell, what's going on?"

"Well, I was actually hoping to talk to you before work…"

There was a long pause before she spoke. "Marley, you can't do that cryptic shit to me. You know it makes me a nervous wreck. What's this about? Are you mad about the creep last night? Are you upset that I ditched you? Are you—"

"No, no, no," I said quickly. "It's nothing you did, Lana. I just—it's just kind of serious, and I didn't want to tell you over the phone. But I can if you want me to."

"I honestly think that's preferable," she said.

"When I got back to the house last night, the door was open, and the lights on the porch and the back walkway were busted," I said.

Again, another long pause. I swore I could hear her processing on the other end of the line. "Someone broke into your place? Was it your ex?"

"I don't know. It was a male wolf. Cole confirmed that much. But he's never scented Wyatt, so there's no way for him to confirm that it was him," I said.

"Holy fuck, Marley, are you okay? Why didn't you call me yesterday? You could have come and stayed with me."

"I didn't want to bother you on your night out with Paulette and Travis, especially when you seemed to really be hitting it off with him. And Cole made a good point that a male wolf could still overpower a female wolf. I didn't want to put you at risk."

"Oh, fuck him! I can hold my own, thank you very much. Next time I see that ass, I'm going to tackle him," she said.

"So, you could have held a male wolf off?" I asked nervously. Maybe this whole thing was a big manipulation after all, then. Maybe Cole had just said that because he wanted me to spend the night at his place. Maybe he was the one that arranged for my house to be broken into, maybe—

"Marley, whatever tale you're spinning in that head of yours, stop," Lana said, bringing me back to reality. "Listen, I disagree with Cole that I couldn't have defended you if it came down to it, but he's not wrong that male wolves tend to be stronger than female wolves. It's just that you can't really calculate the variables. Like when a female is protecting her pack mates."

I blinked, taken aback. "Pack mate? You consider me a pack mate?"

It was kind of antiquated these days for anyone to be considered a pack. Wolf packs hadn't really been a thing for a few decades—it was considered uncouth and a little toxic when wolves formed packs in the present day, at least in the eyes of most humans.

But having dated a shifter, I knew wolves still referred to treasured family and friends as pack mates. It was sort of like referring to someone as your chosen family.

Lana didn't say anything at first, and I could almost imagine the embarrassed look on her face.

When enough time had passed that I thought the call had disconnected, I said, "You there?"

"I'm here," she said before the speaker blew out with the sound of her forceful exhalation. "Listen, Marley. You know I'm not the sentimental type. I don't get mushy and gross with people—"

"See also, vulnerable."

"Whatever," she retorted angrily before giving a soft laugh to let me know she wasn't really angry. "But yeah. You're like a sister to me. I've been so impressed with how resilient and positive you are in the face of everything."

"I don't think I'm a particularly resilient and positive person," I said. "I feel like I'm just...broken, damaged goods. It's not like I'm happy-go-lucky or keeping a gratitude journal or something."

"Bitch, that's not positivity. That is *toxic positivity,"* Lana insisted. "Positivity is continuing to move even when your life is falling apart; positivity is getting out of bed feeling like shit but trusting that you will one day wake up feeling amazing. That's what true positivity is, and it's just how you are."

My throat tightened, and my eyes started to burn. "You really feel that way?"

Lana's tone softened. "Yeah, I do. I could fucking see it in your face the day I found you in the bus terminal. You barely had anything, just an old laptop, your phone, and a backpack full of old clothes, but I could tell you were a bad bitch the moment I met you. You just needed a chance to see it for yourself."

I bit back a sob as I remembered that day.

I'd felt so broken. After leaving the hospital, I'd gone to my parents' house just to be turned away. I went back to the apartment I shared with Wyatt just to find the locks on the doors had been changed.

Wyatt had everything put in his name, even my bank account. When I dumped him, he canceled all the cards and canceled my phone plan. All I had left was my old school laptop, the clothes I'd taken with me to the hospital, and a few bucks in my wallet.

I was so heartbroken and distraught and felt like a pariah in my own hometown. So, I took what few belongings I had, spent my last money on a bus ticket, and wound up stranded in New Middle Bluff.

"I was so hungry when you found me," I said.

"I remember," she said, emotion laced in her tone. "Standing in that convenience store trying to make one quarter become two. It was fucking pitiful."

"I still can't believe how lucky I was to just run into you that day."

"It wasn't luck, Mar. That shit was fate," she said. "Anyway, we're off on an emotional tangent here, but the point is that I would go down swinging for you, got it? Regardless of how likely I'd be to win, I would at least draw some blood before I let that abusive prick or anyone else lay a finger on you."

And, strangely enough, after all of the stress of the last twenty-four hours, the knot of tension in my chest uncoiled at hearing that.

"Yeah, I got it," I said. Deciding to get off this emotional tangent before I burst into tears and drove my car into a ditch, I told her what Cole had proposed about enhancing the security.

"So, what kind of price tag are we looking at for these security enhancements?" Lana asked.

"Oh, uh... well, Cole said he already has all the equipment on hand and a couple of favors to call in that he can make use of. He said he would cover it," I said.

"Girl..." Lana said, sounding almost shocked. "Girl, did you give him the blowjob of the century or something?"

"Don't be gross!"

"God, you really are a kindergarten teacher sometimes, Mar," she said. "Well, I guess Cole is just in love with you, then. Because that ass never works for free."

"He isn't in love with me," I said in exasperation. He's just a really nice, respectful guy who...might be...attracted to me or something."

"Hold the fucking phone. Wait a goddamn minute. I just realized—where did you stay last night?" she asked.

I groaned.

"You stayed at Cole's house? And you weren't going to tell me?!"

"I didn't say I stayed at Cole's house," I said.

"But you did! Didn't you?"

I didn't answer.

"Marley, answer the damn question, or I'm going to call Cole."

"No, no, no. I don't want him thinking I was bragging or something. Don't call him! It's too embarrassing."

"Fine, I won't call. But you better get your cute little ass over to my place and tell me *everything*," Lana demanded.

"Ugh. All right. I was looking for a way to kill time, anyway," I said.

***

By the time the school day ended, I felt like a train had hit me. The day had been so long and chock-full of planning and talking. If I wasn't telling Lana every single anti-climactic detail of my night with Cole, then I was telling Paulette about the break-in. If I wasn't doing that, then I was making arrangements with Cole for the new equipment for the house—including him asking about colors for fixtures he supposedly already had.

I didn't like the idea of him spending money on me, but I tried my best to think of the numerous times he'd promised that he liked taking care of people. Still, Lana's words—about him never working for free—made me nervous. I hoped I wasn't writing a check I couldn't cash.

The kids were especially rowdy all day, too. It was a common thing after the first day of school. They'd gotten their nerves out of the way the previous day and were now fearless and confident that they had already learned everything. I'd always taken exception to the idea that teenagers thought they knew everything. It was really the five- and- six-year-olds who thought they had the wisdom of the universe at their backs.

Paulette and I spent most of the day being corrected by kindergarteners who wanted to show their teachers how clever they were, which was very cute in theory but very hard to manage when twenty students wanted to do it all at once.

By the time the playground cleared and left only me, Paulette, Cole, and Noah, exhaustion had sunk deep into my bones.

I slumped into one of the tiny chairs at one of the tiny tables and propped my chin on my fist.

"You good?" Cole asked as Noah gave him a detailed tour of my classroom.

"Long day," I said. "I think once I get a good gallon of coffee in my system, I should be all right."

"Ah, yes, moderation is key," he said as he smiled at something Noah showed him. "Wow, bud, did you make that?"

"No, my friend Hannah did," he said. "She's not a shifter, but she's really good at playing pretend with us."

"She pretends to be a wolf?" Cole asked, his smile one of pure joy. "Is that true? The human kids are pretending to be wolves?"

I smiled, unable to escape the magnetism of his happiness. "Yeah. You know, kids are really remarkable and adaptable. They're full of love and wonder, so it's no surprise that when they meet other children who can transform into what look like puppies, they want to emulate them. It's real-life magic, you know?"

"Man," Cole said, looking visibly emotional about the idea. "That's just...that's so beautiful. Growing up as a shifter, I never thought I'd get a chance to experience something like that. See human and shifter kids get along with each other and admire each other like that."

"A lot more people admire wolves than you realize," I said. "Hopefully, even a lot more if we manage to do things right."

Cole nodded and followed Noah to the miniature kitchen I had set up in the corner. Noah started to make pretend pancakes. As he did, Cole glanced at me, then looked outside to make sure Paulette was still tidying the playground outside.

"Imagine my surprise when I went down to lunch today and found someone had cleaned up after breakfast," he said softly as he accepted a plastic plate filled with play food from Noah. Apparently, today's menu consisted of a slice of mushroom pizza topped with sliced strawberries and a plastic can of lemon-lime soda.

"Maybe that someone didn't want you to think she was taking advantage of you," I said, keeping the language just barely above Noah's ability to comprehend. "Maybe she thought you'd done enough."

"Maybe she shouldn't be so worried about keeping score," he said, his tone sobering a bit even though his easy smile remained.

Maybe she can't not be worried about keeping score, I wanted to say. But Paulette had just walked in, and I didn't want her to know about me staying at Cole's place. Paulette was sweet, but she was a bit of a gossip. She'd find out in due time, but I didn't have to bring it to her. Hell, I hadn't even really brought it to

Lana. She just picked up on it because she was a freak of nature.

Then again, it was more than possible that Cole's scent was all over me from cuddling with him all night. Paulette was likely just keeping her mouth shut for my benefit.

I sighed internally. Sometimes friendships with shifters could be really darn complicated.

"You ready to get to work on the house, Marley?" Cole asked me.

"Yeah, I think so. Paulette, do you need anything before we go?" I asked.

"No, I'm just gonna prep a couple of things for tomorrow's lessons before heading home. Call if you need any help putting things together."

"We should be good, thanks, Paulette," Cole said. "Between me, Marley, Noah, and Travis, there probably won't be much room to move around."

"Rude!" I said, tossing an unsharpened pencil at him.

"Rude, Daddy!" Noah echoed.

"Great," Cole said, shooting me a dry look. "That one's going to be fun for the next month."

"Consider it retribution for your crimes against my adorable, spacious house," I said, groaning as I to my aching feet. "I'll meet you over there."

"Just wait in the car till I get there, all right? No reason to tempt fate," he said.

For just a moment, I rankled at the command. Then I calmed myself—he wasn't commanding me—just making a suggestion. Cole wasn't Wyatt. Cole was easier than Wyatt.

"Yeah," I muttered as I left, heading toward the faculty parking lot with Cole on my heels, carrying Noah. "I'll see you there."

I didn't wind up having to wait long in my driveway before Cole pulled up behind me, his truck laden with new doors, fixtures, and what looked like miles of cables I would never know what to do with. He hopped out of the truck from the passenger side, and I spotted Travis in the driver's seat. He must have been in the truck the whole time Cole and I were in my classroom. I hoped he wasn't annoyed at having to wait for us.

But as Travis approached, the only thing clear about him was his mild hangover and the faint trace of blond stubble on his face.

"Hey, Marley," he said a little gruffly. "Sorry to hear that the night ended utterly shit for you."

"Bad word, Uncle Travis!"

"That's right, kid," he said, rubbing his hand over his eyes. "All right, let's make this house more tightly sealed than—"

"Trav," Cole warned.

"What? I was going to say, Fort Knox," he said, shaking his head at Cole. Then he looked at me, his face derisively exasperated. "Can you believe the dirty mind on this guy?" he muttered.

I gave a genuine laugh. I really liked Travis. He had a way about him that made him easy to be around, which was welcome at the moment. "Let's get started. What do you guys need me to do?"

"Supply beer and pizza," Travis said as he walked past me.

Cole rolled his eyes as he came up, holding Noah on his hip. "Sorry about him. Travis can be quite brusque after a night of drinking."

"It's nothing to apologize for. It's funny. Besides, pizza and beer is the least I can do," I said.

He gave an apologetic smile. "Only if you don't mind."

I gestured for him to go into the house and followed behind him.

For the next five hours, chaos reigned in my house. It was a cacophony of Noah's questions, old emo music from the early 2000s, and Travis and Cole bickering. Even with all the chaos, though, I couldn't help but feel like my house finally had a little life in it.

I usually tended to be a little lonesome, which I guess was just how things went after cohabitating with someone for a few years and then suddenly having to live on your own. I missed that sort of companionable mundanity of the day-to-day. Someone to eat meals with, someone to debate pop culture with, someone to lean on while binge-watching old sitcoms.

It had been part of what made leaving Wyatt so hard... losing out on the good times. Sure, the bad times certainly outweighed them, but the good times still existed. That was why I'd stayed. The good times were like tiny diamonds in a pit of black tar. Perfect and unblemished.

But this? Sitting with Noah and watching cartoons while his dad and Travis fixed up my house... it sort of felt like the moving experience I never got to have coming out here where all your friends came together for a barn-raising and helped you get your life situated, only accepting pizza as a form of payment.

It made this house I was borrowing feel like home.

It made Noah, Cole, Travis, and Lana feel like family.

So, even though I was nervous as I watched Cole set up what was, no doubt, well over a thousand dollars worth of security equipment in my home, I couldn't help but feel eternally grateful.

Perhaps Lana was right. Maybe everything I had experienced was for the purpose of bringing me here, to this moment. Maybe I needed to experience the hell I'd been through to know what real friends and family were.

By the time everything was done, Noah was passed out on my couch, snugly tucked in a thick blanket to shield him from the cold ocean breeze coming in through the window as Cole and Travis installed restrictors that would keep the windows from swinging fully open if someone slid something through the opening to unhook the latch.

When all was said and done, Cole wanted to do a full walk around the place to make sure everything was in working order. Travis, clearly, did not want to do that. Instead, he offered to take Noah home.

Cole accepted his offer and carefully got Noah's sleeping form into his car seat without waking him. It was impossible not to be endeared by Cole's tender care for his son, but as he quietly shut the door and walked back toward me, my heart rate spiked, and my stomach flipped.

We both watched the truck recede down my driveway, and once it was out of sight, I looked up at Cole with a tight smile. "Shall we?" I asked.

"In a sec," he said, putting a gentle hand on my arm. "How are you doing?"

"F-fine, why do you ask?" I lied.

"Because your heart started racing like a speeding motorbike when I started walking toward you," he said. "I don't smell fear, but that's certainly a response. Not the same response you were having last night."

Heat crept up my neck, and I quickly dropped my gaze to my feet. He tucked a finger under my chin and tilted my head up.

"Marley, tell me what's wrong," he said.

"I'm just worried about this whole thing brewing between us. I don't want you to feel like I'm leading you on or like you're giving more than you get. I don't want you to feel resentful when I can't do the stuff you're doing for me."

"Marley, I already told you—"

"I know. You like taking care of people. I got it," I snapped much more harshly than intended. Cole's face took on a wounded expression, and my heart sank. "I'm sorry, but could you maybe tone it down a bit? It just makes me feel really uneasy. I know we have this crazy chemistry, and I know you're smoking hot and that we almost—"

"I got it."

He echoed my words back to me, but he'd softened them considerably. They sounded more like forgiveness than a frantic exclamation.

"No more grand gestures. We'll let this whole thing breathe. I'll give you some space now that the security measures are in place. We'll order some new windows and get those installed—so maybe just that last grand gesture, and then you can take the lead, all right?"

"What if I don't want anything with you, though? What if I just want to be friends?" I said.

He inhaled sharply through his nose and let it drain out of him slowly. "That would be hard to believe, and I'll be a little disappointed that we won't get to finish what we started last night, but I think I'll live," he said. "Marley, I'm not trying to force something on you. I thought we were on the same page of enjoying each other's company."

I twisted my fingers together.

We were. We had been, at one point. But now I didn't know what I felt. I was starting to panic. The break-in had confused everything. I couldn't tell if this was intimacy or possessive obsession. What if I was falling into old patterns and looking for comfort?

"I'm sorry," I said, breaking eye contact. "I just don't really know what I want. I thought I was doing well enough to have fun again, but I keep looking for old patterns and freaking myself out."

He nodded. "Say no more, Marley. We'll pump the brakes."

"Do you hate me?" I asked.

"Absolutely fucking not," he said emphatically. "Marley, you don't owe me anything. You don't owe anyone anything in exchange for freely given kindness."

I let out a shaky breath and nodded. "I guess I'm still learning that lesson out..."

"The teacher becoming the student, eh?"

Despite the confusing emotions running through my body—all the guilt and anxiety, all the infatuation and excitement, all the fear and worry—I laughed. A full belly laugh, the same way I had when I'd learned the name of Cole's company.

God, it wasn't even that funny, but I couldn't stop laughing.

This silly lumberjack, timber wolf, handsome man was just a weird dork at the end of the day. And even though my fears were getting in the way of any real intimacy between us, one thing remained abundantly clear.

"I'm really glad I ruined your coffee yesterday," I said. "It's the best mistake I've ever made."

He grinned. "It's the best mistake that's ever happened to me, too."

After we got that emotional conversation out of our system, we fell into an easy-going rhythm as Cole walked me through the security system. Both the front and back doors were fitted with the same biometric scanners as in his house. The doorbell also had a camera on it now, so if someone came up to the door, I could check who it was before opening the door.

"This scans your retina and your fingerprint. You can set it to open with both or with one or the other. You can set that up in your phone too."

"The future is a wild place to be," I said.

"Tell me about it. The only time it's a bitch to deal with is when it rains. We can put a man on the moon, but we can't make rain-proof biometric scanners. Worst-case scenario, you'll have to get an authorization code in the app to unlock the door. Just don't share it with anyone."

It was a lot of information, but I was sure I would figure it out...eventually.

"Why don't you give it a try?" Cole asked. "It's set to work with your fingerprint for now."

I pressed my thumb to the reader. The door beeped three times before the lock clicked open.

"There we go. Easy as pie," he said, winking at me.

A half-laugh escaped me. “Thank you again, Cole. For everything. You’ve done so much to help me, and I can’t tell you how much it means to me.”

“No problem. A little security goes a long way.” He hesitated for a moment, and that awkward feeling hung in the air between us again, like we should embrace or kiss before he left for home.

“So, uh... I think I’m going to try to get ready for bed,” I said.

“Good call, it’s getting late,” he said, but he didn’t make a move to leave. His eyes danced over me uncertainly. Finally, he brushed a hand through his hair. “Sleep well, Marley. Call if anything feels amiss—I’m not far.”

“I will. Thank you again. Good night,” I said.

We turned from each other, Cole going to the beach to shift and me going into my house and making sure to lock the door behind me. I went to the back windows just in time to see Cole shift into his lupine form and tear off down the beach.

Now, in the silence of my newly-secure home, I felt strangely isolated. My house suddenly felt too quiet.

Unnervingly quiet.

I doubted I'd get any sleep tonight, but I desperately needed it. I had work in the morning.

Putting on some relaxing music, I poured myself a glass of wine from a bottle Paulette had left here. I sipped at it as I did a little swooning dance on my way to the shower.

I downed the glass before stepping into the steaming water, letting the warmth of the alcohol and water relax me.

My thoughts drifted to Cole, my traitorous brain bringing the kiss into my mind's eye. For a moment, I could almost feel his rough hands squeezing my thighs, feel the pleasant scruff of his beard against the delicate skin of my neck, and feel his hardness pressing between my legs.

I couldn't decide if I regretted my earlier outburst. I couldn't decide if I wanted him or if it was just a self-destructive impulse.

I shut off the faucet, warm and tipsy enough to want to tumble straight into bed. After drying off and braiding my hair, I dressed in some shorts and an oversized T-shirt, I did just that.

I dreamt of Cole's lips pressing reverent kisses against every inch of my body.

***

“Fuck, fuck, *fuck,”* I whined. “Paulette, how could you let me forget?”

“Me? You’re the one who is always reminding *me* of what needs to be done! I could have sworn you knew,” Paulette said.

“I’ve been a little distracted,” I said as I frantically labeled multi-colored folders with the names of my students’ parents.

“By a hot shifter daddy who wants your gams?” Paulette asked.

“By a scary shifter stalker breaking into my house,” I snapped back.

“Right,” Paulette said. “Makes sense. Here, tear the list in half, and I’ll do the other ones.”

It was lunchtime at POSHA, and the kids were all sitting out on the picnic benches with either their lunch boxes or the trays of lunch the school provided. We had approximately twenty minutes to get all of these folders labeled, stuff them with hastily written teacher bios, come up with an icebreaker game, and figure out what refreshments to offer our parents.

It was parents' night, which usually happened three or four weeks into the school year. But since POSHA was an integrated school and the parents were leaving their children in the care of adults who were both shifters and humans, there would be plenty of questions to address at the end of the first week.

I was already anticipating a few questions from Hannah's parents, the girl who had taken to pretending to be a shifter with the other wolves in class. I was sure there were other mishaps Paulette and I had missed that would need to be addressed. Nothing serious, but enough to make parents worry.

So, it was a major, major oversight that Paulette and I had done nothing to prepare for the event.

After lunch, Paulette and I did something I wouldn't usually do—instead of teaching the intended lesson, we put on an educational cartoon. I disliked using cartoons to educate, but I worried that if I didn't get the preparations done for the parent night, I would be facing a much larger disaster than parents being miffed at a bit of extra screen time.

While the kids were absorbed in the cartoon, we cleaned the classroom, ordered food for the event online, and printed a parent bingo card for the parents to get to know each other before they started bickering over whether their human child should be howling.

I wasn't fully present at pick-up. Mostly I just smiled and told the parents I'd see them that evening. My mind was glued to where the food delivery was.

Once the kids were all cleared out, Paulette and I prepared adult-sized seating in the room. I kept checking the clock as we got everything set up.

"Marley, I promise you, the time will still be pretty close to the same when you look up a few seconds from now. You need to chill out. You're going to give *me* a panic attack," Paulette said.

I flashed an apologetic smile. "I'm so sorry. I'm really nervous about making a good first impression."

"The kids love you, so don't even worry about it. I know these things can be a little intense the first time, but it's also not my first rodeo. I promise I can keep things from spinning out of control."

"You think so?" I asked. "Well, yeah, you probably know so."

"Parents mostly just want to know that their kids won't turn into wild animals or forget how to shift. I promise. It's easy to handle."

I nodded and took a forceful breath to center myself.

The phone rang, making me yelp.

Paulette gave me a withering look after jumping herself, and I gave my most-innocent grin. "Sorry, I'll get it."

I hurried over to the phone and picked it up.

"Miss Cage's room," I said.

"Hello, Miss Cage, I just got back to the office after running around the school to see if there were any last-minute disasters," a kind older woman said on the phone. Probably Cindy, one of the human volunteers. "There's a delivery here with your name on it."

"Thank God. Just in time, too," I said. "I'll be right over, thank you."

"See you soon."

I hung up the phone and looked over at Paulette. "I think they delivered the food to the office. I'll be right back," I said.

"Yay! I can't wait to eat."

Laughing, I left our classroom, hurrying through the side door to the lobby and into the office. When I arrived, Cindy handed me a small brown package that definitely couldn't be the food for close to forty people.

When I got back to the classroom, Paulette was standing outside with Lana and Cole, who had just arrived. Cole was holding two tin trays in one hand with shocking ease.

"Cole ran into our confused delivery boy in the parking lot and took the burden off his hands," Paulette said.

"Yes, so you'll just have to tip me instead," Cole joked, but one look at me had his face falling. "Marley, you look like a ghost. What's wrong?"

I unwrapped the package with trembling fingers. Inside was a stuffed wolf toy.

Something stuck out of a gash in the wolf's gut. I tugged at it and found a crumpled Polaroid.

It was a photo of the very same stuffed wolf, only it had a knife sticking out of its belly, impaling it on a wooden cutting board. My wooden cutting board.

The photo had been taken in my kitchen, stuffed in the very gash created by my chef's knife. I handed the picture off to Cole, who took it and read the words scrawled on the Polaroid out loud.

"'Come back home, Marley,'" Cole read out loud. "'Back where you belong.'"

Chapter 10 - Cole

Marley had insisted on going through with parents' night. Regardless of how much I could see her fear on her face, regardless of how we could all smell it seeping from her pores, she refused to cancel.

"Marley," I'd said, trying to appeal to her sense of reason. "This is a very clear and horrible threat. You need to take it seriously."

She'd only shaken her head. "No, it's impossible. You beefed up the security. You said yourself that people can only get in with a special code, and I haven't given that code to anyone, not even Lana. They probably just took the photo the first time they broke in and saved it to try and scare me."

"Do you really want to take that chance?" Paulette had asked, and for the first time, I was grateful for her. I nodded my agreement. "Why don't you just stay with me or Lana tonight?"

"I think that would be a good idea," I'd said.

"Cole, you were the one who told me that if I cave into these sorts of threats, it'll only get worse," she said. "I can't let whoever this guy is, rule my life."

"I also said that you should rely on me, Lana, and Paulette when you needed to," I pleaded. "Marley, please."

"The parents are arriving," she'd said. And then she just walked away and started greeting them, and I'd had to drop the subject.

So now, I was milling around the classroom, trying to check off boxes on this stupid parent-night bingo card while my mind raced with the frantic instinct to protect, protect, protect.

The stuffed wolf tucked behind Marley's desk reeked in the small, stuffy room. As I worked my way around the room trying to find a parent who was a doctor and one who ran marathons, I also sought out any potential stalkers.

But we made it through the inane party games, the stupid, pointless questions about basic shifter biology, and the elbow-rubbing at the end of the night with no creepy stalker in sight.

I stayed near Marley and Paulette as the other parents all said their goodbyes and filed out. Marley smiled and waved as the last one left, then whipped her head toward me.

"*What* is your *problem?*" she seethed.

I was taken aback. "What are you talking about?"

"You spent the whole night glaring, huffing, and prowling, and now you're standing next to me like my own personal protection detail. Do you think the guy is one of the other parents?" she asked. "You're acting like a crazy person."

"Well, excuse me for being fucking worried about you—and yeah, actually, the creep could be one of the parents. This shit didn't start happening until school started, right?" I said. "Doesn't hurt to rule it out."

I looked at Paulette for backup, but she just lifted her brows and turned away as if to say, *you're on your own, guy.*

"Marley, you're being needlessly reckless. If you'd just stay with Paulette or Lana until we can check the house—"

"Cole, you said you would pump the brakes," she shouted. "You *promised* me that less than twenty-four hours ago. And now you're acting like you're going to rip off the head of the next male who tries to shake my hand."

"Why does it bother you so much that I want you to be safe?" I snarled, backing her against the wall. "Why am I not allowed to protect the people who matter to me?"

I'd overdone it. I could see it as soon as her head thumped against the wall. Fuck. I'd frightened her. I could smell it, that acrid, salty stench of fear—fear of me—and I felt fucking horrible for it.

I immediately backed off, taking two big steps back from her.

"Marley, I'm so sorry. I just—"

A breeze whipped through the open door at my back, carrying the scent of night-blooming jasmine, salty sea air, and *him*.

It was very faint, barely there, but my senses latched onto it. It was the intruder's smell, the smell of whoever was leaving these sick threats for Marley.

And I was going to kill him.

"Paulette, call the police and ask for Detective Lucas. Tell her I've caught the scent of the shifter who broke in at Marley's house. Marley, Travis is on his way with Noah to pick me up. When he gets here, just tell him you want a ride to my place and stay there until I see this through to the end," I said as I made my way outside.

"Wait, where are you—"

The rest of her words drowned out as I shifted and took off down the street.

I tracked the scent for a mile to the entrance of the shifter reserve. It was closed for the night, but the scent was behind the locked gates. I paced back and forth in front of the gate. My fur prickled as I dug my claws into the ground with every heavy step I took. Snarling low in my throat, I forced myself in through a gap beneath the wrought-iron fence.

Raising my nose to the air, I sniffed, but instead of his scent hitting my nostrils, I heard a cruel laugh behind me.

I whirled around. A lanky figure stood ten feet away. A dark, slouchy beanie covered his head, and the rest of him was dressed all in black: oversized coat, hoodie, and jeans. Heavy black boots protected his feet—military-grade from the looks of them. The lower half of his face was obscured by a cloth face mask, but I didn't have to see his mouth to know he was giving me a shit-eating grin.

"Oh no, someone sent her guard dog after me," the prick said. "How'd you like the stuffy? I thought they made it in your spitting image."

I bared my teeth and growled, the sound reverberating deep in my chest. He was taunting me, and I knew that, but it was fucking working. I was going to rip his throat out.

"You just going to stand there?" he challenged.

No, I was not.

I bolted toward him, and he shifted into his wolf form, taking off at a clip I couldn't keep up with. The kid didn't match me in size or brute strength, but he had me beat for speed.

The trick was to pace myself. The whelp was sprinting, but even with his smaller stature, he could only do that for so long. I ran fast enough to keep tabs on him but didn't try to match his pace. Sure enough, after pursuing him for about ten minutes, I caught up to him, careening into him with as much force as I could.

We became a tangle of fur, flesh, and teeth. Our snarls bounced off the buildings around us. I tried my hardest to subdue him, but he was scrappy. I lunged for his throat, only to have him dig his hind paws into me and fling me over his head.

He tried to scramble away again, but I closed my jaw on his hind leg and tore at it, drawing a whimper from his throat.

He turned on me, biting down on my shoulder hard enough to draw blood. I opened my mouth, and just as I was about to go for his throat again, he shifted back to his human form, making me stop short.

In my momentary stupor, he scrambled to his feet. My brain clicked into place, and I shifted too, tackling him to the ground, his head hitting the hard-packed dirt with a loud thud. His eyes rolled to the back of his head at the impact.

"Why are you trying to scare Marley off? Who are you? What do you want from her?"

He wheezed. "I don't know what the fuck you're talking about."

"Bullshit. I smelled you all over her place. I smelled you all over the stuffed wolf," I said. "You're coming with me. We're going to the station, and you're going to turn yourself in."

He laughed, his eyes curving with sadistic pleasure.

"With what evidence?" he said. "They don't use scents as evidence in criminal cases yet, and even if they did, I didn't commit a crime."

My fist connected with his face. Once. Twice. I was about to bring it down a third time when a hand caught my wrist. I turned, ready to pull the offending person down into the fight if I had to, but stopped short when I met my sister's angry expression.

"What are you doing, you idiot?" she hissed. "Get off him."

"But—"

"Don't make me put my own fucking brother in handcuffs," she said. "Get off him and hope he doesn't press charges for assault and battery."

"Charge *me?!*"

Sirens wailed through the air.

"You have five seconds to get off this guy before I can no longer vouch for you. If they see you on top of him like this, and he claims assault and battery, there's nothing I can do. Get off. Then it's our word against his."

The stalker beneath me gave a derisive laugh. "New Middle Bluff's finest, eh? A little bit of collusion and corruption to go with your idyllic beach-town life."

"Just because I can't use your scent against you in court doesn't mean I don't know you were somewhere you shouldn't have been. I'm going to let you get scarce, and you're going to be glad I allowed it. You got that? And if you even try to show up at the precinct to file a report, I will be so far up your ass that you'll taste me in the back of your throat." Ginger gave a menacing growl.

He narrowed his eyes at her, then grumbled sourly, "Get the fuck off me."

I stood up, my sister helping support my weight with an arm around my back. The creep adjusted his coat a little indignantly, flipped us both the bird, and ran off, shifting when he was about five feet away.

I glared at Ginger.

"Don't give me that look," she snapped as police started to approach us from behind. "You're lucky you didn't get arrested. How would I have explained to Noah that his father was in jail for assault, huh? You ever think about that? *Your son?!*"

The question was a blow to the gut.

I hadn't thought about that. I hadn't thought about Noah at all.

I had been so obsessed with Marley and her safety that I'd pummeled a stranger into the ground without a single thought for the consequences.

"Didn't think so," she said. "Hold tight and keep your mouth shut while I smooth this whole thing over. You woke up half the damn neighborhood with that stunt, Cole. Do you know how many calls we got?"

"Wait, you came because other people called?" I asked. "Did you get a call from Marley or Paulette?"

"I don't know who Paulette is, and Marley didn't call."

"I have to go," I said.

"You can go when we say you can go," Ginger snapped. "I'm already sticking my neck out for you. Stay here and keep your mouth shut, or—or—"

I waited for the threat.

"Or I'm going to fucking tell Mom, you ass," she said, my old kid sister, coming out from under the detective demeanor.

In spite of everything, I snorted. But I nodded my acquiescence. "I'll stay put. Just...try to hurry, will you?"

With a heavy sigh, she turned away from me to talk to her good old boys.

That left me with nothing to do but worry about Marley and her stalker that we'd just let loose.

Chapter 11 - Marley

Cole could go fuck himself.

Okay, maybe that was a little strong. But who the hell did he think he was? We'd just had a heart-to-heart about boundaries the night before, and now he was commanding me to let his buddy take me to his house. Trying to force me into taking advantage of someone else's hospitality? He had *no right*. I could take care of myself.

As we watched Cole streak into the darkness of the night, I looked over to Paulette. "Don't call the cops," I said.

"But, the wolf toy," Paulette said. "What if it's something serious, Mar?"

"The cops aren't going to do anything, Paulette. Trust me. I have firsthand experience with this. And the last thing I want to hear right now is how this is just a stupid prank, or field questions about my past or my family, or anything like that."

"But—"

"Paulette, I am asking you, as my friend, not to call the cops. I'm asking you to respect me enough to listen to what I want."

Paulette frowned at me and set her phone down. "Marley, if something happened to you, I would never forgive myself."

"Nothing is going to happen. Let's just get all this stuff cleaned up and head home, all right?"

Paulette and I set to work packing up the leftover food—some of it went in the mini-fridge for lunch, and the rest we'd take home with us for dinner. As promised, Travis showed up with Noah, and I told them that Cole was chasing down a scent. Travis seemed mildly annoyed, and I joined him in solidarity. I fed him and Noah for their trouble, then sent them off with a friendly hug and a ruffle of Noah's hair.

Paulette walked me to my car, and before we parted and she walked to her own, she pulled me into a tight hug.

"Hey, what's this all about?" I stammered.

"Just... just don't forget that we're your friends, and we care about you, okay?" Paulette said next to my ear. "I know you're used to strings being attached to every ounce of kindness shown to you, but not everyone is like that, Mar."

She held me at arm's length and flicked me on the nose. "Get home safe. It's supposed to rain tonight. Text me when you're inside, and the door is locked good and tight. And text Lana too. She's probably still screaming at the security company people on the phone."

"It certainly is something, isn't it?" I asked. "All the cameras in the school were working, but the one we needed."

"Seems like too much of a coincidence," Paulette said just as thunder rumbled above our heads. "Okay, I'm out of here before my hair becomes a rat's nest. See you tomorrow, Mar."

I laughed and waved as I slid in behind the wheel. "See you tomorrow!"

As I drove, I saw a group of cop cars pulled over on the side of the street, red and blue lights flashing, but I didn't give it much thought. I was too preoccupied with what Paulette had said.

I knew I was pushing Cole away, and the reason for that was pretty obvious to me. But was I pushing my friends away, too? I had always considered myself a burden to them, but it wasn't like I'd been able to do anything but accept their kindness. Without Lana helping me get on my feet, I would have quite literally been living on the streets or in shelters. Paulette was technically my teaching assistant, but she'd helped me interview for the job at POSHA after Lana introduced us.

Since then, they had done everything from fronting me for meals, paying for drinks, and even helping me build up my wardrobe as I scraped money together.

Since finding some independence, I really had kind of pulled away. Aside from going out to The Night Shift the other night, we hadn't really hung out much over the past few months.

Was I isolating myself? I had just been feeling sorry for myself for feeling lonely, but maybe I was at fault for that.

The rain really started to come down, striking my windshield in big, fat drops. I had to crank my wipers up to the highest speed so I could see the road. The traffic lights streaked across the glass in great, broad lines, like a million tiny sun rises on a million tiny horizons. Red, green, yellow.

I loved the sound of the rain, loved the light refracting through the water. I could probably sleep in my car with background noise like this, but then I thought of how wonderful it was going to sound paired with the sound of the ocean just outside my window.

I hummed to myself. Yeah, it was good that I was going home.

Maybe I had been too harsh with Cole, and I would apologize for it when the opportunity presented itself. But I also needed to learn how to stand on my own two feet without help from the shifters in my life. I couldn't stay afraid of shifters forever, and I couldn't always hide behind other people.

That bolstered me... until I pulled into my driveway.

The automatic lights on my porch weren't turning on.

Before the break-in, the lights turned on pretty much as soon as I pulled to a stop. I had been so distracted with kissing Cole that I never noticed they didn't come on. But now that I was alone and that creepy stuffed wolf had been delivered to me, it felt like a deadly omen.

That familiar feeling of being watched came over me again. It was more intense than the other day on the playground or when I'd gone on my run.

I looked through the rear window to see if I could spot anyone, but the sheeting rain obscured my view. I leaned forward over the steering wheel and squinted at the house. But the house was too dark to see if anyone was moving inside.

Suddenly, I remembered the app that controlled the security and fished my phone out of my purse. The screen remained black when I tried to turn it on. Damn it, the battery was dead! Why hadn't I gotten a car charger like I'd promised myself I would?

Okay, okay. *This was fine.* My door was only a few feet away. I just had to get to the door, jam my thumb against the reader, go inside, turn on every single light, and check every single lock.

I opened my car door and hurried out into the deluge. I was shocked at how much water was falling from the sky. Freezing cold rain sluiced through every layer of my clothing before I even managed to make it to the driftwood walkway.

I stumbled my way along the wet gravel, finding it flooded from the sudden downpour, but I did eventually make it to my porch.

I pressed my thumb to the reader, and it beeped in protest.

"What?" I groaned at it. "Come on. It's me!" I jammed my thumb against it again, and it again refused me access.

I felt a presence looming somewhere behind me and quickly turned my head, scanning my front yard and the darkened windows of my distant neighbors. It looked like I was in the clear.

My gaze swept to the pampas grass and the trees across the street. My body went rigid, icy terror gripping my bones. Set in the stormy darkness like a pair of milky white pearls, two eyes reflected the light from the moon back at me.

My heart leaped into overdrive, and I jammed my thumb against the scanner again, again, and again. Each time it refused entry.

Tears poured down my cheeks. Big, ugly sobs shuddered out of my chest. A crack of lightning split the sky, and the world around me plunged into darkness as the streetlight flickered out. I threw myself against the door, looking frantically over my shoulder.

The eyes were gone, which was somehow worse than them staring at me. God, I was so stupid. I should have listened to Cole. I should have just gone home with Lana or Paulette. Now I was going to die here alone in the cold and wet.

Or worse, Wyatt would rush out of a bush and shove me into his car. God knows where he'd take me. He would never let me out of his sight again if he found me. He would finish what he started, and I might not survive it this time.

I thought I heard a voice, but it spoke at the same time that the thunder boomed so loud it shook the glass in the windows. My shoulder was starting to hurt from the force I was putting behind getting into my house.

Then it happened.

A rough hand, huge and warm, grabbed my arm, tugging me away from my door. I screamed as I turned and slammed my fists into my captor's chest. Muscular arms wrapped around me, crushing me into a large expanse of chest as I wept. I pushed against him, and as my ears stopped ringing from the thunder, I heard his voice.

"...arley, Marley! Calm down! It's me! It's me," the voice said.

"No, no, no," I cried.

"Shhh, shhh," the voice said, hands smoothing wet hair from my face. "Hey, look at me. Look at me."

I did, expecting to see a shock of blue. Instead, I was met with amber-brown eyes.

It wasn't Wyatt. It wasn't a stranger.

My fear-addled brain calmed, and I slumped against Cole's chest. Cole kept smearing hair away from my face. "There we go," he cooed. "You're okay. It's just me."

My surroundings became clearer. We were standing in the middle of the front yard, both of us soaked to the bone. My chest rose and fell in deep, centering breaths as I looked around.

"I thought. I thought I heard..." I said. "I thought he was here."

Cole bent at his waist to look me in the eye. "Your ex?" he asked.

I nodded. "Or whoever is torturing me. Whoever just won't let me rest, catch a break or live my life. Whoever is getting some sick sense of satisfaction from...from..."

I'd managed to work myself up again, and my whimper turned into sobs.

I curled into Cole. "I just want to live a normal life. I know I made a mistake; I know I keep making them, but I just want to live a normal life."

"I know, Marley," Cole said, resting his cheek on my head. "I know. And I promise you will. But for now, will you please just come home with me so I can keep you safe?"

I was so exhausted, so beat down and scared and sad that all I could do was nod. He rubbed a hand over my back. "Just one or two more nights while we get this sorted, and I promise I'll leave you alone."

I let him lead me to my car, where he got me situated in the passenger seat. He buckled my seatbelt with the same tender care I'd seen him use with Noah.

He paused to pet my hair and pierced me with his gaze. His expression was a strange combination of worry and fury. "You good?"

"Don't leave," I begged.

"I'm not leaving. Let's go get you warm and dry, all right?" he said.

I nodded, and he closed the passenger door. He went around the car and settled in the driver's seat. With expert precision, he navigated the car to the road.

In the close proximity of the car, I could practically feel the exhausted sigh leave his body. I sniffed and looked up at him.

"Are you okay?" I asked.

"You were just sobbing in my arms, and you're worried about me?" he said with a weary smile.

"You just seem...worn out. Angry."

"Perceptive," he said softly. "Yeah, I'm a little bit of both. I wound up tracking down your stalker, but I had to let him go."

"Wh-why?" I asked, my voice wobbling more than I wanted it to.

He scrubbed a hand down his face, the other clamped tight on the wheel. "Because our justice system hasn't caught up to us. Because scent-based evidence isn't permissible in court yet. Because if I didn't let him go, I could have been charged with assault."

The reality of that shot through me like a bolt of lightning.

"You fought him?" I asked in a whisper.

"A bit," Cole said. "Nothing to write home about, really. Landed a few blows, and so did he."

My distress must have been palpable because he smiled at me again. "I'm fine, Marley."

"I should have just listened to you when you told me to go with Travis."

"I would have liked it if you did, but even if you had, I still would have tousled with that prick. Don't beat yourself up about it, Marley," he said. "At least I know what he looks like now, and we can keep an eye out for him going forward. What did your ex look like anyway? Was he kinda scrawny? With black hair?"

"No," I said, my brow furrowing. I didn't know if it was better or worse that the person harassing me wasn't Wyatt. "My ex has blond hair, and the last time I saw him, he was pretty muscular. Kinda like you, but slightly less."

"Well, I guess that answers that," he said, frowning ahead. "I'm sorry the answer isn't easier. It'd be a lot simpler if it were your ex, I guess."

"Yeah..." A question sprang to my mind, something that had been gnawing at me for a few days now. "Could I... ask you something?"

"Sure," he said, coming to a stoplight and flicking on the heat in the car.

"Why do you even care?" I asked. "About me? About this creep who's harassing me? We only met a few days ago, and you've already taken it upon yourself to protect me."

The light turned green, and Cole continued driving. Two blocks passed before Cole answered.

"I don't know," he said, scratching his beard. "I keep asking myself the same thing."

I fiddled with my hands in my lap, touching my thumbs to each finger in turn, grateful for the heat now blasting in the car. My clothes were sticking to me like a second skin, and I was aching from the cold. I'd asked him to pump the brakes on us, but it was getting harder and harder to separate myself from him—especially when he kept coming to my rescue like this.

All the frustration and anger I'd felt earlier had evaporated as soon as he got me safely tucked in the car, and that strange confusion and the too-strong feelings were making a comeback now.

Perhaps it was my fear or the warmth from the heater making the smell of him—vanilla and leather—

permeate the air in the car, but whatever it was, I found myself wanting him to hold me again. I wanted to wrap myself up in him, kiss him, feel those strong arms around me, content with the knowledge that he wanted nothing more than to keep me safe. He'd practically begged me for it.

I knew I should just call Lana—knew I should tell Paulette that I'd take her up on her offer of letting me stay with her. Accepting the offer of another night at Cole's house was going to be my undoing. I couldn't tell if what I was feeling for Cole was love or simple infatuation. But I knew for certain that the link between us was stronger than anything I'd ever felt. Stronger than my bond with Wyatt, stronger than the fear I was feeling over repeating past mistakes.

Maybe it was okay not to know what was going to happen and to put myself at risk again. Maybe Cole was the real deal.

The conversation drifted off naturally—I wasn't sure what else to say, and I thought Cole didn't, either. We pulled into his driveway ten minutes later, and he opened his door using the same app he'd installed on my phone.

"Scanner probably wouldn't have worked for me either," he said with a tired smile.

He opened the door, letting me enter ahead of him. He followed right behind me and locked the door again. Travis was sitting at the breakfast bar. He raised his brows inquisitively as he looked at us.

"You two look like a couple of cats that fell into a bathtub full of water," he said.

"Polite as ever, Trav," Cole said flatly.

In spite of everything that happened, I laughed.

Cole's hand rested on the small of my back, and I looked up at him. "Why don't you go hop in the shower to warm up? I'll get some pajamas for you and leave them outside the door. If you want, I could go back to your place tonight and pick up a change of clothes for you."

I shook my head. "My overnight bag from the other night is still in my car. I should have another outfit in there," I said.

"Go on. I'll get your things from the car."

I wandered down the hall the same way I had last time. It was oddly comforting to be in his bedroom again—almost like coming home in a way that returning to the bungalow didn't. I stepped into the bathroom, closed the door behind me, and got the shower running.

Steam rose to the ceiling as the water heated, and I peeled my soaking clothes off and did my best to leave them in a tidy pile, but it felt like leaving a bathing suit on the bathroom floor after going to the beach. I wasn't really sure what to do with it until I washed it.

I stepped under the spray of water, relishing the heat and water pressure. Something between a moan and a sigh burst out of my throat. Seconds later, I heard the loud crash of something in Cole's bedroom and a grumble from the other side of the door.

"Fucking hell," Cole said.

Instinctively I lifted my hands to my chest, covering my breasts—my nipples peaked from the abrupt shift in temperature.

"You okay?" I called.

"Yeah. Just, uh, hit my head on a cupboard," he said. "Clothes are out here when you're done."

I nodded, then realized he couldn't see me. "Thank you."

I showered quickly, my body not as stiff and frozen as it had been the other night. I didn't have that same deep-set chill in my bones. When I was done, I dried off, wrapping the towel around my body before I retrieved the clothes set outside the door.

As I dressed, I got a clearer idea of just how large Cole was. I was swimming in the T-shirt and joggers. The shirt fell past the bottom of my hips, and the sweats were bunched up between the waistband and the elastic around my ankles.

I caught a glimpse of myself in the mirror and gasped in mortification. Would I ever have the forethought to come to Cole's house in any of my sexy pajamas? Hell, at this rate, I would even just settle for ones that would make me look anything like a woman instead of a kid or a dorky teenager.

I quickly brushed my hair and went to the living room. Travis and Cole were deep in muted conversation. When they caught sight of me, Travis let loose a snort of laughter before clapping his hand over his mouth.

Cole shot him a warning look, and Travis dropped his hand.

"Oh, come on. Tell me that's not equal parts adorable and ridiculous."

I blushed, fussing with the hemline of the shirt. I *knew* I looked like a little kid. "I… Do you have a washing machine? I left my clothes in a pile in the bathroom, but I'd like to wash them so they don't get all mildewy or something if that's okay?"

"Sure, let me help," Cole said. "Travis, maybe you should head out before you wind up with a foot in your ass."

"She wouldn't hurt a fly," Travis said easily.

Cole's eyebrow rose in warning. "I wasn't talking about her."

"Right," Travis said, drawing out the syllable. "Off I go, then. Noah's tucked in bed, thanks to this babysitter extraordinaire. I'll be waiting for my pay—twenty bucks an hour sound fair?"

"Yeah, why don't you go ahead and hold your breath until I send it. It will be a fun game," Cole retorted with a grin.

"You sure you wanna hang out with this guy, Marley? Seems like a cheap prick," Travis said, winking exaggeratedly.

"Go home, Trav."

"Fine, fine," Travis griped. "See you next time, Marley. Oh, say hi to Lana for me when you see her again."

"Sure," I said, lifting my hand to wave.

Once Travis had left, Cole shrugged apologetically. "Sorry about him. He's my best friend, but he's an asshat a good seventy percent of the time."

"A loveable asshat," I said. "Don't worry about it. I'm not offended. I do look kind of ridiculous in your clothes."

"You look perfect in my clothes," Cole said, his eyes heavy on mine.

There was a sudden seriousness to him that I didn't know what to make of. I swallowed, feeling warmth rise to tinge my cheeks with a sudden flush. I forced myself to look away.

"Come on. The washing machine is downstairs."

I went to get my wet clothes, and he led me down the stairs to a sunroom—or at least I assumed it was a sunroom when the sun was out. This level of the house was where someone could leave the house to get straight to the beach. He had a little cookout area set up on a patio that was protected from the elements by the overhang of the main floor. In the room framed entirely by windows, there was an air hockey table, a couch to lounge on, a shower for rinsing off after a dip in the sea, and a stacked washer and dryer.

"Your house has new surprises every time I come in here," I said.

"This part of the house rarely gets used during fall and winter. Maybe just a few times in spring. I only remember it's here because this is where the laundry happens."

I looked at a small hamper filled with Noah's clothes and a larger one filled with some of his. "Do you want me to do a load of your wash? I'd feel bad only washing a few things—wasting water and detergent and all."

Cole shook his head. "Nah. The washer is eco-friendly, and a little bit of wasted soap isn't going to put me in the poor house. There's a quick wash setting for smaller loads."

"Well, that's good," I said. "We won't have to stay up until the crack of dawn to swap it over..."

I was acutely aware of the fact that our conversation was entering that strange banality that happened when you were avoiding the elephant in the room. Except, I wasn't sure which elephant we were trying to ignore.

Was it the fact that I was staying at his house again even though I had offers of other couches to crash on? Was it the fact that I'd not listened to him and once again put him in the position of having to come to my aid? Was it the conversation I'd let fizzle out in the car that we never quite finished? I couldn't be sure.

"Well, uh—" I waddled awkwardly over to the washer and propped it open. "Let me just get this going so we can get a move on for the night."

Cole nodded faintly and stepped aside. I put the clothes in the washer and threw a single detergent sheet in with it—the kind that dissolved in the water. I made a mental note to get myself some—they were remarkably convenient. I looked up at Cole once I got the washer started, and my stomach twisted.

He looked pale.

"Cole? What's wrong?"

His lashes fluttered, and he wobbled on his feet. I hurried to support him, and the movement seemed to wake him from whatever trance he was in.

He winced. “I guess I didn’t come out of that tumble as unscathed as I thought.”

“Are you hurt?” I said as a flutter of panic twisted my heart.

“Just some pain. My ribs mostly.” His palm was pressed against his shirt, and when he removed it, it was red with blood. “Well, that’s probably not good,” he said.

He swayed again, and I moved until I was under his shoulder, supporting as much of his weight as I could. I prayed he wouldn’t faint on me down here. I didn’t think I could drag him up the stairs. “Come on, let’s get back up there and take a look.”

Chapter 12 - Cole

"Marley, I'm fine," I said, pressing a hand to my aching rib. "I've got some salve upstairs. I probably just got something lodged in there."

"*Lodged in there?!*" she cried, and I winced at the high pitch of her voice. An ache was growing in my head, pounding at my temples like a prisoner trying to escape. "Cole, just how bad was this fight?"

"I had to really chase after him, had to kinda barrel into him like a linebacker," I said through gritted teeth. The second half of the stairs extending ahead of us felt more like a gauntlet than a little stride through my house. It wasn't so much that I was in enormous amounts of pain, more that the adrenaline of the day was finally beginning to fade and emphasize my injuries.

I could feel my lats trembling. Something was definitely stuck in there. Shit.

With Marley's help, I made it to my room. It still smelled of steam and soap from her shower. Even in my woozy haze, I couldn't help but think of her as she rinsed the fear and trauma off her naked body. I couldn't help but imagine how perfect and pert her ass must look, how her sandy hair must glue itself to the delicate curves of her back, and guess at the muted color of her nipples.

She sat me down on my bed.

"Where's your first aid kit?" she asked.

"Bathroom, under the sink," I grunted back, doing my best to will the fantasy of kissing my way down her body out of my head.

"Stay there," she said before hurrying away.

While she was gone, I stripped my coat off, then my shirt, marveling at how much blood there was. The rain had soaked me so thoroughly that I'd not felt the moisture from the bleeding wound. It still gushed out of a garish-looking wound on the side of my ribs. My fingers brushed over it, and I sucked in a breath. Christ, it fucking hurt.

"Don't mess with it," Marley murmured as she came to kneel between my legs. I knew it was just to get a better view of where my injury was, but I did love the image of Marley kneeling between my legs.

Unbidden fantasies flashed through my mind again; my fingers twisted around her golden hair, her perfect mouth around my cock, those stunning eyes looking up at me to make sure she was doing it right. It would be just like her to make sure she was doing it right—it would be just like her to—

Stop it. Stop it right now, you fucking pervert.

"It looks like it really smarts," she said, frowning in concentration.

"Doesn't feel great," I grunted as I adjusted my hips, trying to hide my growing erection. "Really, Marley. I can handle it if you want to go to bed."

"No, I want to help. You were injured trying to protect me. It's only right," she said.

I grunted again. She pulled out a roll of gauze, some medical tape, a pair of frightening-looking tweezers, and some antiseptic.

"I wish I had some numbing antibacterial with me," she mumbled.

"I didn't know they even made that."

"Oh sure," she said. "It's a lifesaver when it comes to scraped knees and elbows. Gone are the days of dousing scrapes in hydrogen peroxide and alcohol to clean them. They even use it in some tattoo parlors."

I lifted an eyebrow in curiosity. “Now, what does a sweetheart like you know about tattoo parlors?”

She blushed scarlet before dabbing my wound with a wet rag. “I have a couple of tattoos,” she said.

Her expression was all the pain management I needed. I felt a hungry smile curl my lips. “Oh yeah?” I asked, “And just where do you hide those treasures?”

“M-my leg...and my hip...” she said. “I got them when I was younger. One when I was nineteen, the other when I was twenty-two.”

She grimaced as she studied the wound, then took up the tweezers. “I’m sorry, this is probably going to suck a little.”

“I can handle it, sweetheart,” I said, immediately regretting the pet name. “Sorry, I’m really out of it.”

“I know,” she said softly before looking up at me again. “We’ll get this out and get you in bed.”

She tugged at the thing under my skin, and I inhaled sharply through my nose, curling my fingers into the edge of my mattress. I felt it move a bit, then a bit more.

"Almost there," she said apologetically. "One last good tug."

"Fuck, just do it," I gasped.

She gave another hard tug, and the offending object pulled free. She quickly dropped it onto the bed of wet gauze she'd used to clean the wound, then pressed some new gauze to the open wound. "Hold that there," she said.

I nodded, pressing my hand to my side as I tried to catch my breath. Even though it hurt like hell, it was already starting to feel a bit better. "What the hell was that anyway?"

Marley glanced at the object as she doused another square of gauze with antiseptic. "Looks like a wood chip. Kinda big—must have slid into you at just the right angle."

"Lovely," I grunted. "So, before you do anything else, there should be some shifter ointment in the first aid kit. Can you take a look?"

She looked in the kit, pushing things around and pulling out a small blue tin with a winking cartoon wolf on it.

"Shifter Stitches," she read, her head tilting like she was a pup herself. "I've never seen this. What is it?"

"Shifters don't really need stitches," I explained. "We heal so quickly that our major concerns have to do with an overabundance of scar tissue. This just has a mix of arnica and some other homeopathic agents to help the healing process."

"That's fascinating," she said in almost a whisper. "Okay, lift up that gauze. We'll get you cleaned up and apply this."

I tried my best to go to a happier place in my mind as she disinfected the wound and smeared the oily balm over it. When she taped another square of gauze over the gash, I felt like I could finally breathe again.

"All done," she said as she gathered the soiled supplies and stood. "I'll be right back—just gonna toss these in the trash."

I felt her absence keenly when she left the room. I still felt her gentle hands on my skin, her steady gaze on my body. It was difficult not to think about those secret tattoos or about her kneeling between my legs.

I was clearly still out of it—exhausted emotionally or physically. Marley had careened into my life, and I hadn't had a moment of rest since.

Or maybe it was that my biology had finally taken over the last remnants of my good sense, and I was slipping into something I wasn't entirely prepared for. I just couldn't stop wanting her. I couldn't even remember a time when I hadn't wanted her.

Did I really only meet her a few days ago? It felt like it had been years.

Marley returned a few moments later with a glass of water and a few ibuprofen. "Here, take these. It'll help," she said as she dropped the pills in my hand. "I don't remember you eating much at POSHA. Are you hungry?"

I tossed the pills into my mouth and swallowed them down with a gulp of water. All the while, my eyes were glued to her.

I could smell the fresh soap on her hands where she'd washed off my blood, probably in the kitchen sink. I could smell her honey-like scent mingling with my own from the clothing I'd lent her. I set down the glass and brushed a covetous hand up the side of her leg, relishing the smooth curves buried beneath the sweats she borrowed.

“I am hungry,” I said.

Marley’s throat bobbed, her hands coming to fold over her heart. I let my eyes fall there and saw the delicate curves of her breasts hiding under my shirt. Her scent shifted in the air—not with fear or nerves—but with lust. The pleasant musk deepened her natural scent of honey and roses to something more like bourbon and perfume. It was intoxicating.

“Do you want me to stop?” I asked as I brought my hand to a stop at the curve of her hip, hooking my thumb in the waistband. The absence of a lacy waistband of panties or the more practical plain elastic that I should be imagining her in was a pleasant surprise. The flash of black lace in the bundle of clothes she’d just thrown into the washer came into my mind. She was completely bare under my clothes, and fresh desire surged through me. I had to stifle the growl that rumbled in my chest. I knew I was being a degenerate, but my appetite had been whetted to a razor’s edge.

“I... should want you to stop,” Marley said, her voice small and timid. I wanted nothing more than to shower her with the care she deserved, show her how much I could protect her, how I could please her.

"But you don't want me to stop," I ventured.

"No," she said. "I don't."

I used that hooked thumb to pull her closer to me. She didn't fight me as she came to stand in the exact spot where she had been kneeling a moment before. Her hands left their perch over her heart to fall softly on my shoulders, eyes dancing over my face.

"How am I supposed to say no to you?" she whispered. "How am I supposed to stop wanting you so badly?"

It felt almost surreal to hear her echo my own thoughts back to me like she was reading my mind and putting those feelings out in the world. We couldn't avoid this anymore, this undeniable tension—this unending need for each other. This went beyond simple attraction. There was something more between us, something worth exploring.

Marley cupped my face, her thumb tracing a soft line just under my eye before smoothing a circle around my lips. They parted for her as she dragged the tip of her finger over my flesh.

Her breath caught, then shuddered out, and I kissed her thumb as I brought my free hand up to seize her wrist. It was so small, so delicate. I could easily wrap my hand around it, clamping loosely in a loving manacle. I kissed the palm of her hand, the contact slow and dragging. I heard her shudder again and felt her tremble. I moved my mouth to her wrist, kissing the sensitive skin of the underside of her arm. My hand on her hip tucked up and under the hem of her shirt. I curved my hand around her waist, holding her firmly to support her. I loved the smoothness of her—the dip and curve of her, the soft skin. I moved up her arm once more, kissing the slope of her bicep.

Her breaths were leaving her in soft pants now, the musk of her arousal filling the room with that lovely scent. Bourbon, perfume, and *her*. I brushed my hand lightly up her arm before gently cupping her breast in my hand, handling it as delicately as a ripened peach.

"Do you know how badly I've wanted to touch these?" I asked her. "How badly I've wanted to *taste* them?"

Her lashes fluttered, her gaze on me dreamy and drunken. "N-no," she sighed.

“Sometimes it’s all I can think about when I’m looking at you—that first day outside the coffee shop and when you came to the club dressed in lace. I’ve wanted so badly to explore every curve of you,” I said.

“I want you to,” she admitted. “I want you to see me.”

My cock twitched against the fly of my jeans, begging to be let loose, to be buried to the hilt in this beautiful woman before me.

“Show me,” I breathed, soft as a prayer.

Marley bit her lower lip, and I resisted the urge to do the same. I couldn’t claim her mouth yet, not when she was dropping her hands to the hem of her shirt. I watched with rapt attention as she gathered the fabric. I watched the knit fabric ascend past her beautiful stomach, exposing her navel. Watched as she coaxed it up and finally, gloriously, above her breasts.

They were perfect—round and pert, the nipples the same color as her lips. My breath left me in a rush, and I wrapped my arms around her waist, drawing her closer to hold her tight against my chest. From this position, her head was slightly higher than eye level for me. She tilted her head down, and our lips met in pure need.

I lifted a hand to cup the underside of her breast, kneading with tender firmness until I coaxed a precious squeak out of her throat. The sound made my blood run hot, sending my pulse hammering in my ears.

My skin tingled as she combed her fingers through my hair, her nails dragging gently against the sensitive skin of my scalp.

God, this was heaven. I could die happily die right now.

I rolled her nipple between my thumb and forefinger, increasing the pressure so that her knees buckled, but I kept her upright.

She broke from the kiss long enough to gasp out, "*Bed.*"

I didn't need to be told twice. I scooped her up in my arms, lifting her from her precarious lean into me. I stood with ease and turned to lay her gently in my bed. There was no break in the momentum, though. My need for her was too great.

I climbed into the bed, positioning myself above her before I leaned down and sucked her nipple into my mouth, circling it with my tongue as I let my hand take care of its twin. When her back arched, it took everything I had in me to keep my hips from bucking.

How long had it been since I had a woman in my bed? How long has it been since I had my head between a woman's thighs? Too long—all at once, it had been entirely too long. I wanted to show her the meaning of pleasure, wanted to ruin men for her forever. I wanted to be the best she'd ever had.

Her moans indicated it shouldn't be too hard.

I moved to give her other breast the same care, letting the first peak against the ambient air in the room. When I encountered the frustrating scuff of her shirt getting in the way, I retreated from my worship of her breasts. I reached for the shirt gathered above her breasts and tugged it off her.

She looked at me, anticipating what I would do next. I had plenty of ideas of what I would do and where I would start.

And then I saw her shoulder.

Every spare ounce of desire in my body transmuted into something white hot and heavy in my gut, morphing into absolute rage.

A patina of white and red scarring extended from the delicate curve of her shoulder past her collarbone. It was not a clean scar—I'd seen mating bites before, but none so mangled as this one. It looked like he'd tried to get her, and she'd fought against it tooth and nail, requiring him to bite more than once.

I brushed my fingertip over a divot in her skin where she hadn't quite healed, where part of her would always be missing.

"Who did this to you?"

The question came out far harsher than I'd intended. I had never heard myself sound so bloodthirsty. My eyes met hers, and I saw her expression shift.

Gone was the willing warmth, the need. Shutters lowered over eyes. She crossed her arms over her chest and rolled out from underneath me.

"Marley—" I said.

She shook her head, scrambling for the discarded shirt. When she'd covered herself again, she sat on the edge of the bed. "This was a mistake," she said.

"No, no—Marley, it wasn't a mistake. I'm sorry. I shouldn't have even said anything. I just…I saw it, and—it's a failed bite, right? A failed mating—"

"It's none of your business," she said. The harsh words didn't match her tone. She sounded sad, maybe a little broken. She was hugging herself like she was trying to hold herself together.

I sat back on my knees, but she wouldn't meet my eye.

I'd made a huge mistake. I might as well have just bitten her myself with how I tore open the old wound. She'd clearly healed externally, but that wound was still bleeding in the depths of her soul. I cursed under my breath and shuffled forward to sit on the edge of the bed.

I didn't get too close, leaving about four feet of distance between us. I bit the inside of my lip before leaning forward and resting my elbows on my knees. An awkward silence grew between us, and all I could hear was the sound of Marley's forceful breathing and her heart hammering against her ribcage.

"The ex you mentioned…" I said finally when I had found some measure of calm. "Did he do that to you?"

Marley was silent for a long time. So long that I thought she might not answer me. Then I saw a faint movement from the corner of my eye. She nodded.

"Yes." She sounded like she was a million miles away.

"I'm sorry," I said again.

"For what?" she said.

"For making a comment, for bringing all that pain back when you made yourself vulnerable with me, for the fact that it even happened to you..." I said. "For all of it."

"I thought...I thought you were angry with me," she said, her voice shaking with her fear.

"What?" I said. "Marley, no. Not ever."

"I thought you saw it and thought I was mated. I thought you were furious with me for betraying him... I thought—"

"Shhh, shhh," I said, hurrying to my feet. It was my turn to kneel now. I rested my hands on her knees very gently as if the slightest touch might spook her away. My relief was tangible when she didn't flinch or try to shy away. "Marley, a failed mating mark is obvious. Even if he had been successful, I would never be angry at you for being a victim of someone else's abuse."

She looked so small sitting there, her arms still curved around her tiny, fragile body.

"Please forgive me, Marley," I said in a soft whisper.

She nodded, though she didn't look entirely convinced.

"I think… I think it might be best if we stop doing these kinds of things until Noah is in first grade," she said. "We keep playing with fire, and we're starting to get burned."

My wilder side rebelled against that idea—the side of me that wanted her, the side of me that needed to protect her, to take her into the fold. But the human side of my mind knew she was right. She'd told me numerous times now that she wasn't sure what she wanted, what she needed. She wasn't sure she even wanted to see another shifter in a romantic capacity, really.

I'd promised to cool my jets, and maybe it was finally time to keep that promise.

"If that's what you want. I'll respect that," I said.

Marley seemed to relax at that, and I wondered what she had gone through to make her so tense. Sometimes it felt like she was waiting for the shit to hit the fan like she expected me to blow up at her. I thought about those scars on her shoulder again and drew a hand from Marley's knee, flexing it to get my temper in check.

I had half a mind to kill the asshole who harmed her, but I would keep it to myself. My fury wouldn't make Marley feel any safer, and it wouldn't do anything to show her that I was hitting the brakes, either.

"Why don't we go to the kitchen, have a snack and some tea, then just take it easy for the rest of the night? We can put some stupid movie on or something," I said.

"What movie?" she asked, her voice small and sullen.

My lips twitched. Even at her worst, she was adorable. God, I wanted to wrap her in my arms and never let go. I knew better than to do that right now, though.

I eyed her. "Something tells me we need to watch an animation."

She gave a hint of a smile, demurring slightly from my scrutinizing gaze.

"I like to think I'm not so obvious," she said.

"That's the thing, Marley when it comes to you, I make a guess that would surprise me. Because you always surprise me in all the best ways."

Her smile widened a fraction, and I could feel some of the tension in my shoulders unspooling.

"You should put some clothes on first," Marley said. "You're a little...distracting when you walk around like that."

I looked down at my bare chest. "Right, very unbecoming of me," I said.

"You really must leave more to the imagination. What will the eligible bachelorettes of New Middle Bluff think about you showing so much skin, Mr. Lucas?" she said with a sort of prim snootiness.

And just like that, there she was. Silly, sweet, funny, Marley.

That was worth far more to me than whatever might have happened tonight.

I went over to my dresser and pulled out clean clothes. "You're welcome to watch if you'd like the show." I grinned at her over my shoulder. "But if that's a little too much for you, I'll meet you in the living room."

She gave me an adorably shy smile. "See you out there," she said.

I nodded. "See you out there."

My side was feeling better already now that the splinter had been taken out. Dressed in dry clothes, I yawned as I made my way down the hall, my heart warming a little more than I liked to admit when I saw Marley's head resting on the back of the couch.

In the kitchen, I switched on the kettle. "You want some blankets or anything?" I asked.

Marley smiled at me. "Yeah, that sounds nice. Do you have anything other than tea?"

"Hmm, I have coffee. But no decaf. Oh, wait. I can make hot cocoa," I offered.

She bit her lip. "Do you have marshmallows?"

Her sweetness was so endearing. "I do, fancy ones, in fact."

"Fancy ones? What are fancy marshmallows?"

"Ones made with vanilla beans for the really bougie clients," I said through a chuckle. "So, hot cocoa with fancy marshmallows?"

"Yes, please," she said.

"All right, blankets first, then hot cocoa, then a movie. Sound about right?"

"Sounds perfect."

Obliging her, I dug into the hamper near the sofa, where I kept a myriad of warm blankets. I grabbed the one I thought was the coziest and brought it over to her, covering her in the soft micro-plush, then handed her the remote. "Why don't you find us something to watch?"

I went back into the kitchen as the kettle clicked off. Travis would have a fit if he knew I was making hot cocoa with water instead of milk, but Travis wasn't here to be a picky asshole, so I could do what I wanted.

I poured the water over the powdered cocoa, stirred it, then plopped one of the artisan marshmallows in the mug. It was always satisfying to use those things; they looked like little icebergs with their rough-cut edges. When I handed the mug to Marley, her face lit up.

"Ooh! You weren't kidding. These really are fancy marshmallows."

"Only the best for you, sweet Marley," I said with a wink. "You want anything to eat?"

"Honestly, not really. I'm not hungry at all," she said.

"Pretty standard after such an anxiety-ridden night. How about comfort food?"

She pulled her lower lip slightly into her mouth. "I feel like you're going to judge my comfort food."

I quirked an eyebrow at her. "Is it weird?"

"It's a little weird," she admitted.

"Like tuna and peanut butter, weird?"

"Ew," she said. "Not that weird."

I laughed, immediately grimacing at the pain in my side. I pressed my hand against it. "All right, then, what are we talking?"

"You can't just move on like nothing happened. Do you know someone who would eat a PB and T sandwich?" she pressed.

"Oh God, we have an acronym for it now?"

"Listen, tuna and peanut butter sandwich has at least three too many syllables to say for a single, cursed dish. Now, stop avoiding the question," she said.

"My mother may or may not have eaten PB and T sandwiches when she was pregnant with my sister. I can neither confirm nor deny," I said. "Now, spill, what's your weird comfort food?"

"Now I'm self-conscious that it isn't weird enough," Marley said, shifting her position on the sofa.

I dropped my hands to my sides and looked up at my ceiling. "Marley, I am begging you to let me make you something to eat. If you don't tell me what you want, I will make you a PB and T sandwich."

This, of course, was a bluff—I didn't keep canned tuna in the house. Couldn't stand the stuff.

"Jeez, okay," she said, flustered. "Boxed macaroni and cheese mixed with tomato soup...and cut-up hot dogs."

I gave it some thought. It was a weird group of ingredients, but it didn't sound half bad. And since all those ingredients suited a five-year-old's palate, it meant I had the ingredients all on hand.

"You are judging me so hard right now," she accused.

"No, no. I'm not. I was just thinking that as weird as it sounded, it also sounded really good," I promised. "I think I have everything on hand."

She took a sip of her cocoa. "Do you want me to help?"

I shook my head. "I think I can handle boiling water and cutting up some hot dogs," I teased. "You just pick our narrative journey for the night."

It wasn't all that difficult to put the dish together. I had to make a couple of substitutions—I didn't have regular tomato soup, only a can of tomato bisque—and the hot dogs had been conquered by my son, so I used a few bratwurst links instead.

Carrying two bowls filled with the strange dish, I went to join Marley on the sofa. I offered one up to her, and she smiled. "You got some, too?" she asked.

"Like I said, it sounds kind of good. I had to make a couple of substitutions, but I hope you still like it," I said.

She set her cocoa on the coffee table and accepted the bowl, scooping up a bit in her spoon before blowing on it and taking a bite. I sat down as she chewed, waiting for her expert assessment.

"It's like you made my weird toddler meal a gourmet experience."

I laughed. “I hardly think canned bisque and grocery store brats are particularly gourmet, but I’m happy you approve.”

I took a bite and hummed. It reminded me a little of eating grilled cheese with tomato soup, though I wasn’t sure where the hotdogs factored into that equation. “It’s good.”

“Happy to convert you to my religion,” she joked.

“So, what are we watching?” I asked.

“I’m stuck between Detective Doggo and Adventure Hour,” she said.

“Detective Doggo is a classic, but I don’t care for how they represent my kind,” I said.

She looked at me like I’d just told her she’d kicked a kitten. “Do they have lousy shifter representation in Detective Doggo?”

I couldn’t help it. I cracked up. “I’m sorry, it was a bad joke,” I said. “But, oh my god, you are adorable. The expression on your face is priceless. There’s no poor representation of shifters in that show. I was just making a stupid joke about it being about a dog and me being...you know, part wolf.”

"Oh." She chuckled. "You really do love a good dad joke, don't you?"

"It would be a waste not to make dad jokes while being a dad, don't you think?"

"I'm sure it has everything to do with not being wasteful and nothing to do with the fact that you are a humungous, impossibly attractive dork," she said, punctuating her teasing with a bite of her food.

"Detective Doggo it is, then?"

"I think you've lost that privilege for making me panic like that. So, Adventure Hour. And that has nothing to do with the fact that I love the dumb humor in that show, nothing at all."

"I see. I see," I said, nodding sagely and taking another bite. "Damn. I would definitely get high-blood pressure if I ate this every day, but it's fucking great."

"I told you. It's weird, but at least it's not peanut butter-and-tuna weird. This at least tastes good," she said. "No offense to your mom."

We started the show—a strange fever dream of a cartoon involving a collection of kingdoms themed for food and a boy whose dog was his brother.

Marley explained the inside jokes, the histories between the characters, the motivations, and the inspirations of the show's creators. She was really into this show—this wasn't just something she indulged in when she was sad—it was something she genuinely loved.

"It's cute how into this show you are," I said, taking her empty bowl from her and putting it on the coffee table next to mine.

Even in the bluish light of the television, I could see her blushing. She kept her eyes glued to the screen, nervously chewing on her lip.

"My ex always hated this show," she admitted quietly. "Near the end, I could hardly do anything without his permission. So, when I finally got away from him, I binged this show and gorged myself on a gallon of ice cream. I'd laugh and cry and remember that even this little joy in my life—this dumb cartoon—was something I'd taken back from him with my own hands." She heaved a sigh and glanced at me. "I guess that's kind of dumb."

I shook my head, taking her hand in mine and lifting it to press a kiss to one of her knuckles. "It's not dumb," I said. "When we're with people who don't give us what we need, people who expect more from us than we can give, it's important to take every ounce you can back for yourself."

"You don't think I'm stupid for still watching cartoons?"

"I think it makes perfect sense that someone who works so well with children is still connected to their own inner child," I said. "I don't think it's stupid. On the contrary, I think it's special. I like seeing a piece of you no one else gets to see."

She dropped her gaze from mine, but not before I saw the gratitude in her eyes. "Thank you. Not... not just for saying that, but for everything tonight. For not being mad at me when I clammed up, for not teasing me about my comfort foods, for not making me feel stupid—"

"For treating you with basic respect?" I said.

She looked up at me with surprise.

"I guess...I'm still learning what basic respect looks like," she said. "Sometimes I'm worried this is all a plot to get me to put my trust in you. But maybe that's just because my ex used it that way."

My heart ached for her. I didn't know who this prick was, but I'd happily punch his teeth in if I ever got the opportunity to come face-to-face with him.

"It can be hard to get past those old wounds. The pain stops, but there are still internalized beliefs about something. It really colors the world around you in ways you're not cognizant of until someone brings it up to you," I said. "I'm lucky to have always had a supportive family, but Noah's mother... she had me believing a lot of things about women after she betrayed us."

"How did you come out of it?" she asked me. "How did you learn what was real and what you'd internalized?"

"Time. And friends like Travis that told me I was being a sexist numbskull," I said. "There are still times I worry about it, but I can always come back to the touchstone of realizing that Noah's mother just wasn't a very nice person."

"Neither was my ex," she said, looking back at the screen. "It took me a long time to realize he was just mean."

A sort of companionable silence fell between us. In the quiet, I heard the washer chime down the stairs, signaling that the wash cycle was done. Marley didn't seem to hear it, so I stood.

"Your laundry just dinged. Do you mind if I go and change it over to the dryer?" I asked.

"Are you sure you can do it with your side like that?"

"It's already mostly healed, just a little tender. Don't worry about it," I promised.

In the laundry room, I quickly tossed her clothes in the dryer. All the same, by the time I made it up the stairs and back to the sofa, Marley had fallen asleep.

I thought about moving her to the guest room, but she looked so peaceful and comfortable all snuggled up in her blanket that I didn't want to risk waking her up. And the dishes could wait until the morning.

I studied her for a moment, the way her eyelids fluttered, and her chest rose and fell. I turned away before I gave in to the urge to carry her to my bed. I needed to pump the brakes. I needed to remember to pump the brakes.

Chapter 13 - Marley

I woke a few hours later to the theme song for Adventure Hour. It startled me. Everything felt too loud, too much.

Groaning, I lifted my head from where I'd slumped down onto the couch. I tried to remember falling asleep, tried to remember how I'd gotten into Cole's house again. The details came back to me in a slow drip, my brain booting up after the stressful evening. I sat up fully and stretched my arms over my head.

The remote was on the coffee table next to the abandoned bowls from the dinner Cole had made for us. I turned off the television and grabbed up the bowls, carrying them into the kitchen and placing them in the sink. I checked the time on the stove's digital clock—it was the early hours of the morning. I could still get a few hours of sleep before I had to get up for the day.

I rubbed my forehead. I felt like I was forgetting something important.

Then it dawned on me that it was Friday night—I wouldn't have work the next day. The first week of school had put me through such a wringer that I had a lousy concept of time. I laughed at myself as some of the tension in my shoulders eased. The weekend hadn't come a moment too soon. I desperately needed a couple of days to collect myself.

Just then, I heard a little sniffle behind me.

I turned to see Noah holding a small blanket close to him and dressed in spaceship pajamas. He looked so tiny in the enormous space.

"Are you my mommy?" he asked.

The question took me entirely by surprise, so much so that I could do nothing but stare at him. Then I realized that it was quite dark in the house, and I probably wasn't entirely visible to a bleary-eyed child, even with his night vision helping him out.

"No, Noah," I said softly. "It's me, your teacher, Miss Cage."

"You're having a sleepover at our house?" he asked.

"That's right," I said. "Just for tonight. I had a scary dream, and your dad said I could stay over so I didn't feel scared all alone at my house. Is that all right with you?"

Noah blinked blearily, then nodded.

"I had a bad dream, too," he said.

"Oh yeah? What was yours about?" I asked as I knelt on one knee so that I could be at eye level with him.

"I had a dream that Daddy and I got stuck in a big cage," he said. "And that people were calling us mean names. I got stuck as a wolf and couldn't turn back into a little boy."

I frowned. I wasn't sure if dreams like that were coming from some inherited trauma from past generations or if these were really the things that shifters, even as young as Noah, thought about. Either way, there was a sadness to the reality of it. "Did you come out here looking for your dad?" I asked.

He nodded, wiping his eyes with his little balled hand. "I heard the dishes and thought he was out here," he said. "Then I saw you and thought Daddy finally brought home a mommy for me."

I pressed my lips into a tight smile. I probably should have just gotten a hotel room for the night. Noah seeing his teacher spending the night in his home, wearing clothes that belonged to his father, would only confuse him. Kids his age didn't really see nuance; it was why so many children had boyfriends and girlfriends at this age—for children, it was very simple: if you liked someone, they were your partner. Internally, I apologized to Cole in advance. This would not be easy for Noah's mind to rationalize.

All the same, Noah was in distress, and I was his teacher. I could be of some help.

"Do you want to go and get your dad?" I asked.

He shook his head. "Can you come and tuck me in?"

"Sure I can." I opened my arms to him.

He wrapped his arms around my neck, and I picked him up, hitching his small frame on my hip. I shuffled down the hallway, finding his bedroom by the décor and toys scattered across the floor. I went to sit on the edge of his bed before setting him down.

His arms tightened around my neck in panic, and his body went rigid.

"What's wrong, Noah?" I asked.

"What if I have more bad dreams?" he whimpered. "I don't want to have more nightmares." His voice was thick with tears.

I shushed him softly and rubbed my hand gently over his back. “You’ll be fine, Noah,” I said soothingly. “I’m not going anywhere. I can stay here as long as you like.”

“Promise?”

“Promise,” I said. “You want to lie down?”

“Okay.”

His arms loosened just enough for me to lay him down on his bed. I pulled the covers up over him and tucked him in, just as he requested. Then I lay down next to him, brushing my fingers through his hair. I didn’t quite fit on the bed, and I didn’t want to impede his ability to sleep, so I stayed propped up against the headboard as I comforted him.

Eventually, Noah rolled over onto his stomach, and I took to rubbing soothing circles over his back as I took in his room. Spaceships, dinosaurs, glow-in-the-dark stars. He was every bit the normal boy I usually worked with. It was so hard not to be baffled by why anyone would ever be afraid of a sweet little shifter like Noah.

It got me thinking about my own biases, my promise to myself not to date a shifter again, and not to open my heart to another person while I was still healing.

Maybe I was wrong about that. Maybe I was looking too deep into this whole thing with Cole. It didn't have to be as serious as I'd been making it out to be. Sure, it could be said that things were moving quickly, that it was too soon to be involved with another man so soon after Wyatt. But maybe I needed to open myself up to healing these old traumas by letting a good man into my life.

I couldn't deny that Cole was a good man. Not when he'd shown that he had an empathetic heart and a thoughtful nature time and time again. Some of those things were easy to fake—Wyatt had been a master at manipulation and charm. There were so many times, too many to count, that he'd gaslighted me into thinking I was the one who had made the error when I brought any complaints to him. He made me feel selfish and superficial for wanting basic respect.

Cole had regularly shown me, even pointed out to me, when I was surprised by basic compassion.

Maybe he was the real deal. Could Noah have turned out so sweet if his father was an abuser?

I didn't think so.

My eyelids grew heavy as I thought about these matters, about the intricacies of our relationship, the hazards, and possibilities of a future with someone like Cole. I eventually fell asleep and dreamed of waking up to breakfast in bed served by Cole himself—only to forget breakfast entirely when another hunger took over.

He had just been wrapping his arms tightly around my waist when I woke up.

I was being lifted out of the bed by strong, warm arms. Cole's arms. I was so certain it was him, even with my eyes closed. I wanted to open them, to look up at him, to pull him down to me for a kiss. But I didn't want to break the sleepy spell.

I felt so safe in his arms, so treasured.

A few moments later, I was placed on a soft bed, the blankets pulled up to my chin and tucked gently around me.

Cole kissed my forehead, and I heard him huff a soft laugh.

"Thank you, Marley," he whispered so quietly I almost couldn't hear it.

As he left me in his guest room, I couldn't help but think that I should be the one thanking him.

Chapter 14 - Cole

I woke the next day thinking of Marley.

Against my will, I might add.

Every time I tried to divert my thoughts away from her, I somehow wound up wondering about her ex, or wanting to do some sort of sweet gesture, or wanting to kiss her…yeah, just kiss her.

When I finally worked up the nerve to come out of my bedroom and look for her, I found the guest room empty. Noah was still fast asleep in his room, likely from whatever sleep he'd lost when he'd gone to find Marley and wound up conscripting her to put him back to bed. I felt oddly disappointed as I walked out to the kitchen, finding all the dishes washed and set in the drying rack.

I thought she would have at least waited to say goodbye.

Just when I was about to let her fleeing sour my mood for the day, however, I found a note written in her bubbly script on the counter.

Thank you for everything you did for me last night. I can't tell you how much I appreciate it. I put your clothes in the washer—I just figured it would be easier to explain to Noah if I wasn't here when he woke up. Text me when you're awake.

I read the note a few times, trying to find a hidden message or code in the words, like her handwriting would somehow tell me the innermost workings of her heart. I shook my head and tore up the note, then tossed in the trash. The last thing I needed was for Travis to find it and bust my balls about Marley thanking me for what I did.

I knew exactly where that prick's dirty mind would go, and I wasn't keen on wearing my rejection on my sleeve.

I sent Marley a quick text to make sure she was okay. She texted back almost immediately, sending me a photo of her sitting on her back porch in a fluffy sweater with an open book pressed to her chest.

Decided it was a good day for some much-needed self-care. I hope your morning is going decent.

I smiled down at my phone even though I told myself not to. She was just too damned cute. I fought myself on it for a few moments but ultimately decided to save the photo to my phone. I nearly put it as my phone's background, but that would be over the top. I said I would pump the brakes, so I needed to pump the damn brakes.

I decided to focus my energy on caring for my son—it would benefit me in many ways, the least of which was getting my mind off Marley and how badly I wanted her.

I grabbed a bowl and got to whipping up some eggs and adding a splash of cream, cinnamon, nutmeg, sugar, and vanilla extract. I dipped thick slices of bread into the mixture and threw some sausage in a frying pan. French toast was one of Noah's favorite breakfasts, and it was just enough of a pain to make that I could focus on it completely.

As I took the sausage out of the pan to drain, I heard the tell-tale tipping and tapping of Noah's claws against the hardwood flooring. I turned to look back at the hallway, finding Noah sitting at the edge of the kitchen and tilting his head left and right like a confused puppy. He lifted his nose to sniff the air, and I realized he was looking for Marley.

"Sorry, kiddo. Miss Cage went home. You just missed her," I said. "She didn't want to wake you up to say goodbye when she left."

Noah lay down on the floor, nestling his snout between his large paws. He let out a small whimper, and I ignored the jolt of guilt as I put the French toast in the skillet.

Noah shifted back into his human form and ran over to hug my leg. "Daddy! You're making French fry toast!"

"It's just French toast, buddy. French fries are a different food," I said through a laugh. Honestly, I could let him call it that for the rest of his life if he wanted to, but I didn't want him to blame me in the future for getting teased about it, so I did my due diligence.

"Yay!!" he said, bouncing up and down. "French fry toast. French fry toast!"

I laughed again. "Go and pick a cartoon to watch while you eat your breakfast."

"Then school?" he asked.

"No school today, buddy. It's Saturday," I said.

He pouted. "I wanted to see Miss Cage."

"You'll see her on Monday, buddy," I promised. "How about you and I go do something fun today, hm? You wanna have a nice day with Dad?"

"Day with Daddy!" he shouted, bouncing on the tips of his toes before running over to the living room.

I served breakfast, complete with powdered sugar and maple syrup. I had sausage and eggs.

Noah picked up where Marley left off with Adventure Hour, which was impossible not to love. It seemed they had a lot in common. That, and having seen her curled up around Noah in his bed, made it difficult not to think about Marley stepping into the role of Noah's mother.

I shook that thought from my head and returned my attention to Noah. He needed his dad to be present.

After breakfast, I got him dressed up for our day out.

Five-year-olds were pretty easy to satisfy—a movie, a little ice cream, a trip to a park with a swing set. But I'd be switching it up with a trip to the arcade instead.

He was already growing so fast, and I wanted to make sure I enjoyed these experiences with him before he hit puberty and thought he was too cool to hang out with his old man.

I buckled him into his car seat, and once I was in the driver's seat, I took a sneaky photo of myself with Noah looking out of the car window in the background. I sent it off to Marley and tapped out a message.

The pup and I are off on an adventure today. If you were a five-year-old boy, would you want to go to an arcade or a movie?

I started up the car and turned around to exit the long driveway. As I reached the street, my phone chimed with a text.

Definitely an arcade. Way more interactive and engaging for growing little brains. You can teach rules like taking turns and instructions. You can practice colors and shapes. Ski-ball helps with hand-eye coordination too!

Smiling, I shook my head. It was just like a kindergarten teacher to bring all of those points up. Arcade it was, then.

When we arrived at the arcade, Noah was practically jumping off the walls, pointing out this and that game that he wanted to try. I put fifty dollars in the token machine, knowing that with his energy level, we would have no problem burning through them.

We played whack-a-wolf (which I tried not to think too hard about when we were done), ski ball (per Marley's suggestion), and I showed him the ancient art of the coin-pusher game (a family tradition passed down from my father).

Unsurprisingly, after a few rounds of putting tokens in for only very little to happen in the coin-pusher, Noah asked to do something where he could win a prize. Seeing that we'd only won a few tickets to trade for prizes so far, I thought it would be better if we played one of the games where we spent a little more money but had an easier time getting a prize.

I took Noah over to a counter where garish clown faces all stood in a row with water guns across from each one about five feet away.

"All right, Noah," I said, picking him up and hitching him on my hip so I could show him how the game worked. "We have to do is aim our water gun at the clown and try to get the water in his mouth. You see how his mouth is open there?"

Noah nodded, his gaze a little wary—he was probably developing a fear of clowns at this very moment, but that could be handled in therapy when he was older.

"When you get enough water in his mouth, a balloon will grow on top of his head, and then it will pop! The first person who gets their balloon to pop wins. Sound like fun?"

He nodded again and hugged my neck. I could tell he was a little nervous, but he'd enjoy it once we sat down and got to it.

I paid the teenage attendants for two plays, one for me and one for Noah. We sat down, and just before the teen cued up the game, another man approached wearing a suit. He had black hair combed back with product in a standard gentleman's cut. His sunglasses were pushed up into his hair like he'd wandered in from outside.

"Hey, can I hop in on this one before you start?" he asked, his tone warm.

The teenage girl running the booth flushed a little as he offered his cash. She nodded, taking the money and sliding it into her apron.

"Sit wherever you like," she said.

As the man sat, a breeze from outside wafted his scent toward me. Shifter. He looked over at me and smiled before nodding a little hello.

"I haven't played this since I was a kid and couldn't pass it up when I spotted it outside. I hope you don't mind," he said.

"No, not at all—can't beat the old memories, right?"

"Exactly," he said as he rolled up his sleeves to his elbows. "May the best man win."

His tone was friendly, but something about him saying that to me and my son rubbed me the wrong way. Maybe I was just being sensitive after Marley snuck off without saying goodbye. I gave him a tight smile and nodded. "Yeah, good luck," I said.

I showed Noah how to use the water gun—which button to press and where to aim—while the worker ensured all the balloons were ready to go. A bell sounded, and we were off.

Noah loved the game. He got so excited as his balloon began inflating—he was all giggles and bouncing. I split my time between helping him aim and aiming at my own target.

A balloon popped, prompting Noah to cover his ears and wince. He was still learning how to block out the stimulation of sudden loud noises with his sensitive hearing.

Unfortunately, it was neither my balloon nor Noah's that had popped. It was the stranger's. I looked over at him, a little miffed that the jerk couldn't just throw the game for a kid, but some guys had weird complexes about losing.

"C-congratulations, you won, sir," the teenager stammered to him. "Which prize would you like?"

"I think we ought to be asking the man at the table, eh?" he asked before looking over to my son. "What do you think, big man? Which prize will it be?"

I blinked, surprised by the act of kindness. Here I was thinking this guy was an ass for not throwing the match. "You don't have to do that," I said.

"Nonsense, what am I gonna do with a little tchotchke, anyway? I'm here for business, and I wouldn't even be able to fit it in my suitcase."

Noah looked up at me in silent question. I gave him a nod. "Tell the nice lady what prize you want."

"Can I please have the orange dinosaur?"

"Sure!" she said happily as she reached into a bin under the counter to produce the small stuffed animal.

Noah took it and hugged it happily, beaming at it and beginning to ramble off names for him.

"What do you say to the nice man, Noah?" I asked.

Noah looked at me, then at the stranger, still squeezing the little orange dino tightly around its neck. He looked down a little timidly, kicking his feet and mumbling a quiet, "Thank you."

I ruffled his curly hair with endearment. "Attaboy," I said, then turned to the man. "Thank you for doing that."

"No problem," he said.

"So, you said you're in town for business? What kind of business?" I asked.

"Oh, you know, this and that," he said. "Mostly, I'm looking for a place to open a new law office in the area. I just got my license to practice in South Carolina after starting my business in Pennsylvania."

"No kidding? Well, I just got done looking for a new place for my contracting company, so I can give you a list of the places we looked at or put you in touch with a great realtor if you're interested. What's your name?" I asked.

He held out his hand to me, and I took it, giving it a firm shake. The man had a grip on him. "Wyatt. Wyatt Pierce," he said. "You know, I have a meeting later, but I'm feeling a bit peckish. Would you maybe want to get some lunch and talk about the area? It'd be great to get another shifter's perspective."

My gaze slid over to the girl running the booth, only to see her skin blanching.

"Sorry, could you guys move on? We have to make room for the other players," she said stiffly.

Wyatt's face flashed with what looked like rage for a split second, then it was gone. He stood, buttoning the middle button of his blazer and straightening his lapels.

"Sure thing," I said, picking up Noah before Wyatt had the chance to retort and cause a scene. "To answer your question, there are a few restaurants around, so we can definitely grab something. What do you think, Noah? You hungry yet?"

"I want dino nuggets," he said.

"I don't know if we'll be able to find dino nuggets, buddy, but we can get you chicken fingers, okay?"

He nodded and hugged me around my neck again, clearly still shy.

"You all right with a little burger joint? Sorry, probably not the ideal place for a lawyer from out of town, especially so close to the ocean and the fresh seafood, but you know."

Wyatt put up a hand and smiled. "No problem," he said. "I totally get it. You gotta give them what they'll eat, right? Pick your battles and all that."

I laughed and nodded. "Yeah, thanks. Come on. I'll show you around the area. Restaurant's not too far."

As we walked through town, I pointed out a few office buildings that might work for his needs and some nearby restaurants I'd liked. He made some joking remarks, asking where I liked to take women to wine and dine them.

Marley popped into my mind when he asked, and I felt strangely ashamed when I gave him an answer in earnest about good spots for dates. Like I was somehow cheating on her, which made no sense at all since she wasn't mine, and I was not hers.

Finally, we arrived at a tasteful little bistro place called CJ's Brewery. They offered standard American fare, an extensive collection of beers, and plenty of choices for picky five-year-olds. It felt bizarre to sit at a table with a man I'd just met, but he had a way about him that made you not want to refuse him.

After ordering, Wyatt unfolded the cloth napkin on the table and placed it on his lap before leaning back to rest an arm on the back of the empty seat next to him in a comfortable sprawl. "So, it was Cole, right? What do you do? You seem knowledgeable about the states of the buildings in the area and their owners."

I nodded. "I'm a contractor—been working in this area going on almost ten years. I spent a little over seven of those years with my own business. Fur Sure Solutions."

His brow creased before he gave a scoff. "Cute," he said flatly. "But that's actually great news since I'll be looking to update whatever office space I pick out around here. It must have been fate for us to meet like this."

"Yeah? What kind of updates are you considering?"

"I'm so bad with verbalizing this kind of stuff. Do you have an online portfolio I can look at? Maybe that will help me sus out exactly what I want."

"No online portfolio, but you're welcome to come by the office when you have a moment. I'm down in New Middle Bluff near the ocean, about a half hour away from here, if it's not too much trouble for you to go that far."

"No! Not at all. That actually sounds perfect. I've been dying to see the beaches here. I will probably be looking for a small temporary home down here as well."

"Sure, well, there are lots of great bungalows in the area. I'm sure you'll find something that suits you," I said. "Here, let me get you a card."

I opened my wallet, and just as I was fishing one out, our food arrived. I said a quick thanks to the waiter after she told us to flag her down if we needed anything before finally handing the card over to him.

"Just give us a call on Monday any time. My receptionist will take care of you. Her name is Sylvia. She's brilliant."

"Nice," he said, tucking the card in his coat pocket. "So, tell me about your company. Why'd you start it? What kind of projects do you guys usually work on? Are you a licensed contractor?"

"Yep," I said. "As for why I started it, I noticed there was a lack of shifter-friendly construction companies in the area, and that was a niche I knew I could fill. We've worked on everything from shifter-friendly office spaces to the Polar Shift Academy, which is the local integrated school."

"I think I saw that one on the news. How's the faculty?" he asked as he started cutting into his steak.

"Great so far. Noah loves his teacher, and she's fantastic with the kids. It's honestly refreshing to see a human so attuned to the needs and psychology of other shifters."

Wyatt's knife scraped loudly against his plate, the sound grating enough that Noah and I both had to clench our teeth. Noah brought his hands up to his ears again like he had in the arcade, and I gently coaxed them back down before patting him lightly on the back.

"That's nice to hear," Wyatt said, though the words sounded strangely tight.

"Yeah," I said. "Got any kids?"

"I haven't had the privilege yet, but I'm hoping I'll get the opportunity soon," he said.

"Parenthood is wonderful," I said. "Noah's the best thing that ever happened to me."

Wyatt smiled as he took a bite of his steak and chewed. "There's nothing more important than the relationship between a father and son, is there?"

"No, there really isn't," I said, looking down at Noah and petting a hand through his hair.

Wyatt got quiet for a little while after that. I used the silence to focus on eating my own meal and making sure that Noah ate his. There were a lot of distractions in the restaurant. He was a bit fussy about his chicken not being dino-shaped, but after some careful negotiation, I got him to eat two of the tenders along with some shoe-string fries.

When we were all done, Wyatt and I argued over the bill before I relented to him paying because I'd spent so much of my day showing him around town. I didn't feel right about it, but I let it slide, telling him I'd get the next one.

Something about Wyatt was off-putting. He was more than friendly and generous enough and hadn't done anything to cause me or anyone else offense—but something about him put me on edge. It was like every question he asked was an assessment, an evaluation.

Then again, he was a lawyer. I felt the same way about Olivia's lawyer during the custody settlement. Hell, even my own lawyer made me feel like an idiot from time to time. It was probably just part of the bravado they had to put on to be successful in court.

We left together, pausing at the door so we could shake hands again.

"I hope you'll give us a call on Monday," I said.

"Oh, you'll definitely be hearing from me. Don't you worry about that," he said. "Thanks again for all your help. And thank *you*, Noah, for letting me win earlier today. It did wonders for my ego."

He winked at Noah, who I was certain had no idea what he was talking about. I petted his hair comfortingly, letting him know with that little non-verbal communication that he hadn't done anything wrong.

We said our goodbyes and parted in opposite directions, Wyatt back toward where we had come from, Noah and me heading further into the shopping area. I figured I owed Noah a little more fun after diverting our father-and-son day into a business meeting of sorts.

I squeezed Noah's hand. "I'm thinking we go and get some ice cream for dessert, and then maybe we go see a movie. You up for that, kiddo?"

"Arcade AND a movie? Yeah, yeah!!"

I was relieved to see him excited again after I felt like I'd been part of his deflating.

I picked him up and saddled him onto my shoulders, relishing the feeling of his tiny fingers curling into my hair. These moments were fleeting; soon enough, Noah would be too big to carry on my shoulders.

Wyatt was right. There was nothing more important than my relationship with my son. There was nothing that could replace the importance of that—no woman, no friend, no business partnership. I would never love or care about anything more than I cared about Noah.

My mind drifted to Marley and my bruised feelings from the morning.

Maybe it was time to set the feelings I had for her on the back burner, officially. There would be time for romance when Noah was older. For now, I needed to prioritize raising my boy to be a good man.

Besides, that was what Marley wanted anyway.

Right?

Chapter 15 - Marley

The weekend passed way too quickly.

It wasn't like me to think that way right at the beginning of the school year, but I felt like I'd lived an entire month in the last five days. Regardless, I'd had just the weekend I'd needed. I read romance novels, drank wine, and talked to Lana over the phone about Travis—which was more like talking to a stone wall, to be honest.

Still, when my alarm went off on Monday morning for my daily jog, I ignored it. My bed was far too seductive to leave behind, and I was completely at its mercy. Even when my second alarm went off to get ready for work, I snoozed it twice.

As I brushed my teeth, I wondered if I wasn't sleeping as deeply because I was subconsciously hyper-alert after the break-ins at my house.

Whatever it was, I needed to do my best to act as normally as I could, even though I felt like a zombie. I was looking forward to one thing, though—seeing Cole when he dropped off Noah.

I tried to tell myself that I wasn't, but as I welcomed the kids into the classroom, I kept looking for him every time the door to the playground opened. I wanted to smack myself. What was I doing? I could lose my job thinking like this. Hell, it was a miracle I hadn't already lost my job.

Finally, he appeared, holding the door open for Noah.

Our eyes met as Noah ran onto the blacktop, and my heart lodged in my throat. It felt like I was reuniting with someone after weeks or months instead of a couple of days. In a moment of utter surprise, I realized that I had missed him.

I had missed him over the weekend.

I raised my hand to wave, but before I could get a chance, Noah rushed me at full speed.

"Noah, wait!" Cole called.

It was too late. Noah tackled my legs with enough force that I almost toppled over, even though he was only five. Giggling, I patted his back.

"Hey, Noah!"

He nuzzled my leg. "I missed you, Miss Cage!" he said, nuzzling my leg.

I picked him up. "I missed you too, Noah."

Cole approached—his eyebrows high as he rubbed the back of his head. "Sorry about that. He's been asking about you all weekend."

"It's fine," I said. "How was your weekend?"

"Uh, it was good. Yeah, had a day out with Noah—met a potential big client. Yours?"

"Too short."

The conversation trailed off into an awkward silence. I set Noah down on his feet. "Why don't you go play inside?"

"Okay!" he said, turning to hug his dad goodbye. In the nature of all five-year-olds, he raced from one place to another.

I looked around to make sure no adults were within earshot. Then I looked up at Cole. "Is everything okay? You seem a little distant," I said. "Did something happen?"

"I think you need to be a little careful about how excited you get about seeing me when you're here at work, you know?" he said. "We can, uh, scent that kind of thing."

My face flamed. "You can smell when I'm excited?"

"Yeah, it smells a lot like another kind of excitement, if you catch my drift. I know the difference because, well. You know, but..." he trailed off.

"Oh, God." I covered my face with my hands. "I'm so mortified."

He laughed, his strange mood cracking softly. "It's all right," he said. "Like I said, I'm particularly well-attuned to you, Marley. I just want you to be careful—plus, if I'm gonna be pumping the brakes..."

"Right," I said quickly. "If you're pumping the brakes, I need to do the same. It's only fair."

"I have an important meeting this afternoon, so my mom will be picking Noah up. She's registered with the office, but I didn't want you to worry if you saw an unfamiliar face at the bell today," he said.

I nodded. "Thanks for the heads up," I said. "Is this the client you met this weekend?"

"Nah, different guy. One I've been helping over time with some smaller projects. His budget is a little tight, so we work out payment plans and such," he said, checking his watch. "Well, Miss Cage, it's call time for you. I'll see you tomorrow morning."

I bit my lip, wanting to hug him goodbye or give him a smooch on the cheek—or something. Something more than an awkward wave.

But an awkward wave was all I had to give.

"See you tomorrow," I said.

We parted ways to return to our mundane lives.

I supposed the clock had struck midnight, and my carriage had turned back into a pumpkin.

The lesson for the day was about families. Paulette and I explained what each family member was in relation to the other and helped the children draw their family trees with crayons and colored pencils. We went around the room, helping each individual student figure out their special circumstances. Some families had two daddies, some of them had two mommies, some were all lycans, and some were mostly human with a few lycanfolk sprinkled in.

It was an important lesson. It helped the children understand how families came together and also taught them to be tolerant of one another and to understand families that worked differently than their own. At the end of it, we always had a room full of different family trees, and we always made a point of showing the kids how beautiful it looked, regardless of how different their families were.

By the time I got to Noah's seat, it was nearly time for recess. I was surprised to find him staring dejectedly at the blank sheet of paper.

I squatted next to him and tilted my head. "What's goin' on, Noah? Did you not want to draw your pretty tree?" I asked.

He didn't meet my eyes, only rolled a green crayon back and forth under his fingers. He shook his head.

"How come?" I asked.

He gave a non-committal shrug, continuing to roll the crayon.

I lifted my gaze to Paulette, who was helping another kid across the table. Paulette could be a little out there sometimes, but one thing I really appreciated about her was her talent for deciphering non-verbal communication. As soon as I lifted my eyebrows and flicked my head toward the door, she clapped her hands together and stood to her full height.

"All right, everyone, let's take a break from our trees for recess. We'll come back to finish when recess is over!"

The other children started to get up. Some walked, and some ran out to the playground. Noah seemed to understand that I was clearing the room for his benefit, though, because he stayed seated.

Once all the kids were cleared out and we sat in the quiet of the empty classroom, he sniffed, a deep frown etched on his forehead.

"Everyone has a mommy except for me," he said.

"That's not true, Noah," I said. "Some children have two daddies, and some of your classmates live with their grandmas and grandpas."

"Why did my mommy leave?" he asked. "Did she not like me?"

That shattered my heart. These conversations were never easy. No matter what I said, the answer wouldn't be satisfactory. I'd talked to other children about this sort of thing before, and it was always so hard to explain the complexities of adult relationships, and the different kinds of love people felt for each other.

It was much harder knowing what I did about Noah and his father.

How could I explain to a child that even though his mother hadn't stayed, it didn't mean he was missing out on anything? How could I explain that different wasn't the same thing as bad?

"You know, Noah," I said. "I don't know why your mommy left, but I do know one thing for sure."

Noah's big brown eyes looked up at me.

"I know that it had nothing to do with you. It wasn't because of anything you did or didn't do. Your mommy left when you were just a baby, right?"

"Babies can't really do anything," he said.

I nodded and smiled. "That's right," I said. "Which means you couldn't have done anything to make her not like you."

He nodded, and I took his blank sheet of paper and placed it in front of me.

"Okay," I said. "Let's start with the seed. That's you. Do you remember how to spell your name, Noah?"

He nodded. "N-O-A-H," he said.

"*Very* good," I said as I drew a little brown seed with a colored pencil and wrote his name next to it. "Now, who do you spend the most time with?"

"Daddy," he said.

I drew a tree trunk up from the seed and wrote Cole's name there. "Who else?"

"Uncle Travis, Auntie Ginger, and Auntie Sylvia," he said.

I drew another branch off from the trunk and added Travis's and Sylvia's names.

"But Daddy says Auntie Silvia isn't my mommy," Noah said. "He says she's a really good friend but not my mommy."

"That's true," I said. "But there are other family members that aren't your mommy and daddy, remember?"

Noah nodded.

"Who else do you spend a lot of time with?"

"Nanny and Gramps," he said.

"That's right! I heard your nanny is gonna pick you up from school today," I said. "Do you remember who your grandma and grandpa are in your family tree?"

Noah shook his head. I wasn't surprised that he'd not picked up the lesson totally. He was experiencing a lot of feelings. If it was hard for me to focus when I was experiencing feelings, I could only imagine what it felt like for him.

"So," I said as I drew two branches off from his Cole's branch and wrote down the Nanny and Gramps on two separate lines, "Your nanny is your dad's mom. And your gramps is your dad's dad."

Noah's brow wrinkled, and I could tell he wasn't quite getting it, so I tried explaining it a different way.

"You know how your mommy and daddy came together, and they made you?" I asked. He gave a subtle nod. "Well, your nanny and gramps came together and made your dad. Once upon a time, he was a baby and then a little boy, just like you."

"I'm not little! I'm big," he said.

I chuckled softly and nodded. "That's right. You're a big boy."

"Daddy used to be a kid? Just like me?"

I nodded. "That's right, and Nanny and Gramps are his mommy and daddy."

Noah's eyes lit up with recognition, and he nodded. "Does that mean Nanny and Gramps had mommies and daddies too?"

"Yes. Or maybe one of them only had a mommy or only a daddy. Because families are all different shapes and sizes, just like how no two trees are the same."

We spent recess adding other people to his family tree. We added his aunt Ginger and a couple of fictional characters, too. It was more important to me that Noah understood a family could look however he needed it to than to stay strictly secured to reality. Finally, when we had a beautiful family tree sitting before us, I slid it back over to him.

"So, what do you think, Noah?" I asked.

"What about you?"

"You want to see my family tree?" I asked as I grabbed another sheet of paper from the pile in the center of the table.

He shook his head. "No, I mean, where do you go on my tree? Aren't you part of my family?"

I froze, surprised and blindsided by the question. I swallowed and looked over at him, feeling foolish for not seeing that I was careening right for this question.

"You want to put me on your family tree?" I asked, still shocked. Perhaps I misunderstood him.

He nodded and looked at the paper as he colored a few leaves. "Yeah, Miss Cage. You're part of my family too. I spend lots of time with you."

I knew it was inappropriate to allow him to do that—well, maybe not entirely inappropriate, considering my relationship with Noah's father, but that relationship was not one I was supposed to have. I didn't want to confuse him or make him feel as if I was rejecting him.

"Where would you like to put me on your tree, Noah?" I asked.

"Hmm," he said, tapping his lips with his pencil. "Right here."

He pointed to the spot on the paper that sat directly opposite Cole's. The spot that might be for a mother.

My heart sank, not because I didn't want him to see me as a mother figure, but because it didn't feel like my right to take that role. Not when things were so up and down with Cole—not when I wasn't even sure what I was to Cole.

I reached over and wrote my name where he asked to have it. I would just have to text Cole later and mention the situation, explain what had happened, and why I did it. I would just tell him that I wasn't trying to insert myself in their lives, just that I didn't want to make Noah feel even worse.

Noah seemed content with his tree and excited to color it in with all the colors of the rainbow. It was just as well, too, because recess was basically over. When the other children came into the room, he was once again the talkative, friendly boy I was used to.

I was the one who had become uneasy.

"Okay, that's it—Marley, what the *fuck* is wrong with you?"

I jerked my head up from poking my lunch around in the teacher's lounge. I'd brought some leftover pasta and quick-steamed veggies but had to take a bite.

"What? What do you mean?"

"Paulette and I have been trying to hold a basic conversation with you for the last ten minutes, and you are being a damned space cadet. What the hell is up?" Lana clarified. "Did you not get enough sleep last night? Is your pasta making you sad? If you're broke, I'll buy you lunch. It's no big deal."

I shook my head and waved a dismissive hand. "Sorry, I'm sorry. I was just...I have a lot on my mind."

"About the stalker?" Paulette asked.

I blinked.

That's probably what I should have had my mind on, but I'd begun to feel safe after Cole had cared for me, and the rest of the weekend had passed without incident. Cole really did make me feel better, like no matter what happened, he would be there to save me every time. He was already two for two. Three for three if you counted the weirdo at Night Shift.

"Uh," I said, feeling my face warm the same way it had that morning. "No. About Cole and about Noah."

Paulette gave an audible gasp and clapped both hands over her mouth.

"You're falling in love with him, aren't you?"

I hadn't thought it possible, but my face grew even hotter.

"Maybe not that serious, but..." I wasn't sure what to say. Did I love him? Surely that was too much to decide so soon—we'd known each other less than a week, and our relationship had been steeped in stress and trauma. "Well, Noah asked me to put my name on his family tree, and I didn't really know what to do. So I did."

"Oh, wow. In what spot?" Paulette asked.

"Noah didn't specify, but it was the spot right across from his dad's," I said quickly, already feeling embarrassed and ashamed. I braced for a lecture, for gasps of shock and disgust, but they didn't come.

"The biology of lycan pups is kind of complicated," Lana said. "I know they don't require in-depth lessons on that in childhood development classes, but it's not terribly uncommon for a wolf pup with only one parent to start imprinting on whichever mother or father figure is closest and most present. Or the one who most closely resembles what they see in their mind as ideal for that role."

Paulette nodded in agreement. "It's possible you're just perfect for the image he has in his head of what a mother would look and act like."

I pressed my lips together. “Cole and I only just met last week. I know there’s a lot of chemistry between us. You know, with things like our senses of humor and physical attraction, but I have no idea if Cole even sees me as someone with whom he’d want to pursue a relationship. I know he’s interested in me, but I don’t know enough about him to know if that’s just some weird protective instinct or if it’s real.”

“I mean, I’ve known Cole for a long time, and even though we’re not *that* close, I know he hasn’t even shown interest in dating someone since his ex. I think it’s safe to say he wants to pursue something with you,” Lana said.

“But, to do something serious, I’d have to swap Noah out of my class. I don’t think he’d understand that. What if he thinks I’m kicking him out because I don’t care about him? What if it messes with the friendships he’s already formed with the other kids?”

Lana and Paulette both quieted down, looking at their own food in what I could only assume was deep thought.

“When you put it that way, there’s no way to know for sure that you and Cole would even work out long term. Like, you could go out to dinner and find out he had a foot fetish or a sex dungeon or something."

"Sex dungeon? Really?" Lana said in a deadpan.

"I mean, it wouldn't be a problem for me, but Marley seems a little vanilla. Who's to say that wouldn't be a problem for her?" Paulette said.

I inhaled to retort, then thought better of it. I didn't need to be discussing my sex life with my friends during lunch on a school campus.

"Point being, you want to do the most good with Noah. Have I got that right?" Lana said, ignoring Paulette's hypothetical.

"Yeah," I said.

"Then it might be best to just save getting serious with Cole until the summer. That way, if things go south with him, you won't have to traumatize his son while dealing with a breakup."

I nodded. She made a lot of sense.

But the summer was eons away.

"Get through the school year, keep your job. Have your fun with him, sure. It's about damned time you got to experience some nice *quality* time with a man. But just try not to insert yourself into their lives at home. Try not to be at Cole's place while Noah is there. Just keep it simple," Lana directed. "Think of it as a probation period for you and Cole. If it goes well, you get all the benefits of doing this thing for real."

"Keep it simple," I repeated with an exhale. "Right."

Never mind that not a moment of my life since meeting Cole had been simple in any way.

Despite the simplicity of the plan, my worries over Noah and Cole haunted me for the rest of the school day, my drive home, and the night. I lost more sleep than I cared to admit to myself or anyone else, and it made dragging myself to work even harder on Tuesday than after my too-short weekend.

It was a huge relief when it was finally time for recess the next day. After a morning of being half-dead amongst a sea of children, I was looking forward to ten minutes to just close my eyes and decompress.

After the children filed out of the class with Paulette, I slipped off my shoes beneath my desk and rested my head against the back of my chair. I yawned, my inhale slow and steady as I considered getting a little power nap in before recess ended.

Just as I was about to let myself doze off, though, there was a tap on my forearm.

I opened one eye and found Noah's big, sweet eyes staring up at me.

"Noah, why aren't you outside playing?" I asked, sitting up straight from my reclining position. "Is something wrong?"

"Can I play with you during recess from now on?" he asked.

I forced myself not to grimace. This was exactly what I had been worried about: Noah choosing to focus his energy on me rather than socializing with the other children. "I'm a little too big to play on the jungle gym, Noah," I said.

"We can play in here," Noah suggested, reaching up to me and trying to get me to pick him up to sit him on my lap.

I stifled a sigh and offered him my hand. "You know what? Your dad told me you're really good at getting super high on the swing. Why don't we go outside, and you can show me how you do it? I've been wanting to learn how forever," I said.

Noah's face lit up. "Okay!" he said, taking my hand and pulling me along.

I laughed warmly. “Hold on! I just need my shoes,” I said as I hurriedly tried to slip them on. I had barely gotten the back of the second shoe on before I had to leap to my feet and hurry along with him.

I was grateful for my short stature, at least. It meant I didn’t have to hunch over while we ran.

Noah led me out to the swing set that held several varieties of swings. As he started to extol the virtues of each different type of swing, I felt the tingle of awareness on the back of my neck. I tore my eyes away from him and spotted a familiar figure in dark clothes staring at me from across the street.

I had been so focused on the anxiety and stress I was feeling over Cole and Noah that I had forgotten about the very real stressors that still existed in my life. Stressors like this stalker.

My heart started to race so quickly that I thought I might pass out. The day had been cool, the marine layer clinging to the sky like a needy lover, but my skin felt hot and flushed.

“Miss Cage, are you okay?” Noah asked.

I remembered myself and looked down at him. I tried to force a smile onto my face and get air into my lungs. “I’m fine, Noah,” I lied.

“You smell like you’re afraid,” Noah said.

That response only made me more anxious. I was supposed to be the one keeping a steady head. I was the one who was supposed to be keeping these children safe. How could they feel safe with me if I was clearly afraid of something?

I looked up again, but the figure had vanished.

“I thought I saw someone about to fall,” I lied again. “You know how sometimes when you see someone about to hurt themselves, you get a little scared for them? That’s all that happened.”

Noah didn’t look convinced. “I won’t go on the swings then, Miss Cage. I don’t want you to be scared,” he said with such uncharacteristic seriousness that I had to laugh.

“That’s probably for the best. Thank you for thinking about my comfort, Noah,” I said. “How about you show me the slide instead?”

“Okay!” And then he barreled off toward the slide.

There was an adorable irony in him thinking the swings were too risky for my fragile state but that the slide wasn’t. It was certainly possible that Noah didn’t realize he could fall from both pieces of playground equipment. Regardless, I was so relieved that I'd effectively explained my fear away that I didn't care.

I couldn't help but keep a wary eye on my surroundings, watching for the dark figure. Maybe it was foolish to do it—I had no way of knowing if I'd still be letting off the scent of fear—but I didn't want to let my guard down. Especially if it meant I could finally get a visual on this guy.

I thought of texting Cole, letting him know I'd seen a mysterious figure. But he had already almost gotten himself arrested on my behalf once, and I didn't want that to happen again. Plus, if the person was just curiously examining the POSHA campus, as many people did during recess, I would feel absolutely terrible.

As we returned to the classroom, I did my best to shake off the worry and fear. Regardless of whether the figure had been a stalker or not, I had no way to confirm it. Might as well just try to go about my day with as much normalcy as I could.

When we got inside, the children were vibrating with almost as much intensity as they were before recess. In truth, I blamed Paulette for this because she was the one who let everybody know that there would be snacks after recess. It was normally the parents' responsibility to provide snacks for the kids, but Paulette had been on a baking kick and had brought a variety of different treats for the children.

She had been careful to make things with as little sugar as possible and avoid common allergens, yet she had somehow managed to find a way to make things that looked like cakes and cookies. The container Paulette took out was packed to the brim with all of the goodies she'd baked.

"We're going to take turns getting the snacks, and then we're going to watch a cartoon about numbers and letters, okay?" I called out to the class.

The children all cheered—even kindergarteners loved movie days. Truth be told, so did Paulette and me. It gave us a chance to work on lesson plans during school hours, which allowed us to get home sooner.

Paulette began doling out the snacks on square napkins with baby animals all over them. We called the first child down to grab their snack, but when that child stood up, so did three more. Multiple children standing up at the same time emboldened all the rest of the children to step up as well, and before long,

Paulette and I were caught in a tidal wave of children reaching for snacks they couldn't wait to eat.

It was utter chaos. Paulette and I kept trying to correct the behavior, trying to use this as an opportunity to teach the children about what it meant to take turns and wait in line. But we couldn't seem to get a word in edgewise between the children arguing over which one of them was there first and trying to tattle on their friends for getting two servings of the snacks.

"Everyone, everyone! One, two, three, eyes on me!" I called.

It was a call-and-return phrase that usually ended with *four, five, six, button your lips*. It fell on deaf ears. Paulette tried, her voice carrying a little farther than mine did, but before she could even finish, a loud growl came from somewhere in the throng.

Children started falling at the back. Then someone yelped in pain about a scratch. Finally, a tiny wolf pup with adorably large, clumsy feet came bowling through the front of the group. I thought for a moment that it was just a too-eager kid wanting to get to his snack, but then he turned and faced down the crowd.

His haunches were rankled, and the skin on his back puffed up aggressively. His little teeth were bared in a fierce, feral snarl.

Perhaps it was just a wolf pup, but he still had the size and strength of a pit bull.

Oh no. The wolf snarling and snapping in front of me was Noah.

Noah was trying to protect me from the children he should have considered his friends. Noah thought I was afraid of my students.

Paulette quickly stopped plating snacks and shifted. A few of the children screamed—mostly human ones who had never seen a fully grown wolf up close before. One of them ran and hid behind the bookshelves, and a second one wet her pants.

It was pandemonium.

It was disastrous.

And it was entirely my fault.

Paulette picked Noah up by the scruff of his neck and left the classroom through the back door. While she handled the lycan child, I would have to handle the rest of them.

"Everyone get your BUTTS in your CHAIRS," I said, allowing my more assertive voice to come out. I would have to work a little harder today to let the children know that I wasn't mean and scary, but the last thing I needed was for more shifter children to take Paulette's absence as leave to do whatever they wanted. I didn't need a room full of shifter children using the human children as chew toys.

The children all sat down, and I willed myself to regulate the warring emotions twisting in my chest. Guilt, shame, and anxiety all balled up in the same place.

Once the kids had settled down, I started doling out the snacks. My heart hurt with the error I'd just made. I'd let Noah scent my fear—let him worry about me.

If I wasn't careful, Noah might end up imprinting on me.

Then Cole and I would really be in a huge mess.

Chapter 16 - Cole

"Are you trying to tell me you miss me?" I chuckled. "Does stoic, lone wolf Travis miss little old me?"

"You're making me regret asking if you want to get an early lunch," Travis's annoyed voice came through my phone speaker. "It's not my fault you've forgotten the age-old edict of bros before h—"

"Don't. Do not finish what you're about to say. I know you would never imply Marley is a h—"

"Wholesome kindergarten teacher?" he interrupted in turn. "What's wrong with that? Wait, did you think...Coleson Lucas, you should be ashamed. What would your mother think?"

I laughed, the sound warm and full. In the chaos of my professional life and the tasks required of me as a father, it was easy to forget that Travis and I had been best friends since boyhood. "I guess you're right. It has been ages since we hung out just as friends and not business partners."

"Yeah. So, lunch?"

"I've got a few errands to run first. Let's meet up at... I don't know. What sounds good?"

"How about a steakhouse? We'll get some ribeye and brews."

"Wow, you're really wining and dining me," I teased.

"That's right, so you better put out," he said.

I snorted. "See you in a couple of hours, man," I said. "Try not to work too hard."

"When you're paying me? Hell no."

I was still smiling when I ended the call. There wasn't too much to do, thankfully. I just needed to run by some of our smaller projects to make sure they were going smoothly. Namely, that doorways were being properly widened in one client's condo and that the floor door releases had arrived in the larger shifter gym that was being built across town.

Between all the driving and putting out small fires, it took a couple of hours. The door releases weren't compatible with the doorframes installed at the gym, and the doors didn't have locks. I called Sylvia to get things moving toward fixing that and dealt with soothing the gym owner's frayed nerves. She'd been stressed throughout the entire process of setting up her business, and I regularly had to talk her off a ledge and promise her that even with the hiccups in planning, she would still be a great business owner.

We needed other young shifters to keep establishing themselves in this world and help shape the future. This one was fresh out of college and needed a little encouragement that challenges went hand in hand with being an entrepreneur.

I stopped to fuel up on caffeine. I still had about half an hour to kill before I had to meet up with him, so I bought a local newspaper too. Maybe I'd sit out on the coffee shop's front patio and take a little rest before lunch.

I was just about to sit at one of the outdoor tables when I got a text message. I fished my phone out of my back pocket and took a look at it.

On the screen was a text message from Wyatt, the shifter I'd met the other day.

Hey. You free? Found a great business just out of town that has a lot of great features I'd love to include in my law office when I open up in New Middle Bluff. Let's meet for lunch and talk biz?

I pursed my lips. I had really been looking forward to having some lunch with Travis and catching up as friends. We'd been unable to do that lately. It seemed like every time I went out with him, I'd gotten caught up with Marley in some way.

But I also needed to keep my business running and keep food on the table. We were mostly getting small-fry clients these days. Being responsible for an entire law office could really be a solid injection of capital into Fur Sure Solutions. I couldn't pay Travis if we weren't making any money.

I felt terrible about it, but I sent off a message to Travis.

Hey, Mr. Hot Shot Lawyer just texted me. He wants to meet to discuss plans for his office. You mind if we rain check on Beef'n'Brews?

I got a sad emoji in response, then a few moments after that:

Nah, I'm just kidding. No problem, dude. Work is work. We'll try for this weekend.

I was relieved not to have to prostrate myself and ask for forgiveness. Travis had never been a particularly high-maintenance friend, but I still didn't like taking that for granted. I agreed quickly to weekend plans, then shot off a text to Wyatt.

Sure thing. I can leave in ten. Send me the address.

He responded in a flash.

Excellent! See you when you arrive.

He sent a ping for a location. It was just outside of town in another suburb. From what I could tell, it seemed to be some sort of combination of a country club and golf course, which was surprising. I hadn't even known there was a shifter-friendly place around here that functioned in that way.

Granted, I wasn't much of a golfer, but I stayed abreast of the shifter-friendly businesses in the region.

Regardless, I shrugged and tapped my navigation app, then gathered up my coffee and my newspaper. I headed for the work truck and started the drive over.

The place was in a more rural area than I was expecting, but I supposed it made good sense, considering the amount of land needed for a golf course. Eventually, I pulled up to a pair of wrought-iron gates. Each gate had a detailed depiction of a wolf howling up at a full moon in the center. I saw an intercom and rolled my window down, looking back at Wyatt's text to see if I missed a code I needed to get in. I didn't see anything and was about to call him when a voice came through the telecom.

"Welcome. Do you have a membership, or are you here to meet another member?" said a young man.

"I think I'm meeting a member," I said.

"Please scan your ID just beneath the intercom," he said.

"Excuse me? My ID?"

"Non-shifters are not permitted on the premises. We must confirm that you're a shifter, sir."

I was certainly taken aback to hear that—I'd heard of places catering to shifters, but I'd never heard of a business disallowing humans before. I wasn't sure what to make of it.

"Sir?" the voice asked. "If you're not a shifter, we're going to have to ask you to leave."

The youth's voice had taken on a harsh, unwelcoming edge that startled me enough to reach into my pocket for my ID. Right next to my demographic information was a small symbol of a full moon partially obscured by clouds. An easy-to-see indication that I was a shifter. I turned the card over and scanned the barcode on the back.

"Excellent, thank you, Mr. Lucas. Gates opening now," the man said.

Sure enough, the gates slowly opened on silent hinges while I tried to shake off the strangeness of having just had someone scan my information off my driver's license. I had no idea if they saved that information or if they sold the data to anyone. I supposed I'd learn soon enough.

I pulled up the drive, where a valet ran around to the driver's side of my car. He opened my door and beamed at me.

"Good day, sir. I'll be taking care of your car today. Here's your valet ticket. Just make sure you hold on to that so we can bring the right car back to you when you're all done."

"Uh, sure. Thanks, kid," I said, putting the car in park and turning off the ignition. I handed the keys over to him and hopped out of the truck, coffee in hand.

The building was nice. It looked like it might have been a ranch house before and was comprised of exposed beams, warm natural wood, and stone with mortar—the real stuff. It wasn't just a façade. I wasn't really sure where I was going when I entered the building, but as soon as I stopped to take my phone out and text Wyatt, I saw him approaching from the other side of the room.

He was dressed in a white suit, brown loafers, and a pale blue shirt. He had a tan pocket square in his jacket and no tie on. His skin looked tanner than I remembered it being, and I wondered if he'd gone to a tanning salon or had just spent more time on the beach lately. He smiled. His perfect too-straight teeth were blindingly white against that tan.

"Cole, my man! Good of you to come," he said, approaching and clapping his hand into mine for a hefty handshake. "I was worried you'd have trouble finding the place. You doing okay?"

"Yeah. Honestly, I'm just surprised I didn't know about this place sooner. I'm usually on the up-and-up about all the shifter-friendly places in New Middle Bluff, but this is a new one for me. What was it called again?" I hadn't caught the name, only tapped on the address to get an idea of how far I'd need to drive.

"Alpha's Eighteen," he said. "No women or humans allowed. Nice, isn't it? The sweet sound of silence. No nagging, no nasty smell of fear. Pure heaven."

To hear that no women were allowed in the place shocked me. The man over the intercom had made no such mention—then again, he'd only mentioned the fact that humans weren't allowed when he asked to scan my identification. Maybe it just wasn't information they wanted to say out loud.

"Ah, I see. I guess it's always good to have a space dedicated to masculine energy, right? Space to just be a guy," I said. "Why don't you show me the parts you like. I can snap a few photos and get back to the office to start sourcing materials. Have you scoped out a property for your office yet?"

"Whoa, whoa, whoa, pal. Slow down," he said as he wrapped an arm behind my neck, pulling me to his side. "Take off your shoes and stay a while, yeah? Let's hit the green, have some Scotch, and eat some good food. Yes, I'm a potential client, but I'm your friend first."

Was he? I was usually pretty good about compartmentalizing and distinguishing between friends and clients. Though I supposed there was nothing wrong with someone being both. I gave a non-committal shrug. "Sure, I guess so. I have to tell you, though, I'm not much of a golfer."

"No golf, then. Just food, drink, and a little guy time," he said, patting his hand hard on my chest.

I didn't see what other choice I had, so I agreed.

As we walked through the halls, I took a look at the décor and the internal build of the place. My work hat was on, figuring out where to find the contractors and workers for a large-scale project in case he really had something exactly like this place in mind.

The ceilings were high and vaulted with an open floor plan. If I hadn't known better, I'd say we were at a luxurious cabin up in the mountains. Heads of deer and elk were mounted on the walls, as were modern paintings done in deep, moody colors depicting wolves in serious poses.

"Great, isn't it?" Wyatt asked me as I looked up at one depicting a wolf mid-howl.

I nodded absentmindedly. "Yeah, they're nice," I said. "I take it these were commissioned by some big-shot shifter artist?"

"Real visionary," Wyatt said, confirming my assumption. "Have you ever heard of him? Young guy named Curt Fowler. Come on, restaurant's right over here—I'll tell you all about him."

He led me into a little bistro that looked like it should be in Las Vegas or New York. We were immediately sat down at a table by a young shifter woman who never made eye contact. I guessed she was just having a rough day.

"So, this Curt guy…" I said as I opened up my menu. "You a big fan, or do you know him personally?"

"I know him," he said. "Actually, he encouraged me to open my practice out here. Said I could do a lot of good with the shifters of New Middle Bluff."

"Sounds like a nice guy," I said.

"He is. Real dedicated to shifters," Wyatt said. "He's a huge advocate for a return to the more traditional pack dynamics of the old days before we started assimilating into human culture."

"Yikes," I said, flipping through the menu to the page with the beers. I was starting to think I would really need this drink. "Kinda backward by today's standards, don't you think?"

"Backwards?" Wyatt said, "No way. Listen, Cole, my man. You have to admit there's a certain appeal to being an apex predator among *the* apex predator, right? Humans have evolved to be at the top of every single food chain—shifters evolved even above them. That's something to be proud of!"

"Sure, there's a certain appeal to being at the top, but aren't we past all the food chain and pack dynamic bullshit? I figured we exited that era when we learned how to cultivate the land and domesticate animals for food," I said.

"Of course," Wyatt said, though he paused when another restaurant worker, a young man with a too-perfect smile, came by. "Oh, excellent. Two ribeye steaks, medium rare, and a pitcher of ahh… I don't know. What do you recommend for beers here? Something full-bodied."

"We have a wonderful Belgian Ale with some citrus notes. How's that sound?" the young waiter offered.

"Perfect. Let's do that."

I wondered if Wyatt ordering for me was some kind of power move, but I told myself I was just being paranoid. He was just a jerk who liked to be in control. I was sure it had nothing to do with some weird dominance he was trying to exert over me.

The waiter asked if we needed anything else, but Wyatt dismissed him.

"Anyway, where was I?" Wyatt said to himself. "Ah! The food chain."

I fought the urge to groan and nodded.

"You're right. We have evolved past the real need to relate to the world in those contexts—prey and predators and so on. But we still have those structures in our bodies, right, man? Like, you know how the anxiety epidemic is just our brains reacting to non-life-threatening situations the way our minds would an actual threat, right?"

"I'm not sure I follow," I said.

"Anxiety. It's our fight-or-flight, our self-preservation. Back in the hunter-gatherer days, that would keep us from getting eaten by a saber-tooth tiger or a T-rex or some shit."

"I don't think dinosaurs walked the earth when we were in our hunter-gatherer stage," I pointed out.

"No one likes a pedantic bastard, Cole. You get what I'm saying," Wyatt said.

I resisted the urge to roll my eyes and nodded instead because I did get it. And I could tell this was heading somewhere I wasn't going to like. He didn't seem perturbed, though, just kept talking.

"But now that we're not being hunted by giant cats or lizards, our brains give us the very same fight-or-flight response when we, say, get in an argument with our boss or when someone tells us to go fuck ourselves."

"People tell you to go fuck yourself a lot?" I asked a bit dryly.

Wyatt gave me a deadpan stare. "Cute, Cole—real cute. But no," he said. "My point is just like our bodies are hardwired to protect us from being eaten, shifters still have predatory instincts."

"I don't know about that, man," I said. "I mean, I guess I could see some of what you're talking about, but, at the end of the day, we're still human. We still have the ability to choose how we react to something."

"Do we, though?" Wyatt asked. "I mean, you saw the hostess, right? She didn't even make eye contact as she led us to our table. Why do you think that is?"

I looked over to the entrance of the restaurant, meeting eyes with the woman he was talking about. She quickly looked away and made herself scarce. "I mean, I just assumed she was shy or maybe having a bad day."

"It's because she's a *female*," Wyatt said. "Because she's biologically encoded to listen to us, to look at us for guidance and protection. Non-shifters are the same. It's why the regulations are so piss-poor for us. Humans are reacting to a fight-or-flight. They know they have to domesticate us or *be* domesticated. That's why we naturally separate—with a few exceptions for human women who make great breeding stock."

I shifted in my seat a little, uncomfortable at the turn the conversation had taken. Breeding stock? Domestication? What the fuck was this guy going on about?

"I've got some great friendships with human men," I said flatly. "I've never felt the need to separate myself from humans. Just the opposite, actually. My parents actively avoid the pack life they came from. Hell, my best friend is a human, and we've never had any issues with power dynamics or any of the stuff you're talking about."

Wyatt inhaled to speak, but just as he was about to, our food and drinks were delivered to the table. I thanked the waiter and tucked into the steak, happy to have something that might shut Wyatt up.

Except it didn't work. He only took a bite, and then while chewing and pouring beer into the two pint glasses on the table, he continued.

"Your best friend is a human?" Wyatt asked me, his brow furrowing and his expression taking on an almost skeptical air. "How the hell does *that* work?"

My temper flared, and I placed my fork and knife down on my plate a little too hard. His gaze flitted briefly to my plate. He gave me an apologetic smile.

"Listen, listen, that came out the wrong way," he said. "I don't mean there's anything wrong with having a human as a friend, a best friend, even. But you know how different our biology is, right? From humans?"

"I don't see why something like that would matter," I said. "The woman I'm seeing is a human, as is my son's mother."

"Your son's mother? The one that's no longer around?" Wyatt asked pointedly.

My expression must have belied my rage because he held his hands up in a non-threatening way.

"Listen, I rub a lot of folks the wrong way. I learned to talk straight in law school and never unlearned it," he said. "I'm being a real bastard, and I realize that, but please know my heart is in a good place. It's not like I'm saying you *can't* be friends. It's that I think you can do better."

"Travis has been my friend since we were kids. He's never once made me feel bad about what or who I am," I said. "As for Olivia—there are plenty of awful shifter partners too. The woman I'm interested in now used to date a real piece of work."

Wyatt's expression tightened in a way I didn't understand. It wasn't so much that he looked mad—he was still smiling—but there was a bit more of a feral edge to it than I expected.

"She told you that, huh?" he asked. "Was he a piece of work? Or was he just a shifter with the heart of an alpha?"

"Listen, maybe this is getting too heated," I said.

"No, no, no," Wyatt said. "This is *good*, man. You need to have these outlets, these moments where you can just have a good verbal row with someone. And we're getting to something good here! We're getting to the core of the thing."

"The core of what?" I asked.

"The core of you as a man, as a shifter. Listen, shifter integration into the general population is still new, and I'm not entirely sure it was all for the best," he said. "Did you know that rates of depression and suicide have been steadily climbing among shifters every year since we all came out of the clawset?"

"I mean, isn't it a little early to really analyze what those statistics mean?"

"Maybe." He shrugged. "And sure, correlation isn't causation, but I think those numbers speak volumes. We did better as a people when we could hide in the shadows, and we didn't have to pretend to be good little domesticated animals. Pack life almost disintegrated completely as soon as we started to play nice. Wolves aren't *meant* to be alone. Even in the wild, a lone wolf usually dies."

He carved a bite off his ribeye and popped it in his mouth, chewing as he let me think on that one.

"I'm not a lone wolf. I have my parents, my kid, and plenty of shifter friends."

"Friends or acquaintances?" he asked, pointing his knife at me. "Are the most important people in your life the ones who will always ask you to be something else? Something less wild, something less strong, for their own comfort?"

I picked up my utensils, shaking my head. I wanted to say no, wanted to retort that, of course,

Travis would never expect something like that from me. Marley wouldn't either, of that I was certain.

But as I ate and really let myself think about it, I had to admit that it wasn't really true. The only times I'd really experienced strain in my relationship with Travis was when I still hadn't figured out those biological impulses to be aggressive and protective.

Even Marley had been frightened and worried by my instincts to protect her, to keep her safe. She'd halted every interaction we'd had so far. While I supposed that was better than Olivia, who spent our entire relationship worshipping only the parts of me that came from my lycan biology and rolling her eyes at anything that didn't fit her mental image of an alpha, it wasn't exactly wholehearted support.

"You're thinking about it, aren't you?" Wyatt asked. "I can see the gears turning."

I looked up at him as I chewed the bite in my mouth and swallowed.

"I am," I said. "But also, if we want to live freely in this world, we have to play by this world's rules."

"Yeah, we do. For now," he said. "But that's part of why I brought you here, man. The owner of this place, he's a rare breed. A guy who really gets it.

He sees how we need to embrace the feral parts of ourselves, which is why he created this place as a safe haven for us. Here, we can cultivate these aspects of ourselves and figure out how we're going to shape the world going ahead."

"Shape the world?" I asked. "You sound like you're talking about some weird shifter-centric society."

"It's not weird, Cole. It's the natural way of things. It's *evolution*. Survival of the fittest. I predict people will soon be biting at the bit to become shifters. We're the apex predators."

I waited for him to say he was joking—waited for the punchline. But as the seconds started ticking by, I realized it wasn't coming. He was entirely serious. He meant every word.

Just as I was about to speak, my phone rang.

I kept my phone on vibrate, and there was only one number I kept a ringtone on for—Sylvia's private phone number.

Sylvia was obsessive about keeping life and work separate, which I'd learned pretty early on in our relationship. When Sylvia called me during business hours from her own phone, it was because something was either really wrong or really right.

My phone rang when Olivia went into labor with Noah, it rang when Sylvia's son got in an accident and she was frantic about getting on a plane to California to check on him, and I was certain as I looked down at my phone that whatever was waiting on the other line wasn't good news.

"Excuse me," I said. "I have to take this."

I stood and paced toward one of the panoramic views of the golf course outside. "Syl, what's wrong?" I asked when I answered.

"Hey," she said. "Don't panic. No one is hurt. But I just got off the phone with Miss Cage over at POSHA."

"Is she okay?" I asked, panicking anyway.

"Uh—" Sylvia sounded almost confused by the question. "Okay, we'll circle back to that later. But as far as I could tell, yes. She's fine, but Noah is having a bad day. He shifted shortly after the first recess, and no one has been able to get him to shift back. They've been trying for hours. They need you to go talk him down."

I pressed my forehead against the cool glass of the window. It wasn't a great scenario, but Sylvia was right; no one was hurt, and that was good.

"I'm on my way," I said.

"Do you want me to call them back?" she asked.

"No," I said. "I'll call from the car. Thank you, Syl. You're a lifesaver, as always."

"Sure thing. Drive safe."

I made a sound of acknowledgment and ended the call.

When I returned to the table, I took my wallet out of my back pocket and started pulling some bills out.

"Whoa, whoa," Wyatt said. "You're not leaving?"

"I'm sorry," I said. "My son's school just called. I have to handle a little emergency. Thank you so much for today. You've given me a lot to think about. Let's meet up again soon and get the wheels in motion for your office," I said, setting down the cash.

"Don't worry about that," he said. "I've got it. Go and take care of your son. I'll come to you next time."

"Yeah, appreciate it. Thanks," I said, tucking the money back into my wallet. Normally I wouldn't let a client treat me, but I had no time to do that social dance, and I knew where it would end up just from the kind of guy Wyatt was. Best to just accept the foregone conclusion.

I hurried out to my car and cursed when I remembered I'd used the complimentary valet—not that I had been given a choice. I tried not to be a jerk about having to wait for my car. I handed the youth a ten-dollar bill as I hopped in the truck and tore off.

I needed to help my son.

###

I arrived at Polar Shift Academy a few minutes before the lunch break ended. I hurried in through the front door and walked to the office. When I got there, I was relieved to see Marley there, talking to Lana in hushed tones.

"Hey," I said.

Lana gave Marley a look, brows lifting, then left the office. Marley grimaced apologetically at me.

"I'm so sorry," she said. "I'm afraid this might be my fault."

"How so?"

"When I was out with Noah on the playground during recess, I saw someone and got frightened. I think he sensed my fear, so when the kids crowded me during snack time, he got really protective. I wanted to go talk to him, but...they said it wasn't a good idea," she said. She looked down the hall toward the infirmary and frowned. Her guilt was pretty clear on her face. I wanted to tell her to go and talk to Noah, but it probably *wasn't* a good idea for her to be around him when he was already feeling territorial over her.

"Don't worry about it, Marley," I said. "I'll go talk to him and touch base with you later on tonight. I'll probably just take him home for the day so we can work this out in the comfort of our home. But don't beat yourself up. This is just biological malarky, you know?"

She didn't look entirely convinced, but she nodded. I wanted to hug her and let her know everything was fine, but this wasn't the time or the place. I resolved to do so later instead.

"He's in there with Paulette. If you need anything, just have the ladies at the desk call me," she said.

I nodded and gave her the most convincing smile I could. "Will do. Thank you, Marley," I said.

We turned from each other at the same time. I walked down the hallway toward the infirmary, and she left the office to return to her classroom.

When I stepped into the nurse's office, I saw my son curled up in his lycan form on one of the vinyl cots. Paulette sat on a stool a few feet away, looking exhausted and exasperated. When she saw me, she perked up.

"Noah, look who's here," she said, overly eager. "It's your dad. Think you can shift back to talk to your daddy?"

My son's snout was nestled between his paws, and he gave me a forlorn look. Then he stood, padded around to turn his back on me, and curled back up on the cot.

Paulette's expression puckered with frustration, and I squeezed her shoulder. When she looked up at me, I smiled.

"I can take it from here," I said. "I'm gonna take him home. I'm sure you need to recoup before the kids need you again."

"Are you sure? If you need me here—"

I shook my head. "I've got it. Thank you for taking such good care of him. I'm sure it was a frustrating situation, and I'm glad it got handled as quickly and simply as it did."

I couldn't be sure, but I thought Paulette flushed as she nodded. She gave Noah a final look before standing and giving me an encouraging look. She walked out of the infirmary, leaving Noah and me alone.

When the door shut behind her, Noah whimpered. I'm sure he thought he was in trouble now that I was here. I approached the cot and sat on the far edge. Noah inched even farther away, his whole body heaving with his sigh like a put-out old dog.

"You don't wanna shift back to a little boy, huh?" I asked.

A tiny whine rumbled out of him.

"That's a shame because only little boys get to have ice cream with their dads. Little wolf pups can't eat ice cream, you know?"

Noah turned his head, giving me a sidelong look. His little bushy tail flapped against the cot in an irregular rhythm, like he was happy about the idea of ice cream but trying to hide it.

I smiled, reaching over and ruffling his fur between his too-big ears. "Come on, kiddo. Can you please use your words? You're not in trouble. I just want to know what happened."

He studied me, then whimpered again. With a slow blink, he shifted back to boy Noah. His curly hair was a mess—his face flushed with emotion. He was feeling a lot, of that I was certain. It was my job to help him figure out what those feelings were and how to tackle them.

"C'mere," I said. "Come tell Dad what happened."

He gave an almost cartoonish frown, but I could tell I was chipping through the distance he'd put between us. He looked at me, hedging on whether or not he wanted to accept the offered olive branch. Sniffling, he hurled himself toward me. He climbed into my lap and wrapped his arms around my neck, hugging me with that strange strength only children seemed to have.

I curled my arms around him, patting his back and swaying in a comforting rhythm. His tears soaked through my shirt as I held him, but I let him cry it out. Sometimes kids needed space to just feel their feelings, and I didn't think I was wrong about assuming that was what he needed.

"Attaboy," I murmured. "There you go, get all that gunk out. We can talk about it when you're done."

He gripped me tight, his small body shaking as he cried.

After about ten minutes, he finally spoke.

"Miss Cage was scared, Daddy," he said, his voice muffled against my shoulder. "She was scared during recess, and then the kids all gathered around her feet, and I didn't want her to be scared again. I just wanted her to be okay. I didn't mean to get in trouble," he wailed.

"You're not in trouble, kiddo," I promised.

"But they brought me to the office. Only bad kids come to the office."

I patted his back in time to our swaying. "Sometimes—sometimes we come to the office when we don't feel good, or when we need help, or even when you get to leave school a little early to get ice cream with your dad. It's not a bad place," I said.

"I didn't want to shift because I didn't want to be in trouble," he said.

"Well, sometimes wolves get in trouble, too," I said. "Trouble isn't just for boys. It's also for wolves."

"But I'm not in trouble?" It was half a question, half a statement.

"No, you're not in trouble. But you worried a lot of people today. You worried me, Auntie Syl, Miss Paulette, and Miss Cage. We didn't know what was wrong, and sometimes it's scary when we don't know why you're upset, Noah."

"You were worried?" he asked.

"Mm-hm," I said.

"I worry about Miss Cage a lot," he said. "She seems scared all the time. I want to help her not feel scared."

"That's very brave and very grown up of you, Noah," I said. "But why don't you leave taking care of Marley to me? Grownups are usually scared about grownup things, and even though you're super strong, that's a lot for a little boy to take on."

"Yeah. I didn't know what to do when the other kids wouldn't leave Miss Cage alone," he said. "It made me really mad. And then I wanted to fight with them."

"Yeah, and you don't want to fight your friends, right? You want to play with them, but you don't want to fight them like that."

Noah was quiet for a long time. Then he drew his arms back from my neck. He pushed himself back a little bit so he could look me in the eyes.

"I would fight my friends if I had to. If they were hurting Miss Cage, I would fight them," he said.

I couldn't help but laugh as I brushed my hands through Noah's curls in an effort to fix where they still were a little messy. Like father, like son, I supposed.

"Me too," I said. "So just leave the fighting to me, all right? Because getting in fights *will* get you in trouble, and we don't want that, do we?"

Noah shook his head. "Will Miss Cage be okay? She won't be scared if we leave?"

"I think she'll be very safe and happy, even if we have to be apart from her sometimes," I said. "So, why don't we go pick up some ice cream and go see Nanny and Gramps?"

At that, Noah finally cracked a smile and nodded. "Yeah!"

"There we go," I said, standing up and hitching him up on my back for a piggyback ride. "You better hold on tight, little monkey man!"

He giggled. "I'm not a monkey. I'm a wolf!"

"Of course, my mistake," I said as I opened the door and headed back out to the office. "No monkeys here, only silly little boys."

"And silly dads!" he shot back.

"Ah, you got me, kiddo," I said.

Because, really, I was a silly fool to have put me and my son in this position.

And to keep us in it.

Chapter 17 - Marley

My thoughts were consumed with Noah as I drove home.

I had never seen Noah so distressed. I hadn't been scared when the children swarmed around me during snack time, but it was as if Noah had been frightened for me. Paulette had been so quick to shift and take Noah away, and I knew that was likely to avoid the risk of Noah biting a human child and causing a big media mess, but I wished I'd had the time to try and help him.

I hoped the incident—being taken away for shifting to protect me—wouldn't hinder or damage him in any way. I didn't like the thought that he might associate shifting with punishment. I heaved a sigh as I turned down my street. I had to trust that Cole would take care of his son and make sure Noah didn't feel bad about himself.

After parking in my driveway, I got out of my car with my things. I scanned my thumb with the biometric scanner and realized suddenly that it was the first time in a while that I hadn't felt scared or had that sensation of being followed. It felt like any other day. My neighbors were grabbing their mail, and I waved at them as other familiar faces from the neighborhood speed-walked past me. Perhaps it was foolish of me, but I hoped my life was returning to normal.

I went into the house and examined the place. As far as I could tell, nothing had been tampered with. For the first time in a long time, the place was utterly peaceful.

After the day I'd had, I wanted to indulge in self-care. One of the parents had given me a bath bomb as a start-of-school gift, and I'd been saving it for a special occasion. A day of feeling safe was a special occasion, as far as I was concerned.

I got the water running in the bath and added some lavender bath oil. I collected a few of my candles from around the house and stationed them on the lip of the tub. Finally, I grabbed my current read and a sizable glass of wine.

I lit the candles and dimmed the lights, turning on some calm music on the waterproof speaker that Lana had gotten me for my birthday last year. Finally, I added the pièce de résistance—the bath bomb.

I watched with giddy glee as it bobbed and fizzed in the water, violet and pink clouds pluming off it like an aura.

I undressed, sliding into the water just as flower petals started to break off from the fizzing bath bomb. It smelled like freesia, honey, and vanilla. When those fragrances blended with the lavender, I was in absolute heaven.

I took a sip of my wine, and my bones seemed to melt as a feeling of complete relaxation came over me. I picked up my book, thumbing through it to find the spot I'd left off on. Maybe it was a little embarrassing, but I loved goofy romances. Reading about a woman waking up from a night where she was so drunk that she couldn't remember marrying the devil was more entertaining than all the reality television in the world combined.

I don't know how long I soaked in the tub, but I'd finished my wine and read through several chapters of my book when the water started to cool. I rubbed my soft towel over my skin, which felt blissfully soft after soaking in moisturizers and oils. I hadn't washed my hair, but I'd be going for a run in the morning, so I'd be showering before work, anyway.

I pulled on my robe and grabbed the speaker before walking back out to the kitchen and opening the fridge. I was peering into it, wondering what to have for dinner that would be quick and require little cleanup, when the doorbell rang.

The change in my body was instantaneous. I went from calm and content to anxious in a heartbeat. My heart began racing even as every nerve in my body grew heavy. I had the urge to run and hide.

Stalkers and criminals didn't typically ring the doorbell before they harassed you, but nonetheless, I picked up my phone with shaking hands and paged to the security app. I looked at the feed from the doorbell camera and saw Cole hovering outside, shifting awkwardly on his feet.

I had no idea why he was here, but just as quickly as I'd slipped into a panicked state, I suddenly felt like I needed to go and let him in right away. I slammed shut the fridge and hurried to the door.

I was about to open the door when I remembered what I was wearing.

The silky, baby-pink bathrobe left little to the imagination. My nipples were hard under the thin fabric. I flushed, looking at the screen on my phone once again. I pressed the mic icon to speak through the doorbell.

"Hang on. I need to get dressed."

Cole's eyebrows shot up, and he smirked. "Don't go out of your way on my account," he said suggestively.

I rolled my eyes but couldn't help the smile in my voice. "You kiss your mother with that mouth?" I asked as I hurried to my bedroom and threw on a pair of panties, some comfy sweats, and a knitted sweatshirt in a similar pink to the robe.

I hurried back to the door and threw it open, panting slightly.

"Cole," I said. "To what do I owe the pleasure?"

He smiled sheepishly before producing a bouquet from behind his back. "I came to give you an apology—from both me and Noah."

"Apologize? You have nothing to apologize for," I said as I accepted the flowers from him.

"I think I do...I don't want to presume, but could I—" he gestured to the door.

"Oh, yeah, of course," I said, quickly moving aside. "Come in."

He nodded in thanks as he stepped inside. I shut the door behind him and gestured toward the living room. "Make yourself comfortable. Are you hungry? I was just about to make dinner."

"Do I smell...wine?" he asked from the other room.

"Oh! Yeah, let me get you a glass," I said. I walked into the kitchen and poured him a generous glass of the cabernet I'd been drinking.

When I turned to return to the living room area, Cole was standing in front of me. I almost collided with him. As I stopped short, the wine undulated in the glass like the sea in the middle of a storm. "Oh," I said. "I thought you sat down."

"Is it weird to admit that I have a thing for seeing you in the kitchen?" he asked. "Wait a minute, that came out entirely wrong. Let me start that again."

He took the wine glass from my hand and set it on the countertop. My heart jumped into my throat as I looked at him. It was the first time I really saw the resemblance between him and his son. Noah's eyes may have been larger, but they were about the same shape, and he had the same color of freckles that dotted Cole's skin, though Cole had a deeper tan than his son. I realized he hadn't been in my house since the time he set up my security system. It had only been about a week ago, but it felt like forever. I tried thinking back to that day, but I couldn't remember if I'd felt this tense.

It wasn't an uncomfortable tension; if anything, it was filled with promise.

My mind drifted to Noah and all the questions he had asked me about his mother. Noah needed a mother figure, and I desperately wanted to be that mother figure for him, but it wasn't my place. For all of the kindness and affection Cole had shown me, I didn't know if he was interested in having me in his life as a permanent fixture or if he was just looking for some affection after being a single father for so long.

It was hard to believe I was even here, honestly.

I had spent so much of my adult life wanting to get out from under Wyatt's thumb, and it was still hard to believe that I had finally managed to do it. Not only that, but I had somehow managed to find even children who were more willing to protect and appreciate me than Wyatt ever had.

Still, I couldn't be entirely sure that Cole felt something more for me than just the urge to protect me. Who was to say that once the threat of the stalker was no more, there would even be anything between us? What if all of these feelings were only present because I was weak and vulnerable, and that awakened some protective instinct that I didn't understand?

Cole took one step toward me and cradled my face in his calloused hand.

"Tell me what's going on in that gorgeous head of yours," he said, his voice soft as a prayer. "You look like you're waging a war with yourself."

I laid my hand on his cheek, brushing my thumb over the scruff on his jaw. "I'm thinking that I wish I'd taken the opportunity to kiss you for hours when it'd been offered to me that time after back-to-school night. I'm thinking that it was foolish of me to be afraid to share everything with you because you've always been so forthright with me," I said.

His long lashes dusted the edge of his cheek as he looked down at me, his eyes hooded and glossy like an icon in an oil painting. God, he was a beautiful man.

I'd once thought the same thing about Wyatt, but Cole's beauty was something more natural—more real—than Wyatt's contrived and cultivated beauty. Cole was just...wholesome. Perfect. There were no words to accurately describe it.

"Well," he said, his voice barely a gust of air. "It didn't feel right for you then. What feels right for you now?"

I searched his eyes, my heart racing. I was certain he could hear it in such close proximity. I wondered if he could tell what was coming.

I rose to my toes, pressing the length of my body against his. I smoothed my other hand over his broad chest and slipped my fingers into his hair. Then, I closed the narrow distance that remained between us and kissed him.

And it felt right.

Chapter 18 - Cole

The kiss blew me away. It was strangely intense in its slowness.

Her lips were soft and pliant, opening just enough for me to seize her lower lip between both of mine. She tasted of wine. I wanted more of it, more of her, as I traced my tongue along the curve of her full lower lip.

Marley's sigh crested sweetly out of her throat, and I swallowed it. The sound awakened a sharp hunger in me that I hadn't felt before. My pulse hammered in my neck. I wanted to pick her up and wrap her legs around my waist and—

I tore my mouth from hers, breaking the kiss.

"Marley," I said in a gentle, chastising tone. "I came over to apologize for Noah's behavior."

She shrank away from me, dropping back down to her heels.

"I'm sorry," she squeaked.

"Don't be. I want to do more of that. Hell, I want to do more *than* that. But I just... I told Noah we need to be careful about expecting too much from you before you really even get to know us, and..." I trailed off, going against my own words as I stroked a covetous hand over her delicate waist and growled. "I really ought to adhere to my own rules, don't you think?"

Her skin went pink, and it was perfect. She bit her lip, which only enticed me to do the same.

"How is he? I was worrying about him on my way home," she said before I could lower my mouth to hers to feast on her lip.

I couldn't help the smile that her comment brought to my face.

"Were you?" I asked. "Is that something you do for all of your students?"

She swatted my chest playfully. "Only my favorites," she said sheepishly.

"Oh my, Miss Cage is playing favorites? How lucky for me that Noah's made such a good impression on my behalf," I said.

"Truly, he is your only redeeming quality."

I laughed and cupped her face again. I couldn't bring myself to stop touching her. "I took him to my parents so I could come to talk to you without worrying about hurrying off," I said. "It feels like there's always something forcing us apart. I wanted to catch you at a time when we could actually talk. Besides, my parents spoil Noah rotten. I guarantee you that little pup has forgotten my existence."

She laughed warmly before sighing softly.

"So, what did you want to talk about?" she asked.

Thinking of Noah at my parents' house made me realize something. "You know, I don't know anything about your family, really. I don't think you've even mentioned your parents."

"Yikes," she said, grimacing. "Yeah, I mean...the subject of my parents is a little loaded. I'm going to need to drink some more wine and get a little food in me if we're going to go there."

Laughing, I reached back over to the counter, holding the glass she poured for me. "Here you are. I think you need this more than I do."

###

Half a bottle of wine later, we sat on the couch, some rom-com playing in the background. We'd set out with the intention of watching it, but we were far too busy going back and forth, taking turns being indecisive about what takeout we should order for dinner.

"Thai food," I suggested.

"Nah," she grumbled. "I love Thai, but the noodles make me all puffy and bloated."

"The wine won't do that?"

"Very rude of you to use logic against me," she said, pointing at me before downing the last bit in her glass.

I shook my head. "Maybe you ought to slow down until we get some food in your cute little belly."

"What if we got wings?" she asked.

"I mean, I'm down for that if you are. You women are usually all weird about eating messy food in company."

"Shit, that's a good point," she said. "Okay, no wings. That's definitely a food for couples who don't care about impressing each other anymore."

I chuckled. "We have three more options we haven't covered. After that, I'm calling it, and we're going to rummage in your kitchen for as many snacks as we can find and eat like teenagers."

"Don't threaten me with a good time, Mr. Lucas," she said.

I gave her a pointed look before starting to list the choices. "Italian, sushi, or Vietnamese?"

"Ohhhh, *sushi!* God, that sounds amazing," she said.

"Perfect. I know a place," I said.

We ordered enough sushi to feed a small army. I figured whatever we didn't eat could be parsed out for Marley's lunch the next day. Part of me liked the idea of being able to feed her even after I left her for the night.

The food arrived fairly quickly, and it was a good thing because Marley was getting just a *little* too inebriated. We popped open the containers and quieted down as we ate. I could tell Marley was hungry because she wasn't even really paying attention to the movie.

After filling our bellies, I groaned exaggeratedly.

"Feeling better?" I asked as I stretched my arms up and over my head before resting them on the back of the couch.

"So much better," she said. "You were right. I was getting a little tipsy there. I'm sorry about that."

I shrugged. "I see nothing wrong with a woman enjoying her night off. Especially when her nosy friend is prying into her private life."

"Mmm, right—my parents."

"Marley, you don't have to share anything you're not comfortable sharing," I said. "I asked because I'm curious about you, and I want to know everything I can about you, but that doesn't mean that you owe me anything."

"I want you to know me," she said. "Truth be told, it's probably a boring story. I just...do you remember when I told you my breakup was really horrible?"

I nodded. "Yes."

"They were part of that equation," she said. "My ex was a shifter, a really egotistical, manipulative, entitled asshole. I'd started dating him right before I graduated high school. God, I was so enamored with him. My parents never trusted him, though. They did everything they could to split us up, but my ex was so manipulative that all it did was alienate me from my parents. They made me choose between them and him, and I chose him."

"That sounds familiar," I said. "At least the bit about parents warning you off a partner."

"Yeah? You too?" she asked.

I nodded. "Noah's mother. My mom, my dad, hell, even my own gut told me she was wrong for me. I didn't listen."

"I don't understand how someone could abandon a sweet boy like Noah. I don't understand how anyone can have a child and just forget about them like that," she said. "I try to understand it again and again. I try to run my mind through the scenarios, but every time I think about squishy baby faces, I can't imagine leaving."

It warmed my heart to hear that from Marley. It was nice to hear that she thought about being a mother.

"Olivia...she just—I think she thought of children like a very special kind of pet, you know? She thought Noah would come out and just be an adorable accessory to take with her to parties and play dress up. When Noah came out all colicky and messy, I think she realized she'd bitten off more than she could chew. She hardly even wanted to hold him."

"Every day, I look at Noah, and I wonder how she did it. He's such a smart, sensitive kid. It breaks my heart that he's so confused about where his mom is. I wish I could fix it for him."

I had to stop myself from immediately answering with, *you can.*

I knew it wouldn't be fair of me to put that expectation on Marley. I knew it would be the exact opposite of pumping the brakes on our relationship. My mind, for just a moment, went back to the talk I'd had with Wyatt.

Would this entire situation be easier if Marley had been born a shifter? I wondered if maybe she would find Noah's attachment and my attachment to her a little more endearing and less entrapping.

I must have thought for a little too long because Marley tilted her head toward me.

"What's on your mind?" she asked.

I considered bending the truth a little bit, considered saying something else, but I was never a good liar. So, I tried to deliver the information as truthfully as I could without putting any undue pressure on her.

"You know," I said. "Noah really does love having you in his life. I know he just seems like a silly kid with an attachment, but if that was a role you wanted to fill in his life, even just a little bit, I'm sure he'd love that."

She flushed, looking down at her near-empty wine glass. "I'd be lying if I said I hadn't thought about it, but..."

She trailed off, and I just kept my eyes on her, quiet and patient. I didn't want to rush if she was thinking about playing some key part in our lives.

"My life in Leighton Valley was really wonderful... until it wasn't. New Middle Bluff is finally starting to feel like home, and I don't want to throw that all away if I'm wrong about this again," she said. "Not that you're anything like my ex—but...I don't know. Abusive partners have a way of degrading your own trust, even of yourself."

"Do you..." I said cautiously. "Would you tell me exactly what happened before you came here? It's not that I want to intrude or even that I want you to prove to me why you need the boundaries you've set in place. I just...I want to understand you better,

Marley. I want to know what happened so that I can be a good man to you—hell, a good friend."

She looked at me, searching my face as if looking for some kind of sign that I was being honest. I hoped to hell and back that she'd find what she was looking for.

Finally, after a moment, she let out a long, low breath.

"My ex and I were together for a long time," she said. "When I freaked out when you saw the scar on my shoulder? You were right, that was from him, and it was a failed mating bite."

Even though I'd guessed it, I still had to fight the wave of anger that rolled through me. It wasn't just the brazen entitlement that infuriated me. It was the risk to her life that was evident in that scar.

When people wanted to become shifters, there were particular channels to go through that made it safer. Someone who wanted to undergo the change went to a certified shifter specialist who would inject the DNA directly into their spine to trigger the change. When people did it through a lycan bite, though, that DNA acted like a virus, latching onto every cell it could until it found its home in the spinal cord.

Too many people died when they were changed through a bite. There were so many ways it could go wrong: it could attack the white blood cells and destroy a person's immunity or cause a fever so severe that the person could go into shock or start seizing. A change from a bite had about a fifty percent chance of killing the recipient. Hell, even in a clinical setting, it still had a twenty-percent chance of going horribly wrong.

The idea that someone who had claimed to love Marley would willingly put her life at risk like that was enough to make me that fucker to shreds.

"I'm so sorry, Marley," I said.

She put her hand over the shoulder that was scarred. Her thumb rubbed a soothing stroke over it. "Honestly, that wasn't even the worst part," she said. "It was the apathy of the doctors when I went to the emergency room and told them what happened. It was the questions—they'd asked me why I was partnered with a shifter if I hadn't wanted to be victimized. It was like they thought I'd deserved what happened to me."

She brushed a hand through her hair. "I still feel like it's my fault sometimes, especially since my parents warned me about him. My brother has always been a little playful and flighty, but even he didn't like my ex. I look back and see all the red flags, all the little signs that things were going to end up terrible, and I feel like I was blind to it all. Or maybe just stupid."

"Abusers are charming, Marley. You wouldn't be the only one who ever felt duped by an abuser. Hindsight is always twenty-twenty," I said.

"Well, I wish my parents felt that way. Because when I went to them after my ex locked me out of my own apartment, they told me they didn't have the energy to deal with my 'dramatics' anymore."

"What did your brother do?" I asked.

"Jack has been doing theater over in the UK for the last few years," she said. "I didn't want to bother him. Not when his life seems to be going so well."

"Does he know this stuff happened?" I asked.

"Yeah. Lana forced me to call him after I came out here. He'd just started doing Shakespeare in London and offered to come home to help me, but the damage had already been done. I didn't want to take him away from the success he was having," she said.

She looked over at the movie we weren't really watching.

"I just want love to be easy," she said so softly that my keen hearing barely picked up on it. "I just want to not question every choice I make and not wonder if my heart is making decisions that will hurt me down the line."

"Have you been questioning a lot of choices lately?"

It was a loaded question, I knew, but all this information only made me want Marley more. I wanted to prove to her how wonderful I could be, to her. I wanted to show her exactly the kind of affection she was worthy of and help her trust herself again.

Perhaps that was arrogant of me and made me just as egotistical as her ex, but I was certain I could give her the love she deserved.

And maybe that was what it really was—maybe all of this hot-and-cold, back-and-forth mess with Marley was love.

She looked over at me, her face serious and thoughtful.

"I've questioned almost every choice I've made regarding you," she said finally. "Every time I'm around you, all I can seem to think about is how much I want you, how much I want to believe this is the real thing for once."

My heart stuttered in my chest before hammering against my sternum, in my ears. I wasn't even sure if I could promise her that this would last, but whatever I felt for her was real. I wanted her with every fiber of my being. Maybe this conversation was what I needed to really accept that deeply in my heart.

"I think it is," I said. "Because it seems like all I can think about lately is you. I think about you when I get coffee in the morning. I think about you while I drive around town. While I work. I think about whether you'd like a certain restaurant or your thoughts on an issue I read about in the newspaper. I think of how you looked when I found you cradling my son in his bed and how I'd do anything to stumble upon that again and again."

"What are you saying?" The emotion in her voice straddled the line between panic and exhilaration.

I knew I needed to give her more time, and I could do that. I could move at her pace, but I knew one thing with absolute certainty.

I'd be happy to spend the rest of my life with Marley.

I'd be happy to trust her with caring for my son in the way that even his own mother couldn't.

"I'm saying that I want nothing more than to be whatever you want, whatever you need, whenever you know what that is," I said. "I'm saying that I'll be following your lead from here on out. The only thing you have to worry about is your heart. I'll worry about the rest of the pesky complications."

It was a promise I likely couldn't keep, but it was the closest I could get to telling her I loved her without actually saying the words. It was the closest I could get to having her without really having her. I could serve her. I could protect her. I could keep her from being driven away from her new home until she could see herself being at home with me.

"Do you really mean that?" she asked.

I nodded because I did. I'd think of the practicalities later.

"Every complication? Whether it's Noah, or work, or my ex, or this stalker who's chasing me around?"

"Every complication," I promised.

“How?” she asked. “You can’t promise something like that, Cole. We both know that. There are too many variables—too many ways it could go wrong.”

I raked a hand through my hair. “You’re right. But I want to be able to promise it. I don’t know that I can promise it, but I want to.”

I reached over and took her hand in mine, entwining our fingers together. She looked up at me, her eyes wide and searching.

“I can absolutely promise one thing, though,” I said.

“What’s that?” she asked.

“I would never put you in a position that would make you flee your home, no matter what circumstances arise. Even if we fell out, even if we can’t work as a couple,” I said. “I will always protect you to the best of my ability. Whether the threat is real or imagined, you’re part of my life permanently.”

She squeezed my hand. “Do you know what I want?” she asked, her voice barely a whisper. “Do you know what I’ve been wanting practically since I met you?”

My heart soared with hope. “What do you want, Marley?” I murmured.

“I want… *you,*” she said. “Every inch of you, Cole.”

The blood in my veins heated. God, I needed her. I reached over and took the wine glass she still clutched in her hand. She held onto it only for a moment before relinquishing it to me.

I slowly, methodically, moved the glass over to the coffee table.

Her chest rose and fell as if she’d just come back from a run. I dropped down to my knees in front of the couch, in front of her, just as I had the night things went south in my bedroom.

I cupped her face in my free hand and drew her in for a kiss, claiming her mouth. She moaned softly against me, her lips opening like the petals of a flower unfurling. Her lips were so soft, so sweet—despite the fact that I’d had the genuine pleasure of kissing her before, I still marveled at them.

I hummed against her lips and sucked her lower lip in between my teeth.

Marley let out a sound that ignited a carnal hunger within me. I wanted to taste every inch of her skin, wanted to send her sailing away on a current of pleasure.

"Where do you want me?" I asked her against her lips. "Where do you want to feel me, Marley?"

"I…" she gasped. "God, I want you to kiss my skin."

"Where on your skin?" I asked, chuckling warmly, brushing my nose against her. "You'll have to be more specific."

She flushed so adorably, and her eyes lowered in embarrassment. It was almost enough for me to let her off the hook—almost.

"Come on, Marley," I said, coaxing the minx I knew was hiding inside of her out of her shell. "If you can't tell me, sweet girl, why don't you show me?"

She nodded, biting her lower lip.

With her eyes fixed on mine, she reached for the hem of her shirt and tugged it over her head, baring her beautiful body to me.

Chapter 19 - Marley

Aroused Cole was so unlike what I was used to. When Wyatt and I made love, it was always so aggressive and demanding. He threw me around like I was a toy for him to play with. But when I pulled my shirt off and revealed myself to Cole, it was like I was a painting in a museum that he was trying to interpret.

His brows were low and heavy, his lashes almost shining in the low light. He stared for so long that I almost felt the need to hide myself away from him again. I almost did, lifting my arms from my sides to cover myself in a show of modesty. Even though I was still protected by my bra, I felt like he was staring right through me.

"No. No," he muttered. He reached up, circling my wrists, drawing them away from my breasts and pinning them to my sides. "Don't you dare hide away from me, Marley. Don't tease me that way."

"I'm just... worried that I... didn't look right," I said.

"You look exactly right. There's not a single thing wrong about you."

The intensity of his gaze was overwhelming. That, paired with his strong hands pinning my arms to my sides, made me feel a strange mixture of danger and excitement.

His breath left him in a rush, brushing against the soft, thin lace of my bra. My nipples hardened under the pale, sheer fabric as a chill moved through me. My stomach clenched. The tingling between my legs made me shift slightly.

"Feeling flustered?" he asked me, his tone strangely teasing—like he was having too much fun.

"Yes," I said breathily.

His mouth curved into a smile that bordered on wicked. "If only someone would tell me what they wanted me to do."

I wasn't used to this. I wasn't used to having a partner who cared about me. Wyatt always just took what he wanted. My enjoyment was a secondary experience to him. Wyatt cared about his own pleasure first and foremost.

"I don't... know how to say it," I said. "I can't explain it."

“If I guess, will you tell me if I’m on the right track?” he asked.

I nodded, and he released my wrists. He smoothed his hands up my sides, following the line of my waist and stopping just below my breasts. He nestled his thumbs just under the underwire of my bra.

I arched my back, and he splayed his hand over my back.

“Would you like me to take this cute little bra off?” he asked. “Would you like to show me your perfect breasts?”

I shuddered, my head lolling back onto the back of the couch as I looked down at him. I swallowed, my breath rasping out of me.

“Yes,” I said softly.

He nodded, sliding one hand to the clasp of my bra. With expert dexterity, he pinched the fabric together.

I felt the clasp give, popping slightly. The supportive tension of the bra ceased, and the fabric tented slightly over my breasts. He smoothed both hands up to my shoulders, sliding the straps down my arms.

He had seen my breasts before but in the midst of a moment of passion where we'd both lost control. It felt so different now, sitting in the middle of my living room, in the amber lighting instead of the dim and dark. He wasn't grabbing and taking—he was appreciating and treasuring me.

"God, I love your breasts," he said. "I love their shape, their softness, your glorious nipples. God, Marley, you're just exquisite."

I had to look away from him as my stomach twisted with sheepish timidity. It was so flustering to have his attention solely focused on me and my body.

"Can I touch you?" he asked.

I nodded, not meeting his gaze. I closed my eyes, the anticipation of feeling his hands on the bare skin of my breasts too much to bear. He cupped my swollen breasts, squeezing only a little—enough to feel but not enough to hurt. Then I felt his rough, calloused thumb brush over my stiff nipple.

I tensed, my thighs squeezing together and heat rising to my décolletage, my neck, and my face.

Then, I felt the tickle of his beard against my breast. I started gasping. But before I could say anything, he claimed my breast with his mouth.

I moaned and curled my fingers into his hair. Cole flicked his tongue across my sensitive skin, and then his cool breath coursed over my bare skin. The sensation made me gasp and shiver, and my neglected nipple hardened in anticipation.

"Is this okay?" he asked, his voice low and gravelly.

"God, yes." I sighed.

His breath left him on a laugh. "Just wanted to make sure."

He lowered his mouth to my other breast.

I opened my eyes just in time to see his tongue draw a slow and torturous circle around the rigid point of my breast.

His eyes flicked up to mine as he sat back on his legs. "Is this where you want to do this?"

"D-do what?" I asked.

He tweaked my nipple softly. "Whatever you want, Marley."

"I want...I want you to kiss me."

He lay his palm against my cheek as he rose to his knees again, but I lifted my hand to stop him before he met his lips to mine.

"Not there." I took his hand and guided it down to my thigh.

His thumb pressed into the crease where my leg met my pelvis as a ravenous gleam entered his eyes.

"Here," I said shakily.

One moment I was sitting on the couch with Cole between my legs, the next, I'd been swept off the soft cushions and into his strong arms.

"What are you doing?" I scrambled.

"If I'm going to treat myself to a feast between your legs, Marley, I'm doing it where I can make you good and comfortable. I'm going to make you feel so good you'll be begging me to stop."

The promise in his words made me wriggle in his grasp, my skin ablaze with desire.

He carried me into my bedroom and gently laid me on the bed. His fingers curled into the waistband of my sweats, and then in one swift movement, he tugged them off. I yelped with surprise as he pulled right to the edge of the bed and knelt before me.

"I'm sorry," Cole rumbled. "I've waited too long for this to slow down." He hooked his thumb into my panties and started to pull them down.

“Wait,” I said, hands going between my legs, covering that innermost part of me.

Despite his claim of being unable to slow down, he came to an abrupt and immediate stop.

I knew then that everything he was doing was for my pleasure. Cole was trying to show me just how attentive he could be. But there was one problem making me panic as he nestled between my legs.

I blushed, the heat spreading all the way up to my ears.

“Marley,” he said, his voice gentle and comforting. “If you want to stop—”

“No. I don’t want you to stop. It’s just that...”

I couldn’t make my mouth form the words. I didn’t know if I was embarrassed, ashamed or if it was something else.

“Marley?”

I squeezed my eyes shut and took a deep breath, preparing myself to just spit it out.

“I’ve never... No one has ever done this before,” I mumbled.

He jolted up, his brows high with surprise.

"Your ex never... You're telling me that you're this fucking beautiful, this exquisite, and your ex never gave you head?"

I covered my face with my hands. It was so embarrassing. I was almost thirty, for God's sake.

"Hey, hey. Hold on." He tugged my hands away from my face. "This isn't something *you* should be embarrassed about. This is on him. Frankly, I don't know how he denied himself the absolute pleasure of being between your legs."

"He always made it seem like it was...gross, or dirty, or something," I mumbled.

"So, does that mean you never gave him head either?"

"Well, no. I did it when he wanted me to," I said. "Saying it out loud feels a little stupid."

"*You* do not sound stupid, Marley," he said. "But your ex sounds like an absolute idiot." He released my hands and kissed the soft skin of my belly. "Allow me to take my time, so you can experience it the way it's meant to be."

I nodded, exhaling softly. My voice shook with a mix of excitement and need when I said, "Okay..."

He feathered slow kisses down my stomach, his beard tickling me and making me giggle. The lower he got, the slower he went, driving me crazy with desire. Each slow, undulating kiss wound me tighter and tighter and made my skin tingle more and more.

By the time he made it to the curves of my hip bones, all my nerves and embarrassment of being so stripped bare in front of Cole had eddied out of my body, replaced with an urgency to have his soft lips and tongue caress that most private part of me.

He gave a hungry growl as he closed his teeth over the band of my panties and lifted my hips with his strong, perfect hands. He drew the scrap of fabric off my legs, his teeth scraping along my skin, down my thigh, and my calf.

I was completely naked, my center on display before his very eyes while he was still fully dressed. Something about that was exhilarating and made it seem so blissfully dangerous.

His hand smoothed up my calf to the back of my knee, hitching my leg over his shoulder.

Unbidden, a whimper escaped my lips. My body almost ached with need, with the curiosity of what this would feel like.

“Cole, *please,*” I whispered.

He gave a dark chuckle. “Already begging, Marley?” he said. “We haven’t even started, sweetheart. Give me a little bit of a challenge, at least.”

I lifted my index finger to my mouth and bit down on my knuckle to keep myself from begging again. My head dropped back, my eyes fluttering shut as he hitched my other leg over his free shoulder.

With my eyes closed, every tiny sensation was amplified: the soft knit of his shirt, the rough texture of his hands over the sides of my thighs, the gust of his breath against my core. I bit down harder on my knuckle and whimpered.

He chuckled as he pressed a cruel, teasing kiss to my inner thigh, then to my folds. My breaths were coming in quick bursts, my mind addled and dizzy. Everything thought in my head vanished as my brain focused entirely on the sensitivity between my legs.

Finally, it happened.

It felt like warm, slick silk was being dragged over me. I didn’t know why I had been expecting something taut and acute when this was more like melting. My finger dropped from my mouth as he lapped from my opening all the way to the little bundle of nerves at my apex.

"Oh God...that is heaven," I sighed.

"Hmm?" The vibration of his lips against me tickled.

I gazed at him from under my lashes as I smoothed my fingers through his hair.

As if in answer, he deftly slid a finger inside me, deepening the experience into something entirely new.

"O-oh," I gasped.

"Is this fine?" he said, taking a break to kiss the inside of my thigh.

I couldn't form words, could only nod and tug gently at his hair—a quiet request to continue tasting me. He obliged me, licking slow strokes over my clit as he pumped his finger in and out of me.

Something built inside me, a coalescing feeling from the top of my head all the way to my toes. I crossed my legs behind his head, trying to get it under control. I didn't want to come yet, not when I was in such an utter state of bliss.

But Cole had other plans. A second finger joined the first, and he slowed the rhythmic thrusting of those fingers, taking extra care to make sure I felt the penetration on every nerve inside of me. He coaxed my G-spot as he closed his mouth around my clit and began to suckle with *just* enough pressure that it had me moaning.

"Cole, I'm going to... Fuck."

He hummed in encouragement, his tongue flicking my clit, his fingers speeding up.

I gripped his head with both hands as my toes curled.

A moan escaped me, starting low and long, then shortening and becoming louder and higher in pitch. A wave receded and built. Any moment now, it would crash into me with such force that it would destroy me.

Still, I tried to hold it off, tried to slow it down.

Cole tore his mouth away, his lips brushing against my mound. "Come on, sweetheart. I want to hear you scream for me."

He renewed the contact with fresh vigor, licking and flicking as his fingers fucked me harder and faster.

My back arched, and my whole body contracted as I cried out. Release crashed into me when I squeezed my thighs around his head and pulled his hair. The rhythmic thrusts slowed as he let me come down from my orgasm.

He kissed the inside of my thigh, now slick with my own wetness. “That’s what I like to see.”

His fingers slowed almost to a stop as I lay panting, trying to recuperate and bring my mind back to this plane of existence. Lips brushing over the insides of my thighs, Cole pulled his fingers out of me.

My thinking mind returned to me slowly, then reeled with shock.

“I think...” I said softly. “That was the first orgasm I ever had.”

Wyatt had always insisted that I had, in fact, orgasmed every time we had sex, and I’d always wondered why sex was so unenjoyable. I’d seen so many scenes in movies where women would weep and cry out while they had sex, but for me, sex had always just been a mildly flustering, rough experience.

Cole perched himself over me. His arms braced on either side of me.

“Hold on,” he said. “You’re telling me that your ex never made you come?”

"Not like that, no," I said. "Is it supposed to be like that?"

"Marley, haven't you ever touched yourself? Or played with some toys?" he asked. "How do you not know what an orgasm is supposed to feel like?"

I blushed, biting my lip and looking carefully at the ceiling. "He didn't like when I touched myself or used toys. He never let me get them, anyway."

He brushed my hair away from his face. "Don't be ashamed, Marley. You didn't do anything wrong."

"I mean, you're right. An adult woman should know how her own body works. I was complacent for not trying to learn those things about myself. I was a pretty innocent teenager, and then I met him in high school and never dated anyone else."

"Jesus Christ," he said. "I don't know how a man goes through life willing to let their partner have crappy sex like that."

"To be fair, I don't think he thought it was bad sex," I said.

"Good point. You did say he was egotistical," he said as he settled beside me and pulled me against him. I rested my head in the crook of his arm.

“Do you...um, do you want me to...” I trailed off, moving my hand to his belt buckle.

He closed his hand over mine, then lifted it to his lips to kiss my fingers. “No, that won’t be necessary, Marley,” he said softly. “As much as I would *love* to see those pretty eyes of yours looking up at me while you suck my cock, it’s been a long day for you. I want you to ride the high of your first orgasm as long as you can.”

Hearing him talk so brazenly made me squeeze my thighs together. Again, as much as I didn’t want to think about him in this intimate and lovely moment, I couldn’t help but compare this intimacy to the lackluster physical relationship I’d had with Wyatt.

Wyatt had only ever cared about his own sexual gratification. Whenever I’d desired sex, he almost seemed annoyed with the fact that he had to try—like he was just giving a whining child what they needed to shut up. Eventually, I think I’d convinced myself that I was enjoying myself just to avoid the discomfort of communicating my needs with Wyatt since that conversation always led to some kind of fight where he told me I didn’t respect him as an alpha.

But Cole? Cole seemed to get his own pleasure from giving *me* pleasure. Which I'd never thought was possible.

Just another reason that made me feel safe with Cole.

"Stay the night?" I asked.

He tilted his head to look down at me, kissing my hand again.

"I would love to," he said, smiling. "But if I do, I think we should get cleaned up. I know you took a bath just before I arrived, but..."

I laughed lightly. I nodded. "Yeah, we got a little messy, didn't we?"

"In the best possible way," he said. "I want to spend the night kissing you to sleep, and I guess I won't get to do that if I—uh—taste like you."

My cheeks heated. "I mean, it won't bother me that much, but I appreciate you being thoughtful. Now, if we're going to shower together, we better get you undressed."

Cole's brows shot up, his mouth popping open. "Together?"

I smirked. "It's the efficient choice. We don't want to waste water, do we?"

"Oh, absolutely *not*," he said with mock seriousness. "It's clearly the best choice to shower together—purely for ecological reasons."

I straddled him and took the liberty of undressing him, grabbing the hem of his shirt and inching it up and over his head. The second his arms were free, he gripped my ass and stood up, carrying me toward the bathroom.

"More efficient to undress in the bathroom, isn't it?" he teased.

"The spare toothbrushes are in there, too," I parried back.

"Spare toothbrushes?" he sputtered. "Do you often have overnight guests?"

"No!" I swatted his chest. "It's just for emergencies. Sometimes I find out a student's family is having a hard time, so I make sure I have some on hand. And it's helpful when Lana or Paulette stays over. It's just—"

"Efficient?" he interrupted with a toothy grin.

"I'm the most efficient kindergarten teacher you'll ever meet," I said with a wink.

He walked us into the bathroom and sat me down on the counter.

He brushed his teeth with a dinosaur toothbrush. In his massive hand, it looked like it had been made for dolls. When he felt better about his breath, he got the water running before coming back to kiss me.

As we kissed, I unbuckled his belt and unfastened the button on his dark jeans. He bent at his waist, letting go of my hips long enough to kick off his jeans and underwear.

I broke the kiss to get a good look at him.

Cole laughed and tutted like a scolding teacher. "Dirty girl," he growled.

"You took your time admiring me. Seems only fair," I protested.

"Admire away," he said. "I'll even let you look with your hands if you want."

The dark promise of that got me all worked up again, and it didn't help when he kissed me again. Since he was preventing me from looking with my eyes, I had no choice but to look with my hands.

I smoothed my fingertips from his hair to his shoulders, following the curves and lines of his muscles down to his pecs, over his abs, then lower…and lower…

My hand smoothed down his length and wrapped around his thickness. Cole gasped into my mouth, a little sound trilling out of him as I slid my hand from the base all the way to the tip. He was *huge*.

"Fuck, Marley," he groaned. "Your hand feels so fucking good. Behave. Or you're showering alone."

He grabbed my wrist and pinned my hand, and me, against the mirror at my back. He leaned in close, kissing me with renewed vigor and such calm dominance it was dizzying.

He wrenched away. "Can you keep your hands to yourself, Marley?" he murmured in my ear.

"Yes," I squeaked, though it sounded more like a whine needily.

"Good girl."

The words sent a jolt of pleasure through me, and I shivered. Then, as if he wasn't standing in front of me with a raging erection, as if this was a completely normal situation, he backed away and helped me down from the counter.

"Why do I feel like you're denying me for fun?" I asked.

"I may or may not enjoy teasing you," he said with a roguish grin. "I also may or may not have been with a woman sexually in years, and I *really* don't want to embarrass myself by barely lasting as long as a teenager the first time you touch me."

"Really? You don't come off as the nervous type to me."

"Oh, Marley," he said as he helped me into the running water. "Every man, no matter how strong or macho he might seem, is nervous around the woman he likes. And I like you quite a lot."

Somehow, the sweetness of that admission helped me ease out of my arousal and into something far more comfortable. As I leaned my head back into the water, I heard the pop of my shampoo bottle. Cole gestured to me with a come-hither motion.

I obliged, and he gently turned me around to face the water before lathering the shampoo into my hair.

I hummed as he massaged my scalp and combed his fingers through my hair.

"You're really good at that," I mumbled.

"Lots of practice washing Noah's mop."

"Hmm," I said. "Makes sense."

The simple act of showering together wasn't something I'd ever really experienced before. Showering together was always sexualized. But not with Cole. Once he'd rinsed the shampoo and conditioner out of my hair, Cole washed his own hair and his beard. Even as we washed each other's bodies, it wasn't sexual; we were just having a normal conversation about our schedules for the next day, the restaurants we liked, and the books we wanted to read.

It felt so easy.

Easier than anything I'd ever experienced.

I had been overcomplicating this whole thing. We were just two adults who liked each other. Maybe, if things went right, we'd come to love each other. Maybe I didn't have to think so hard about being in Noah's life.

Maybe I could have my cake and eat it too.

We were still talking as we got out of the shower and dried off. I giggled when I cracked a joke about Cole drying off like a dog, and he responded by whipping his hair around and splashing water across the room.

When all was said and done, I slipped into comfortable pajamas, and Cole got dressed in his boxers and T-shirt before we climbed into bed. He didn't waste any time hugging me close to him.

"I'm going to have to buy that shampoo just to smell when I'm missing you," he said.

"Do you miss me often?" I asked.

"More than I care to admit," he said a bit wryly. "I can't seem to stop thinking about you, Marley."

I smiled into his shirt. "Well, you're not the only one."

"Yeah?" he asked. "Are you also plagued by daydreams of me in a bikini?"

"Yeah, the one with yellow polka dots." I pinched his side playfully.

He yelped and quickly grabbed my hand. "You should know I am incredibly ticklish," he said. "And that I *will* panic if you tickle me. Not in an adorable way—in an embarrassing way."

"You say that like it will make me *not* want to do it."

"Marley, you're not a secret tickle sadist, are you? You're not hiding a collection of feather dusters under your bed or something, right?"

“I can neither confirm nor deny the existence of a tickle-torture dungeon somewhere on the premises,” I said.

“An entire room of red flags,” he said.

I laughed, nuzzling into him. “This is nice. Spending time with you, joking around—I wish we could do it.”

“Me too,” he said. Then he tilted his head, his lips pursed. “Actually, that gives me an idea.”

“Oh?” I asked.

“You know that carnival that comes into town a few times a year?”

“The one that moves around? I’ve heard of it, but I’ve never been,” I said.

“It’s coming to New Middle Bluff this weekend. I was planning on taking Noah as a father-son day, but why don’t you tag along with us?”

“I would love to,” I said, almost giddy. “God, this is probably going to sound stupid, but I’ve always wanted to go on a date to a carnival.”

“Well, it’s a week for firsts,” he said, kissing my brow. “First experience with oral sex, first orgasm, first carnival date.”

“Sounds like we went backward,” I said.

He barked a laugh. “What’s new?” he said. “Our whole situation has been backward, inside out, and upside down.”

“So true,” I said, stifling a yawn.

He kissed my temple. “Sleepy?”

“Mmm.”

He slipped his fingers into my hair and gently stroked my scalp.

“Mmm, evil,” I slurred. “I’m going to pass right out.”

“That, my dear, is sort of the point. You realize that, right?”

I hummed some non-committal answer, already surrendering to the feeling pulling me down toward sleep. I heard a soft, breathy chuckle and felt the press of a kiss to my brow as I drifted into unconsciousness.

Chapter 20 - Cole

My night with Marley carried me through the rest of the week in a blissful haze. Everything about her was tantalizing, adorable, and sexy. I didn't know it was possible for a woman to be the whole package, but Marley definitely was.

What made my week even better was the date I had to look forward to. A *real* date, not just another weird crisis that somehow led to me kissing Marley. We were going on an honest-to-God date. And about damn time.

I couldn't tell who was more excited about the date—me or Noah. He'd asked me about the carnival every day, asking again and again about Marley coming with us. When Saturday finally rolled around, I was just about getting exasperated about Noah's constant barrage of questions. I got him buckled into his car seat, both of us suitably dressed for a day out when he asked again.

"Is Miss Cage still coming with us, Daddy?"

"Yeah, champ. We're going to go get her right now," I said. "We want to make sure Marley has a lot of fun today, too, okay? So try not to climb all over her all day."

"Okay, Daddy! I'm gonna show Marley all my favorite parts of the carnival."

I laughed, fairly certain that meant he was absolutely going to be climbing all over her. "That'll be real nice of you, buddy. Ready to go?"

"Yeah!" he said, kicking his light-up shoes.

I felt like a teenager all over again. The closer we got to her house, the faster my heart raced. My stomach was dipping nervously. I'd been so busy between the meetings with my clients, sourcing the materials for Wyatt's law offices, and handling the end-of-the-month payouts that I hadn't seen Marley since the night I'd spent at her place. Either Travis or my parents had taken on the onus of getting Noah to school while I handled business matters that needed my personal attention.

When we pulled up to Marley's house, I grabbed my phone. She'd told me just to text her when I arrived, which I did somewhat begrudgingly. I preferred walking a date to the car and opening the door for her, but she'd pointed out it would be more work to get Noah in and out of the car. I sent off the text, wondering if she was still getting ready.

With Olivia, it had been a frequent source of contention whenever we had to get ready to go out together. For some reason, we always left an hour later than we were supposed to—the fights over that didn't stop until I'd learned to tell her we needed to arrive two hours earlier than we actually had to.

But just a minute after I'd sent the text, Marley hurried out her door, shutting it behind her and triggering the locking mechanism with her biometric scanner. I got out of the car and came around to the passenger side as she skipped down the driftwood walkway.

She was a vision in a flowery summer dress and a wide-brimmed hat. Her hair was styled in bouncy curls and sprayed with...was that perfume? Her white wedges laced up her calf like ballerina shoes. I found myself smiling like an idiot as she walked over to me.

"Sorry for the wait," she said, angling her head up to kiss me hello.

"No worries." I beamed at her. "You look amazing, Marley."

She smiled up at me, the apples of her freckled cheeks slightly flushed. "You don't look so bad yourself, sir," she said as she climbed into the passenger seat.

I was on cloud nine as I circled the car and got back into the driver's seat. When I did, I adjusted my mirror and caught a glimpse of Noah's face. He was beaming from ear to ear—his shoulders bunched around his ears like he'd just seen something he wasn't supposed to. I almost didn't realize why.

Then I remembered that Marley had just snuck a kiss a moment ago—or not so much snuck as blatantly stole one.

"Are you guys boyfriend and girlfriend?!" he practically squealed.

I winced.

It was only natural for a five-year-old to jump to that conclusion after seeing two adults kiss. After all, there was very little room in a child's mind for the shades of gray between the black-and-white notions of together and not together.

I made to answer but floundered and choked on my words. I didn't even know how to answer the question without risking breaking his heart and taking the wind out of his sails.

In the end, Marley came to my rescue.

"Your dad and I like each other very much, Noah," she said. "But more than anything, we both *love* you."

His brow furrowed. "But you just kissed Daddy," he said. "I thought kisses were only for boyfriend and girlfriend."

"Doesn't your grandma kiss you sometimes? And your dad?"

"Yeah," he said, his little wheels turning as he tried to make the connection between the situations she was listing. "And sometimes Miss Sylvia does, too."

"Mhm," she said. "So, we're not boyfriend and girlfriend right now, but we're getting to know each other kind of like how you're super close with Miss Sylvia."

Understanding started to light up Noah's face. He gave a nod. Relieved, I pulled away from the curb and got us on our way to the carnival.

I looked over to Marley and mouthed a quiet *thank you*. She smiled and gave a little nod, offering her hand to me on the center console of the car.

My heart squeezed. I'd forgotten just how much I missed little things like this: holding my partner's hand while I drove, doing fun activities with my partner and son, and picking someone up for a date. I couldn't remember a time I'd been so happy.

I took her hand, our fingers lacing together.

I didn't let go the whole ride over to the carnival.

Halfway through the drive, Noah asked Marley if they could sing some of the songs she'd been teaching the kids about colors, shapes, and numbers. I worried that she wouldn't want to fuss with it on a day off, but she surprised me once again by seeming more than content to do it.

I felt like I'd never stop grinning. This was the mother I'd always wanted Olivia to be, the mother I'd always hoped my son would get to have.

I was still smiling when we arrived at the carnival grounds. This year, they'd set up the festivities in a depot of baseball fields usually used by the local mini-league baseball teams and sometimes by high-school kids who played club games. A grassy field was much better than hot asphalt. At least if Noah took off running, her wouldn't fall and break his teeth or scrape a knee.

I got Noah out of his car seat and carefully set him down on the pavement.

"All right, kiddo, stay right here while we get your lunch bag out of the back seat and your water, okay?" I asked.

He looked like he was biting at the bit to run into the colorful chaos, but he did wait—a marked improvement from his old habits. I had to wonder if learning how to line up and take turns at school was starting to sink in a little more than I'd really noticed.

Marley took Noah's hand, engaging him in conversation about what he most wanted to do at the carnival.

My heart sank with fatherly futility over the fact that most of what he wanted to do was eat junk food. I didn't know why I'd even bothered bringing peanut butter and jelly sandwiches and cut-up fruit. There was no way he would let me get away with anything less than a carnival-sponsored sugar rush.

I set the lunch bag back into the car, taking just a backpack with a change of clothes and a few water bottles. You never knew when a five-year-old would have an accident, and there was no way in hell I was going to pay eight dollars for a bottle of water that I could buy at the store for a buck. I shut the car door and hitched the backpack on my shoulder.

"No lunch bag after all?" Marley asked me.

I shrugged. "Just trying to be realistic about what this one's going to let me get away with today. Would you eat PB and J when corndogs were on offer?"

"Daddy, Daddy, I want a corndog!"

I heaved a withering sigh. "Case in point," I said a bit dryly.

"Fair enough. I'm relieved you didn't bring a peanut butter and tuna sandwich," she said.

I laughed, remembering that conversation with fondness. "Oh, wait, you didn't want to eat that today? Damn, I had a whole dinner planned and everything," I teased.

"Peanut butter and tuna?" Noah asked incredulously. "That's gross!"

"Yes, it is," I growled as I picked my son up and blew a raspberry on his cheek. "And if you don't behave, that's all you get to have for dinner!"

"No. Yuck." He giggled and pressed his hands against my face.

"For a week," Marley said, playing along.

"Forever," I chipped in.

Noah devolved into a fit of giggles that warmed my heart. He was already having fun, and we hadn't even gotten into the carnival yet.

Of course, when we did get into the festivities, he was even more excited.

We did just about everything the carnival had to offer. We played games, and Noah even managed to get Marley to go on the teacup ride with us, even though she swore she'd throw up all over both.

She, of course, did not vomit. Marley was a champ the whole time.

After a couple of hours of playing around, we went to the food court to grab some lunch. The carnival organizers had really thought of everything when they set up the layout. Right next to the food court was a gated playground for the kids to run around and play in while the adults ate. It was perfect because Noah ate approximately two bites of his corndog and French fries before begging to go back to playing games and going on rides.

"Buddy, you gotta remember that Marley and I are old people. We gotta take a break before we can have more fun. Otherwise, we're gonna fall asleep, and *you'll* have to drive us home," I said as I ate some of my street tacos. "You wanna go play with the other kids in the playground over there?"

He kicked his feet and looked over to the other children bouncing in jumpy castles and going down slides. He nodded slightly, and I set my food aside. "Watch the table?" I asked Marley.

"Mmm, I'll consider it. Maybe someone more charming will wander over, and I'll let him eat your tacos," she said.

"Marley, don't let anyone eat Daddy's food. He's a big strong guy. He has to eat."

Marley clicked her tongue and shook her head as if she'd forgotten. "Gosh, Noah, you're so right. We don't wanna deal with your dad when he's cranky and hungry, huh?" she asked, bonking her forehead with a flat hand. "Good looking out, Noah."

Noah gave a sage nod, and I couldn't help but laugh. "I'll be right back," I said, walking away with Noah in tow.

The playground was close enough that I'd be able to see Noah while Marley and I ate. It was covered in a bed of hay and some tumbling mats so if any of the kids fell, they'd at least have a soft landing. I paid the gaggle of girls running the playground and acting as informal supervisors. We chatted a bit, and I learned they were an all-shifter softball team. They were running the playground to raise funds for equipment and uniforms.

"The local leagues don't allow shifters to join," one of them said. "So we had to make our own league, and since we have to travel so far to play games, we didn't have a lot of our sponsor money left after renting a bus."

I nodded, plucking a business card out of my wallet and handing it to them.

"When you have a chance, give my office a call and talk to Sylvia. I'll let her know you're calling. We'd love to sponsor you," I said.

"Fur Sure Solutions?" another of the girls snorted. "So dorky."

The first girl swatted her on the arm. "Dude, *shut up*," she hissed before looking up at me. "Sorry about that. We'll totally give you guys a call on Monday. Thank you so much. It means everything to us."

"No problem, and no worries. I'm happy to help some enterprising shifters. We need kids like you to pave the way for us old-timers. I'm Cole, by the way. Let me know if my son gets too rambunctious for you, will you?"

"Yes, sir! Thank you!"

I left the playground and looked toward the table. To my surprise, my spot had been filled. Jealousy flared through me. I thought she'd been joking about replacing me.

As I neared, I saw a familiar platinum blonde bob.

It was Lana. Travis and Paulette were also seated at the table.

"Well, what are you crazy kids doing here?" I asked as I approached the table.

Lana looked up at me and gave me a devilish grin. "Same as you," she said. "Travis and I are on a date."

Paulette was munching on Noah's crinkle-cut fries as she said, "I'm third wheeling."

"Unfortunately," Travis grumbled from his spot between the two shifter women.

Paulette flicked his nose. "Enhanced hearing, dickhead," she reminded him. "I can hear you."

"Yes, I'm fully aware. That's what you call intentional, Paulette."

"Poor, poor Travis." Paulette pinched his cheek. "You think I'm gonna let Lana date just any loser? This is an interview."

"Then why do I have to pay for you?" Travis grumbled.

"Because I said so," Lana said, sounding almost bored.

Marley grimaced. I could see she was feeling empathetic toward my old friend. Still, I couldn't blame Paulette for wanting to make sure Travis was a decent guy. I knew he was, of course, but if shifter men had it bad when it came to humans fetishizing them, shifter women had it even worse. I'd seen the forums online claiming shifter women wanted nothing more than to be dominated and "bred." Women often watched each other's backs when they met up with human men for romantic entanglements.

Travis was aware of that as well, which was why he was putting up with it in the first place. He was just whining out of principle. Marley scooted over on the bench and patted the seat next to her, inviting me to sit with her.

I sat down next to her, resting my hand on the small of her back.

"So," Lana said. "Is this thing happening?"

As she gestured between us, Marley shrank away from me a bit.

"Is it really that big of a deal?" I asked.

"No," Lana said. "I mean, it could be problematic if any of the parents learn about it, but I don't think it would blow up too much even if they did. But what I mean is... are you guys sure you wanna seem so close in front of Noah?"

Anger stoked in my gut. "I know you're not telling me how to parent my son, Lana," I said.

"God, don't be a drama queen," she snapped. "Of course, I'm not. But I just know that things have been a little funky for little Noah between the shift last week at school and how much you've been stepping up to protect her."

"I don't think we do know for sure," Marley said, surprising me a little bit. "But, I mean, how can we be sure unless we get to know each other?"

Lana's expression softened. "Fair," she said. "Just... don't you dare hurt her, Cole. I know you're a good dude, but I also know how protective and territorial men are when it comes to our kind."

"I promise that I'm on my best behavior," I said, fighting not to roll my eyes. "When did you guys get here? Got any plans after eating?"

"Speaking of eating, I'm going to go get food. Trav, Lana, you want something?" Paulette asked.

"Surprise me," Lana said. "You know what I like."

"Cool," she said.

Travis opened his mouth to make a request, but Paulette interjected before he could. "I'll surprise you too. Don't be a picky bitch," she said.

Travis closed his mouth and gave me a deadpan look like he wanted to pummel me for the crimes of all lycanfolk.

"Anyway," Lana said. "We've been here a couple of hours, thought we'd get some food, play a few more games, browse around the craft stalls, then head back home."

"That sounds fun," Marley said, looking at me. "We're almost out of ride tickets, aren't we? Why don't we join them?"

"Yeah, sure. I'm sure Noah would love that. It will be like an impromptu double date."

"Exactly!" She grinned.

God, to see her smile like that, I'd cut off a limb if she asked me.

We shot the shit for a while, finishing our food and waiting while Travis, Lana, and Paulette ate. I loved watching Marley with Lana and Paulette. I wasn't sure if she noticed how Lana and Paulette doted on her like wolves caring for a pup, but they did. Lana's edgy sharpness was a little duller, and Paulette was gently indulgent of Marley's curiosity.

It was clear to me that wherever Marley went, people fell in love with her in their own little ways. Her students, Lana, Paulette, my son, and me... Marley's earnest sweetness had ensnared us all, and we had happily fallen into the trap.

We fell into the common pattern of the three women taking over the conversation with gossip, inside jokes, and planning future outings and girls' days as Travis and I observed and communicated with our eyes in the way only best friends could. Little paper boats full of fried food gradually emptied, then I heard a familiar voice calling from the playground.

"Daddy," Noah called, his face smooshed against the gate. "Daddy! I GOTTA GO PEE."

I choked on my laughter.

"Well, at least he's discreet," Travis joked.

"Duty calls," I said, kissing Marley on her temple. "Be right back."

"'Kay!" she said, her eyes bright. "I'll be here."

I took Noah to the restroom. When Noah and I got back to the group, it seemed like everyone was done eating, which worked out perfectly because Noah was eager to go on more rides.

As a group, we went on a handful of the carnival rides—the Ferris wheel, the merry-go-round, and the dragon swing.

The dragon swing had been a little too intense for Noah, and he insisted I carry him after the scary ride. It made it a good time to go to the market and peruse the wares. I kept Noah up on my shoulders while Marley, Lana, and Paulette looked around.

There was a very cute moment where Lana and Paulette insisted on getting matching friendship bracelets with Marley. I was starting to realize just how much I appreciated the silly, childlike parts of Marley and the way she brought that out in other people. I couldn't think of another person who could get Lana to buy a friendship bracelet.

Once the girls were done shopping, Noah wanted to go on another ride.

"We only have two more ride tickets," I said as I took him down from my shoulders. "Which ride do you want to go on?"

"Teacups! Teacups!"

"That works out perfectly," Marley said. "My stomach was just empty enough not to hurl the first time, but now that my belly is full, I'm going to sit this one out."

"Just you and me, kiddo," I said.

"Okay!"

We went to the teacup ride, which really worked out in our favor, considering it was so close to the exit. We got in line while Marley waited at the gate where we'd come out. Travis, Lana, and Paulette decided to join us on the ride. Travis joined us in our cup, and we had an informal battle of the sexes as to who could make their cup spin faster.

I don't think anyone really "won" the competition because we were all varying shades of green as we stumbled off the teacups. Well, all of us except Noah, who was still too small to feel the full force of gravity working against him and his digestive system.

Still, we were all in good spirits as we came off the ride, chattering about the plan for the rest of the night—Travis and his dates would stay a little longer to watch the live music and have a few drinks in the beer garden.

I was looking forward to a blissful night of Marley's company, maybe curled up on the couch and watching cartoons with Noah, when we exited through the gate, and my son asked a question that made my blood run cold.

"Daddy, where's Marley?"

I looked around. She was nowhere to be seen. I lifted my nose to the air to catch her scent. It took a moment to find it through the cacophony of smells surrounding me.

Finally, I caught her rose-and-honey scent. It was tangled with the pungent stench of her fear.

"Trav, can you watch Noah for a moment?" I asked in as calm a voice as possible. "I'm going to go look for Marley. Maybe she ran to the bathroom or something, but I just want to be sure."

Travis's jaw clenched. I knew he sensed something was off, but he nodded nonetheless. "Sure, man," he said. "Come here, little dude. Let's go play a game while we wait for your dad."

"Yay! Games!" Noah punched the air. I was relieved he hadn't noticed the shift in my demeanor.

I watched as Travis walked away with my son and the two shifter women. When I was sure they were out of earshot and eyeshot, I started searching.

It was a pain to single out the thread of Marley and her fear among the chaotic landscape of fragrances around me. Garbage, food, sweat, sunscreen—everything clashed with everything else, leaving me straining and struggling to find the whiff I'd caught by the rides.

It was maddening and terrifying. The idea that I might lose her scent before I found her was enough to make me want to shift into my lycan form to go looking for her.

But eventually, I managed to find her scent again—stronger this time. She was near. I was so close to winning this game of hot and cold. I followed the scent through the food tents, almost losing it again. Honestly, I think I would have lost it completely if it weren't for the acrid, burnt smell of her fear.

Horrible visions of what might have happened flashed through my mind. I thought of her stalker finding her and carrying her off. I thought of her shoved into the trunk of a car while children screamed with delight—while Noah and I rode the damned teacups without a care in the world.

That scent was becoming stronger—so strong that my stomach churned with nausea. I followed it all the way to the edge of the fields, beyond the rides and booths and shops, all the way over to a copse of trees that hemmed in the baseball fields and offered privacy to the nearby residential area.

As I neared, I heard the soft hitching of Marley's sobs, heard her sniffling and murmuring to herself.

"You're okay, you're okay, you're okay," she was saying to herself over and over again.

Then I spotted her. Relief swept through me. She was in one piece, uninjured, and alone. Thank God something terrible hadn't happened. Thank God she was still here. She was bent over, hugging her knees. Something had clearly upset her, but she was still whole and physically unharmed.

"Marley?" I said softly, not wanting to frighten her.

Despite the careful way I approached, she still let out a yelp and whipped her over her shoulder to look at me.

Upon recognizing me, though, her fearful expression immediately melted into some mixture of relief and distress.

"C-Cole," she said. "I-I'm sorry. I saw him. I saw him, and I just..."

"Your stalker?" I asked, anger already boiling over, hot and sharp.

She shook her head, her expression crumpling in dismay.

There was nothing to prepare me for what she said next.

"I—" she said, breath hitching so much that she almost couldn't get the words out. "I think I saw Wyatt... My ex."

Chapter 21 - Marley

Cole sank down to the grass next to me, stroking my back. "You saw him?" he asked me. "What did he look like? Are you sure it was him?"

"Oh, I'm sure," I sputtered. I hated that I couldn't get a grip on myself. "I think I'm sure. H-his hair is a little shorter, but he's still getting that stupid tan and—and..."

I rubbed my shoulder where the pain had suddenly become overwhelming, a searing heat that had sensed his arrival.

"I was watching you guys have fun on the ride. Everything was fine, and then it was like I felt him—my shoulder started hurting. When I turned, he was standing ten feet away."

"Did he see you?" Cole asked, barely contained rage lacing his every word. "Did he come after you?"

"I don't know. I don't think so. I was so afraid that I didn't think. I just ran as far and as fast as I could," I said.

"Marley." His voice was steady but cold. "I have to ask you a question, and I don't want you to jump to conclusions before I explain everything."

The sudden intensity, the seemingly random shift in his expression, baffled me. His lips were flattened into a thin line, his brow taut. I worried that he was about to accuse me of the same things the people in Leighton Valley had. What if he didn't believe me? What if he thought I was being overdramatic just to get his attention?

Regardless, I swallowed my terror and nodded.

The muscles in his jaw jumped as he dropped his gaze from mine. "Is your ex's name Wyatt Pierce?"

I jerked back a little. Had I never told Cole my ex's name? I searched through my memory. But no, I hadn't. I'd only ever called him my ex. I didn't want to say his name. Saying his name out loud almost felt like inviting his cruelty back into my life. It almost felt like a betrayal of my own self.

Which meant that if Cole knew his name...

"How do you know that?" I asked.

Cole's intake of breath was sharp. He couldn't meet my eyes.

"He's been talking to me about setting up a law office out here in New Middle Bluff," he said.

My blood ran cold.

This was all my nightmares manifesting. This was everything I didn't want. This was the end of my new life here.

Cole had been working with him. They'd spoken with each other, probably laughed together. What if Wyatt had already convinced him that I was some lycan-fetishizing psycho? What if now that Cole was putting two and two together, he didn't want me anymore?

The point of my heart chipped off.

"If he told you anything about me," I sobbed, choking on my breath. "I promise none of it's true, Cole. Please don't cut me out of your life. Please don't—Please—"

"What?" Cole said, bracketing my face in his hands. "Marley, no. God, you silly woman. I wasn't asking you that because he'd told me something terrible about you or because I have any plans of cutting you out of my and Noah's life."

"Y-you weren't?" I asked, trying to steady my breaths.

"Of course not. You think I'd side with your shitty ex over you? Beautiful, amazing you?" He gave an exasperated shake of his head. "No, Marley. I was asking because when I realized I'd been talking to him, I thought for sure you would never forgive me."

Tears still streamed down my face. He huffed a soft laugh and wiped the wetness off my cheeks.

"I'm afraid you're stuck with me, Marley," he said. "At least until you really get sick of me."

I couldn't imagine something like that ever happening. I couldn't imagine ever being sick of him. I wanted to tell him as much, but for some reason, I choked on the words.

"I'm going to call Lana and Paulette and have them take you home, then I'll go looking for Wyatt and—"

"Cole, please don't leave me alone. Not when he's so close." I despised the desperation in my voice. "God, do you think it *is* him? The stalker?"

Cole pressed his lips together and shook his head. "I'm afraid not, Marley. Their scents are entirely different, and I've seen both Wyatt and your stalker up close. I hate to suggest it, but it might be completely unrelated."

The laugh that left me was devoid of humor. "What kind of luck do I have that I have an abusive ex and a stalker? What is *wrong* with me?"

"There's nothing wrong with you, Marley," he said. "Unfortunately, people who have been victims of domestic crimes once often experience them again. Predators seek out sweet, caring people like you because they think they can take advantage. They mistake kindness for weakness."

My tears refused to stop, no matter how much I wished they would.

"Maybe I am weak," I said quietly. I certainly felt weak at the moment. "Maybe I am."

"You're not, Marley. You're one of the strongest people I know. Only strong people can be beaten down by the world, by their families, by the very people who should care for them and still rise to the occasion every day and still find brightness in the world," he told me. "Don't sell yourself short."

I searched his eyes. Did he really mean what he was saying? From what I could tell, he did.

Had I actually found someone earnest for once? Maybe I wasn't doomed to repeat the same mistakes over and over again. I wanted to tell him that looking into his face, into his son's face, made me feel like those things might be true. But it didn't feel right to say it now, not while I was such a horrible mess.

"What do we do? I don't want Noah to see me like this. I don't want to worry him," I asked.

"I'll have Trav take him to my parents' house. He won't mind, and Noah always likes spending the night with his grandparents," he said. "You can come and stay with me tonight. Hell, stay with me as long as you like. But tonight, we'll give you some time and space to process."

I wanted to run the hell away, pack my bags and flee.

But another part of me wasn't ready to let go of this new home I'd built for myself. I had worked so hard to build myself back up from nothing. I'd done everything I could to learn who I was without Wyatt.

"If you're sure you don't mind doing that for my benefit," I said. "I would really appreciate having you close by tonight. I'm terrified of Wyatt, but I don't think he would stand a chance against you."

Cole's smile was bright and radiant before he touched his forehead to mine.

"That's right, Marley," he said. "I'd tear him apart if he so much as tried to touch you."

Despite the violent sentiment, despite the fact that I'd just spent who knew how long crying and quivering, I found myself smiling back at him. For some reason, Cole always managed to make me laugh or smile, even when it felt impossible.

"Thank you," I said. "I wish I could tell you how much that means to me."

###

Noah was more than eager to spend more time at the carnival with his Uncle Travis, Lana, and Paulette. I could vaguely hear Travis asking Cole if I was okay, and Cole, thankfully, kept his answer vague enough that I didn't have to feel too embarrassed about my outburst and by my fleeing.

When that was handled, Cole held me close and walked me back to his car. He made sure I was situated safely in the passenger seat before rounding the car to get in the driver's seat. Before long, we were on our way to his house.

When we were a few minutes away from his house, a question popped into my mind and nagged at me until I had no choice but to ask.

"Cole, did Wyatt ever ask about me?"

Cole's jaw worked for a moment. He kept his eyes on the road as he spoke. "Not outright, but he had his way of getting information out of me when we met up. Marley, I didn't even tell him your name. I promise you."

I nodded, trying to unravel the mysteries surrounding my life.

"Do you think he's serious about opening a law office out here?" I asked.

"I don't know." Cole rubbed his jaw. I'd noticed him doing that whenever he was thinking deeply. "I've met a lot of potential clients over the years. I can usually sniff out whether they're serious about hiring me. With him, though, it's hard to tell."

I nodded. That sounded like Wyatt. He always had a way of seeming equal parts committed and lackadaisical.

"Sounds like him."

"We don't have to talk about him, Marley," Cole said. "As far as I'm concerned, I don't think he's even worth a passing thought. And I definitely won't be working with him. He can get another contractor."

"I just don't know what I'd do if he moved out here," I said. "I didn't even know he had a license to practice law in South Carolina."

"We'll cross that bridge when we get to it," he said. "Hopefully, once he realizes he can't get to you through me, he'll fly back home to Leighton Valley."

"I hope so."

He parked at his home and came around to the passenger side to let me out. Inside, I found myself wanting to check every nook and cranny of the place to see if Wyatt was hiding somewhere, just waiting to hop out and scare me.

"Was Wyatt ever here?" I asked. "I know your office is upstairs."

He shook his head. "No, the first time I met him was when I took Noah to the arcade. The second time, we met at some demented country club."

I was too exhausted to ask about the details of that second meeting. "You only met the two times?"

He nodded. "And I have no intention of meeting with him ever again, Marley."

I exhaled, letting that fact soothe my fraying edges.

He locked the door. "Let's see if we can get your mind off him. I don't want that asshole ruining our whole night after we'd had such a lovely day?"

Cole brushed his hand down my arm before he caught my hand with his and lifted it to remind me of the cute friendship bracelet I'd gotten with Lana and Paulette.

It *had* been a lovely day. It was the first time I'd ever felt valued as a partner and doted on by a man I was interested in. The carnival had been so fun and exciting. Noah was adorably eager and happy to be there. Maybe there was still a way to salvage this day.

"Wanna order food?" I asked him.

He grinned. "Just tell me what."

We ordered Chinese and watched more Adventure Hour on Cole's couch. It was funny. Just the week before, we'd done exactly this, yet everything was already so different from then.

We drifted closer to each other with each episode until we were cuddling. Cole laying behind me, his arms wrapped around me, his warm hand drawing a slow, lazy path from my forearm up to my shoulder and then down again. Our focus was on the television, but Cole yawned periodically.

It was getting late, but I wasn't sure I'd be able to sleep. I didn't want to face a borrowed bed and knew I was about to spend the night tossing and turning, jumping at every little sound I heard in the house. Maybe Cole realized that. Maybe that was why he stayed up with me even though he was clearly awake past his bedtime.

"Do you mind if I take a shower?" I asked. "Maybe it would help me fall asleep, so you don't have to stay up all night with me."

"It wouldn't be the first time I stayed up all night because someone couldn't sleep," he pointed out.

"Fair point, but I'm not a child," I said.

He smiled before yawning again. "Also fair. How about a bath instead?"

A bath would probably be better. Nothing made you sleepy like soaking in hot water.

"That actually sounds perfect," I said softly.

"I'll start running a bath for you. In the meantime, you should check my dresser—second drawer."

I tilted my head to the side. "How come?"

"If I *told* you that, it wouldn't be a surprise," he said, flicking my forehead.

I snorted a laugh and nodded before I got up from the couch. I stretched, my muscles stiff and sore from being so tense the last few hours. Cole stood, and I followed him down the hall to his bedroom. As he went into the bathroom, I wandered over to his wardrobe.

I opened the second drawer, not really sure what I'd find. When I did, I found a small collection of soft, fluffy fabrics in pastel shades.

"Cole," I said. "Did you buy me pajamas?"

He poked his head out the doorway, grinning brightly.

"You've been staying over with *some* regularity," he said. "I thought it'd be nice for you to have some comfy clothes here. Do you like them?"

The particular set I was holding was pale blue and covered with stars and moons. They were so cute and, inexplicably, perfectly *me*. I would have picked them for myself had I seen them in a store.

"I love them," I said.

"Good," he said. "I wasn't sure if I got the right size. You can exchange them if you want."

“They look good to me,” I said, bringing the pajamas with me as I walked over to the bathroom. “How is the bath coming?”

“Just about full,” he said.

I nodded, already looking forward to sinking into that steaming water.

“Could you help me out of my dress?” I asked, turning my back to him. My dress was kind of a pain to get on and off. It had a button closure instead of a zipper, which always made things hard.

I felt him behind me even though he hadn’t said anything. Despite their size and strength, his hands were gentle as he unbuttoned my dress.

The hairs on the back of my neck stood on end as he leaned forward and pressed a kiss to the curve of my shoulder.

“I’m convinced you’re trying to torture me,” he said quietly. “How am I supposed to bear it? Seeing your beautiful neck and back and being unable to touch you? To taste you?”

I trembled with my own aching desire.

“Why aren’t you able to touch me?” I said breathily.

"I don't want you to think of your ex every time we make love, Marley," he murmured against my skin as he unhooked the last button. "I don't want you to think of crying, of being afraid, when I touch you."

I turned toward him slowly, and he cupped his hand to my cheek. "Another night, all right?" he said.

I nodded even as disappointment speared me.

He leaned down and pressed a kiss to my forehead. "Enjoy your bath. I'll be in bed waiting for you when you're all done."

My eyes followed him as he left and closed the bathroom door behind him. Setting the pajamas down on the counter, I pushed the straps of my dress off my shoulders and let it fall to the floor. My underwear followed.

I got into the bath, sighing at the delightful heat that sank into my bones.

I kept my hair up and out of the water and mulled over Cole's words about not wanting me to think of Wyatt every time he touched me.

That annoyed me, and I wasn't exactly sure why.

I kept thinking it over as I scrubbed my body and enjoyed the water jets that kept the water hot and bubbling. It took me a while to figure it out, but I eventually arrived at the conclusion that made the most sense.

It was annoying to me because I had finally gotten away from Wyatt. I had finally done all the work I was supposed to do to move on from my broken heart and the ways that he'd let me down. And yet, here he was, still controlling my life in a way he couldn't even guess at.

Why should he have power over when I enjoyed the company of a man?

Especially one who actually cared about my intimate experiences, one who could actually make me moan and curl my toes? One who cared as much about giving—no, cared *more* about giving than receiving?

A fire roiled in my belly. The feeling was unfamiliar. New.

Anger.

Even though I'd been apart from Wyatt for a while, I'd never gotten truly angry about what he'd done to me. Even today, when I realized he was trying to sabotage my new life by inserting himself into the fabric of my new home, I had gotten sad, not angry.

But now he was keeping me from the man I possibly loved?

I refused to put up with it.

I stood up out of the bath too quickly, almost slipping and falling right back in. I managed to catch myself and stepped over the lip of the tub. I grabbed a towel and dried my body rigorously, catching my flushed face in the mirror and telling myself not to lose my nerve.

I put on the pajamas, forgoing the underwear.

I threw open the door and found Cole lying in his bed, one arm pillowing his head, the other scrolling through his phone. At the noise, he glanced over at me.

"Everything okay?" he asked, raising an eyebrow in concern.

I was breathing hard, I realized.

"I—" I started, swallowing dryly. "I don't want Wyatt to prevent me from living my life."

He blinked in confusion. "I don't want that for you either."

My face ignited.

Don't lose your nerve, Marley, don't lose it.

"I mean..." I groaned. "I mean that I..."

He turned the screen off on his phone and set it aside as he sat upright and swung his legs over the edge of the bed.

"Marley," he said. "Whatever you're thinking, you're safe to say it here."

But the fact of the matter was, I didn't know how to say what I was thinking. My thoughts weren't coming to me in sentences. They were flashes of feelings, visions of intimacy. It was the faint memory of the smell of him, the feeling of him hard in my hand in the bathroom of my house. The raw desire I'd had for him but not acted upon.

So, instead of attempting to verbalize it, I acted.

I stalked over to him, stopping between his legs and pressing my palm to his cheek. I angled his chin just enough to meet my eyes. Even with him seated, I only barely stood above his eye level. I lifted my other hand to bracket the other side of his face, then I leaned in and pressed my lips to his.

He ran his hands over my legs before gripping my hips. I traced his lower lip with my tongue.

His fingertips curled into the soft flesh of my ass before he stroked and cupped me.

He broke from the kiss, and his gaze was dark with hunger.

"No panties?" he whispered. "If I didn't know any better, I would think you were *trying* to be cruel to me, Marley."

"Why put them on if I don't plan on wearing them long?"

I wanted so badly for those words to come out of me sounding like they were coming from a different person. Someone who was sensual and confident, someone sexy.

Instead, they sounded like the breathy wish of a nervous wreck.

Even so, Cole's lip quirked into a crooked smile.

"My, my," he said in a low growl. "Are you trying to take advantage of me, Miss Cage?"

A lump rose to my throat, catching there and almost rendering me silent as he looked up at me with a challenge in his eyes. My confidence and bravery fluttered away like a moth in the dark. Was I taking advantage? Was I being too pushy? What if he just didn't want to have sex tonight, and I was trying to force him?

I dropped my gaze to the floor and bit the inside of my lip. I was a horrible person.

He tilted my chin up. "Show me what you want, Marley. Anything you want. I'm here to provide it."

I exhaled shakily as relief washed over me like a cool ocean tide.

I closed the distance between us, kissing him again.

This kiss was slower, warmer, wetter. It opened quickly, and we were soon a tangle of lips and tongues. I straddled him, and his erection pressed against me in a way that made me salivate.

I wanted to taste *him* now. His mouth, this body, everything.

His hands traced a slow and cautious trail over my legs, my waist, and my arms. He wasn't trying to take over, just enhance the experience I was taking charge of, taking for myself.

I bit down gently on his lower lip, dragging my teeth just enough to pull. His eyes were hooded and dreamy as he looked at me when I released his lip.

"Can I have you inside of me?" I whispered, lips brushing over his.

"God, yes."

"Lie down," I said softly, but my tone held the command.

He obeyed, wrapping his arms around my waist and supporting me with his strength as he rearranged our bodies. He moved me like I weighed nothing before lying back against his pillows, eyes glued to me like I was the only thing in the world that mattered.

That gaze, that desire, made me feel like I was on top of the world.

"Hands to yourself, Cole," I said, echoing his teasing remark from the night in my bathroom.

He reluctantly let go of my body, crossing his arms under his head instead.

I lifted the hem of the shirt I was wearing, little by little, teasing him.

His awed breath when I revealed my breasts was nothing short of miraculous. He reached out to touch.

"Ah, ah, ah," I said. "What did I just say, Mr. Lucas?"

"Mmn," he said, grinning wickedly. "Maybe there is a good application for Mr. Lucas after all. I think I'd like to hear you call me that while I bend you over one of my desks upstairs."

I wagged a scolding finger at him.

"You better watch that mouth of yours," I said.

"Yes, ma'am," he said, brows lifting as I started slinking off his lap and wedging myself between his legs. "Fuck—Marley—"

"Shhh," I said, my focus centered on the single region of his body that I'd been unable to stop thinking about.

I tugged at his sweatpants down, and he lifted his hips to accommodate me, his breathing ragged and uneven.

I pulled his sweats and his boxers down as a unit, biting my lip when his impressive length sprung free, standing at attention. I brushed my hand up his silken shaft softly, watching it bounce and bob as his stomach clenched and tightened.

"Fuck." He almost whimpered.

I pressed a soft kiss to the underside of his cock, then a second, and a third, until I came up to the tip. I met his ravenous gaze.

I took him into my mouth, tasting him, learning the unique lines and ridges of him. He was so large that I couldn't fit all of him into my mouth, so as I focused the loving care of my mouth on the head of his cock, I pumped him slowly and rhythmically with my hand.

He hissed through his teeth. I met his eyes once more, and I watched with satisfaction as he started to bring his hands down before remembering my little rule and correcting himself.

I smiled around him, rewarding him by taking him deeper into my mouth until he brushed the back of my throat. I bobbed my head back up, pulling him from my mouth with a little pop as I worked his length with a gentle yet firm hand.

“I didn’t know you were capable of being such a mean little thing.” His voice was rough and breathless.

I bit my lower lip, trying to hide my pleased grin. Wyatt had never said much about my prowess in bed. He’d taken everything about me for granted.

“Is it good?” I asked. I wanted to hear his praise, wanted to know I was driving him as mad as he did me when his head was between my thighs.

His eyes never left mine. “You’re fucking incredible.”

I saw the briefest flash of his tongue on his lower lip like he was looking at something he wanted to devour. I tightened my grip around his shaft, pumping slightly faster.

"Can I have you inside me, Cole?" I asked.

I could feel my own slickness between my thighs, feel the ache of the absence of him. My body yearned for him, but I didn't want him to do something he didn't want.

"Marley," he said, wetting his mouth like he was parched. "Marley, you can do whatever you want with me."

I nodded, backing away to slide off the foot of the bed. I pushed my pajama pants down, letting the fabric pool around my feet before I stepped out of them and back onto the bed.

Riding him would be a little tricky. It was a tighter fit, a deeper thrust. But I wanted to feel him deep inside me.

I straddled his pelvis, and his brows shot up as I positioned his cock at my entrance.

"Marley, are you sure you want to start like that? I don't want you to hurt yourse—"

"I'm sure."

I angled my hips, feeling that initial press into me. When I was sure the trajectory was secure, I supported my weight against the firm planes of his abs and lowered myself onto him.

We moaned in unison as I slid down his length. He filled me completely, my neglected core panging as it stretched to accommodate him. Once he was fully seated inside me, I sat there for a moment, catching my breath as I reveled in the fullness. I could feel him pressing against my cervix.

I could imagine him being sweet and soft with me and foregoing his own pleasure so he didn't hurt me. But I wanted my body to remember his. I wanted to be able to take every inch of him.

"Are you okay?" he asked.

I nodded once, twisting my hips to allow my body to get used to his girth. When I started feeling that slickness build between us, I drew myself up and down in a slow, steady rhythm. Each time I slid back down his length, Cole let out a blissful moan, watching the space between us, watching his cock vanish into me again and again, faster and faster.

Pleasure and need set my skin ablaze.

Cole curled his hands into his pillow above his head like it was all he could do to keep from latching onto me.

"Marley," he gasped. "Fuck, you're a goddess. You're a goddamned angel. You're riding my cock so well."

His praise emboldened me. Grinding my hips, I rode him harder. My knees started to ache, my thighs shaking as my lack of practice caught up to me, but my need for release was greater than my fatigue. Leaning slightly forward, I shifted the angle so I could ride him even harder, even faster.

"Marley," he begged. "Please let me touch you."

I couldn't form words, could only gather enough sense of mind to give a clumsy nod. His hands immediately grabbed my hips.

"You're still in control," he said. "Tell me what you want."

"I need you deeper," I gasped.

He tightened his grip on my hips, keeping me in place as he drove up and into me, slow and hard.

I cried out in time with his thrusts, each one bringing with it a wave of pleasure that wiped all coherent thoughts from my mind.

"*More*," I pleaded. "*Faster.*"

He grunted in assent, hands shifting their angle, guiding me upright before he took over for my shaking legs. The bands of muscle in his arms contracted as he used his considerable strength to slide me up and down on his hard cock. I whimpered as he thrust into me hard and fast.

"Good girl," he coaxed. "Come for me, sweetheart. Come for me."

"But you... God." I couldn't think straight.

"I'm on my way with you there, baby, but I need you to get there first."

The thought of him coming inside me as I orgasmed was enough to push me over the edge. My breaths and moans came together in a bright crescendo as glorious tingling lanced out across every inch of my body.

I almost wept with pleasure as I slackened on top of him. Seconds later, Cole groaned, low and sonorous, as his thrusting slowed. I could feel him twitching inside me as he came.

His panting slowed to gasps as he dropped back on his pillow. I collapsed forward onto him, and he wrapped his arms around me, running his hands over my back and squeezing me against him as he peppered soft kisses on my head.

"You're something else, Marley," he said, almost laughing. "I didn't know that...I didn't think it could feel this good."

My heart wanted to burst even though I was fairly certain he was only flattering me. Still, it was nice to hear the praise of someone you loved.

I blinked as the realization set in. Love. That was what I was feeling. I'd considered it a possibility and had guessed it was starting, but now I was staring it in the face and couldn't deny it.

Cole was like a tattoo across my soul. My love for him had grown in a matter of weeks. It was unlike anything I'd ever felt for anyone else. It was nothing like that tenuous, fearful devotion I'd felt with Wyatt. This was different. It was easy. It was clean. It was true.

Cole was the most supportive man I'd ever met, and I'd been waiting for the shoe to drop, for the chink in his armor to reveal itself, for the cruelty hidden behind the kindness in his eyes to make itself known.

But maybe this actually *was* Cole. Maybe Cole, by the very nature of his being, was a generous, caring person. Maybe I loved him.

Maybe he could love me too.

"Marley? You okay?" he asked when I hadn't spoken for a long time.

I rested my chin on his chest and smiled. "Yeah," I said. "I'm more than okay. I'm so incredibly happy, Cole. So happy I met you. I still can't believe that I just bumped into you at random."

"Me either," he said. "You literally ran into my life and flipped it on its head in the best possible way. I'd been so determined never to date again after Olivia, and now here I am, absolutely obsessed with you."

He craned his head to kiss me again.

I laughed softly, propping myself up on his chest.

"I should go clean up," I said. "Because, well, you know."

Cole grimaced, and sudden panic flared in his eyes. "Oh, God. Condom. Fuck. I completely wasn't thinking."

"It's okay, Cole. I have an IUD."

He looked relieved. "Not that I wouldn't want to have a child with you—er—not that I *do* want that."

I snorted. "Don't worry," I said. "Believe me. I'm not trying to have a child with a man I met less than a month ago."

I sat up, and when he slid out of me, I felt the ache of his absence. There would be more opportunities to make love to him. This wasn't a casual hookup, a one-and-done. Cole was actually interested in me. For real, at least as far as I could tell.

Cole loped after me, scooping me up into a bridal carry and making me yelp in surprise.

"Never instruct me not to touch you again," he said, burying his face into my neck and giving me a half-dozen rapid-fire kisses. "I can't keep my hands off your precious, perfect body."

I giggled as he set me gently onto the bathroom floor.

We took a few minutes to clean ourselves up, which was slightly embarrassing but quite comfortable. It was starting to feel like a real relationship—like we'd known each other for years.

When we were done, I went to grab my pajamas, but Cole stopped me, curling his arms around me from behind and swaying me softly.

"Leave them," he said, nibbling on the shell of my ear. "I want to feel your skin on mine."

I turned to face him. "Has anyone ever told you that you're adorable when you're smitten?"

His grin grew as he brushed his nose against mine. "If you think smitten is cute, wait until you see absolute devotion, Marley."

My heart clenched as that word echoed through my psyche. Devotion.

Devotion was something I had never experienced in my life from someone else. Even my own parents failed in their devotion to me. Could Cole really be that person for me? Was this actually happening?

I wanted to believe that it could be real. Wanted it so desperately, I allowed myself to believe.

Trailing my fingertips over his cheek, I pressed a soft kiss to his mouth. He smiled into it, and I did too. Only Cole could take some of the worst days of my life and turn them into some of the best; turn them into my happiest memories.

If he was devoted to me, then I was devoted to him.

I parted from the kiss and nuzzled my nose against his.

"Cole," I said, my voice as soft as a prayer. "I think I love you."

He pressed his forehead against mine, closing his eyes.

"You know?" he said. "I was just about to say the same thing."

Chapter 22 - Cole

My weekend was euphoric, filled with love, laughs, and amazing sex.

Really amazing sex.

Marley was an active and generous lover, taking an interest in what I liked and what I didn't care for. Though, that second list was growing shorter and shorter by the day. I was starting to realize that many of the things I thought I disliked were only because of Olivia's piss-poor attitude when it came to pleasing me.

I derived a good portion of my enjoyment of sex from making it good for my partner, so it had never been a deal breaker when Olivia wanted to be a pillow princess—but I'd vastly underestimated the enjoyment of sex with a partner who cared about *my* experience as much as I cared about hers.

I woke on Sunday tangled in Marley's perfect, naked body. I didn't move, simply admiring her until she woke.

She couldn't stay long, citing the need to go to Paulette's house to work on lesson plans and make calls regarding a field trip to the library at the end of the next week. She seemed particularly excited about the field trip. Apparently, she'd had a long-standing love of libraries ever since she was a kid. I was already formulating plans in my head for converting the office upstairs into a library for her once we opened the office in town.

I thought about it throughout the day as I handled a few chores around the house before I went to get Noah.

I phoned my sister to talk about Marley's stalker situation, but she didn't have much to report. Maybe the prick had decided to move on and bug someone else. I could only hope so, anyway.

While I was on the phone with Ginger, my call waiting beeped. Wyatt's name flashed on the screen, and I cursed.

"What's wrong?" my sister asked me.

"Marley's chump ex-boyfriend is calling me," I said. "I forgot to block his number."

"Why do you even have it?" she said.

"Because he pretended he wanted to hire me. The guy's a manipulative asshole. I think he's going to try and turn me against Marley. Either that, or he's trying to figure out what I'm doing with her."

My sister was quiet for a moment, then she said, "Well, what *are* you doing with her, exactly?" Ginger asked. "You've been weirdly hush-hush about this new human girl you've been keeping around. You seem weirdly protective of her—to the point where you're putting yourself at risk of being arrested and shit."

"Are we talking about my romantic life? Is that what we're doing as siblings now?"

I could practically hear her eyes rolling. "If I have to put up with an interrogation about Marley every time I call Mom, then you have to deal with me farming intelligence for home base," she said dryly.

"You know, you were way more fun before you went to police academy."

"Police academy was fine. It was the force that jaded me," she grumbled. "Nice try changing the subject, asshat."

I sighed and rubbed my temple. "If I promise to talk to Mom, can we drop it? I'm not really in the mood to have your pragmatism ruin my day."

She laughed. "Damn, you really *must* have gotten laid then."

"All right, that's where I draw the line. I am not discussing sex life with my baby sister," I grumbled. "I'll see you later."

"Yeah, sounds good. Go and pick up my nephew from Mom's. He's running her ragged."

"Will do," I grunted before hanging up.

A little later, I hopped in the car and headed over to my parents, strategizing how to bring up the fact that I was dating again.

I wondered if it were a universal thing not to want to do what your mother urged you to do, if only because of the annoying smug expression she'd have when she was right. My mother had been nagging me to date for months, to get out there, see what there was to see—all those little clichés that make me want to break things. Every time, I'd gently refused.

Then Marley stumbled into my life, and everything changed in ways I would never have guessed.

And I knew my mom was going to take credit for it.

Even so, as I pulled into my parents' driveway, I found I was eager to tell my mother about Marley. I wondered if this was what it felt like when you knew you'd met "the one." I thought I'd met the one before, but I didn't really know anything back then. When I met Olivia, I'd still been a kid, really.

Though this thing between Marley and me was still in its early stages, I couldn't imagine these feelings going away. I couldn't imagine ever wanting anyone but Marley.

I walked up the stairs, stepping into the house. Just as I did, Wyatt called again.

I ignored the call, remembering to block his number this time instead of leaving it to ring for what I could only assume would be the whole damned night.

"Mom?" I called.

"We're in the backyard, honey!"

I found her sitting on a porch swing with my father. Noah was lying next to them, fast asleep, his head nestled on my mother's lap.

"Wow, you guys must have worn him out," I said.

"He wore himself out," my mother said with a chuckle. "He spent the whole day talking about his adventures at the carnival with Daddy and Miss Cage."

"Little tattler," I said as I sat on a patio chair across from them. My mom had a mischievous twinkle in her eye that told me I was in for it. I was sure Noah had mentioned Marley before, what with her being his teacher and all, but it was a lot harder to write off spending a Saturday with her. "I was going to tell you about her today anyway."

"Well, it's about dang time," she said. "I've been trying to get your sister to talk to no avail."

"Yeah, thanks for that, by the way. I love talking with my sister about the intricacies of my dating life," I mumbled.

"Well, if you didn't keep secrets, there'd be no reason for me to snoop," she said primly.

My dad shook his head but smiled nonetheless. She looked up at him, doing that old smile that crinkled her nose.

"You know your mother just wants you to be happy, Cole," my dad said. "To the point where she'll bother you about it until you are."

"Well, it's a good thing I decided to share," I said. "I've sort of been seeing Noah's teacher. It all started very unexpectedly. It took us both by surprise, but things are getting more serious."

"Is she the shifter teacher? I don't remember their names," my mother said. "I know I've seen both of them—"

I shook my head. "No, she's human. The pretty blonde teacher."

My mother looked over at my father, a look of concern flashing over her face.

I let out a frustrated sigh. "Mom, I told you, when you make that face, it gives you up pretty much instantly," I said. "What is it?"

She had the good grace to look a little sheepish as she patted Noah's head softly.

"It's just that, well, *you-know-who* just did such a number on you when you both broke up. And—well, you know. I thought from the very get-go that she wasn't right for you. She was always so awful and demanding. I just don't want to see you go through that again."

"Did you get the same feeling when you met Marley at the school?" I asked patiently.

"Well... No, but isn't it too early to give anything any labels?"

"I didn't say anything about labels, Mom," I pointed out. "I wanted to wait until I knew if I was interested in pursuing this before I told you about it. Now I'm sure that I am certain of it. So, I'm letting you know."

My mother gave a nod and glanced at my father.

He studied me with narrowed eyes. "You like this girl? Noah likes her?"

"I like her a lot," I said. "Noah adores her. Can't seem to get enough of her attention or her company—frankly, that makes two of us."

"Then that settles everything." my father said, patting my mom on the shoulder and squeezing her close. "If our kids are happy, then we can be happy for them. Right, honey?"

She pursed her lips. "Bring her by to meet us soon," she said. "I don't like feeling like a stranger in your life, Cole. It's like you're keeping secrets."

I smiled, huffing a soft laugh. "No secrets, Mom," I said. "I just wasn't sure there was anything to tell until recently."

One of her eyebrows curved upward, but she dropped it and shrugged. "I'll never get used to not knowing everything about you kids," she said. "Sometimes I miss the days when you were this age."

She petted Noah's back, and he wiggled a little in his sleep before settling down again. "You were both just perfect little kids, just like baby Noah," she said. "You better remember to appreciate this time you have with him, Cole. It'll be gone before you know it."

"I have been," I said, nodding. "It's part of why I waited this long to pursue anything romantic. But it just kind of dropped in my lap, you know?"

"I'm looking forward to meeting her. Bring her over so I can make her some dinner."

"I'm sure she'd love to meet you," I said.

The assurance of that seemed to lighten my mother's mood. Her existential nostalgia gave way to the normalcy that was somehow always so comforting. As we talked about television dramas and stories about the pack in Georgia, I relaxed in the comfort of my family.

For old time's sake.

###

We started the demolition of the old dental office a few days later. I'd done everything I could to be on top of all of my other clients and make sure Noah was set up at school so that I could devote my attention to the project. I wouldn't be doing it by myself, of course. I hired my usual guys—a few shifters from a couple of towns over who always had a rough time getting work—to come in and work with me.

I had to sort of be "on" the whole day to make sure no load-bearing walls were getting knocked down, see to it that everyone ate and took the required breaks, slap wrists when my crew tried to use buckets and chairs as ladders instead of, well, ladders.

It was good, old-fashioned destruction, which was a lot of fun and very helpful if you needed to work out some frustration. But it also required so much focus that it could be a little exhausting.

At the end of the day, I was sitting on the floor, covered in dust, sweat, and sawdust. Travis had picked Noah up from school, and I was sad to have missed seeing Marley's beautiful face today, but I'd see her tomorrow.

I stretched my shoulders, waving goodbye to the crew as they made their way out to their cars. As I rested, I munched on a few stale French fries and sipped watered-down soda, trying to gather enough energy to go home. I'd need to get some caffeine in my system if I wanted to keep up with Noah for the night.

Just as I was about to get back up to my feet and head outside, though, I heard the door open. One of my guys called into the empty building.

"Hey, boss man, some guy is out here looking for you," he said.

"Oh?" I said, coming around the corner. "I'm not expecting anyone."

"Says he's some big shot lawyer or something," he said.

I had to school my features to keep from losing it.

"Thanks, man. You guys have a good one. I'll see you next week for cleanup, all right?"

"Sure thing. Thanks again for the work, boss," he said as he took his leave.

As my crew climbed in one truck and rolled out of the parking lot, I saw him.

Wyatt Pierce. Grinning like the cat who'd just caught the canary.

“What the fuck do you think you’re doing here?” I said, slamming the door behind me. “You got a fucking death wish?”

“Oh, going to kill me?” He seemed genuinely amused. “What did Marley tell you? That I’m some abusive psycho? Please. Come on, man. We were just talking about how unhinged human women can be. They mistake dominance for abuse.” He shrugged. “Happens all the time.”

“So, you didn’t try to bite her?” I seethed. “You didn’t try to force a shift on her that might have killed her?”

The humor faded from his face, his eyes becoming steely and hard. “She would have been fine. She’s practically *built* to be a wolf,” he said.

More rage started to color his face, his skin actually turning red.

“Imagining how I might have seen the scars?” I asked, giving him a sharp, cruel smile.

Wyatt cracked his neck once, twice, then shook out his arms. “No,” he said. “She’s got a type, as you can tell. I figured she’d gotten to you if you were ignoring my calls. I just wanted to warn about the kind of woman Marley is.”

“Get the fuck off my property,” I said, stalking closer to him. “Get the *fuck* out of my town.”

He didn’t budge.

“It’s a free country, Cole Lucas. I can set up a law office wherever I like,” he said. “If you don’t want to help me renovate, that’s fine by me. But I’m not going anywhere.”

I grabbed him by his tacky suit, lifting him up from the ground and slamming him against the stucco walls of my building. His hands clasped over my wrists, pulling at them as his feet dangled in the air.

I gave a derisive snort. “Of course,” I said. “You’re one of those pitiful so-called ‘alphas’ who might be able to hold their own when they shift but don’t know their ass from a hole in the ground when it comes to a fistfight.”

He looked frightened for a moment, but then his lips curled back in an ugly snarl. “If I’m so pitiful, why don’t you shift and show me just how superior you are?”

I tossed him to the side. He stumbled, falling back on his ass. I stared down my nose at him, my lip curling with disgust.

"You're not worth it," I growled. "You're like shit under my shoe. I wouldn't even track you onto my carpet."

Wyatt got back up to his feet, straightening his lapels and dusting himself off.

"You're both going to regret this," he said.

"Yeah. I'm sure I will, tough guy," I said, shoulder-checking him as I passed him.

I got into my car, turned the ignition, and sped away.

I didn't even bother sparing him a glance in the rear-view mirror.

Chapter 23 - Marley

The problem with only feeling safe when Cole was nearby meant that ninety percent of my life was still woefully devoid of him.

I'd spent the week looking over my shoulder. I'd thought the comfort and intimacy I'd shared with Cole would be enough to make me feel invincible against Wyatt. But the more time I spent away from Cole, the less I was able to calm myself down.

I had been jumpy all week. Whatever time I didn't spend trying to control my urge to text and call Cole every waking moment, I spent examining every shadow in the corner of my eye and checking all my locks too many times to count.

Part of me wanted to ask Cole if I could stay at his place again, if for nothing else but to get a good night's sleep. But things were still so new, and I didn't want to confuse Noah and risk him telling the other children at school about his dad and the teacher being boyfriend and girlfriend. Not only that, but part of me feared that coming on too strong too fast would make it so that he didn't want to keep seeing me. And frankly, that was a reality I didn't want to deal with.

My mind was so consumed with it that even airy Paulette was getting a little exasperated with me.

The field trip to the library marched ever nearer, and I tried to use it as a lifeline. Despite all the sleepless nights, the fear, and the confusion, I was *still* excited to be the one to introduce the children to the library.

I just needed to be on top of things for one day. Just one teeny tiny day.

The night before the field trip, I was putting together the packets for the scavenger hunt in the kids' section of the library. It was a simple list that would help them understand how the library's sorting system worked. I'd already called ahead and learned that very young children's books were marked with shapes of animals and fruits to help non-readers find the kinds of books they liked. The hunt only had a few tasks like "find a book about a bear" and "find a book about a princess." Hopefully, it would show the students how fun a library could be.

I was finishing up the last of my prep work when my phone rang.

As usual, I flinched when the phone rang. I picked it up, my heart pounding in my ears from the sudden lurch of fear. But with the name on the screen, my fear dissipated.

My brother Jack's face smiled up at me from the screen. It had been months since I'd heard from him. As far as I was aware, he was still in the United Kingdom performing in Shakespeare plays. I quickly swiped my phone to answer.

"Look who has decided to grace his sister with a phone call," I said warmly. "Let's see, is it King Lear? Or maybe Romeo?"

"Romeo, Romeo, wherefore art thou, Romeo!" a dramatic voice said on the other side of the line before a laugh escaped him. "How's my favorite little sister?"

"Your *only* little sister," I said. It was an obvious joke, but we'd been running with it since we were kids. "To be honest, I've been better."

I heard Jack say something to someone, then heard the crackle of him moving his phone to his other ear. I could only imagine that he was hanging out with friends or maybe a guy he was interested in.

The background noise quieted, and I heard the click of a door shutting.

“What’s going on?” Jack asked. “Are Mom and Dad being dicks again? I can call them.”

“No, no. Nothing like that,” I said. “Uh… When I was out the other day, I saw Wyatt. Apparently, he’s been talking to the guy I’ve been seeing about opening a law firm here?”

“Since when does that prick practice law in South Carolina?”

“Your guess is as good as mine,” I said as I plopped down on my couch. “I’m trying not to read too much into it.”

“Uh,” he said. “I think you should *absolutely* read into it. He’s clearly stalking you. Why don’t you get a restraining order?”

“Do you know how hard it is to get those?” I said. I’d done the research. “You practically have to be on death’s doorstep before they’ll give you a piece of paper to forbid someone from coming near you. Besides, it’s the first time I’ve seen him, and it’s been almost a year since we broke up. Maybe it’s just a coincidence.”

“I guess it’s not like he’d even abide by a restraining order anyway,” he said. “Marley, I wish you’d told me about everything sooner—about Wyatt and our parents. Everything you've been through just makes me feel like the world's shittiest older brother."

"I didn't want you to throw away everything you've been working for because of Wyatt. Ruining one life was bad enough, don't you think?"

"But now he's just showing up and ruining your ability to recover and move on? And you think it's a coincidence? I doubt it," Jack said.

"You're right," I said, smoothing my hand back through my hair and checking over my shoulder. Part of me thought talking about Wyatt this way would somehow conjure him out of thin air. It gave me a little chill. "Still, though. You know how Wyatt is. The best course of action is just to avoid him until I can't ignore him anymore. I'm moving on anyway."

"Yeah, don't think I didn't notice that, by the way. Spill the beans," Jack said. "So, we've got a new guy on the board. What's the deal? Situationship, friends with benefits, sugar daddy?"

"Jack!"

"Oh, shut up. I know the books you read, you degenerate. Like you wouldn't want some daddy shifter billionaire to sweep you off your feet."

"Well, you're two for three."

"Oh my god. He's a billionaire!"

I cackled. "No, Jack. I mean, he seems to be decently well off, but he's a shifter and the parent of one of my students. So, I guess...a daddy? Literally?"

Jack laughed, and I could almost see his dimple pock his cheek in my mind's eye. It hit me suddenly. I missed my brother.

"I hope I get to see you soon," I said. "When are you coming to visit?"

"Actually, that's why I'm calling. I'm back in the States. I want to come and visit you and see your new life. If you have time for me," he said. "My production doesn't start for a couple of weeks, so I thought I'd come to see you and maybe visit Mom and Dad—give them the stink eye for you."

I laughed, even though it stung to think of them. That was what was so special about Jack, honestly. He could even make dismal things feel better just with this sharp humor and his lighthearted way. "I would love to see you."

"Well, it's settled then," Jack said. "You and I will go have a relaxing staycation at one of the little resorts just out of town over there."

"That sounds amazing." I meant it. "When are you coming to town?"

"I can be there in a couple of days. Just before the weekend. You can show me around town and stuff."

"Perfect," I said. "Just send me the itinerary when you have it."

"Don't think I'm done with you yet. You still have to tell me about this guy, and I have to tell you about my romantic adventures through London."

We talked for hours, catching each other up on our lives. As was always the way with my older brother, it was like no time had passed. Jack had certainly been *busy* in London for the last year or two and had left behind a daisy chain of broken hearts, both men and women.

I liked to think that in a different time, my older brother would have been a poet or a bard, just like Shakespeare himself. Writing sonnets for lover after lover, enjoying whirlwind romances before taking off on the road with his troupe of performers and bohemians. He was apparently seeing a guy that got him his newest job—a documentarian gig, actually. Jack was the producer and host, which meant he'd get some time in behind the camera as well as in front of it.

They were still figuring out exactly what subjects they wanted to cover, but they had some time to workshop it with the studios over in New York and might even go to Hollywood to see if they could get someone to option their series.

I told him about all the new parts in my life, which sounded much more boring in comparison to his life. All the same, Jack showed genuine interest in everything I told him. He asked about Lana, teased me about Cole, and asked me to introduce him to Ginger because she sounded hot.

I fell asleep talking to him. I had ached for the family connection I'd lost since leaving Leighton Valley. I tried to remember the last time I'd felt that familial love and care from my parents, and I had to go all the way back to before I'd ever met Wyatt. Before he took me aside and started paying such special attention to me that I couldn't see anything else but what he wanted for and from me.

I woke the next morning with my phone nestled between the pillow and my face. I scrubbed the indentations off my cheek and got ready for the field trip. I was excited about every part of it: the bus ride, the scavenger hunt, and the picnic lunches. I hadn't gone on a field trip in ages, and there was always something so exciting about it, if not a bit daunting.

We gathered in the parking lot instead of on the school playground.

My stomach twisted with anxiety. When Cole arrived with Noah, he ushered Noah onto the bus with Paulette, then approached me, his expression taking on a worried softness.

"Hey," he said. "You doing okay? You seem a little tense."

"Ah, yeah," I said. "I'm fine. I'm a little worried I might run into Wyatt again. Probably just being paranoid."

Cole looked around before lightly touching my back between my shoulder blades. The touch wasn't overly intimate, but intimate enough to make me feel better.

"Everything is going to be fine, Marley," he said. "Even if he does show up, he can't do anything to you in public, especially not in front of a bunch of kids. And he seems like the type to be obsessive about appearances, judging from his fake tan and whitened teeth."

I sputtered a laugh and looked up at him incredulously. "God, now that you're pointing it out, it does seem kind of ridiculous."

He beamed down at me. "Not to toot my own horn here, but I think you made a major upgrade," he said with a wink.

I had to resist the urge to stand up on my toes and kiss him. "I think I did, too," I said. "What have you got going on today?"

"Work. Maybe lunch with Travis or something."

"Well, you better be prepared for library visits after today because I think Noah is going to love it."

"I'm sure we will have even more to do and more ways to spoil him the more you spend time with him," he said.

Something about him saying that *we* would have more to do sent my heart fluttering. It was like I suddenly had a family again. It felt almost foolish that I'd missed family the night before. "Have a good day," I said. "I'll hold down the fort here."

"You too," he said.

He lingered before he dropped his hand from my back and left. I watched him go, sighing wistfully.

Paulette came up behind me. “Okay, lover girl. Time to take your heart off your damned sleeve. The parents are watching.”

I jumped, whirling to look past her to the other parents, who wore expressions varying from skepticism to curiosity.

“Crap,” I muttered under my breath.

“Yeah,” Paulette teased. “Come on. It’s time to leave anyway.”

“Thank God,” I croaked before climbing onto the bus with her.

It was strange to be on a school bus after so long. I’d forgotten how nostalgic it was to ride in the front. Paulette and I waved to all the parents as the bus pulled out of the parking lot. The children were practically buzzing with excitement at being away from school for the day.

For many of them, this was the first time they’d been on an outing without a relative. It was their opportunity to learn how to follow instructions and experience going somewhere new without their parents for the first time since the beginning of the school year.

Noah sat next to Hannah—the human girl who liked to pretend to be a shifter, and they were talking spiritedly about something I could only guess at. It could be anything from superheroes to the virtues of dino nuggets. Overall, I was proud of how much Noah was blossoming as a boy. Every day he was more perceptive, more empathetic, more thoughtful.

I looked forward to watching him grow, not only as his teacher but as his family—at least if things kept going as wonderfully as they had been.

Paulette nudged my shoulder, and I looked at her. "Someone looks like they're about to start *nesting*," she said teasingly. "What's the deal with you and Cole? Something big happen?"

"Uh..." I said, my face warming. "Yes."

"Ooooh, you *dirty girl*," she said in a conspiratorial whisper.

"I don't think we should talk about this stuff in front of the kids," I said, looking back at them nervously.

"Ugh. I hate it when you're right," she said. "Okay, fine, but you better spill the beans later. I need to know if he's as good at uh—*dancing*—as I think he is."

"Rest assured in the knowledge that Cole is an excellent *dancer*," I said, giggling at the sneaky word choice.

"Oooooh! I can't wait," she said. "Sleepover at my place tonight?"

A laugh bubbled from deep in my chest. "What are we, thirteen?"

"You're never too old for a slumber party, Marley," she said, her expression hilariously serious.

"Of course, my mistake."

We arrived at the library twenty minutes later. It was a bit of a task to get all the children off the bus and keep them focused on us. A few of the children saw the park and playground just in front of the library and tried to take off running for it, but we managed to get them back before they got more than a few feet away.

We instructed everyone to find a buddy and hold their hands.

"It's your job to make sure your buddy stays safe and follows the rules, all right, everyone?" I said to the gaggle of kids after everyone had scrambled to find their favorite friends. “Make sure you guys stay together. What do you do if you need the restroom?”

“Ask the teacher!” the children chorused.

“That’s right. Great job, everyone,” I said. “Now, let’s go see the library.”

Paulette took up the rear of the double-file line, and I took the lead up front. As I looked back over the kids, I started to feel like we may have bitten off more than we could chew. We should have roped some of the parents into chaperoning.

Then again, it wasn’t like we were going to a zoo or a museum. Once we made it into the library, we wouldn’t be going far. We’d be spending the day indoors until lunch, when we would go to the playground and let the kids blow off some steam after having to be very courteous and quiet.

At the library steps, I turned to all the children to instruct them on the usual rules of a library: the need to be quiet and whisper when they needed to talk, the fact that there would be no running allowed, and that they were to mind their manners with the librarians and the other people in the library.

"And since we have to be quiet, I need you to make this sign with your hands when you see me or Miss Stevens making it!"

I held my hand up, bringing my two middle fingertips to meet with the tip of my thumb, making the shape of a little wolf snout. I left my index finger standing up straight to resemble ears. "Do you know what this hand symbol is called?" I asked.

No one answered, which was just fine as it was meant to be rhetorical. "This is the peaceful pup. And when we see the peaceful pup, it means it's time to be quiet so we can open our big ears and listen, okay? Let me see everyone's peaceful pups!"

The children all raised their free hands to show me their little pups, and I smiled widely. "Excellent work! Look at all those perfect, peaceful puppies! I know you will all do great today. Just keep close and listen to instructions."

I turned and opened the door to the library before stepping in and holding the door open for all the children.

Once properly inside, a librarian guided us to the children's section of the library, which I was relieved to find was within an enclosed space. It didn't have a separate door or anything, but it would be easier to keep the kids looking in the section that was meant for them.

There was only a sprinkling of people here and there as we walked in, but for the most part, the library was empty. It made sense, what with it being a workday in the middle of the morning.

The librarian had the children all sit on a plush carpet covered in an oversized game of chutes and ladders—I made a note to pick up a few copies of that game for the classroom to show the kids how to play games with one another and learn the value of being a good sport.

The librarian started talking about the library—how it worked, what kinds of things the kids could do at the library with their parents, the history of libraries, and even how to look for books that they wanted to read. She taught them about coming up to the counter to ask for help from the librarian any time.

While she gave her age-appropriate lecture, I looked up and examined the rest of the space. The children's section was contained in a small alcove, which was hemmed in by walls on the lower level and railings on the second floor. From what I could glean from looking up, the upper floor near the children's section seemed to be an area for teenagers.

I saw rows of comic books, young adult novels, and reference books, along with posters advertising free tutoring and the rules for maker's spaces and the like.

I was quite impressed with the library and was considering volunteering my time as a tutor when I saw him.

My stalker.

Was it? As soon as my eyes fell on his form, he was already vanishing into the rows of books up above us.

My blood ran cold, and the room suddenly seemed stuffy and crowded. I scanned the top floor obsessively. It wasn't until the children all started getting up that I realized the librarian was done talking. How long had I been distracted?

"Hey, what's the matter?" Paulette asked.

"Huh? Nothing. I'm fine. Why?"

"Your fear is stinking up the place," Paulette said.

"Sh—crap. Really?" I asked. "I'm sorry, I just thought I saw something. Noah's going to freak out."

I scanned the room for Noah, making sure I caught him before he went into protective pup mode and we had to call his father again. But I couldn't see him anywhere.

"Paulette, where's Noah?"

"Huh?" She looked around the room. "When was the last time you saw him?"

My heart dropped to my stomach, sending waves of nausea rolling through me. "W-when we sat down?"

"Marley, how long have you been staring up at the second floor?" Paulette asked, her tone serious.

"I don't know." My voice took on a high pitch. "Weren't you here the whole time?"

"I stepped away to take a couple of the girls to the bathroom," she said. "Shit. Let's ask the librarian."

The librarian was passing out the scavenger hunt packets when we asked her about Noah.

"The boy with the curly hair?" she asked. "Yes, I saw him get up and follow you out of the room when you took those other girls to the bathroom. He was holding hands with a little blonde girl with pigtails. I just assumed they were siblings and that their parents had picked them up when he didn't come back with you, dear."

"Oh my god." Panic sluiced through me. "We need to look for him. He's with Hannah."

"One of us has to stay with the kids so we don't lose more of them," Paulette snapped in annoyance.

I couldn't blame her—I'd completely dropped the ball.

"Okay, you stay with the kids, and I'll start looking," I said.

"I'll have the other employees start looking, too," the librarian said. "Why don't you go check outside? A lot of kids run over to the playground when people aren't looking. Hard to resist the enticing prospect of a jungle gym nearby."

I nodded even as I tried not to spiral into hysterics. I wouldn't be able to find Noah if I was sobbing and wailing.

Paulette nodded. "Go on. I'll call the school and have them get in touch with Cole and Hannah's parents. I'll stay with the kids and keep them all corralled and focused on reading a story together. It will be okay, Marley. They can't have gone far."

I tried to tell myself the same thing, tried to stay calm when it felt like everything was crashing down on me all at once.

I hurried out of the library and went straight to the playground. It was nearly empty except for a few mothers sitting and chatting while their children played on the jungle gym a few feet away. I asked if they'd seen a little boy with curly brown hair or a blonde girl with pigtails, but no one had.

"There's a toy store the opposite direction from here, right behind the library. Why don't you check there?" one of the mothers told me. Her other friends, however, were looking at me like they wanted to ask where I worked so they could be sure not to send their children to go to school there.

I couldn't think about that right now. I couldn't think about my reputation as a teacher—I couldn't even let myself fret about Cole being upset with me. I needed to concentrate on finding Noah and Hannah.

I ran past the library, down about half a block to the small shopping area the mother had told me about. Again, I took to asking each and every person I could find about Noah and Hannah. Again, no one had seen either of them.

I hoped against hope that they had found him in the library while I was gone because each passing moment felt like another terrible nail in the coffin.

Every horrible scenario entered my head. What if the children had gotten kidnapped? What if they'd wandered into the street and gotten hit by a car? What if Noah had lost his cool when he realized he and Hannah were lost and started attacking Hannah?

No, I couldn't think that way. Noah was a good kid. Even if he did freak out, even if he was scared, he wouldn't hurt Hannah. I forced myself to breathe slow, steady breaths as I ran back to the library.

I was grateful for my penchant for jogging because even with all the running I was doing, I wasn't winded. And if I was winded, it wasn't from the hurrying.

Panic attack? That was an entirely different story.

I turned the corner and headed for the library again, but in my hurry, I'd failed to notice the person right in front of me. I slammed into them before falling squarely on my backside and backsliding a few feet.

“I’m so sorry. I wasn’t paying attention, and I—
”

I stopped short when I looked up and found Cole’s familiar face above me. Every other time I’d run into Cole had been such a relief, a happy accident. I couldn’t help but notice the strange discrepancy between this moment and the moment I’d met him. That day I had run into him, ruined his coffee, and gotten it all over his shirt, and he was all smiles and charming jokes.

The Cole that stared down at me now was a complete stranger to me. Gone were the smiles and winks. Gone was the gentle kindness in his eyes. With the absence of all those things that I loved so much, there was only one thing that remained.

Rage.

Chapter 24 - Cole

“You all right?” Travis asked me as we drove over to the new office building. There wasn’t much left to do by way of demolition, so I was bringing Travis in to go over the budget for the infrastructure in the office: hardwood floors, cabinetry, swatches—stuff like that.

“I’m fine,” I said. “Just been a stressful couple of weeks.”

“Yeah, no kidding,” Travis said. “What even happened that night at the carnival? Lana and Paulette seemed to know something, but they wouldn’t tell me.”

“It’s Marley’s business, and I don’t want to divulge information she might not be ready to share,” I said.

“Fair enough,” Travis said as he pulled down the road our new building was on. “I wasn’t trying to pry.”

“Nah, I know. How are things going with Lana?” I asked, trying my best to change the subject. “Did you pass quality control?”

"I think so?" He sighed. "To be entirely honest, Lana's kinda tough. Like I'm not trying to get into her pencil skirt or anything, but she treats me like I am all the time. Sometimes I'm not even sure if I'm actually a good guy."

"You're… not trying to get into her pencil skirt? Really?"

He leveled me with a deadpan glare before looking at the road. "Listen, I know I have a reputation as a flirt, but I would like to remind you that I am nearing my forties. It might be time to consider settling down," he said.

"Travis. You're thirty-two," I said flatly.

"And already with one foot in the grave."

He pulled into the parking lot, and we got out of the truck. I lifted my brows at him. "I don't think Lana would take too kindly to being your 'time to settle' kinda girl."

"No, that's not… for fuck's sake. I really do *like* her," he said. "She's smart. She's sexy. She's kind of a bully."

"Just like your mother," I said.

"Yikes," Travis said, clutching at his heart. "You don't have to wound me so hard. Also, I'm going to tell Marley you think my mom is sexy."

I laughed as I unlocked the front door, stepping aside to let him in. "Go ahead, see if she even believes you."

Travis walked in and looked around, nodding with approval. "Still smells like a dentist's office, but I'm happy to see that ugly linoleum is gone."

"You and me both," I said, slipping my hands into my pockets. "I think we can do something nice with the space, but I need my numbers man to go over things with me."

"Numbers man is here and reporting for duty," he said as he walked into the area where we knocked down three walls to create a larger office space out of the four examination rooms in the dental office. "What are we thinking?"

"Well, for starters, we need flooring—I'm thinking real wood because it will increase the overall property value. It will be a pretty penny but worth it, I think."

"How much of a pretty penny are we talking?"

"Eh, ten bucks per square foot," I said.

Travis gave me an incredulous look. "Cole, it's a three-thousand square foot space."

"Yeah," I said. "It's not too bad."

"That's thirty-thousand dollars just for the flooring. The thing we'll be tracking mud onto and spilling coffee on—"

"It's an investment!"

"One we wouldn't see a return on for...Christ, possibly never?"

"Are you telling me we can't afford it, or are you telling me you want to be cheap."

"Well, with the cash infusion from the work with the hotshot lawyer, I think we can manage it. I just, as ever, question your business sense when it comes to shit like this. Why not use that money for something more...I don't know...fun? Buy a boat or something."

"A boat?"

"Or whatever it is wealthy people get."

"Well, let's say we don't get the hotshot lawyer job," I said. "Could we still afford it?"

Travis's face shifted from incredulity to bafflement. "Why wouldn't we get the job with the lawyer?"

"Because I decided not to take it."

"Dude! What the fuck?" Travis said. "Were you going to talk to me about that before you made the decision? Or am I just your little human punching bag that's the butt of all your jokes?"

"Whoa, whoa, whoa! Where the hell did that come from?" I asked. "And last I checked, I don't have to run any of my business decisions by you before I make them."

"Did you forget that I'm your chief financial officer, Cole? We're *partners*. I know you have a new girl and a new lease on life, but we can't just throw jobs away because you want to snuggle all day."

"Have I *ever* been that way, Travis? Have I ever been someone to put anyone before taking care of my family and my business? If I turned down work, assume it's for a good fucking reason," I snapped.

"Maybe you haven't ever been that way before, sure. But lately, I feel like I don't recognize you. You're distracted, stressed out, and you've started fucking canceling plans on me left and right. Like I said, I'm glad you're happy, but—"

"God, is this really over the lunch I canceled? Travis, it was a *business lunch*."

"Yeah, it is about the fucking lunch. Because if it was a business lunch, why didn't you invite me?" Travis shouted.

"What?" I stumbled.

"Because you're embarrassed, right? Embarrassed to cart around a human business partner when everyone else that matters in your life is a shifter?"

"Travis, we've been best friends since we were teenagers. We've been business partners for ten years," I said.

"Then why do you treat me like a glorified personal accountant?"

My phone started ringing, and I checked it, brows knitting. It was Sylvia's personal cell phone again.

"Hold on, I need to take this," I said.

"Great, go right ahead," Travis said, his tone soaked in derision.

I shook my head and turned, stepping away from him to pick it up. "Syl, what's wrong?"

"Noah's gone missing," she said, her voice cracking. "They lost him somewhere on the field trip."

The door to the building slammed behind me, and I looked over my shoulder to see that Travis had stormed out. There was so much going on internally and around me that I didn't pick up on what Sylvia had said.

"I'm sorry. Say that again?"

"They lost Noah on the field trip, Cole," she said, the emotion in her voice reaching its crescendo. "They can't find him anywhere!"

Ice filled my veins as my stomach dropped. "What? How?"

"They don't know. They said he vanished during the librarian's presentation. He was with another little girl. They're both missing. Uhm, the police have been called, and... Cole, should I go help? What if someone grabbed him?"

My phone beeped, letting me know there was a call waiting. I pulled the phone away from my face to see who it was. It was my sister, probably calling about the same thing.

"That's Ginger on the other line," I said. "Sylvia, just stay where you are and try to get a hold of Travis. He just stormed out on me, and he has the fucking truck."

"He did what?!"

"No time. Feel free to bite his ear off if you get a hold of him."

"I will. Keep me updated," she said, fury replacing the worry in her voice.

I hung up without saying goodbye, quickly taking Ginger's call.

"Hey," I said.

"Okay, you've heard," she said. "I wanted to make sure you knew Noah got called in as a missing child."

"I did. Where are you?"

"Over by the coffee place, why?"

"Can you give me a ride? Travis just took off with my fucking truck," I said. "I take it you're heading there anyway."

"That's right," Ginger said. "Where am I going?"

"Remember that dentist's office—"

"Yep," she said, not bothering to listen to what I had been about to say before she turned her sirens on. "Be there in three."

People could say whatever they wanted about the response rate of the New Middle Bluff Police

Department, but I knew that when shit hit the fan, I could trust Ginger to make it to wherever she needed to be as quickly as she could. She told me three minutes, but she was there within ninety seconds.

There were times I doubted Ginger's attachment to me and Noah. But as I ran out to the cruiser and got in the passenger seat, she had the same determined, worried expression that I had. "You good?" she asked as she peeled out of the parking lot before I even had my seatbelt buckled.

"Not in the slightest," I said.

Now that I was sitting. Now that I had nothing to do or say that was particularly active, my thoughts ran wild. What if some shifter-hating extremist got a hold of Noah? What if it was one of those disgusting people who ran pup-fighting rings and wanted to groom him to be a fighter?

I'd heard so many horror stories of what people had done to exploit shifter children. The possibilities were endless. Very few of those stories ended on a happy note. Labored breaths surged out of me as I tried to understand how this could have happened.

He had been with Marley. How could she let him wander off? How could she let him get taken, and not only him but another child as well? What if it was a human girl?

What if Noah was fine and something happened to the girl? Would Noah be blamed for it? Would his life be over before it even started?

I regretted allowing him to go on the field trip. I regretted letting Marley get close. I regretted that I'd trusted her to care for my son. How could I have been so blind? I let another woman in my life just for her to let me and my son down all over again.

"Breathe, Cole," Ginger said next to me, shaking me out of my doom spiral. "You're hyperventilating."

"My son is missing, Ginger!" I screamed. "What if something happens to him? What if someone hurts him?"

"I know you're fearing the worst right now," she said. "But you need to remember that, statistically, situations like this turn out just fine. There aren't nearly as many child predators as we are led to believe. Noah probably just wandered off or thinks he's playing a very exciting game of hide and seek."

“I just don’t know how the hell something like this could happen,” I said. “He has two teachers, and there’s definitely a bunch of adults around the library—in the library. Is it even likely at all that he just wandered away?”

“People, by nature, don’t interfere with people. It’s just the way they are. Unless Noah or Hannah was showing some kind of distress, it’s probable that they just looked like a couple of kids walking along with their parents.”

“You really think they’re okay?”

Ginger chewed on the inside of her cheek. “I’m a little too jaded by my work to say whether I think Noah is fine or not. But you won’t be able to look for him if you can’t keep your head about you, and at least for these first forty-eight hours, statistics are on our side.”

It wasn’t a perfect encouragement, but it would have to do.

Her sirens made our drive to the library quick. I jumped out of the car before it had even stopped moving and ran to the library. I lifted my nose to the air and started sniffing to see if I could catch Noah’s scent. Unfortunately, though, the seas had been choppy, and the wind was high and strong today. It was unlikely that I'd be able to catch even a whisper of his scent.

As we neared the doors, someone slammed into me so fast that I almost lost my footing. They tumbled to the floor, and I glared over at them, ready to throw the next person who inconvenienced me or even slightly irritated me into the damned street.

But sprawled there on her backside was none other than Marley. Sweat glistened on her face, her eyes wide and worried, the scent of her fear and anxiety twisting together in an acrid miasma that made me want to shield my nose from it.

"C-Cole," she stammered.

"What happened?" I asked. "How did my son get out of your sight?"

She flinched, her face crumpling and eyes welling with tears. I couldn't even look at her. Disgust, rage, and guilt muddled into a sour cocktail in my gut.

"Cole, I'm so sorry. It's my fault. I thought I saw the stalker, and then I got distracted looking for him, and when I brought my focus back to the kids—"

"Your focus should have never even *left* those children, Marley!" I shouted.

She flinched again. The guilt that pitiful reaction kindled in me only enhanced my fury. I felt like I was going to explode. A pain speared into my chest. I wanted to pick her up and shake her.

"If you can't focus on your job because of the baggage you picked up from your shitty ex, then you're a danger to these children. To *my child*, Marley."

"I know," she said, her voice like a mouse's—small and broken. "I've been trying not to be scared."

"Trying isn't good enough anymore." I pinched the bridge of my nose. "Just tell me where you've looked so far."

"The playground, the shopping area," she said. "I was just about to go inside and see if they found him anywhere inside the library."

I nodded and walked away, going up the shallow steps into the library. I didn't have the energy or the desire to watch Marley sulk—besides, it didn't matter how bad she felt. My kid was fucking missing. I hurried to the front counter.

"Hi there," I said to the worker at the front desk. "I'm the father of the missing boy. I just wanted to check in and see if he'd been found."

The woman behind the desk, a young girl with a fretful face, shook her head while she bit on the side of her thumb. A nervous habit if the scarring on her skin was any indication.

"No, sir. I'm so sorry," she said. "We're still looking around, but unless he's in the archives..."

I nodded and flexed my hands, taking a deep breath to keep myself from losing it. Ginger followed after me a few moments later, and I turned to her.

"I need to go looking for him," I said.

"No need," Ginger said, her smile relieved. "Just got the radio that he's been found. Both of them."

"W-where? Where is he?"

"In a squad car on the way over right now," she said. "Apparently, Noah wanted to show Hannah where I worked. They walked right into the precinct."

A wave of relief washed over me so forcefully that I lowered my head on the front desk.

My son was safe. He was with someone who would keep him safe until he made his way back to me. His friend was safe. No kidnappers, no pup fighting, no crazy extremists or crimes pinned on my son. Everything would be okay.

“Thank fuck,” I said.

“Yeah,” Ginger said. “And, on that note, you might want to go talk to your girlfriend outside. She’s trying to pull herself together out on the steps. Been a wreck since you walked away from her.”

I looked toward the front door and saw her folded against her knees, her shoulders shaking with her sobs. I didn’t know if they were sobs of relief or self-pity.

“Yeah,” I said as I stalked toward the door. “I’ve got plenty to say, that’s for damned sure.”

Chapter 25 - Marley

Noah was going to be okay. They found him, and they were bringing him back. I still had a reckoning coming my way for letting two children wander away, but thank God, they were both okay. I didn't know if I could ever have forgiven myself if something had happened to them—not just because of Cole or Hannah's parents, but because I would have failed at the fundamental responsibility I had as a teacher: protecting the children.

The tears streaming down my face wouldn't stop, though. I'd failed by even letting kids wander away like this. I'd gotten lucky they didn't go far. I'd gotten lucky that they walked into a police station instead of somewhere awful, but the fact remained that they'd walked away in the first place, and that was wholly on me.

I heard the door open behind me and looked over my shoulder at Cole.

Guilt gnawed at my intestines. I thought I might vomit. I looked away from him to hide how ashamed I was of myself.

He sat down next to me and heaved a long, tired sigh.

"Marley, we need to talk this over before Noah gets here," he said.

His tone was soft and slightly defeated—I didn't need to have been dumped before to know what was about to happen.

"All right," I said softly.

"Marley," he said. "It's really warm in that library—it's not a big building. If your stalker had been in there, I would have smelled him, but..."

"But he wasn't in there," I said.

I wasn't looking at him, but I could see the slight nod of his head from the corner of my eye. I dragged in a shaky breath and let it out slowly. So, I'd just been reacting to ghosts, phantom threats that didn't exist. And because of my paranoia, two children went missing.

I could blame a million things. I could have said it would never have happened if Wyatt hadn't been around, that it wouldn't have happened if I hadn't experienced the discomfort and terror of being followed around and harassed by a stranger. But the fact of the matter remained that I had shown up to work. I was expected to do my job and do it well. And that job was watching and teaching children, not letting them wander off while I was freaking out over nothing.

“I’m so sorry,” I said.

“So am I,” Cole said. “I’m sorry for treating you cruelly when I got here, and I’m sorry for scaring you.”

There was a tension in the air that let me know he wasn’t done speaking.

“But?” I asked, my throat painfully tight.

He sighed and looked ahead.

“Marley, this is becoming too dangerous,” he said. “It’s one thing for me to be in the line of fire when it comes to your ex-boyfriend and whoever this psycho stalker is. But now it’s putting my family, my friendships, and my business at risk.”

I hated that my mind clung to the hope that he would change the trajectory of this sentence, hated that since he hadn’t told me it was over, part of me still thought this wasn’t coming to an abrupt and painful end.

“Can you just...say it? So I know you mean it?” I asked.

His breath left him in a tremble, and he was quiet for long enough that I really hoped I had it wrong. That he'd take my face in his hands and tell me what a silly woman I was like he had at the carnival when I'd run away from Wyatt.

"Marley, look at me," he said.

I did.

What I saw in his eyes was a man who knew what he wanted and what he needed were not the same thing—a man who knew he couldn't have both at the same time.

"This isn't working out," he said. "We need to stop seeing each other."

It was shocking how much it hurt to hear it. The pain folded in on itself a thousand times over. I felt feverish and cold at the same time. I wanted to cry. I wanted to run away. I wanted to throw myself into the ocean and let it carry me away.

I wanted to beg him to give me another chance.

But I didn't.

I only looked ahead and nodded.

"I understand," I said through a stream of tears. "I just hope you know how sorry I am."

"I do," he said. "It's what makes this entire thing fucking gut-wrenching."

Two police officers approached, carrying Noah and Hannah. The kids were eating ice cream. One of the cops held a grocery bag in his hand with what I could only assume was more ice cream for the rest of the kids inside. I sniffed and wiped my face, trying to plaster a smile on my face as Noah waved at me.

I waved back as Cole got up and hurried over to them, taking Noah out of the police officer's arms and holding him close like he might have never seen him again.

At the same time that Noah and Cole had their reunion, I heard a car door slam and looked to the right to see Lana striding over with quick, clipped footsteps. I got to my feet to explain as she got closer, but she jabbed a manicured finger at me.

"You need to make yourself scarce before you cause any more drama," Lana said curtly. "Hannah's parents are on their way over, and they're fucking pissed."

"But the other kids... getting back to the school."

"I'm going to handle it. We have more faculty on the way, but I need you and Paulette not to be here when Hannah's parents show up. It's only going to make it all a giant pain in my ass."

Guilt flooded me again, and I nodded, pressing my lips to keep them from quivering.

Lana sighed and pulled me into her embrace. "Marley, I know you feel terrible, and I know that you would never let something like this happen if it weren't for all the bullshit going on in your life. Mistakes happen—I've seen plenty of them. But if they show up and see you and Paulette feeling sorry for yourselves, it's going to be a shit show."

"Yeah, I get it," I said.

"Good," Lana said. "Now you get out of here with Paulette, and I'll meet up with you later tonight."

"Okay," I said.

Paulette and I took a cab back to the school to pick up our cars. I was worried that Paulette was furious with me too. After all, she was in hot water, thanks to my stupidity.

But finally, when we were halfway to the school, Paulette said, "Man, what a fucking disaster of a day."

"No kidding. Paulette, I'm really sorry for dropping the ball. I should have been paying attention the whole time."

"Listen, Marley. You're only human. No, shit, that didn't come out the way I meant it to," she said, waving a hand as if to erase the words. "I don't mean that like 'you're only human and humans suck compared to shifters', you get that, right?"

I snorted. "Yeah, I knew what you meant."

"Good." She smiled, pleased with herself, then suddenly worry creased her brow. "I noticed you didn't say bye to Cole or Noah...everything good there?"

I bit down hard on my tongue to stem the threatening waterworks. "Uh, well, understandably, Cole doesn't want to see me anymore. He didn't say so, but I imagine he'll be pulling Noah out of the class, too," I said.

Paulette looked genuinely taken aback. "What the fuck? For God's sake, why?"

"Well, because I let his son walk away on my watch, obviously," I said.

"Does he not realize that even parents can lose their kids? And they only have to watch one of them.

What a prick! Next time I see him, I'm gonna fucking wallop him," Paulette griped. "What are we supposed to do? Grow one eye for each kid? We'd look like boogeymen!"

"Wallop?" I asked, surprised at the laughter that escaped me. "What are you, an old-timey British grandma?"

"Well, maybe I fucking should be! I'll put a brick of fudge so heavy in my purse that Cole won't know what's coming."

I laughed again, grateful at that moment for Paulette's irreverence and loyalty, even if I felt every bit deserving of what happened. "I get where he's coming from. His son is and should be his top priority. I let my fears and trauma get in the way of taking proper care of Noah. Cole's allowed to be furious and want to end things."

"Marley, I know that you're prone to taking way too much responsibility for fucking everything that happens to you and to everyone else in your life, but the point is that Noah was found safe."

"But he wouldn't have gone missing if I hadn't been distracted—"

"You wouldn't have been distracted if you weren't being terrorized by an abusive ex and a stalker creep, either. Like, fuck—you're doing pretty good, I think," she said. "The kids always have so much fun. The humans and the shifters are getting along. Hannah and Noah being the ones to get lost together in the first place is a testament to how well you're doing."

"Maybe," I said. "But Paulette, I am... I'm just always afraid. I'm constantly worried and uncomfortable. I can't focus. The happy things that happen in my life are always eclipsed by this all-encompassing fear. I thought I was ready to go back to work, and maybe I would be if not for everything that's happened so far. But these things *have* happened. And I've had no time to process them or recover from them," I said. "I just keep putting my nose to the grindstone and being surprised when things don't work out."

Paulette looked at me thoughtfully. More thoughtfully than I'd ever seen her look at me, really. She pursed her lips and looked over my shoulder as the school came into view. "Why don't you take a leave of absence? For the rest of the year, if you must. Get this stuff sorted out, get your head on straight, then come back when you're ready."

"The school year just started," I said.

"I know it did, but it's not as if you can know how long it will take to free yourself of all of this stress and fear. And I hate seeing you beat yourself up like this for things that are really out of your control." She shrugged. "Anyone would be scared. Anyone would be distracted if they thought someone was following them around. Maybe the consequences weren't ideal, but there's only so much you can do."

I rubbed my hand over my forehead as the cab pulled into a random parking spot in the school lot. "Yeah," I said. "Maybe I really ought to."

"We'll talk with Lana about it when she gets to my house to hang out with us," she said cheerfully.

"Are you sure you still want to have a sleepover tonight?" I asked.

"Uh, duh, bitch. Of course, I fucking do. I never *not* want to have one. Don't you dare try to back out now," she said.

"I wasn't trying to back out. I just don't want you to feel like you have to hang out with me."

"If you girls don't get out of my cab in a few minutes here, I'm going to come to the sleepover, too," the driver said gruffly.

"You wanna come?" Paulette said, teasingly sweet, then shifting to a ruder, more clipped tone, "Don't be an impatient asshole."

For all the complaining he was doing, the driver actually gave a rough laugh. "God, I love girls like you, Miss. Let me tell you—if I were twenty years younger."

"Don't worry, I know," Paulette said, patting his shoulder. "Come on, Marley."

We got out and watched him drive off. I huffed and shook my head. "You and Lana are so brave and sure of yourselves. I wish I could be like that," I said.

"You want to know our secret, Marley?"

"Yeah," I said.

"We're terrified all the time, too," she said. "I think all women are: human or shifter. It's only that Lana and I get mad before we let someone hurt us. We learned to fake it until it felt real, and when something rattles our confidence, we turn to each other and build it back up."

She grabbed my arm and tugged me into a sideways hug. “Even with everything going on in your life, Marley, you still try to do everything by yourself. You still haven’t learned that you’re allowed to rely on other people.”

“Rely on other people...” I repeated almost absentmindedly.

She made a valid point. When I thought of all the people I could lean on, one person leaped out in my mind before everyone, even before Lana and Paulette.

Maybe Jack could make it to town a little bit earlier.

Chapter 26 - Cole

I took Noah directly home after we talked things out with the police and faculty at the library. My rage had ebbed pretty quickly once I was holding Noah in my arms, but I knew I'd have to deal with some emotional fallout later.

I needed to switch Noah over to another class, both for his sake and Marley's. I didn't want her to have to see me every day while we were both nursing broken hearts. I didn't want to deprive Noah of having his dad drop him off at school, either.

I considered that we might be better off getting a homeschool instructor for him and structuring a play-date schedule of some kind for him to help him get his socialization in.

When we got home, I talked to Noah about the changes that would be coming down the turnpike for him—for us.

"Listen, buddy," I said to him as he munched on dino nuggets. "Marley won't be coming over for a while after today, okay?"

He stopped mid-bite and put his nugget down on the plate, his head tilting to the side like a confused puppy. “Is it because I took Hannah to the police station to show her my auntie?” His voice turned to a wail of distress. “Daddy, I didn’t know it was bad. The teachers said that we were safe with our buddies. I didn’t mean to make her mad. I can say sorry. Let me say sorry, and maybe she’ll keep coming over.”

“What? Buddy, no,” I said, taking his hand. “Baby, it had nothing to do with you. It’s because she has a lot of grownup problems right now, and she needs to focus on those before she can make sure that she’s taking good care of you.”

The corners of Noah’s mouth pulled into a frown as he pressed the back of his hand to one of his eyes and, to my surprise, started crying.

“Marley takes good care of me. Marley takes the best care of me,” he said through tears. “Please, Daddy? Can I please say sorry? I don’t want her to hate me.”

“Noah, no one hates you,” I said, my voice tightening. “Marley loves you.”

“Then why doesn’t she want to be my mommy anymore?” he wailed, his voice cracking. “I could tell she was part of our family. She liked dinosaurs and

Adventure Hour. She took my nightmares away. What did I do, Daddy? I can fix it. I can..."

My heart shattered, my own tears burning my eyes as I cradled my son in my arms. How could I explain such a complicated thing to him? How could I convey that even with how much we both loved Marley, the things in her life put him in very real danger?

How could I convey to a five-year-old that I was breaking on the inside and that if I had the ability, I would have her with us in the house right this very moment? It was too hard to explain, but the only thing that made sense to Noah's sweet mind was not that Marley had made an error but that he had.

There was only one way to do it—and I knew that it would hurt just as bad as everything else I'd had to do that day.

"Noah. Marley isn't coming over anymore because I told her she wasn't allowed to," I said in the most assertive tone I could muster. "It's not because you did something wrong. It was because she was distracted, and because of that, you were in danger."

"She didn't know I left!" Noah cried out. "It's not Marley's fault."

“I know you think that, kiddo. I know you do. But sometimes when parents tell a kid not to do something, it’s not always because we want you to not have fun, but because we are keeping you safe,” I said. “If Marley had been paying attention, she would have stopped you from leaving.”

“Let her come over again!” Noah demanded.

I paused at the demand in his tone. It was the first time he’d ever talked to me like that.

“No. I’m doing what’s best for us.”

“Daddy! You let Marley come back!”

“Noah. No.”

My temper surged, and with it, a touch of resentment toward Marley. Couldn’t Noah tell that I was also heartbroken? Couldn’t he see how fucking awful this was for me? If Marley hadn’t let my son waltz out of the library and into the world by himself, I wouldn’t have had to do this.

Noah struggled out of my grip, then picked up his plate of nuggets and threw it across the room. The plate was plastic, so it didn’t shatter, but it did leave a mess of ketchup and food everywhere.

I looked back at the mess, then over to him. I was getting ready to give him the lecture of the century.

But the boy beat me to it, as he usually did.

"I hate you!"

It was a sucker punch to the gut. Noah had never in his life told me that he hated me. I'd known it would happen eventually. I'd just assumed since we'd made it through most of the toddler years without it happening, I would be in the clear until he was in his teens.

But to hear it now? When I'd had the world's worst fucking day, when I'd argued with everyone from my best friend to the woman I loved, to end the night with my son—my very reason for existence—telling me that he hated me?

It shattered me.

He glared at me as I stared at him in stunned silence, then he slid off the seat and ran away to his room, slamming the door behind him for emphasis.

I heaved a soft breath out and leaned back against the island in my kitchen, sliding down against it until I sat on the floor.

Then I buried my face in my hands.

And I wept.

Chapter 27 - Marley

"To men being absolute babies!" Paulette said as she lifted her fourth glass of wine.

"To parents who think we're all incompetent assholes," Lana said dryly as she raised her own.

"To TSA agents that take your two-hundred-dollar skin-care product and toss it in the fucking garbage," Jack chimed in.

I giggled at all of their lamenting toasts as I lifted my own glass, my face flushed from the alcohol. I was finally starting to feel a little better. I didn't want to bury myself in the ground and become a tree anymore.

"To friends who don't let you wallow in self-pity," I said before clinking my glass with all of theirs.

We all drank, and as Lana took her glass away from her mouth, she pointed a finger at me. "You cheated—we were toasting complaints."

"Sorry, I'm having a hard time finding my sour mood now that Jack is here," I said. "Also, I'm pretty wine drunk, so if you want me to sulk, you're going to have to put some food in me."

"Fuck, I keep forgetting to order the pizza," Paulette said.

"Ugh, pizza is ruined for me after—"

"Living in New York," the three of us interrupted.

We broke out in a fit of giggles. It was becoming a running joke to tease Jack as much as possible for how often he mentioned living in New York.

"Poke your fun all you like, but when you come from po-dunk Pennsylvania, living in the big city is fucking magical," he said.

"I still can't believe how quickly you got out here," Paulette said. "Did you just have a plane waiting for you on the tarmac?"

"When your sister calls you with a broken heart, you make it happen," Jack said. "Also, we got incredibly lucky with a standby ticket. Paulette, order the damn pizza."

"Shit, right," she said, staring blearily down at her phone.

"Maybe we should slow down. We're supposed to educate the future of the world tomorrow," Lana said.

"Fuck them kids," Paulette said. "Wait, not really. I do love them. I just trust myself to bring my a-game, even when I'm hungover."

"We managed all right after Nightshift, I guess," Lana said.

I felt a pang in my chest at the mention of the shifter club. It must have shown on my face because Lana grimaced.

"Sorry," she said. "I wasn't thinking."

"It's fine," I said. "Honestly, since we're on the subject, I think I want to go on a leave of absence while I sort out this stuff with my ex and the stalker."

"That sort of sounds like an indefinite leave of absence," Lana said.

I nodded. "Yeah, I guess it would be. But Cole was right about one thing. I'm too distracted to be a good teacher to these kids. They deserve a more attentive teacher—one who won't let them wander off into the street."

"You're being too hard on yourself. These parents are experiencing their kids being in someone's care for the first time, so their expectations are a little unrealistic. It's true that it could have been terrible, but it wasn't. No harm, no foul," Lana said.

"I know," I said. "Still, I have been distracted, and I've had a hard time staying focused on work. With Wyatt in town, I'm worried it's only going to get worse."

"We'll have a good spa day, get you in with a good shrink, and come up with a game plan for the worst-case scenario," Jack said, cradling his wine to his chest. "But I agree—in the meantime, we need to get you away from the stressors so you can heal before you have to worry about caring for the future of the nation."

"You're not going to run off, are you?" Lana asked cautiously. "I mean, it's obviously your prerogative to do whatever you need to do to protect your sanity, but...I've gotten a little attached to you and your bubbly nonsense."

I reached a hand out for Lana's. She reached out across Paulette's coffee table, and I took her hand, squeezing it.

"I love it here," I said. "I'll stay as long as I can. Hopefully, Wyatt showing up in New Middle Bluff is just a weird coincidence. Maybe he's just acting like a tough guy with Cole because he feels threatened. I mean, I'm not even convinced Wyatt ever liked me, you know?"

"No one can do anything but love you, Mar," Jack said.

I choked on my wine. "I guess Mom and Dad didn't get that memo, huh?"

"Can we maybe limit the number of depressing subjects we bring up?" Paulette griped. "Focus on something else. Like helping me order this pizza."

"You're such a boomer. Give me that phone," Jack said.

"I resent that," she said but handed over the device anyway.

"Let's get stuffed crust—and extra cheese," Lana said.

"Sinful," Jack said. "So many empty calories."

"Not all of us have to watch our girlish figure," Paulette teased.

Despite the back and forth and the constant ribbing, we did finally manage to get the pizza ordered. We spent most of the evening talking about exes, looking at pictures of spas, and watching movies with a common theme of women getting their revenge on jerk exes.

I didn't feel like Cole was a jerk. The breakup felt surreal. Hell, it even felt weird to call it a breakup. We hadn't even defined what we were to each other, hadn't talked about exclusivity or anything else. I'd made an error, and the consequence of that error was losing the most important thing to me.

Still, despite the fact that I only had myself to blame for the way things ended between me and Cole, I realized that this was the first time that I had friends to support me when I was going through a heartbreak. When Wyatt had locked me out of my apartment and I had been chased out of town, the pain was so great that I thought it might suffocate me. Lana was the lifeline I held onto, and she'd seen me at my absolute worst.

Yet, even though this hurt was greater than it was when I lost Wyatt, having a group of people who supported me, whether I was in the right or in the wrong, was such a beautiful thing that I could still smile, still laugh.

My friends had become my family. And having my older brother here to help me made everything feel like it might actually turn out well, even though I knew this was only the start of my grieving period.

By the time the pizza arrived, I'd been quiet for a while. Jack placed a healthy serving of pizza on a paper plate and sat next to me on the floor. He wrapped an arm around my shoulders and pulled me against him with a sigh.

"Penny for your thoughts, Marmalade?"

I huffed at the old nickname but leaned my head onto his shoulder.

"I'm just glad you're here," I said. "I missed you tons."

"Missed you too," he said. "And you and I are going to have the best time ever during Sibling Spa Retreat."

"Oh, we have a name for it?" I asked.

"Trademarked and everything," he said.

I smiled down at my hands. "You have a lot of exes, right?"

He scoffed a little laugh. "Yeah, I guess that's one way you could put it."

"Does this ever get easier? The hurt when you lose someone you really liked? The awkwardness of it? The feeling of loss?"

"No," he said plainly. But he didn't sound sad. "I don't think I'd ever want it to get any easier. If it was any easier, it would mean I wasn't really connecting with people, you know?"

"Maybe—" I said. "But shit, dealing with this is so fucking disruptive. I can't even remember what it's like to function."

"You know how I think of love, Mar?"

"How?" I asked.

"People go through life trying real hard not to get hurt. They refuse commitment, give themselves reasons not to date, nitpick little things on first or second dates and call them red flags, look for shadows of unhappiness in a future that hasn't come to pass," he said. "But I think love—real love—is finding that person who you *know* will hurt you at some point. Someone who can shatter you completely. But they're just so wonderful and so perfect *for you* that you're willing to be hurt if it means you get to have them in your life."

I looked over at Jack and saw something that I'd not seen in his face before. I'd spent so much time talking with him about his string of broken hearts, about his romantic escapades, that it never occurred to me that he might be experiencing his own heartbreak every time something fell through.

"Are you telling me that love is an act of emotional masochism?" I asked to lighten the heavy mood.

"Clever as always, Marmite," he said before trapping me in a headlock and mussing my hair. "Clever, perceptive, and just enough of a smart ass to make it worth the trouble of bullying you."

I squealed as I fought against his grapple. "Let me go! Let me go!"

He did, promptly fixing my messy hair. He squeezed my cheeks and pressed a brotherly peck to my forehead.

"Point is, Mar," he said. "I don't know much about this Cole guy, and I don't know how stubborn he is or how much he meant what he said when he ended things today. But from what I've heard, it seems like he really cares about you, and you really care about him. If it's real, if you really do love each other, it might be worth putting yourself in the line of fire one more time."

My heart hurt from the ups and downs of the day, the week, the month.

"Maybe," I said. "Either way, I think we could both use a little space before I show up at his house holding a stereo over my head and playing a sappy love song, begging him to come back."

"Of course. Mar, we gotta make him sweat. Let him come to you."

"I highly doubt that's going to happen," I said derisively.

"Okay, that's enough self-loathing. Eat your pizza," he said, flicking me on the forehead.

Laughing, I bit into my pizza.

The rest of the night followed the same predictable rhythm that sleepovers always kept to. We ate and gradually became more and more lazy as the hours ticked by. Our energetic conversations tapered down to quiet whispers and giggle fits.

We eventually fell asleep on a pile of blankets on the floor with a movie playing as background noise.

Even with everything going on, with all the heartache twisting my stomach in knots and all of the uncertainty looming in the future...

It was the best sleep I'd gotten in a very long time.

Chapter 28 - Cole

The week went from bad to worse. If it wasn't the fight with Travis, it was little fires going on with my clients. If it wasn't that, it was Noah giving me a silent treatment his biological mother would be proud of. If it wasn't Noah's silent treatment, it was the nagging feeling that I was missing something.

I couldn't tell if it was the general feeling of missing Marley or if I was just feeling off-kilter because my kid refused to talk to me. But I had the nagging feeling in the back of my mind that there was something I was forgetting or not understanding.

I'd had similar feelings before when I was with Noah's mother. Feelings I'd ignored because I was so smitten with her. But they ceased as soon as we broke up, and she left our lives in a more permanent fashion. This was the opposite. The longer I was away from Marley, the more confused and agitated I felt.

I stayed stuck in this muck of my own making until a few days after the incident at the library.

Sylvia had just gone downstairs to put Noah down for his nap. I'd been distracted and irritable all day, and Sylvia stomped into my office.

"That's enough of all this bullshit."

I looked up from where I sat, hunched over in my chair, my forehead braced on my hand.

"Excuse me?" I said a little too sharply.

"You can excuse yourself," she said. "You are a grown-ass man and a father. You own a business. You need to stop sulking and get your shit together," she said.

I dropped my hands on my desk and looked up at her. "And what is it that you think I've been trying to do, Syl? Huh? You think I'm just sitting around sulking?"

"That's exactly what you're doing. Sulking, giving your best friend the silent treatment, and getting on my last nerve," she said. "Noah is miserable. You're miserable. Travis is miserable, and I'm starting to get miserable, too."

"Travis doesn't want to talk to me," I said dismissively. "Evidently, Noah hates me so—"

"Oh, *stop it*. Noah is five years old. If I believed my kids every time they told me they hated me, I'd be a miserable, lonely creature by now. He's just feeling too much right now, and the only way he knows how to express it is by getting pissed." She slapped her palms on my desk and leaned forward, leveling a look at me. "Now, who do you think he got *that* from?"

I bit my tongue and refrained from rolling my eyes. "Syl, I'm not in the mood."

"Call Travis. Invite him out for drinks. You do this, or I will submit my resignation right this second."

I narrowed my eyes. "You're bluffing."

"You wanna call that bluff? Be my guest. Let's see how long this office runs without me mothering you and Travis," she snipped.

I winced and rubbed my temple. I was starting to get a headache from how much I'd been clenching my jaw.

The worst part about this whole conversation was the fact that I had the urge to insist that the argument with Travis wasn't even my fault—that he didn't give me a chance to explain, that it should be *him* that called *me* and invited *me* out for drinks.

Of course, saying something like that would be ridiculously juvenile and immature...and prove Sylvia right.

"I don't have a sitter," I tried to say.

"Do not. Bullshit. Me. Cole Lucas," she said. "Call your mom. I'm sure she'd be happy to see Noah."

I resisted the urge to heave a great, put-upon sigh. "All right," I said. "I'll call him."

"Right now!"

"Yes, yes! Right now," I griped. "Some privacy would be nice."

She squinted at me like she was trying to sus out if I was lying. I was certain it was a skill only mothers had.

She must have found whatever she was looking for, though, because she gave a curt nod and left my office.

When she was gone, I rubbed both hands down the length of my face and let out a low growl. I hated fighting with Travis. I hated it even more when I had to extend the olive branch.

Regardless, I forced myself to pull my phone out of my pocket and tap his name on my list of favorites.

I put the phone to my ear, hoping it would go to voicemail. Then I could just leave a voicemail and have the ball be in Travis's court. But he picked up on the second ring.

"Hey," he said, sounding none too happy to hear from me.

"Hey."

An awkward silence extended between us for close to fifteen seconds. Then I heard the crackle of Travis's sigh against the receiver of his phone.

"A little birdy told me you went and fucked your entire life up after you fucked things between us."

Rage flared inside me, but I bit it back. This was just how Travis was when he wasn't ready to drop a conflict. He liked adding fuel to the fire.

"Yeah," I said. "Guess I did. Is that really what you want to rub in my face right now?"

Another silence. Another sigh.

"No," he relented. "It's not."

The tension in my shoulders loosened with that admission. "Listen, I'm sorry for not talking to you about Wyatt. It was a complicated situation. Not telling you about it had nothing to do with how I see you. I would never be embarrassed to call you my friend, you know that."

"Yeah," he said, sounding a little sheepish. "Actually, Lana told me about Wyatt. I've been feeling like a dick since our argument. I didn't know how to call you about it because I'd made such a fucking idiot of myself. Not to mention I took the truck right before Noah went missing. I was sure you were going to be fucking done with me."

"So, this whole silence treatment was an anxiety thing?" I asked with a bit of a chuckle. "Man, we've been through thick and thin together. Shit happens. We always work it out."

"Yeah, I just didn't know if I'd gone over the edge or not this time," he said. "I thought I pushed past the limits of your magnanimity."

"You make me sound like some kind of rage-fueled tyrant," I said.

"Nah, you're not. But I can tell you that I'd hate to be on the receiving end of that rage. I've seen it as a bystander. It must be like looking into the abyss when you're at the other end of it."

The memory of Marley flinching as I barked at her flashed into my mind and made me feel nauseous. That coil of tension returned to my shoulders.

"You all right, man?" he asked.

"Not really," I said. "You got a few hours tonight to help me sort through some shit?"

"Yeah. Where do you want to meet up?"

"You pick. My treat," I said.

"Oh, big spender. How about that dive bar that has two-dollar pints on weeknights?"

"That sounds good. Shouldn't be too crowded," I said.

"My thoughts exactly. When do you wanna meet? I, uh, obviously have a free day."

I snorted. "Fucking worst CFO ever," I said. "Seven? That will give me some time to get Noah to my mom's and put out all the dumpster fires I've been working on today."

"Sounds good to me."

We said our goodbyes, and a few seconds later, Sylvia was leaning against the doorframe.

I shot her a withering look, bracing for the lecture.

"Was that so bad?" she asked me.

"It stands to be a lot worse if you come and lecture me even more about being an idiot," I said.

She smirked. "Want me to call your mom about babysitting?"

"If you don't mind."

"Sure," she said. "I haven't talked to her in a while, anyway."

"No gossiping about my life being a mess!" I called after her as she went back to her desk.

"Wouldn't dream of it, kid!" she called back.

I wasn't sure if I trusted her in that.

###

Noah was still persisting in his silent treatment as we reached my mother's house, though he did finally crack a smile when his grandmother scooped him into a big hug and nuzzled him. She caught up with him a little bit, asking what he wanted to eat, which to no one's surprise, was dino nuggets.

When my mother saw my face, however, she encouraged Noah to go find his grandfather and ask to see his coin collection. Noah nodded and ran off, knowing that a visit to my father's coin collection usually meant receiving his own collection of treasures in the form of quarters and dollar bills.

When Noah was out of earshot, my mom looked at me.

"Rough time with the kiddo?" she asked.

"Syl tell you?"

"No, I just remember what it was like when you guys were little and we fought," she said. "He seems a little sour, and you look exhausted. And sad."

"Things got a little complicated with Marley, and I told him we wouldn't be seeing her anymore," I said, my heart still aching from the open wound. "He told me he hates me for taking her away from him."

My mother gave me a sympathetic look before reaching out and rubbing my arm. "He'll get over it," she said. "These things happen when they're at this age. It'll keep happening at every big stage in their lives. Middle school, high school... both you *and* Ginger were that way."

"I don't remember ever telling you that I hated you," I said.

"You sure did," she said. "And even if you don't remember, your father and I sure do."

"Really?" I asked.

"Yeah," she said. "First time for you...let's see. You were seven, and you wanted to join a sports team. Naturally, with the state of things back then for shifters, we said no. You told us you hated us and were going to run away."

I cringed. I remembered the argument, but I still didn't remember telling her I hated her. "I'm sorry, Mom."

"Honey, it's fine. You didn't mean it," she said. "Kids—especially shifter kids—have feelings that are so overwhelming that they often don't have a place to put it, you know? The only outlet they have is to hurt you back."

My eyes burned from unshed tears. My mother cooed softly and pulled me down into her arms for a hug. I bent and let her wrap her arms around my neck. She patted my back. I'm sure I looked ridiculous, but sometimes you just needed to hug your mom.

"My poor son," she said sweetly. "You've been put through the wringer these last few years. Go and enjoy a night out with your best friend and let us cheer Noah up."

"I feel like I don't know if I'm making the right choices anymore," I said. "It feels like every choice is the wrong choice for someone. For me. For my business partners. For my son."

"That's just life, honey," she said. "I don't think we ever know for sure. We just do the best we can."

I nodded and straightened my back. My mother kept her hands perched on my shoulders and smiled at me with such love.

"You're doing fine, Cole," she said. "Just keep following that gut instinct of yours."

I blew out a breath. "You mind keeping Noah for a couple of days?" I asked. "I wasn't planning on asking, but now that we're talking about this..."

"You could use a little time to ponder?"

I nodded again.

"Sure, just make sure you call to say goodnight to Noah."

"Yeah, of course," I said.

She patted my arm and nodded toward the door. "You have a good night. Call if you need anything," she said.

"You too, Mom," I said.

I spent most of the drive thinking about what my mother said—one piece of advice in particular.

Just keep following that gut instinct of yours.

Sometimes it was hard to tell if the force fueling my decisions was based on anxiety or actual instinct. When I'd ended things with Marley, I really thought I was following my protective instincts. But the longer I went without a text or a call from her, and the more I thought about how heartbroken and guilty she looked, the less certain I was about it.

I was still thinking about it when I arrived at the restaurant to meet Travis. When I entered, a hand shot out from the edge of a booth, waving me over.

I tried to put my dreary thoughts away as I made my way over to the booth. It was obnoxiously large for just two guys meeting for dinner, but the high walls of the booth afforded us some privacy to hash out our issues.

"Hey," I said as I sat across from him.

"Hey, how's the day been?"

I scoffed. "Come on, dude. We don't need to do the small-talk thing."

"Fair," Travis said, blowing a breath out of his chest. "I'm not trying to be awkward, I swear."

"You've never had to *try*."

"Okay, yes, we all know that you have always been more capable and prolific when it comes to social graces," he said dryly. "But what I lack in social prowess, I have always made up for in a sharp and quick wit."

"And let us not forget your humility," I said.

"Do you think Lana would date a *humble* kinda guy?"

I tilted my head in thought. "No, probably not," I said before laughing. "So, uh, she told you everything, huh?"

"A good amount, yeah," he said. "She said you dumped Marley after Noah went missing on her watch."

The verbiage was a lot harsher than I would have used, but I supposed those were the facts. Marley made a mistake, and I told her we couldn't keep seeing each other. "Yeah."

"So why do you look so torn up about it? You look like you kicked a puppy by accident," he said.

I started to answer, but we were briefly interrupted by a waiter taking our orders. We ordered two pints, asked to keep them coming, and then ordered some finger food. Simple fare, which was great because my appetite wasn't what it usually was.

I looked across the table at Travis and pursed my lips. "I feel like I can't tell if I'm doing what's best for Noah or if I'm being an asshole," I said. "I can't tell if I'm angry at Marley or angry at myself."

“Could all of those things be true?” Travis asked. “Sure, it’s good to be protective of your son, but it’s also possible to be a little too harsh sometimes. It makes sense to be mad at Marley for being too distracted to notice Noah walking off, but it’s also partially on you for not teaching him the importance of staying with an adult—for not volunteering as a chaperone—”

I raked a hand through my hair. “Isn’t it Marley’s job to think about her own limitations due to her trauma, though? She knew she was easily distracted. She should have taken time off. She shouldn’t have planned a field trip in the first place.”

“Sure,” Travis said with a shrug. “But how would you react if the life you’d been building for yourself after an abusive relationship was at risk of falling apart? Would you just lie down and take it? Or would you try to live as normal a life as possible?”

“Fair point,” I said. “But Noah could have gotten seriously hurt—he could have been kidnapped.”

“I’m not saying those things aren’t true. But Marley has never seemed the complacent type to me. And I mean, I wasn’t there, so I can’t be sure, but I’m willing to bet she was fucking torn up about it," Travis said.

"Yeah, she was," I admitted. "She felt awful about it."

"At the end of the day, those things *could* have happened. But they could have happened with anyone—me, your mother. Hell, it could have happened with you," Travis said. "I'm not saying that you should have just said 'fuck it' and let it slide, but from what I could tell, Noah and Marley seemed to have a sort of pseudo-imprinting thing going on."

"Yeah, Noah took it pretty hard when I told him we wouldn't be seeing Marley anymore," I said.

"Understandable, don't you think?" Travis asked. "Poor kid's been put through the wringer where mother figures are concerned."

"He has"

"But none of that crap really matters," Travis said.

I gave him a confused look. "How so? I think it all matters."

Travis rolled his eyes. "Okay, *yes*, they matter in the way that important things matter. But what I really mean is that when it comes to how you feel and your experience of life in general, none of these things are deal breakers. Noah will move on, and so will you. Marley will move on."

"Right..." I said somewhat skeptically, still not getting what he was getting at.

"The thing that really matters here is whether *you* can be happy without Marley in your life," Travis said. "You guys are only human—or, I guess, uh... humanoid? You're both going to make mistakes. What matters is whether or not that person is worth the frustration and the work to fix those mistakes."

I drummed my fingers on the table. That really was the question, wasn't it?

I thought on it for a while as beers and food were delivered to our table. Truth be told, when it came to the relationship between us, I'd made far more mistakes than Marley had. I'd become protective and possessive way too early. I'd even been a little pushy about pursuing her because I was so dogged about my interest in her.

My intentions were never bad, of course. But...neither were hers. She'd been doing her best to balance everything in her life: the stalker, Wyatt, this strange man and his kid bursting into her life and demanding so much of her time and attention.

We'd fought, and we'd made up. She'd given me so many chances and opened her heart to me even though she had every reason to guard it, to reject me.

And at the first opportunity I had to be understanding of her—the first time she made a big mistake—I'd left her.

I'd left her behind even with all of the lip service I'd done, claiming I'd be patient and understanding of all of her idiosyncrasies and traumas.

"I probably ought to call her," I said finally.

"I guess that's the answer to the question, then. You want her in your life, even though she's got a bit of baggage."

"Hell, I've got more baggage than she does," I said, already taking out my phone and pulling up her number. "Man, I already feel relieved. I must have really been fighting against my instincts."

Travis picked up an onion ring and bit into it. "Only one problem, dude," he said.

"What's that?" I asked.

"Marley hasn't got her phone," he said. "She left it with Lana when she went out of town with her brother."

All of the relief and ease that had flooded into me immediately dried up.

"What about the stalker? What happens if there's an emergency with one of us?"

"Lana and Paulette have Jack's number, I guess. And Jack has theirs."

"Well, I'll call Lana."

Travis shook his head. "Don't even try it. You know how these women protect their own. She'll be back in a few days. Just wait until then."

My stomach was in knots. "What if she decides that she wants nothing to do with me?" I asked. "I want to set things right now."

"You'll have to just trust her and respect her space—just like she did for you," Travis said, his brows lifting with the point he was making. "Patience is not a virtue of yours. You know that?"

I groaned and looked at my beer. "I think I'm going to need to drink something a little stronger tonight."

###

Too many drinks later, I stumbled out of a cab down the long driveway in front of my house. Travis and I had talked through everything and were back to being almost brothers by the end of the night. I was truly lucky to have him as a friend. I'd been stupid to ever feel doubtful of our bond because of Wyatt's manipulations.

I used the biometric scanner with some difficulty and stumbled into my home, down the hall, and into my bed.

In my half-drunk stupor, I thought about Marley. That sweet seduction when she rode my cock like it was her goddamned job. I missed her. I wanted her. I needed her.

I hoped she'd forgive me for being an idiot. Not only because the sex I'd had with her was amazing but because I'd fallen for her. As had Noah. Noah deserved a mother like Marley—and maybe I was worthy of a woman like Marley, too.

Still, something nagged in the back of my mind. It had been since that day at the library, but I'd not been able to quantify just what it was. It sort of felt like having a word or a name on the tip of my tongue—like I was missing something right in front of my face.

I fell asleep thinking about it, but my dreams were just as tumultuous as my waking state.

I dreamt about Marley's stalker and the fight in the shifter reserve. In the dream, there was a sort of tickle in my nose, a scent that had bothered me at the time but that I couldn't really place. It was no shocker to me that I didn't like the smell of the guy—he'd threatened the woman I love more than once. But there was something *to* that scent beyond the negative association. Something that made my eyes water and my nose burn.

I woke up with a start just before I managed to close my maw around the stalker's throat and take him down. The afternoon sun was pouring into my room through the curtains I'd forgotten to close before I crashed the night before.

Damn, I really couldn't drink like I used to.

My head felt too heavy on my neck and pounded furiously as I stumbled into the shower. The echo of that scent was still reverberating through my head. I started to wash my body as I started cycling through smells.

Bleach? No, it wasn't strong enough to be bleach, and I kind of liked the smell of that, thanks to my mother's obsessive cleanliness. The smell of bleach reminded me of being at home.

I thought of some smells I definitely didn't like. Alcohol—like the kind used in the shitty perfumes Olivia used to wear. I used to hate that, but that wasn't it.

I was still thinking of the scent as I toweled off and brushed my teeth.

My phone buzzed in the other room, and I hurried over to it with my heart in my throat, hoping it would be Marley. Instead, Travis's smug face flashed on the screen.

"Hey," I said, trying to mask my disappointment.

"Good morning, sunshine," Travis said.

"You sound way too chipper for someone who drank as much as you did last night," I said.

"Oh, I only had a few beers, dude. You're the one who drank like a fish."

"Why the hell did I take a cab home last night, then?" I said. "You couldn't give me a ride?"

"You insisted when I told you I'd pick up your car from the restaurant for you this morning, you forgetful prick," he said, but amusement laced every word. "Speaking of which, I did you the favor of checking in on the office building after I picked up the car. You're *welcome* for doing your job for you."

"We'll call it even for you playing hooky for three days," I grumbled. "You on your way over?"

"Yep. Don't worry. I called Syl and told her to take the day off so you don't have to deal with that disapproving look for being hungover as all hell."

It hadn't even occurred to me that it was a workday. At least it was nearly the weekend. And I was sure Sylvia wouldn't mind a paid day off, anyway.

"Fine," I griped. "You win business partner of the year. Is that what you want?"

"Man, you're easy. I haven't even told you I picked up some coffee for you," he said.

I huffed a laugh into the phone. "Coffee actually does sound really damn good."

"Good, because I'm here. Come open your door, bitch."

"I'm going to give you one 'get out of an ass-beating free card' for being a good friend, but that's the only one you get. The next time you call me a bitch, I will show you exactly who is the bitch between the two of us," I promised.

"Duly noted," Travis said.

I grumbled and threw on some sweats, putting my phone in my pocket before going to open the door. Travis came in and walked over to my bar counter, placing down the coffee. I followed after him, still feeling like a zombie, as I reached over his shoulder to grab the massive cup of coffee.

Then, in the proximity of my friend, I smelled it.

That nose-burning, chemical smell.

I stiffened, almost crushing the coffee cup.

"Whoa, whoa! It's not going to grow legs and walk away," he said.

"Sorry," I said. "Did you get something on your clothes? Gasoline or something?"

I guzzled the hot coffee. Travis wasn't Marley's stalker, but the smell of that substance threw me entirely off.

"Huh? Gasoline?" Travis said. "No. Oh, shit. Wait, I thought I managed to rinse it out, but one of your guys rammed right into me with an open bottle of turpentine."

"Turpentine?" I asked, somewhat surprised.

"Yeah. Worst part? After he spilled half the damn bottle on me, one of the other guys told him he got the wrong paint thinner. Apparently, straight turpentine is only good for artsy shit like portraits and junk like that."

"I'm glad they caught it. I don't know how well that would have gone over," I said.

"Yeah," Travis said. "Damn, now Lana's going to give me an earful for smelling like a college art class."

"Lana? You guys going out today?"

"Hah, yeah, she pulled in right behind me," Travis said. "I hate to drop and dash but..."

"No, don't worry about it. You guys have a great time," I said. I lifted my coffee just as he grabbed his—an iced coffee that I realized was probably more Lana's preference than his own. "Thanks for the coffee and the tying of all those loose ends."

“Sure thing, dude. By the way, a little birdie tells me a certain kindergarten teacher is back in town. I guess she’s just dropping off her brother at the airport and then heading home.”

I was mid-sip when Travis shared this, and I immediately choked. Travis cackled and patted me halfheartedly on the back.

“Good luck, bro. I’ll call you later,” he said.

I cleared my throat just enough to croak out. “Thanks.”

A horn blasted outside, and Travis stiffened. “Gotta go,” he said as he gave a little salute and ran out of the door, the lock triggering as soon as it closed.

I sighed, shaking my head as I wandered over to the kitchen, my head now a useless jumble of thoughts. Turpentine, Marley’s return, and my son’s anger at me all came together to make the pounding in my head deafening. I hoped some breakfast would help me figure out what the hell I was getting so hung up on.

I blearily stared into my fridge. Pancakes sounded good, but it felt weirdly sad to have pancakes without my son. I could make a smoothie, but the idea of nursing two breakfast drinks at once felt kind of silly.

There were a couple of steaks I'd left defrosting, but ever since Wyatt had tried to exert his dominance over me by ordering my food at the shifter lodge, steak had been ruined for me.

Then it hit me.

It hit me like a damned train.

The painter Wyatt was obsessed with—the one who had encouraged him to open a practice out in New Middle Bluff.

Fuck. What was his name?

I slammed my fridge shut and pulled my phone out of my pocket, doing frantic internet searches for anything that might bring up a popular young shifter.

I was about to chuck my phone across the room when I finally spotted a familiar name in a headline.

Curt Fowler Opens Showing of Controversial New Collection in New York.

My heart rammed against my ribcage as I opened the article and scrolled through it, not even bothering to read it—I just needed to find the artist's photo.

Then I saw it.

I saw him.

Messy hair, black beanie, skinny jeans, and a smug smile with black, hateful eyes.

Curt Fowler was Marley's stalker.

Chapter 29 - Marley

"Do you have everything?" I asked my brother as he got out of my car.

"If I don't, I'll be back in a couple of months with Mom and Dad and get it then."

I grimaced for the umpteenth time, and he gave me a bland look.

"Marley, I'm telling you. It will be good for the whole family. Mom and Dad need to see how they fucked up, and they need to see what it can look like when shifters and humans actually co-exist so they don't just wind up on the wrong side of history forever."

"Yeah, yeah," I relented. "But don't you dare back out at the last minute and leave me alone in this."

"I would never dream of it," he said before leaning in through my window to kiss my cheek. "Call me when you get home safe."

"That's my line. Call me when you land."

"Will do. Love you, Marmalade."

"Love you!"

I watched him walk into the airport before pulling away from the drop-off zone.

It really had been a boon to go to the spa over the last few days. Between all the mud baths and eucalyptus scrubs, I'd done a whole lot of thinking about everything: about Wyatt, about my stalker, about Cole and Noah.

And with all of that thinking, I'd come to a realization of sorts—with Jack's help, of course.

I'd always felt that I'd gotten exactly what was coming to me.

When Wyatt locked me out of our shared apartment, I thought I'd done something to deserve it.

When I went to the hospital and was treated like I was dirty, I thought I'd deserved it.

When my parents told me they didn't have any more sympathy to spare for me, I thought I'd deserved it.

I ran away from my home—from the place I spent my entire childhood and early adulthood—because I thought I had ruined my own life. I thought I'd destroyed everything.

But the fact of the matter was, I'd been in an abusive relationship. And when I finally managed to get out of that relationship, the people who should have been there to catch my fall—the doctors, my parents— weren't there. They all turned their back on me. And the only reason I managed to escape was because Wyatt had tried to teach me a lesson about how much I needed him by locking me out of the house.

I was *lucky* he'd done that. He forced me to finally save myself.

And now that he regretted losing me, he was showing his face again.

I held the power in this whole situation. Wyatt had chased me all the way to New Middle Bluff because he wanted me. He missed me. And at the end of the day, even if he managed to destroy everything from my career to my sense of safety, there was one thing he couldn't take from me.

My friends.

Lana and Paulette had continued to come through for me every single time. Any time the shit hit the fan, any time I made a mistake, they were there to support me and pick me back up off the floor.

I'd had Cole, too, until this most recent mistake. But I was hoping that a proper apology—one where I wasn't crying and freaking out—would somehow enable us to be friends again, if not have a path that would bring us back there.

I was scared shitless that he'd tell me to take a long walk off a short pier, but I had to at least try.

My plan was to get home, get settled, and then give Cole a call to see if we could talk. The drive wasn't far from the airport, maybe thirty or forty minutes. Plenty of time to obsess and rehearse what I would say to Cole.

I was a little nervous that my phone would die before I got to an area I recognized. After Jack and I left on our sibling spa trip, Lana was kind enough to grab the things we'd left at Paulette's so we could pick them up more easily. Paulette lived a little bit out of the way, and I didn't want to make Jack miss his flight out. Unfortunately, we were still rushing even with the closer pick-up point, and, in my hurry, I'd accidentally left my charger at Lana's place when Jack and I stopped by to grab our things.

It hadn't occurred to me that my phone's battery would be out of juice after being dormant for several days while I was off lounging with cucumbers over my eyes and margaritas in my hand.

It had been a lovely time, sure. But I was excited that I was going to be home soon.

In the time I'd spent away from my little bungalow on the beach, I'd realized that New Middle Bluff really had become my home. I had friends here. I had a job here. I was determined to keep things growing here. Wyatt and creepy stalker be damned.

I pulled up just outside of my home and climbed out of my car, reaching in to grab my phone that was holding onto one percent of battery life with everything it could manage.

Just as I started heading for the door, my phone rang.

It was Cole.

I stopped dead in my tracks, my heart rate skyrocketing to a million beats per minute. I desperately wanted to talk to him, but I was still running through everything I wanted to say. I'd planned to practice in the mirror or at least get some wine in me first to build up the courage.

I thought about ignoring the call, but I had no way of knowing if my phone would die before I managed to text him that I'd call him back in a moment. If he called again, it'd go straight to voicemail and seem like I had blocked his number.

I took a deep breath and decided to just answer. I'd tell him my phone was about to die and that I'd call him back once I managed to charge the phone. I started walking again as I tapped the phone to answer the call.

I would just take one second, one chance to take a breath, before putting the phone to my ear. I opened the door and stepped in, just about to lift the phone to my ear.

Then I froze.

Standing in my foyer, casually inspecting a pistol made of metal as black as the clothes he was wearing, was a stranger. A stranger I'd seen from afar so many times but never this close.

His clothes were streaked with gray, red, and black paint. He looked up at me with eyes as black as coal and full of hatred.

"You have been a very tricky woman to get hold of," my stalker said, his lips curling with a humorless smirk. "Lucky for me, you were out of town long enough so I could get past these cheap little window locks."

My heart went into my throat as I fumbled to grab the doorknob behind me.

All humor left my stalker's face as he aimed the gun at me.

"Don't be an idiot," he growled, pointed canines in his mouth bared. "Close the door, sit on the couch, and be a good girl."

I squeezed my phone to my chest, not daring to look down at it. I could only hope that Cole had heard everything and that he still cared enough to come and save me just one more time.

Chapter 30 - Cole

"You have been a very tricky woman to get a hold of. Lucky for me, you were out of town long enough so I could get past these cheap little window locks."

It was the first thing I heard when Marley answered the call.

"Don't be an idiot. Close the door, sit on the couch, and be a good girl."

I was too late.

I was *too fucking late.*

The phone line went quiet, my phone beeping to indicate a hung-up call.

I flew into action, calling my sister immediately as I hurried out of the house and jumped into my car. She didn't answer the first call. I cursed and called again as I peeled down the road.

She finally answered her damned phone on the third call.

"Cole, I am not your private police det—"

"You need to get a car to Marley's house immediately," I barked.

There was a pause on the other line, then her quieted voice spoke again. “What’s going on?”

“Her stalker is in her house. Curt Fowler. He’s a friend of a Wyatt Pierce, her ex-boyfriend, and some lycan supremacist dick.”

“Wait, not the artist?”

My stomach flipped with my irritation. “Yes, the fucking artist. Are you dispatching or what?!”

“Listen, I can’t do much for you here. I have been running around for you and your girlfriend for weeks, and I’m starting to get in some hot water with my superiors. I’ll be on my way over, though. Don’t go over there. Just wait for my call.”

“Like fucking hell will I wait!”

“Fine, do whatever you want, you stubborn asshole. Just don’t get in a fight with him again. I might not be able to save your ass this time.”

“I’ll do my best.” I tossed my phone on the passenger seat and tore down the road toward Marley’s house.

A million thoughts raced through my head as I drove, only slowing down enough so I made sure I didn’t hit a car or a pedestrian before blowing through red lights and stop signs.

I should have called sooner. I shouldn't have been such a sullen asshole. I could have already been at Marley's house if I'd just left as soon as I realized Curt Fowler was her stalker.

I kicked myself for not looking up his name the moment Wyatt revealed what a dick he was or even the first time he ever mentioned him.

I should have just ripped his throat out the first time I caught him instead of trying to clean up this mess after the face. Now Marley was in danger, and I was the only one to blame. It was because of my negligence that this was happening right now.

I'd dropped the ball so much more than Marley ever had with Noah.

I had been such an idiot to let her go. And now my own stupidity might mean I never got to hold her again—never get to apologize for my mistakes.

My car screeched to a stop in Marley's driveway. I leaped out of the driver's seat and ran for the front door.

Just in time to hear a struggle inside the house.

Chapter 31 - Marley

When I'd first arrived in New Middle Bluff, I'd talked to Lana about my panic attacks and nightmares. I was having the strangest responses to the panic—it was almost like I wasn't experiencing fight-or-flight at all—I just became paralyzed. I couldn't do anything. Couldn't move, couldn't breathe.

"That's because there's more than just fight-or-flight," Lana had told me. "There's also fawn and freeze. It sounds like you're freezing."

And that's what I was doing now. Freezing up in this situation that had materialized right out of my nightmares. My stalker rounded the sofa and pushed my coffee table back until he could sit on it comfortably. He leaned forward, resting his elbows on his knees with the gun sort of hanging from his hand casually.

He captured my eyes with his black stare, and I swallowed hard.

“This has been a lot of fun,” he said, the corner of his mouth ticking upward. “When my partner approached me to play this role, I was a little hesitant to take it on, but it’s been way too much fun to watch you and your friends chase your own tails while I fooled around.”

I didn’t speak. Couldn’t speak. My whole body was far too taut with anticipation and fear to do anything but sit there.

“Don’t you want to know who my partner is? My collaborator in this piece of performance art, Marley Cage?”

Again, I didn’t answer him. My lack of response pissed him off. He aimed the gun at me again. I choked on the lump in my throat before forcing myself to answer.

“It’s a little obvious, isn’t it?” I asked hoarsely. “It must be Wyatt.”

“Well, sure. *Now,* it’s obvious. I told him that showing up at the carnival like that would ruin the fun, but you know how he is. Stubborn. Once he gets an idea in his head, he can’t let it go—hence our trip over to sleepy little New Middle Bluff.”

“Why isn’t he here?” I asked.

Curt tutted like a parent scolding a toddler. "I told you, Marley. This is a *performance* piece. And this is only one part of it."

"What's the other part?" My voice broke.

"No spoilers, you stupid girl."

A car door slammed out front. We both jumped, startled by the unexpected sound. But our emotional experiences diverged from there. I was immediately filled with hope and relief. Cole must have heard my stalker threatening me on the phone.

My stalker, though, didn't seem to be nearly as glad as I was to hear the intrusion. His mask of humor fell from his face and shifted into a hateful glare.

"Did you hit some panic button or something, you bitch?" he snapped at me.

I panicked, and words tumbled out of my mouth like clumsy raindrops.

"No. It's probably just the mailman."

"You better hope that's all it is," he growled.

He stood up from his perch on the coffee table and stalked over to my front door. As soon as his footsteps receded, I took the risk of peeking over my shoulder to see where he was.

I couldn't see him. The back door to the patio was only a few feet away. If I could move quietly enough, I could get out of the house and onto the beach. It'd be easier for Cole to help me out there—if it was him.

I just needed to put a few feet between us. I just needed to get somewhere where my stalker couldn't just do anything he wanted. There had to be people on the beach.

But could I make it? What if he heard me and shot me in the back? What if he killed me right on the spot?

Then again...wouldn't that defeat the whole purpose of everything he and Wyatt had been trying to do? If this whole thing was just coming from Wyatt's obsession with getting me back home after losing me, it wouldn't make sense for this guy to kill me.

I thought about the lazy way he had been handling the gun. Real gun handlers didn't play around with firearms like that. My dad had been really into hunting when I was a little girl, and I remembered him talking about never having your finger on the trigger unless you were about to take a shot.

The real question in all of this, though, was whether I was willing to take that bet. Would I stake my life on theories and assumptions?

Did I have a choice?

I counted to three in my head, taking deep breaths at each number.

Then, I was up and running.

I scrambled to the back door, fingers trembling as I fumbled with the lock. I didn't dare look behind me. My heart leaped as I managed to turn the handle and open the door.

Everything came crashing down when a huge hand slammed against it above me, closing it so aggressively that it shook the windows.

"Don't be a fucking idiot," he said, pressing the barrel of the gun into my spine. "Go. Sit. Down."

I whirled toward him, my heart hammering against my temples as I glared into his black eyes. "Go ahead and shoot me," I said, voice wavering. "I'd rather be dead than get back together with that—that—abusive *dick*."

Silence stretched on for a moment between us. A muscle in his jaw told me just how hard he was clenching his teeth. I could hear them grinding together. Five seconds passed, then five more.

I brought my knee up as hard and fast as I could and landed the blow right between his legs.

He gasped, doubling over and trying to grab at me on the way down. He seized my wrist and squeezed so hard that I thought it might break. But the knee to his balls still sent him to the ground, and at this new vantage point, he was close enough that I could fight tooth and nail.

I scratched and thrashed until I landed a blow, an angry red line carved across his cheek where my nails hit their mark.

He screamed, letting go of my hand to grab his own face.

"You bitch! You whore! How dare you—"

I didn't wait to hear him wail and bemoan the fresh wound I'd left on him. I opened the door again, slamming it into his head before sprinting onto the beach. As soon as I made it to the sand, I started screaming for help, making as much noise as I could for whoever had arrived at my home, for any neighbors who were enjoying their afternoon tea, for anyone on the beach to notice me and come to my aid.

I was grateful for my daily jogging routine, even if I'd fallen out of that routine recently. I had much more stamina than I'd expected to have when I came up with this haphazard plan.

Despite my endurance, despite running as quickly as I could, it was only moments later when I heard the heavy footfalls of padded feet behind me.

I burst into tears as they grew closer and closer. I considered then that it really had been the mailman. Not Cole.

Maybe Cole had decided just to leave me to this fate—maybe he thought this was what I deserved for letting his precious, perfect son get into harm's way. Maybe Wyatt really was all I deserved. Maybe no one was coming to my aid because I'd invited all this hurt and trauma into my life and kept making the same mistake over and over again.

My stalker hit me in his lycan form, and we went flying in a tangle of limbs, claws, teeth, and sand. When we finally rolled to a stop, every bone in my body hurt, and the huge wolf was looming over me. He bared his teeth, lips curling back across row after row of frightening-looking teeth. I cringed away from him, shrinking into the dense sand beneath me as he inched closer and closer.

This was it for me. I was going to die right now. This asshole had forgotten his allegiance to Wyatt and was going to murder me.

But before he could even open his mouth to close it around my throat, another wolf came flying through the air.

He careened right into my stalker and tumbled the wolf off me. The two wolves became a mass of gnashing teeth and snarls.

I would recognize that wolf anywhere. The vision of him had been burned into my mind since the very first day I saw him spying on his son from the bushes.

It was Cole.

My Cole.

Chapter 32 - Cole

Good God, it was satisfying to finally dig my teeth into this prick flesh.

I'd chased after him for weeks, dealing with his childish taunting and his smug face.

My heart was a jackhammer, but now that we were facing off against each other as wolves, I had the upper hand. He might have been fast, but he was small, and when he attacked Marley, he'd opened himself up for me like a sitting duck.

He put up a valiant effort. Getting a few strikes in on me before I managed to pin him and go for his neck.

Of course, as soon I did, he shifted back into his human form, screaming and covering his face with his hands like a coward.

"I yield, I yield! Please don't hurt me," he whimpered.

It was so different from what I had expected. The complete opposite to that nasty, sneering jerk I'd tangled with, that I actually did stop, lifting my head to get a good look at him.

“Police! Freeze!” my sister’s voice shouted from the other side of the beach. I looked over to find not only her but a few of the other lycan police officers with her. Just after my sister shouted out for us, they all shifted and closed the remaining distance.

I shifted into my own human form, stepping aside as they arrived. Curt was still curled in a ball on the sand, covering his head with his hands. It was so surreal to see him that way that I almost forgot why I’d even come to fight him.

Then I heard her soft voice like a bell ringing clear and bright against all the noise and chaos on the beach.

“Cole?” Marley said.

She was sitting in the sand. Her knees pulled up to her chest. Tears carved clean streaks through the layer of sand and grime on her face. She looked scared, and she looked sore—but there was no blood. And from what I could tell, no broken bones.

I rushed over to her, Curt completely forgotten now that Marley was sitting here before me. I fell to my knees next to her, dusted some of the sand out of her hair, and swiped tears away with the pads of my thumbs as gently as I could so as not to irritate her skin with the abrasive sand.

"Hey, sweetheart," I said softly. "Good job getting yourself outside and on the run."

"Cole," she said, hitching out little sobs. I didn't think I could keep up with the tears that fell from her eyes. "I'm so sorry. About Noah, and everything. I'm sorry for all of this. I'm so, so, sorry—"

"Shhh, shh," I said, scooping her into my arms and standing. I wanted to get her away from Curt and the police. I wanted to give Marley the privacy she deserved after being violated like this. "Water under the bridge, okay? It was an honest mistake. I just lost my cool because he's my son."

I started carrying her toward the house, and she looked past me to peek at Curt.

"Don't worry about him," I said. "Keep your eyes on me."

She looked up at me. "I... don't take me back to the house. I don't want to be in there right now."

I nodded, turning toward the driveway. I took her to my car and opened up the passenger door before placing her gently in the seat. I reached into the backseat to grab one of Noah's blankets, then tugged it around her as she started to shiver.

"You all right?" I asked, bending at my knees a little to look her in the eye. "Does anything hurt?"

"Not physically."

I kissed her forehead. "Let me go talk to my sister, and—"

One of her hands shot out to cling to my shirt.

"Don't," she said. "Don't leave."

My heart broke, but I couldn't deny the relief I felt that she still wanted me near her after how horrible I'd been to her. I'd thought for certain I'd ruined everything, but just as she always did, Marley surprised me.

Her kindness, her bravery, her willingness to forgive—all of those things and more made me realize how lucky I was to have found her and fallen in love with her. I cupped her face in my hand and leaned down to kiss her.

Her lips were still sandy and a little salty, but they were just as warm and soft as I remembered. Perhaps even more so. I was prepared to pull away, steal this kiss and go back to being whatever support she needed from me. But she gripped the back of my hand and deepened the kiss.

I lost myself in the taste of her as she claimed my mouth. I let her set the pace of the kiss, let her keep control of it. And when it naturally broke a few moments later, I pressed my forehead against hers.

"Forgive me, Marley? For everything I've put you through. —for not being here sooner. For being a coward," I said.

"You arrived right on time, and don't worry, I was a coward too," she said. "I'm so happy you came. And I'm so happy you still... Do you still...?"

"Love you?" I asked.

She stiffened a little but nodded.

"Yes, Marley," I said without a second's hesitation. "I still love you. More than I've ever loved a woman in my whole damned life."

The smile she rewarded me with was nothing short of miraculous.

###

I'd hoped we'd be able to go home—to my home. Instead, we were stuck with the police for near on two hours. Ginger didn't question us, probably just to avoid the trouble with conflict of interest, but the lycan officers kept asking Marley and me the same questions over and over again.

Finally, they walked a whimpering Curt Fowler to the cruiser in a set of cuffs. I could feel the tension unspool from Marley as she watched them place a hand on the top of his head to put him in the back seat.

Ginger approached us. She looked annoyed and exhausted, but that didn't stop me from giving her a hard time.

"Ginge, you wanna explain why it felt like your buddies were trying to catch us in a lie?" I asked. "They kept making us rehash the story, asking us trick questions—"

Ginger put a hand up in my face. "I'm going to stop you right there. It's standard procedure to do that to make sure people aren't misremembering something or embellishing," she said. "Just take her home and get some food in her. I'll call you when I know more."

I wanted to keep pressing her, but when Marley realized we could leave, I could practically feel her relief.

"All right," I said. "Thanks for getting here so quick, Ginger."

"Yeah," she said. "Glad we could stop the kerfuffle before it got bloody."

She patted me on the arm, then got into her cruiser.

Marley and I watched her pull away from the curb, a second, unmarked car following behind hers.

A relieved sigh seeped out of me.

"You ready to go home?" I asked Marley.

She smiled, the expression as tired as I assumed mine must have been but so warm and loving.

"Never been more ready," she said.

Chapter 33 – Marley

I woke to slow, teasing kisses against the bare skin of my shoulder. Each one left a tickling wetness that made goosebumps rise on my arms as Cole's breath blew across it. I hummed softly, a little laugh escaping my mouth as my eyes remained closed.

"Aren't you worried about Noah walking in on us?" I said sleepily.

"Uncle Travis *just* came to pick him up," he said, desire heavy in his voice.

We spent the first few days after the attack healing. We talked through all of our miscommunications, and we apologized properly instead of those clumsy, rambling apologies we'd rattled off when tensions were high.

Finally, on the night we decided to really define what we were to each other, we made love.

He'd wanted desperately to do it again. Hell, I had, too. But a five-year-old with super-sonic hearing down the hallway was a surefire way to kill any bedroom activity.

"Ah, is this what we'll be doing until we soundproof the bedroom?" I teased, my toes curling as he pressed a kiss to the soft skin of my waist. “Mmm—asking for babysitters? So that they can tease us every time we have sex?”

“Don’t worry, the soundproofing is already on the way,” he said as he ducked beneath the covers and coaxed me onto my back.

He lowered himself between my legs, peppering tantalizing, teasing kisses against the soft, sensitive skin of my inner thighs. Kissed the area just beneath my navel. Kissed the edge of my hipbone.

“You’re cruel,” I whined. “Kissing everywhere but where I want it.”

He chuckled against my skin. “Oh, I’m sorry,” he said. “Did you think this was going somewhere? I only wanted to kiss my *mate*.”

I giggled. I’d always thought the term mate was exclusively for people who’d gone through the change or been bitten by their lycan partners. At least, that was how Wyatt had described it. But apparently, it was more than common enough for partners to refer to each other as mates.

It was a relief to learn because what I had with Cole felt altogether too deep and perfect to simply call him my boyfriend.

"Well," I said, my voice becoming thin and reedy with pent-up desire. "Maybe you could kiss your *mate* in your favorite spot."

"Hmmm, what was that again? Was it here?"

He kissed the inside of my knee.

"Or perhaps here?" he said before kissing my opposite calf.

"Cole," I begged.

"Ah," he said warmly. "That's right. It was here."

I hitched my breath just as he dived between my thighs and curled his soft lower lip against my clit. My hips bucked, and he curled his strong arms under my legs, pressing his hands down against my hips to keep me in place.

"Hold still, pretty thing," he said, lips brushing against the delicate skin of my inner lips.

I whined.

He closed his lips around my clit once, twice. Then he licked deeply into me, his tongue plumbing the opening just a little lower. I gasped as he thrust that curling tongue in and out of me with slow, deliberate intent.

I wanted more than his mouth could offer. I wanted to feel all of him inside of me. I wanted to feel him press against the very end of me. I wanted to be overwhelmed by it, maybe have it hurt just a little, tiny bit.

"Cole—" I gasped.

The blanket flew off us as he tossed it aside. He slid to the end of the bed and stood. His erection strained against his boxer briefs, and I had to swallow to keep myself from moaning.

He smirked as he pulled down his boxers, letting the full length of his cock spring free.

He climbed onto me, pausing to nuzzle his nose against mine. His eyes crinkled with a smile. "I love you so much, Marley," he said.

"I love you."

He kissed me sweetly and quickly before coming back up to look down at me. "Say it again," he said.

"I love you," I said.

He reached between us, grabbing onto his shaft and pressing against the wetness waiting for him. *"Again,"* he said, this time in a growl.

My skin blazed with cold fire as I realized what he was doing.

"I love you," I whispered.

He pressed into me but stopped, looking down at me with raised eyebrows as if he was waiting for the answer to a question.

"I love you. I love you. I love you," I whimpered needily.

I said it as much as I needed to until his hips were flush with mine, his cock buried in me all the way to the hilt. By then, I was already panting and moaning.

Then he took each of my hands in his.

And pinned them above my head.

"Hold on tight, sweetheart," he told me.

His hips moved slowly against mine. Each movement started slowly but gradually picked up in tempo and intensity until each thrust brought a slick, wet sound along with it.

I kept asking for more of him. Deeper. Harder. Slower.

Finally, when I whimpered out a particularly frustrated plea for more of him, he pulled all the way out of me.

I let out a soft sound of dismay, of disappointment. But he wasn't gone long. He turned me over, positioning me on my knees and smoothing his hand up my spine until my head rested on the bed, looking to the side, my breasts brushing the sheet beneath me. I curled my arms at my side to support my weight as he ran a hand up my flank, pressing that same hand against the curve of my ass.

I could feel him looking at me, taking me in.

"As much as I want to see your face while you come," he said as he brought his other hand to press the other side of me, opening to me. "I can't deny how much I love seeing you like this. You have the prettiest flower I've ever seen."

He leaned in and licked up the length of me from my clit to my opening, moaning as if he'd taken a bite of a sinful dessert. I curled my fingers into the sheets and bit down on my lip.

He sidled up behind me, his knees spreading my legs a little wider until I was at the perfect height for him to slide into me.

"This is the only way I can give you more of me, baby," he grunted. "But let me know if it's too much."

He slid in tantalizingly slowly, then pulled back until just the tip of him was inside me. Then, he slammed hard into me.

I cried out. It hurt, but God, it hurt good.

It was quick after that. A few more forceful thrusts, then I was begging for faster. He obliged me, moving faster and faster until I collapsed against the bed.

We came together just as Cole's phone started to ring.

I was thanking modern science for birth control as he slid out of me and rolled over beside me.

I rolled onto my back, too, relishing the feeling of him dripping out of me. I looked over as he panted and picked up his phone. "Fuck," he said. "It's Travis."

"Pick it up," I said through heavy breathing. "Make sure Noah's okay."

He smiled at me and kissed my temple.

"Hey, Trav. Is Noah—whoa, whoa. Slow down, dude. Why do you want me to turn on the news?" A pause. "All right, yes, I'm getting up."

He rolled out of bed and quickly slipped his boxers on. He nodded for me to follow him out to the living room.

I grabbed a blanket to cover me and guard my modesty. He got the TV on just as I exited the bedroom. When I stepped into the living room, Cole's hand dropped to his side, the phone hanging limply in his grip.

I could hear Travis's tinny voice trying to get his attention, though. He hadn't hung up.

On the screen was Wyatt, standing next to my stalker, who still had an angry pink scar across his face from where I'd scratched him. He looked small and frightened, nothing like the man I'd encountered.

Then I saw the headline at the bottom of the screen.

Celebrated Shifter Artist Pursues Harassment Case Against Alleged Stalker.

My heart sank into the pit of my stomach, my world tilted on its axis, and time stopped.

"Marley Cage is a serial stalker and abuser. She clearly, from her pursuit of myself, of my client Curt Fowler, and of her current partner, Cole Lucas, prefers to target successful lycans in the hopes of trapping them in marriage to steal their assets," Wyatt said to a crowd of gathered reporters. "If she is allowed to keep getting away with this predatory behavior, we can never hope to advance as a society past the fear and fetishization that is perpetuated against our kind. The state of South Carolina *must* hold this woman responsible for the pain and suffering she has caused these poor men."

My mind went back to what my stalker—Curt—had said to me in the living room of my little bungalow.

I told you, Marley. This is a performance piece. And this is only one part of it.

I could only guess what would come next.

Made in United States
North Haven, CT
14 October 2023

42765279R00374